PRAISE FOR CHRISTOPHER GOLDEN

The Ferryman

"With his customary style and economy, Christopher Golden has penned a powerful and haunting tale."—Clive Barker

"Kept me reading long into the evening on more than one night. Golden delivers...good, old-fashioned storytelling...and he doesn't back away from the consequences of the darkness he has set upon his characters. I liked his deft touch with his characters, his crisp prose, and how he lets the story unfold. And I especially liked the relationship Golden built between his characters.... We should all be so lucky as to have such friends."—Charles de Lint

"*The Ferryman* is a compulsive read, one I finished in a single sleep-deprived night. The characters are easy to care about, the story unpredictable and involving. Rarest of all, Golden conveys the terrible sadness of the supernatural in a way few authors have managed."—Poppy Z. Brite

"An intelligent, compelling ghost story in the classic horror tradition...Harrowing...Superior characterization, an exquisitely detailed setting and superbly orchestrated suspense."—*Publishers Weekly*

"A gripping tale from a genre master."—*Booklist*

"Once in a very long while, a horror novel will come along that is so believable and frightening, it will live on in the reader's mind forevermore. *The Stand* and *The Exorcist* were such books and so too is *The Ferryman*. Christopher Golden is a talented writer who makes the audience give credence to events in his novel as if they occurred in the real world."—Harriet Klausner

"A horrifying, disturbing assault... Tight, focused and almost claustrophobically intimate, it's a must read for those yearning for a really terrifying experience."—*Fangoria*

"Readers [will] wonder if Christopher Golden is actually a pseudonym for a collaboration between Dean Koontz and Peter Straub."—*BookBrowser*

"*The Ferryman* [is] shot through with a sadness that sometimes gently aches and other times deeply wounds. Golden's subtle and clever way with a plot really shines. Spencer makes a stellar second-tier bad guy, the kind of jerk you don't just love to hate; you want to beat him to death with a coal shovel. A year later, I can recall quite clearly the feelings that *Straight on 'til Morning* stirred up while reading it. It's not every book I can say that about, but I fully expect to be able to say the same thing about *The Ferryman* come the spring of 2003."—Brian Hodge, in *Hellnotes*

Strangewood

"In *Strangewood*, Christopher Golden gradually brings into being a world of haunted and perilous fantasy which, while moving into greater and greater solidity, never loses touch with its painful, sweet, embattled human context. This is a notable achievement. Christopher Golden has written a beautiful and wildly inventive hymn to the most salvific human capacity: imagination."—Peter Straub

"If Clive Barker had gone Through the Looking Glass, he might have come up with something as imaginative and compelling as *Strangewood*. Christopher Golden's writing is vivid, making his quirky fantasy world as real as the 'real world' in his story. It's been a long time since I've read such an original novel in the fantasy genre."—Kevin J. Anderson

"A terrific novel. There's a hint of *The Talisman* here, as well as Stephen Donaldson's Thomas Covenant novels, but ultimately it is the strength of Golden's characters that carries this novel and gives it its power. I never do this, but at one point I actually found myself looking ahead in the book to learn whether a particular character made it out of a scrape alive. I cannot give higher praise than that—breaking my own reading habits because I was so involved with the story—and I salute Golden for being able to make me do such a thing. *Strangewood* is an excellent book, an impressive achievement by a fine writer whose message could not be more timely."—Bentley Little

"I read *Strangewood* in one sitting. *Strangewood* the novel is a daring and thoroughly engrossing blend of wonder and adventure, terror and tenderness. Strangewood the place is what Oz might have been if L. Frank Baum had grown up on a steady diet of Stephen King."—F. Paul Wilson

"A beautiful new formulation of genre material. A novel which roots the extremes of imagination in the displacements of the human heart. Lovely stuff."—Graham Joyce

"A fascinating read. It has a lot to say about the nature of creation. *Strangewood* was the most inventive paperback original of 1999. It deserves great success."—*Cemetery Dance*

"*Strangewood* is a treat, and it shouts Christopher Golden's talent with a megaphone to its lips. With a sure voice and a steady hand, Golden weaves a story both deceptively simple and vibrantly realized, and he does it with pure artistry. I believe in his characters, his world and his talent."—Greg Rucka

Straight on 'Til Morning

"Golden's dramatic and funny coming-of-age story evolv[es] into a horrific and ultimately sorrowful thriller. A bizarre combination of *The Wonder Years* and *The Lost Boys*, this fantastic tale entertains."
—*Publishers Weekly*

"Christopher Golden . . . is an imaginative and prodigious talent who never lets genre boundaries hold him back."
—Douglas Clegg

"The print equivalent of *From Dusk Till Dawn*. High praise, indeed. A bizarre trip across the dark fantastic that really, really works. The *Stand by Me*-cum-*The Outsiders* feel of the first half of the novel is real, and honest, and a great read in and of itself; add the twisted fantasy element, and this book becomes perfectly unique. A grown-up, odd, compelling journey through adolescence, and heartache, and of course, Neverland. A fascinating and completely engrossing book."
—*The 11th Hour*

"I defy anyone to read a few of these scenes and not be swept up. Golden's imagination was working overtime when he crafted a way to blend this coming-of-age story with not just a bona fide childhood classic, but Gaelic mythology as well, as the novel progresses from the mundane to the weird to full-blown high fantasy. Golden keeps those pages flying by, without forgetting to bring it full circle and give your heart a tweak or two in the very end."—Brian Hodge

"A clever and touching dark fantasy novel [that is] magic to read. As dark, and as mature, as any good fairy tale is at heart. Golden's storytelling is restrained as he finesses us down the plot's road, and though there is a moral to the story, it's a moral that aches with the revelations of coming of age, and of leaving an age behind."
—Gothic.net

The Shadow Saga

"A politico-religious thriller reminiscent of the novels of David Morrell. A delightful read and a noteworthy debut by a writer who cares passionately about the stuff of horror. Harrowing, humorous, overflowing with characters and plot contortions, abundantly entertaining... a portent of great things to come from Christopher Golden."
—Douglas E. Winter, in *Cemetery Dance*

"A breathtaking story that succeeds in marrying gore and romance, sex and sentiment. A brilliant epic."—*Dark News,* Paris

"One of the best horror novels of the year. Filled with tension, breathtaking action, dire plots and a convincing depiction of worlds existing unseen within our own. One of the most promising debuts in some time."—*Science Fiction Chronicle*

"You can damn near chase me a mile these days with a vampire novel. Then, along comes Christopher Golden. His work is fast and furious, funny and original, and I can't wait until his next book."—Joe R. Lansdale

"The most refreshing books in the vampire genre since Anne Rice wrote *Interview with the Vampire,* [Golden's novels] are completely in a class by themselves."—*Pathway to Darkness*

"Christopher Golden has painted an intriguing canvas, full of action, sweep and dark mythology; a novel that unfolds like a vampiric Kabuki theatre. Golden is smart and savvy; a writer with a bright future."—Rex Miller

"Passionate... excellent... Golden has written one of the best... a deep probe into the inner workings of the church and a surprise explanation for vampires. [A] brilliant vampire novel in a blizzard of bloody tooth bites this year."—LitNews Online

"A promising debut. In his world of vampires and dark magic, Golden presents us with a complex canvas to rival Brian Lumley."
—Craig Shaw Gardner

"Golden combines quiet, dark, subtle mood with Super-Giant monster action. Sort of M. R. James meets Godzilla!"
—Mike Mignola

"The characters in Golden's books are always interesting and carefully drawn. You might care a little too much about some of them. *Of Masques and Martyrs* is a furiously paced, energetic thriller with enough original ideas for three or four of anyone else's books."—*The Plot Thickens*, from Mysterious Galaxy

Body of Evidence

"Golden [has a] sense of the truly morbid, and [a] knack for uncomfortably realistic medical dialogue. Unpredictable."
—*Publishers Weekly*

"Will appeal to teens with a taste for the macabre...Jenna Blake, the series heroine...[is] bright and extraordinarily perceptive...a persistent and plucky protagonist.... Teens will be drawn into the fast action...and gripping suspense. This is a good choice for reluctant readers."—*Kliatt*

"[An] absorbing medical mystery/thriller for older teens. Jenna is one tough cookie and smart as well. Is this what Kay Scarpetta was like in college? Readers won't be able to wait for Jenna's next adventure."—*VOYA*

Buffy the Vampire Slayer
Spike & Dru: Pretty Maids All in a Row

"Suspenseful... the narrative's swift momentum and engaging action sequences make for breezy entertainment. Avid fans of the series will buy the book, of course, but word of mouth could also bring newcomers to this mysterious world of dark creatures and cruel intentions."—*Publishers Weekly*

THE BOYS ARE BACK IN TOWN

CHRISTOPHER GOLDEN

BANTAM BOOKS

THE BOYS ARE BACK IN TOWN
A Bantam Spectra Book / February 2004

Published by
Bantam Dell
a division of
Random House, Inc.
New York, New York

Copyright © 2004 by Christopher Golden
Cover photo © Ian Jackson/Getty Images

BOOK DESIGN BY GLEN EDELSTEIN

Library of Congress Cataloging-in-Publication Data

Golden, Christopher.
The boys are back in town / Christopher Golden.
p. cm.
ISBN 0-553-38207-1
I. Title.

PS3557.O35927B69 2004
813'.54—dc22
2003062216

Manufactured in the United States of America
Published simultaneously in Canada

10 9 8 7 6 5 4 3 2
RRH

In memory of *Dawn Russell*.
The Lost One.

ACKNOWLEDGMENTS

Thanks as ever to my wife, Connie, my partner and inspiration, and to the laughter in my life, our children Nicholas, Daniel, and Lily. Thanks also to everyone in the clan, especially Mom, Erin, and Jamie. To Tom Sniegoski, Amber Benson, Jose Nieto, Bob Tomko, Rick Hautala, Jeff Mariotte, and Pete Donaldson.

My gratitude to Allie Costa, Maria Carlini, and everyone on the various lists and boards, as well as to Jim Cobb for his efforts on my behalf, and to everyone else who lent their enthusiasm and support during this process.

Finally, a very special thanks to my wonderful editor Anne Groell for good vibes, hard work, charts, and most especially, focus.

And, in the end, to John Mayer and Amanda Marshall, whose lyrics provided a great deal of food for thought in the period during which this book was written.

I wonder, sometimes, about the outcome
of a still verdictless life.
—John Mayer

THE BOYS ARE BACK IN TOWN

CHAPTER I

The world was still solid and reliable that chilly October morning, but it would not stay that way forever.

Or even for long.

Will James stepped out of the Porter Square T station amidst the early-morning throng, enjoying the warmth of the sun and the crispness of the autumn air. The other commuters disgorging themselves from the subway were as uncommunicative as always, their eyes downcast or steadfastly focused on navigating their morning routes. But Will caught a vibe off them, a sort of aura that told him that they were enjoying the blue-sky morning just as much as he was.

A heavyset black woman crowded up behind him as he started along Massachusetts Avenue toward his office. Will could feel the *hurry* coming off her in waves, so he stepped aside. As she passed he raised his Dunkin' Donuts cup to her and smiled. She said nothing, but did smile in return as she continued on her way.

Will blew into the hole he'd ripped in the lid of his coffee cup and it whistled slightly. He set off again along the sidewalk, taking his time. Technically he was not due in the office until late in the morning but he nearly always showed up early. Will was a

Lifestyles writer and entertainment critic for the *Boston Tribune*, a tabloid that'd been the third best-selling paper in the city since Lew Orton had founded it sixty-five years before. Will had always suspected that after the first couple of decades everyone at the *Trib* had just given up thinking it could ever be anything else.

It sure didn't look like he was ever going to work for the *New York Times* or win that Pulitzer Prize—his dreams had been larger than reality had provided—but he loved his job and for the most part got along with the people he worked with. And he had learned enough to know that was not the norm. Some days he did not feel like it, but he was a lucky guy.

A police officer directing traffic at the intersection just ahead blew a whistle and waved several cars through. An SUV driven by a perfectly coiffed blonde in sunglasses rumbled by, followed by a Volkswagen Beetle, the windows rolled down, blaring out hip-hop rhythms that nearly knocked over the bicycle messenger who was trying to keep up with the traffic.

The offices of the *Boston Tribune* were not actually in Boston, but Cambridge, and Will had always been pleased with the incongruity. There was something wonderfully avant-garde about this section of Massachusetts Avenue. Porter Square was in the midst of a Bermuda Triangle of Boston's college scene, with Tufts, Harvard, and M.I.T. all near enough to have inspired the secondhand clothing boutiques, specialty bookshops, and unique restaurants that lined the road.

A van went by pumping Aerosmith out of its speakers; under his breath, Will began to sing along. He had a long day ahead, starting with some follow-up phone calls on a Lifestyles piece he was working on, then lunch with old friends who were in town, and finally a pair of back-to-back film screenings, the reviews of which he had to write before nine o'clock that night to hit the deadline for tomorrow's paper.

It was a good thing he loved his work. He did not have time for very much else.

When he reached the *Tribune* building he bid a reluctant good-bye to the blue sky and the scent of October on the breeze, dropped his nearly empty coffee cup into a trash can, and held the door open for a UPS deliveryman. It was just after nine A.M. when he stepped off the elevator on the fifth floor and into the editorial bullpen. Reporters and editors were fond of saying that the fifth floor was the heart of the newspaper. Will disagreed. He figured the actual printing press was the paper's pumping, beating heart. The bullpen was its eyes and ears and sometimes, if they were very lucky, its conscience.

"Morning, Micaela," he said as he swept past the desk of the city editor. She was typing, and her gaze did not even rise from her computer screen, but she greeted him nevertheless. He would've thought she was psychic if he believed in that sort of thing.

Several other people greeted him, but at this time of day the bullpen was anarchy, the entire staff behaving like they were racing dogs and somebody'd just set the rabbit to running. Will slipped off the Somerset University sweatshirt he had worn that morning and slid into the chair behind his desk. Other than the paper clutter of notebooks and bits of research he had printed off the Net, the only things that marked the space as his were a small black-and-white photo of his parents, a harlequin-painted ceramic mask he had picked up in New Orleans, and a framed photograph of Harry Houdini, the great escapist and magician.

Will mentally said good morning to his parents, vowing to call them down in South Carolina later that morning and knowing he would forget to do it. His dad loved the game of golf, maybe more than he did Will's mother, and so rather than Florida they had retired to Hilton Head.

The message light was blinking on his phone so he picked up his voice mail. There was only one message. "Good morning, Will. Do me a favor? Come see me when you get in."

It was Tad Green, the editor in chief of the *Trib*. There was no hint in his tone as to the nature of the impromptu meeting. Will got up from his desk and weaved through the bullpen toward the e in c's corner office. Halfway there he passed the cubicle where Stefan Bruning was busily doing his advance prep for the next day's Sports page.

"Hey. Did I hear right? You going after what's-her-name? The lady who talks to the dead on the radio?"

Will stopped short and looked down at him, brows knitted. "Helen Corsi. And she doesn't talk to the dead, Stef, she *pretends* to talk to the dead and gets paid for it by people who already have enough heartbreak in their lives. It's called *fraud*."

"Ah, man, come on," Stefan replied, waving him away. "You don't know that. I've listened to her on the radio. I'm not saying I'm going to pay her to do it, but it sure sounds real to me."

With a chuckle Will shook his head. "It's supposed to sound real. If it didn't, nobody would pay her. There are lots of people who think professional wrestling is real, too."

The sportswriter blanched. "You mean it isn't? Next you're gonna tell me there's no Easter bunny."

He managed to keep his face blank for the count of three, and then the two of them laughed. Will walked on toward the corner office as Stefan put his earplugs back in.

Tad's door was open. The editor in chief was dressed in a brown suit with a bright yellow tie, phone clutched to his ear. Will wore a decent shirt and black shoes, but invariably his uniform started with blue jeans. He doubted that Tad was required to wear a suit, but could not imagine why anyone would choose to do so if they didn't have to. It was one of the mysteries of life.

Will stopped just outside the office and rapped on the door frame. Inside, Tad looked up and nodded, holding up one finger to indicate that he should wait. The e in c was forty-seven, but he was thin and his eyes were blue and bright, and that lent him a boyish air in spite of his thinning hair.

"Hey, Will, come on in," Tad said as he hung up the phone. He motioned with one hand but his gaze went back out into the bullpen. "Close the door, will you?"

What gave it away was the fact that Tad did not look at his face as he stepped into the room. Only after Will had closed the door and slid into the chair opposite the editor in chief's desk did Tad meet his gaze. By then, Will had the whole thing figured out.

"You picked a new Lifestyles editor. And it isn't me."

Tad actually flinched. He was a good manager, tough when it came to the job but fair and an amiable enough guy. But he sucked at delivering the bad news.

"You're a hell of a writer, Will. I've told you that a hundred times and it's always going to be true. But there are other things that come into play when making a decision like this, and—"

"Who'd you give it to?"

Tad picked up a pencil from his desk and tapped it on the arm of his chair. He sat back and regarded Will closely. "Lara Zahansky."

Will swore under his breath. It wouldn't have been so bad if it had been anyone else. Lara was a team player, a decent writer when it came to the mechanics of the job, but she had no flair, and her aesthetic judgment when it came to the arts was for shit. But she dotted all the *I*s and crossed all the *T*s and always met her deadlines. Perfect management material, in other words.

"Jesus, Tad," Will whispered.

"You're only twenty-eight years old, Will. Give it time. Work out some of the kinks and—"

Will's head snapped up and his eyes narrowed. "What kinks?"

Tad rolled his eyes. He was losing his patience. "Don't play games with me. You know what I'm talking about. Your age was a factor, but at least half the reason you didn't get the gig this time around is that you've made a rep as an eccentric. You're unpredictable, Will. That might be okay for a crime reporter, but this is Lifestyles."

"I've won awards for my work, Tad. Been in *People* magazine. What's Lara got on her resume?"

The editor in chief gave him a hard look, all the reticence burned out of him now. "For starters, she's got *this* job."

Will ground his teeth and looked away.

Tad sighed. "Will, look at the Lifestyles pieces you've done in your tenure here. At least a quarter of them have this occult angle. Mediums. Psychics. Witches." He paused. "Vampires, Will. You wrote about vampires."

Tired now, Will slipped a few inches lower in his chair, getting comfortable. He had had this conversation far too often for his taste. "I've done stories on mediums and psychics in order to debunk their claims, Tad. I've worked with the state Better Business Bureau to expose frauds and get people their money back. I've done stories on Wicca, a modern religion made up of so-called witches, mainly to explain the difference between them and the hags with pointy hats and broomsticks.

"As for the vampires, that piece was about cults of people who either believe or pretend that they're actual vampires, but who spend their time cutting themselves and drinking each other's blood. There are parties devoted to it, major gatherings all across the country, which you'd know if you bothered to actually read the pieces you're talking about. All right, I confess, the idea that people believe this kind of bullshit gets under my skin. So when I see it out there, I want to shed some light on it. You want to know why? Fine. My grandmother lost her life savings to a woman who helped her *communicate* with my dead grandfather. Is it personal? Sure, but that doesn't make it any less valid. Someone's got to debunk the charlatans, Tad. Why does that make me eccentric?"

Will took a deep breath, gazing steadily at the editor in chief. For a long moment Tad only returned his stare. Then the man reached up and loosened the knot on his tie and leaned forward, elbows on his desk.

"Will—"

"It's crap, Tad. Give the job to Lara. She's competent. I'm sure she'll be fine. But don't tell me I can't do the job because I'm 'eccentric.'"

The editor in chief pushed back his chair and walked over to the windows. The corner office gave him a wonderful view of Massachusetts Avenue. The sunlight flooded the room, brightening the yellow of his tie, the green and red in a painting on the wall, the orange of the ceramic jack-o'-lantern on his desk; yet somehow it made his face washed-out and pale, his thinning hair little more than wisps in the bright light.

He slipped his hands in his pockets. "Look, Will, I'm sorry. Truly. I could've bullshitted you, laid it off to Lara having more years at the paper. But that wouldn't have been doing you any favors. You've got this little crusade going, and with what happened to your grandmother, I guess I understand it. We've gotten some great pieces out of it, I won't deny that. But you might want to tone it down in the future. That's all. I thought you should know why you didn't get this gig, so maybe things will be different the next time around."

For a long moment the two men regarded one another. Then Will took another long breath and shrugged. "I just try to do my job as well as I can. This wasn't the news I wanted today. I guess I'll get back to it."

"Hey," Tad said as Will started to walk out of the office. He waited for Will to pause and look back before continuing. "Stick it out. It'll happen for you eventually. You're too good not to make it work for you. I was thirty-five before I was made an editor."

Will nodded politely. Tad didn't want him to quit. That was almost funny. Disappointed as he was, where would he go? He was a reporter and a critic. It was the only thing he had ever wanted to do.

THE REST OF THE MORNING flew by in a rush of e-mail and phone calls as Will tried to focus on his draft of the story about the supposed radio medium. He did a quick follow-up interview with one of her most avid supporters, during which he feigned interest just long enough to get a handful of usable quotes. By the time he had hung up the phone it was ten till noon.

Tugging his sweatshirt from the back of his chair, he got up and hurried from the newsroom, glancing at the clock as he rushed for the elevator. He was going to be late.

Thanks to Tad Green's bad news, the magic of the October day had escaped him, yet it returned the moment he set foot back out on the street. The air was still crisp, the sky ice blue, and he could smell the smoke from a fireplace or wood-burnin stove on the breeze. Right here; this was the only kind of magic that mattered.

As he walked the four blocks to Carmine's Trattoria—a place he loved for the freshness of its food and the paper map-of-Italy placemats that set off an otherwise sophisticated decor—he took his sweatshirt off and draped it over his shoulder. The lunchtime crowd had hit the sidewalks, milling about and crossing the streets at abandon, slowing Cambridge traffic even further. Will passed a construction site, where surprisingly tactful men in hardhats watched a slender, model-beautiful woman walk her terrier down the street with admiring glances but no rude shouts or whistles.

Will watched her as well. The woman was breathtaking in a sheer, sky blue top and crisply new jeans. Seeing her—and the men loosening their ties and women tying sweaters around their waists—made it feel like spring instead of fall. Will found himself suffused with a feeling of well-being that brought a smile to his face and made him chuckle softly to himself.

When he walked past the front windows of Carmine's he spotted Ashleigh and Eric DeSantis at a table right in front. Grinning, he tapped on the glass. Ashleigh was on her cell phone, but when she looked up and saw him her eyes sparkled and her face lit up with a smile that made her look ten years old again. She wore a deep red cable-knit sweater that brought out the auburn highlights in her chestnut hair and was tight enough to flatter her slender frame. In a white oxford shirt and khaki pants, Eric sat tilted back on his chair and raised a hand to offer a casual wave. That was Eric, cool as could be, letting the world just wash over him.

When Will was a kid, Ashleigh had literally been the girl next door. Their mothers had walked them side by side in their strollers and planned play dates. They had grown up together on the broad expanse of lawn between their backyards, bisected by a row of tall shrubs, and on the swing set behind Ashleigh's house. They had explored the woods that began at the back of their property lines and stretched what looked like forever, into some primordial forest of their imagination.

She was his oldest friend, and he had never thought of her any other way. Even when his buddies at Kennedy Middle School and later Eastborough High teased him, Will looked at her thin, elegant features and lush brown hair and saw the girl he'd gone trick-or-treating with every Halloween since birth, the girl who had cried on his shoulder the first time she had ever kissed a boy, because the little shit hadn't kissed her back. Will had punched Jimmy Renahan in the head for that one, and Jimmy hadn't had a clue as to why.

Will's parents had never had any other children, but in Ashleigh, he had a sister.

When he walked into the restaurant she rushed to meet him. He wrapped his arms around her and lifted her several inches off the ground in a bear hug.

"Hey, Ash. Welcome home."

She grinned and hugged him again. "You have to visit more. I miss you so much. You haven't come down to see us since New Year's!"

Ashleigh and Eric lived in Elmsford, New York, where she was a lawyer and he was the athletic director for a private high school, and where they still somehow managed to be fantastic parents to their twins. Though he knew it wasn't, they made it look easy, and that gave him faith.

Will made an effort to go down and see them a couple of times a year and always came away pleased that Ashleigh had married Eric. It could be difficult at times—when he had been with Caitlyn the four of them had often formed a social quartet—but his pleasure at seeing Ashleigh happy far outweighed whatever discomfort his own regrets might bring him.

With his arm around her he walked to the table and shook hands with her husband.

"Good to see you, Will," Eric said. "Have a seat."

They hadn't been seated for thirty seconds before Ashleigh

leaned over and gave him a conspiratorial grin. "So, come on. You know you want to go."

"I really don't."

Eric shook his head and picked up a sweating bottle of Sam Adams from the table. "You do. You just want to make us all suffer and prove our love by begging you to come along. So no more of that shit." His eyes were alight with mischief. "One comment from me, Will, then we're done. If I was single, I would take this opportunity to spend the weekend banging all the girls I wanted to have sex with in high school but never got the chance to."

Ashleigh leaned over the table, chin rested on her palm, hazel eyes narrowed with interest. "Oh, really. And which ones were those, honey?"

"Nah, I'm not talking about me, sweetheart. But Will, he was a horny dog back then. I'm sure he's got a list."

His wife pretended to look scandalized and Will just rolled his eyes and reached for his menu.

Ashleigh sighed softly. "Is it Caitlyn? Please don't tell me you don't want to go just because you don't want to see her. Otherwise I'll have to lock her in a closet for the weekend."

"No. I don't think I'd enjoy seeing her, but it wouldn't kill me. Time heals all wounds, right?"

He hoped he sounded more confident than he felt. Will's relationship with Caitlyn Rouge had survived high school graduation and four years of college, only to fall messily apart on what was to be their wedding day. It was an old wound, but the truth was that five years after their breakup, it still had not healed.

"So?" Ashleigh prodded, nudging him, knowing with absolute certainty that he loved her too much to take offense.

As he perused the list of salads Will shook his head slightly. Even if Caitlyn did show up, years had passed since the last time they had seen one another. The world had moved on, unmindful of whether or not he still loved her. Which was fine, in a way. A lot had happened in those intervening years, and it was not as though he had any illusions.

"I'll regret this later if I don't go, won't I?" he asked without glancing up from the menu.

"Horribly. Particularly because of the torment you'll suffer at my hands," Ashleigh promised.

Slowly, Will lowered his head to the table and thumped it once against the wood.

WHEN HE RETURNED to the office the first thing he did was check his e-mail. The first of the two film screenings he had to go to started at three o'clock, so he only had about half an hour before he had to fly out the door again. There were twenty-seven e-mails, many of which were attempting to lure him to various pornographic Web sites or to sell him Omaha steaks or crystal penguins. Roughly one third of them were business; a handful were personal.

As he was responding to his e-mail, Will ruminated on the events of the day thus far. His feelings about the reunion did not stem from an actual aversion to attending, but from a general lack of interest. Certainly there was a curiosity about old friends and ac-quaintances, but the people he really wanted to see he had already made plans to visit with while they were in town. Lunch with Ashleigh and Eric had been planned because he had no intention of attending the reunion. He saw Danny and his wife often enough.

His brow furrowed. There was something else he had planned, but it seemed to have slipped his mind. Then, abruptly, it came to him. *Lebo!* He and Mike Lebo had exchanged e-mails the previous week. Mike was flying in from Arizona for the re-union and he and Will had made a plan to get together on Sun-day afternoon.

What the hell's wrong with me? Will thought, annoyed that he had let it slip his mind. Mike had been part of the group he'd hung out with all through high school, along with Danny and Eric, Ashleigh and Caitlyn, and a handful of others. They spoke a few times a year, but he had not seen Mike for ages.

For a long moment he stared at his computer screen, and then he chuckled softly to himself. *Why the hell not?*

Will typed up a quick e-mail to let Mike know that he had changed his mind. Seeing everyone separately was all right, but the more he thought about it the more he realized that having the whole gang together would be really nice. He had to search his memory for Mike's e-mail address, since for some reason he couldn't find it in his computer address book, but it was fairly simple and his recall for that kind of thing had always been good.

He sent the e-mail, confirming that he would be there, but a few minutes later, as he was getting ready to head out to the first screening, he received notice in his Outlook in-box that his message had been rejected because the user name "lebomp01" was unknown to the system.

Will frowned and stared at the screen. It had taken him a moment to remember, but he was certain there was no mistake in the e-mail address he had used. There was nothing he could do at the moment, however. Not if he wanted to make the screening on time. And when he was wearing his critic's hat he was a stickler about promptness. Will James would never write a review about something he had not witnessed in its entirety.

He'd see Mike tomorrow night. Anything they had to say to one another would keep until then.

CHAPTER 2

Sometime during the night it began to rain. Will woke, staggered into the bathroom, and forced his eyes open to slits only wide enough to guarantee his aim. When he returned to the mess of his bed and fumbled to wrap himself in the covers, he became aware of the patter of raindrops on the windows and the sound the water made sluicing down the drainpipes.

Barely awake, he settled his head back into the pillows and let the sound lull him back to sleep, just as he had always done as a child in the small bedroom of his family's home on Parmenter Road.

By morning the rain had stopped but the sky was still overcast, and the air that whispered in through the partially open windows was damp and cold. Will stretched and yawned and stared at the clock on his bureau. It was already a quarter to nine.

For several minutes he just lay there with his eyes closed, hands crossed over his chest as though in deathly repose, and wondered if he would fall back to sleep. He might have dozed a little, but soon enough his eyes fluttered open and he knew he was now up for the day. With the exception of the aftermath of the rare night of drunken debauchery, Will never managed to sleep very late, even if he wanted to.

He scraped his hand across the stubble on his chin and slipped from the bed in his T-shirt and underwear. He snatched up a pair of blue, mostly clean sweatpants from the cold hardwood floor. Balancing carefully, he slipped into the sweats and then ran both hands through his sleep-bedraggled hair. In the bathroom, he splashed some water on his face to help him wake up and tried to focus on the eyes staring back at him from the mirror.

"You're really gonna do this?" he asked himself. But he knew the answer, just as he knew that mostly he was just blowing smoke, even to himself. The truth was, he wanted to go to the reunion. He just wasn't sure what to expect.

His stomach rumbled and he thought about breakfast, but there was something else he had to do first. Will's feet were cold on the wood floor as he went through the living room, but the linoleum in the kitchen was even colder. The archaic radiator hissed and clanked on the other side of the room, but the heat that emanated from it never seemed to warm the floor. The apartment was in an old Victorian in Somerville, just outside of Davis Square, only a single T stop away from the office.

But Will wasn't going in to the office today. If he was going to do this, he was going to do it right, devote the day to the sort of rumination and reminiscence that he rarely indulged in.

He retrieved a glass from the cabinet and poured himself some Grovestand orange juice, the kind with extra pulp. Then he picked up the phone and called the *Trib*, dialing the main number for the newsroom. After three rings, the phone was answered by Ruth Kaplan, who doubled as receptionist and part-time copy editor for the paper.

"*Boston Tribune.*"

"Morning, Ruth, it's Will."

"Hey, there," Ruth said pleasantly. They'd been out a few times, slept together twice, and both knew it was not going to go any further. "I noticed you hadn't come in today. You on assignment?"

"Nope," Will said happily. "Actually, I'm calling in sick."

"You don't sound sick," Ruth mused.

"Oh, but I am. So very. If anyone asks, I'm e-mailing the final drafts of the two features I've been working on to Tad and to Lara. Otherwise, I'm off the clock."

There was a pause as Ruth took this in. When she spoke again he could hear the amusement in her voice.

"Whatever you say, Will. Feel better."

"Absolutely."

They said their good-byes and Will hung up the phone. He downed half the glass of OJ, then left it on the counter as he went back through the apartment to the second bedroom, which he used as a home office. A sense of quiet satisfaction filled him as he drew a deep breath and let it out. Was he disappointed about Lara Zahansky getting the promotion he had hoped for? Shit, yeah. Was he going to let it get in the way of his job? Not at all.

On the other hand, Tad Green probably would have given him the day off if he had asked the previous afternoon and explained why he wanted it. Will wasn't going to leave it up to Tad, though. He liked the man well enough, most of the time. But right about now, he figured Tad Green could go fuck himself.

Will chuckled. *Looks like you need this weekend more than you thought you did.*

In the black leather chair he had picked up for next to nothing at Staples, he turned on his computer and logged on to the Net. More of the usual spam. He answered the few personal messages, but when the in-box was empty he stared at the computer screen for several seconds as though expecting something more. It was the same way he always double-checked the contents of his mailbox; the way Yukon Cornelius in the *Rudolph, the Red-Nosed Reindeer* TV special licked the end of his ice pick and said, "ah, nuthin'."

But there weren't any other messages.

His friend Danny Plumer had been hugely into the music of the seventies back in high school and on countless nights Will had found himself trapped in the passenger seat while Danny drove his father's car, listening to Lynyrd Skynyrd and the Eagles. A line from a Bob Seger song stuck in his head now—and though he could remember sitting in the Jetta, roaring down Route 495 with the windows down, hearing that song pumping from the speakers, he couldn't for the life of him remember the song the words were attached to.

The words, though, he recalled very well. *"See some old friends,"* Seger had sung. *"Good for the soul."*

Will had never really gotten into the old stuff. He was more interested in Nirvana and Soundgarden, and to a lesser extent in calmer bands like They Might Be Giants and Barenaked Ladies. But that didn't mean he couldn't appreciate the stuff Danny listened to. Or the words.

So this weekend he would see some old friends. And maybe, just maybe, it would be good for the soul.

BY THE TIME Will had his Toyota rolling west on the Massachusetts Turnpike, the sky had begun to clear. The cloud cover was dark in places, but there were patches where the sun broke through, revealing blue sky beyond. There might be a few more showers, but Will believed the clouds were on the way out.

It felt good to be away from the city and he kept the window rolled down a few inches, WBCN cranked a little too loud on the radio. The woods that lined both sides of the turnpike were rich with the colors of autumn, the trees bright with reds and coppers and golds that shone despite the overcast sky. He drove on toward Natick and Framingham, and Eastborough beyond, and he could not help but think of Halloween, of trick-or-treating, and raking frosted leaves with his dad, who had always waited late in the season to do the job.

Danny and the guys would have ragged him for romanticizing the suburbs. Parts of Eastborough were rural, but it was not exactly the country. In a way, though, it was still a classic small New England town.

Will spent a lot of his free time hanging out with Zora and Kate, the lesbian couple who lived downstairs from him and who were always trying to fix him up with their straight girlfriends. They shared movie nights with him, went to the occasional club.

There were a handful of people at work he would have a drink or a meal with now and again. And of course there was Danny. Then there was Carlos, his closest friend from college, who lived in Salem and worked in graphic design.

Not a lot of friends, perhaps, but his life was fairly busy just the same. And maybe that was all he had room for. All in all, the job and his handful of friends kept him busy enough that it had been well over a year, maybe closer to two, since he had done anything more than drive past exit 12 on the turnpike. Once his parents had moved, he had no real reason to go back to Eastborough.

It wasn't home anymore.

But as he paid the toll and drove the Toyota around the curved ramp onto Route 9, it sure felt like coming home.

Eastborough was part of a geographical diamond that also included Northborough, Southborough, and Westborough, but the easiest way to reach it was by slipping past Framingham and into Marlboro, then curving slightly west on Old Buffalo Farm Road. The name always made Will smile. The suburbs, sure, but that was the country right there. The scary thing was, there actually was a farm that had buffaloes in its pasture, and penny candy in the general store across the street. It was a little piece of quaint that stuck around mainly because nobody had the heart to let it go.

As he drove into Eastborough, images flashed through Will's mind. He was certain that the occasion of his visit had him feeling more nostalgic than normal, but the images kept coming despite that awareness. He passed Market Street, which would lead down to Kennedy Middle School and Robinson Field, where he and his friends had played baseball and football, making up their own rules.

He guided the Toyota past the strip mall that contained The Sampan, which had the best Chinese takeout in town, and Annie's Book Stop, where he had bought all of the used paperback mystery, horror, and fantasy novels that had intrigued him so much as a kid—right up until the point where he had stopped reading that sort of thing entirely. Still, the memory of the place—the smell of the old books, digging through the shelves—was a pleasant one. He had done the same kind of cultural archaeology in the used CD shop down on Knight Road, and he knew that those afternoons had contributed as much to his chosen career as the trips to the movies in Marlboro and Framingham.

In the center of town he passed the library, in whose study carrels he had first kissed Polly Creedon in the fifth grade. Athens Pizza had been replaced by Giovanni's Pizza & Subs, but other than the sign the place looked much the same. He had taken Sandy Weisman there on the first official date he had ever had with a girl, and he and the guys—Danny, Eric, Mike, Nick, and Brian—had hung out there a hundred times. A thousand times—or so it seemed.

He wondered if any of their graffiti was still legible on the bathroom walls.

Once his mother had driven away from Athens with the two pizzas she had just picked up still on the roof. Will still remembered the thump as the two boxes tumbled down to hit the trunk before flopping into the street. Diana James had sworn like a truck driver while her son Will was laughing his ass off.

Gone completely were Herbie's Ice Cream, where Will and Nick Acosta had worked summers all through high school, and the Comic Book Palace, where Mike had dragged them dozens of times. None of the other guys had been into comics but they'd all go along with Mike if they were out and happened to be passing by. Then, of course, they'd torture him for reading X-Men and Spider-Man, and never mind that they all thought Wolverine was cool.

What disturbed Will was that he could not even remember how long Herbie's and the Palace had been gone. It might have been years or only months. The last couple of times he had driven through Eastborough, he knew he would not have been paying enough attention to notice.

He turned west after the center, down Fordham Street. Video stores, gas stations, and liquor stores lined the road that led, eventually, back toward Route 9 and the pike. An ancient McDonald's stood at the intersection with Weldon Hill, and he had a sudden image of being hungover there after a sleepover at Tommy Berman's, pushing past the other guys to get to the bathroom so he could vomit up an Egg McMuffin.

Farther along Fordham Street there was Liam's, the Irish tavern where they had all tried to get served, and where Nick Acosta now tended bar. The reunion weekend would get under way there at seven o'clock—as good a place as any to kick things off. He wondered how many people would attend the party at Liam's or the football game tomorrow, and how many would just show up for the official reunion gathering on Saturday night.

He wondered which of his classmates wouldn't bother to show at all.

And, much as he tried to avoid it, he wondered if Caitlyn would be there. How she would look. Who she would be with.

They had been over for a long time and Will was not a fool. Not only was he sure there was no chance of reconciliation, he had no desire to attempt one. The woman had not bothered to make an appearance at the altar on what had been intended to be their wedding day. They were history, and Will James had a lot of future to look forward to. A full life to go back to on Sunday night when the reunion weekend was over.

But some of the best memories he had, some of the sweetest moments in his life, he had shared with Caitlyn. Even if there was nothing ahead for them, they were bonded forever by what lay behind. In a way, he supposed that was true of all of them, the entire crew with whom he had grown up. Whatever his life was now, they were part of its foundation. Their collective experiences were a part of him, and would always be, even if he never saw any of them again.

It was almost two o'clock when he turned the Toyota up Parmenter Road. The neighborhood had been built in the late fifties and early sixties, and looked it. Ranches and split-levels dominated, but still it was one of the nicer areas in Eastborough if you didn't count the upscale private developments that had sprung up in the decade since he'd graduated.

All of the homes were well maintained, the lawns neatly landscaped. Soccer moms were out power-walking behind sport-strollers. SUVs sat dormant in driveways. A sixtyish man with thinning gray hair walked his yellow Labrador, the dog hauling him forward with an eagerness that threatened to tug the man off his feet.

Will nearly did not recognize the house he had grown up in.

Number 76 Parmenter Road was a split-level with a large yard and a triangular garden beside the front walk that was almost exotic. Berry bushes and thin trees with an Asian flair had jutted from that triangle of soil. But all of the shrubs that had once lined the front of the house had been removed, with only sod left in their wake. A pair of ash trees was also gone—Will's eyes had itched all the time because of those damn trees, but he was sad to see the bare patches where they had once stood. The current owners had also removed the shutters and painted the house completely white.

It was hideous.

"Holy shit," he muttered to himself as he slowed the Toyota to a standstill.

For a long time he just sat in the car and stared at the house. A while later a bus rumbled past at the bottom of the street, disgorging kids from the high school. When the lanky, redheaded kid rapped on his window, Will jumped, heart pounding, and glared at him.

"Hey. You scared the crap out of me," Will said, putting the window down.

"Help you with something? You lost?"

The kid was maybe sixteen and broad-shouldered, just that age when he thought the world was full of shit and he might have to kick its ass any minute. He glared right back into the car, at this man who was pulled over to the side of the road and was staring at his house.

No wonder, Will thought. *Probably thinks I'm a stalker or something.*

"Lost?" Will considered telling the kid that yeah, he was lost, and then driving off. He surprised himself by telling the truth. "Not really. Actually, I used to live here. That your house?"

"Yeah." The kid's face was impassive, giving away nothing. Will wondered if he and his friends had been that insolent, and figured they had.

Will smiled. "That place has a lot of stories to tell."

Maybe it was the wistful tone in Will's voice or the look on his face or maybe it was his words. Whatever did it, the kid's expression actually changed, his suspicious frown melting into an amused grin.

"Yeah?" he said. "Well, so far it hasn't said a word to me."

"Could be it's keeping its secrets," Will suggested.

"Could be," the kid agreed. "Or maybe it's just pissed that my parents freakin' neutered it, taking down those shutters and all those bushes. Wanted it to look different. I guess ugly is different enough."

Will laughed out loud. The kid had echoed the thoughts he had been too polite to express. For a long moment they just looked at one another. Will thought about introducing himself, then realized there was no point. This was their moment of contact, right here. It was unlikely they'd ever meet again.

"You take care," he said, then he started to pull away.

"Yeah," the kid said—his favorite word—and waved. "You, too."

Will turned around in the Ginzlers' driveway a few houses up, and on the way back down he saw the kid going inside his house and shutting the door. As Will drove away, he wondered if there would ever come a time when the redheaded kid would sit on the side of the road in his car and stare in horror at what some new-owner assholes had done to his home.

WILL SPENT THE AFTERNOON just wandering around town. He knew that some of his friends were showing up early at Liam's for dinner, but he felt a kind of inner quiet that made him shy away. Instead he went into Annie's Book Stop and lost himself in the musty racks of used paperbacks, just glancing through titles. Eventually he found a Len Deighton book about World War II, and that was his sole purchase. He read the first three chapters sitting in The Sampan eating wonton soup and General Tsao's Chicken, careful not to get any food on his V-necked navy sweater or the crisp new blue jeans he wore.

After dinner he left his car in the lot of the strip mall and went across the street to the Brooks Pharmacy. Once upon a time it had been an Osco, and before that a CVS. At the age of nine, with his mother over in the cosmetics section, he had stood in the candy aisle, glancing nervously back and forth to see if anyone was watching him as he debated stuffing a Snickers bar into his pocket. His conscience had won the debate, but even though he had not stolen anything, he had still felt guilty about it afterward.

Now he bought a pack of Altoids to rid his mouth of the dreaded Chinese-food-breath and chewed three of them instantly, then followed them with two more.

When he returned to his car, ready to head over to Liam's, he found that it was still only six-thirty. Though he had not wanted to be early, there was no way he was going to just sit in his car or invent something else to do in order to avoid it. He had enjoyed the afternoon on his own, but he found himself anticipating the evening quite a bit.

Will started up the engine and the radio blared to life in the midst of the Barenaked Ladies tune "The Old Apartment." A smile spread across Will's face as he sang along:

"*This is where we used to live. . . .*"

When he reached Liam's, the parking lot was already nearly full. The place had always been popular, and it was Friday night. There was a room upstairs, which he guessed was where his classmates would be gathered, but the main dining room and bar on the first floor would be packed as well.

While he had been wandering through the stacks at Annie's the afternoon had cleared. There were still clouds in the early-evening sky, but they made a mural of shades of blue and none of them were threatening. There would be no more rain tonight. He climbed out of the car and started across the lot. The air was crisp and cold and he zipped his jacket up to his neck as he approached the restaurant.

Just looking at Liam's Irish Tavern, a rambling old mid-nineteenth-century building with dark green paint and shamrocks on the sign, made him smile. It was good to know that some things never changed.

"Hey, Will!"

Just outside the door he turned to see a quartet of new arrivals moving through the parked cars toward the restaurant. Leading the pack was Joe Rosenthal, who had called out to him. Joe had been their class president all four years and Will had worked with him on the school paper. The two shared the same build, not tall but broad-shouldered. Will had remained fit, but Joe had a potbelly now and his hair was already thinning. There was a pair of women with him, both of whom Will recognized. One was Kelly Meserve, but to his horror he could not remember the other woman's name at all. He doubted if they had ever exchanged words in high school, but he still ought to be able to remember her name. Their class had not been that big.

Tammy? Terri? Something like that. Hell, nobody's going to remember everyone.

The last of the four was Tim Friel, who had been captain of the football team junior and senior year, but was such a quiet, humble guy that nobody could hold it against him. Tim had dated his share of cheerleaders, but he had never fit the stereotype of the football captain made popular by countless idiotic teen movies. The Eastborough Cougars had certainly had their share of dim-witted, cruel-natured assholes on the football team; it was simply that Tim was not one of them.

"No shit," Will said happily as he took a few steps back toward them and shook hands with Joe. "How've you been?"

Joe grinned. "Never better." But there was something in his tone, and in his gray eyes, that gave the lie to those words.

"Good to see you, Will," Tim said quietly.

Will rocked on his feet and regarded the ex–football star, who was just as tall, handsome, and boyish as he had been back in the day. "What about you, Tim? What've you been up to?"

"I'm coaching at Holy Cross." Tim smiled, and there was a sparkle in his ice blue eyes. "It's not quarterbacking for the Miami Dolphins, but it's a great way to spend your days. Almost feels like I never graduated."

Will nodded. "I know what you mean. I talk to my friends from college and listen to them bitch and I figure, hey, I actually like what I do. That's pretty rare. I'm not complaining."

The two of them exchanged a look and Will was surprised to feel a moment of connection with this guy he had never really been friends with. Neither of them had accomplished what they'd dreamed about, but still they counted themselves lucky.

The pleasantries went on for another minute or so before the entire group went into Liam's together. Will had said hello to Kelly, caught up a bit with Tim and Joe, but as they were stepping into the foyer of the tavern, the woman whose name he could not remember smiled at him shyly, even a bit flirtatiously.

"Hey, Will. It's been a while."

Reflexively, he gave a hollow laugh. "Too long." He hoped that nothing in his face would give away how completely clueless he was as to her identity. *Tori? Kerry?* She seemed not to notice and he was grateful when she moved ahead to catch up with Kelly.

Inside Liam's they were enveloped in a cloud of wonderful smells. Waiters and waitresses weaved in amongst the tables, serving steaks that were still sizzling on cast-iron plates that would burn if you touched them. Will hadn't been inside Liam's in a decade, but the smell and the decor were so familiar it was like another sort of homecoming.

The hostess confirmed that their classmates were gathering in the function room upstairs, and Will followed the others along a narrow corridor to the steps that led to the second floor. As he climbed he heard laughter and music drifting down toward him.

Will had one final moment of trepidation; then, as he stepped into the room, it evaporated in an instant. He was a little early, but it seemed as though the party had started anyway. Dozens of people had already arrived, some of them eating dinner at the round tables, others mingling in front of the bar. As Will entered with Joe, Tim, Kelly, and the mystery woman— *Terri, pretty sure it's Terri*—a number of curious faces turned to look at them.

Familiar faces. Older faces.

His mind was on overload, sifting through them all. There was bookish Delia Young, now sleek and elegant, talking with Todd Vasquez. A group of perhaps a half-dozen men and women were gathered around Chuck Wisialowski at the bar. The faces of the guys—all of them ten years past their glory days on Eastborough High's hockey team—were just as pinched and sour-looking as ever. Laughter erupted from the group, and Chuck took that as his cue to knock back a shot of something. He let out a kind of snarl, the very image of a drunken frat boy.

Chuck was the only person Will had ever had an actual fist-fight with. He had always regretted that his history teacher, Mr. Sandoval, had broken it up. In his mind, forever and always, the guys who had been on the hockey team would remain a herd of slack-jawed goons. It was a prejudice he had accepted long ago. And from the looks of things, the years had not done much to alter either his perception or the reality.

As Will mentally sifted through the other faces in the room he noticed something else as well—the spouses and significant others. At the tables they seemed to sit back just slightly, and in groups they protruded from the edges of a conversation as though they might slip away at any moment.

Will waded into the room, into a sea of hard kisses and firm embraces, of compliments and questions and pats on the back. To his relief he found that he could remember at least the first name of everyone he saw, if not the last. Adrenaline surged through him, along with a kind of high he had not expected. It felt good to be around them, to laugh and smile and reminisce. He knew without a doubt that in an hour he would for the most part have forgotten who lived where, had how many children, or did what for a living, but that seemed less important in the moment than the simple act of reconnecting.

He had been shanghaied by a pair of old friends who had also written for the school newspaper when, beyond them, he saw Ashleigh coming his way waving both hands over her head. Will laughed.

"Excuse me, you guys," he said, then he slipped between them.

Ashleigh punched him in the shoulder. "Goofball," she chided him, wearing that mischievous grin that always silently reminded him how much she meant to him. "I've been waving to you for like an hour."

"I've been here for three minutes."

"Well, you're blind. We've been trying to get your attention the whole time."

She gestured toward the far corner of the room, where Eric sat with Danny Plumer and his wife. With them were the ethereally beautiful Carrie Klaussen, whom Will had dubbed "PixieGirl" during high school, and Lolly something, whose real name Will didn't think he had ever known. They were all grinning, waving at him like fools.

Ashleigh took him by the hand and dragged him over to the table, where he said hello to Eric. Danny got up to give him a bear hug—he was a burly guy and could lift Will right off the floor. They spent a minute pretending to reminisce about how long it had been since they'd seen one another—in reality ten days—and each commented that the other looked like shit and had clearly aged very poorly in that time.

Will kissed Danny's wife Keisha on the cheek. Then he smiled over at Carrie, who rose from the table to hug him.

"Hey, Pix," he said as they broke their embrace. He looked into her eyes. "It's really good to see you."

"You, too," she replied, nodding as though to punctuate her sincerity. "But nobody calls me that anymore."

"Except me," he teased. His gaze ticked toward Lolly, whose dark skin and sculpted features were such a dramatic foil to PixieGirl; it had always made their status as best friends that much more fascinating. Two beautiful girls—women now—who couldn't look less alike. "Pix and Lolly. You guys will always be Pix and Lolly in my head. You should've gotten together. As girlfriends, you know? It always seemed so right."

Lolly laughed. "We tried it once. Didn't like it."

Will smiled in appreciation. "You know, I can't tell if you're bullshitting me, but if you are, please just let me go on believing that."

He bent to kiss her on the cheek as well.

There followed just the slightest awkward pause, a silent moment filled only by the music being played at the other end of the room and by the strange feeling that there was a ghost among them. Pix gave him a look that was sort of sad.

She had been there that day—the day he was supposed to have married Caitlyn. Pix had been the maid of honor. Panicked and humiliated, Will had jokingly asked her if she wanted to stand in. And PixieGirl had cried for him.

He smiled at her now and leaned close in so that no one else could hear him. "I'm fine," he said.

"No, *I'm* fine," she teased. "You, you're just okay."

"Will, what'll you have?" Danny asked. "Have you eaten? Want a drink? What's your pleasure?"

Before he could answer something hit him in the back of the head. Will spun just in time to see a maraschino cherry bounce on the ground. When he touched his head where it had struck him, his hair was sticky. He shot a glance over at the bar and could only laugh.

"Hang on," he told Danny.

He marched over to the bar, where Nick Acosta was pouring

glasses of wine for a pair of women who were obviously spouses. Neither of them looked familiar to him at all. When the spouses departed, Will rapped on the bar.

"Barkeep. Captain Morgan and Coke, please."

Nick shuddered with revulsion and shot him a look that wrinkled the thin white scar that trailed down from his scalp across his forehead and through his left eyebrow. The sight of it triggered a memory in Will, images of freshman year, when Nick had lost his footing playing basketball in the schoolyard and careened into a tree, a broken limb peeling his skin back far enough that when he looked up, blood veiling his features, the other guys gathered there had been able to see bone. Even now, all these years later, with his black hair, a mass of curls and cowlicks, and deep olive skin, the scar was like a magnet to the eye, forcing anyone talking to Nick to glance at it at least once.

"Spiced rum. You still drinking that crap?" Nick asked. "Don't know how you don't sick it up."

Will gave him a blank look. "I do. Is that not supposed to happen?"

Nick chuckled and started to fix the drink as he regarded Will. "How you doing, man? Been way too long."

"Doing great. Can't complain, though it usually doesn't stop me."

"Any love in your life?" Nick asked, raising that same scarred eyebrow. He was tall enough that he seemed to loom over Will from behind the bar.

"Comes and goes," Will replied, and though their banter was light, there was a truth to it, just as there had always been in these conversations with Nick. He was the sage of the group. Whenever anybody had a problem, Nick was the one they talked to.

"It always does," Nick replied. "Then again, who knows what fate might have in store for you this weekend? For instance, have you taken a look at her?"

He gestured across the room.

Will turned.

On a raised platform a woman sat on a stool with an electric acoustic guitar and a microphone. Since he had walked in Will had been enjoying her raspy, smoky voice and the way she played. Old Tori Amos songs side by side with The Corrs and Nelly Furtado. But only now did he get a good look at her.

She was slender, with an exotic bronze complexion that was set off by the green silk shirt she wore with plain blue jeans. Her black hair was lush and draped in a sensual curtain across her face when she bent over her guitar to play a break.

"You have got to be kidding me," Will whispered. "Stacy?"

Nick laughed. "Gives you a funny tingle, doesn't she?"

Will glanced at him. "She always did," he admitted. But Nick already knew that. Nick knew the whole story, in fact, for he had gone with Will on the ski trip the senior class had taken to Mount Orford in Canada. On the bus ride north Will had spent more than two hours locked in conversation with Stacy Shipman, the girl with the sweetest, most suggestive smile he had ever seen. Party girl. Pothead. Double trouble. Stacy had been all of those things, but mysterious as well, for she had never really hung out with her classmates. Though there had been a couple of exceptions—mostly tough guys who did too many drugs and didn't graduate anyway.

Caitlyn had been his girlfriend, but Will had always been fascinated by Stacy. All of the guys were. And on that bus ride, for the first time, he had gotten to know her and discovered that she was bright and funny and ambitious, all of the things her reputation said she could not possibly be.

They had never hung out again after that, but at graduation Stacy had written a very long note in his yearbook, thanking him for that talk on the bus, for being "real" with her. He had never forgotten it, or her.

Will thanked Nick for the drink, promised his friends he'd be back to the table in just a minute, and walked straight across the room to slide into a chair right in front of that platform. There, he watched Stacy finish up an old Edwin McCain tune.

Near the end of the song, as she lifted her head to sing the chorus for a final time, she saw him. In the midst of strumming chords, she broke off and gave him a little wave, then her fingers fell right back into rhythm. When she was done and a ripple of applause went through the room, Stacy leaned into the microphone.

"Thanks, you guys," she said softly. "We got started a little early, so I'm gonna take a short break and then we'll kick it up a notch."

Another round of applause followed her as she set her guitar on its stand and stepped down off the platform, striding over to Will. He stood up, drink in hand, but he didn't hug or kiss her. They had never had that kind of friendship.

"Hey," she said, almost shyly, though there was nothing shy in her gaze. It was just her way.

"You're amazing."

She glanced at the ground for a moment. "Thanks."

"It's really nice to see you," he said. "I hoped you'd be here, actually. Of all the people we went to high school with, there are only a couple I really wanted to see again. I'm glad you made it."

"Me, too," she said, nodding. Then she reached out and took his hand, gave his fingers a little squeeze. "I'm going to do a long set, then take a break about eight-thirty or so. Can we talk more then? I want to know what's up with your life."

"I'm not going anywhere."

"Good."

Without another word she drifted off into the growing crowd.

Will took a long sip of his Captain Morgan and then shook his head. He was waylaid several times on the way back to the table by people who had not necessarily been his friends in high school but had been casual acquaintances. Each time, he took a few minutes to be cordial and moved on, everyone assuring one another that they would speak more later that night, or the following day. It was going to be a long weekend, with plenty of time to get caught up.

At last he returned to the round table where he had left his friends. Danny and Eric had disappeared, leaving the four women. Will took one look at Danny's wife, Keisha, and felt bad for her. She smiled politely, but Ashleigh, Pix, and Lolly had known each other for fourteen years.

Will spotted the guys over at the bar talking to Nick and he was tempted to join them, but instead he slid into Danny's empty chair next to Keisha.

"Hey," he said, smiling as he set his drink on the table. "This weekend is probably going to be excruciating for you."

One corner of her mouth tugged upward in a playful half-smirk. "Nah. I love all you guys. We don't get to see you nearly enough, so this is a good excuse. It's all the rest of the stuff that I could do without. If it was just, you know, you guys, that'd be great. But...Eastborough High's Homecoming parade and football game?" Her eyes rolled up. "I think I might have a headache tomorrow."

"You can't!" Will said, eyes wide with feigned scandal. "You'd miss the steamed hot dogs and cotton candy and—"

"And the cheerleaders," Ashleigh said, leaning over to shoot Will an insinuating glare. "Don't forget about the cheerleaders."

Will pressed a hand against his chest and made his face a mask of hurt feelings. "You wound me. They're children, Ashleigh. Seventeen- and eighteen-year-old girls."

Lolly barked laughter. "Oh, please, like you won't be looking."

"At jailbait?" Will scoffed, letting an evil grin slip across his features.

Pix gave Keisha a conspiratorial look and lowered her voice. "They'll all be looking at the cheerleaders. Don't think Danny's innocent."

Keisha waved her away. "Oh, honey, there's nothing innocent about that man." She gave Lolly a pointed look. "Trust me. I know where he's been. And I know where he's going if he ever does more than look."

They all laughed at that and then the chatter began again, but this time, Keisha was very much a part of it. Will smiled. *My work here is done.* The women barely noticed when he excused himself and went over to the bar, where the guys were involved in a conversation about the girls they had secretly—and not so secretly—desired back in high school.

The moment Will arrived they all looked at him. Danny raised his beer and gestured with it toward the empty stage.

"And speaking of secret longings, you two seemed intimate."

Will arched an eyebrow. "Oh, yes. Very."

Nick smiled as he drew a beer from the tap. "Could it be there's a woman in the world you'd go on more than three dates with? Is the Caitlyn Curse over?"

"There's no curse," Will said, no longer amused.

Danny arched an eyebrow. "Do tell?"

But Nick had stopped teasing. He brought the beer to a woman a ways down the bar and then came back to them.

"Seriously, Will. How long are you gonna stay girl-skittish? There's more to a relationship than a couple of weeks of coffee bars and sex."

Will glanced around. "Do me a favor, Nick. Point out your girlfriend or wife in this room."

The bartender winced and glanced away, the jab obviously hitting too close to home. "Okay, Will. We're just friends, looking out for our old bud, but okay. Nobody's trying to start anything. But for the record, I've made it to the pennant race a few times. Yeah, I blew it every time, but that doesn't keep me from stepping up to the plate again. You've got to be in the game."

His expression was so earnest that for a long moment, Will and Danny could only stare at him. The absurdity of it all descended upon them and Will started to chuckle. A moment later all four of them were laughing.

"Romance According to the Boston Red Sox," Danny said.

"Confucius at the Bat," Will added.

Nick shot them a withering glance and moved on to serve another customer. By the time he came back, Will and Danny were on to other subjects. They all began to talk at once, two or three conversations happening at a time. They were laughing, giving each other shit; the drinks kept coming, and soon it seemed like no time at all had passed since they had last done this.

Stacy was back up onstage, doing some more upbeat tunes. Will watched her, and he wondered how much of what Nick had said was true.

After a while, Will became distracted. He would tune the guys out, just for a second, and glance over Danny's shoulder at the door. The first time he looked at his watch, it was quarter to eight. He checked it again seven minutes later. When he checked it the third time, Eric and Nick were in the middle of a debate about the New England Patriots coaching staff, and Danny took Will by the arm and pulled him away from them.

"Hey," he said, brows knitted in concern. "What's with you? So Caitlyn's not here. I thought you didn't want to see her anyway."

For a moment, Will didn't understand. Then he put it together. Danny had seen him watching the door.

"No. I mean, I don't. Want to see her. I mean, I don't care if I see her or not. I figure she'll be there tomorrow night if nothing else. Most everyone will be, right? But it's not her I'm looking for. It's Mike. I got e-mail from him; he said he'd be here. It's been like three years, and I was hoping he was gonna——"

"Mike?" Danny asked, frown deepening. He narrowed one eye, the way he always did when he was trying to work something out in his head. "Mike who?"

Will scoffed. "Mike. Mike, Mike. What do you mean, Mike who? Fucking Lebo. He told me he was gonna be——"

The look on Danny's face stopped him cold. Will blinked several times as though that would help him escape the grave disapproval that had carved itself into Danny Plumer's face.

"Will. I know it was a long time ago, so maybe you think..." Danny shook his head. "That is *not* fucking funny. Sincerely. Not even a little."

Confused, Will tilted his head. "What isn't? What are you talking about? I'm not supposed to want to see him, or I'm not supposed to get pissed 'cause he said he was gonna show and he——"

Danny twisted his head to the left as if suddenly offended by Will's smell. Will was stunned to silence. His best friend had just recoiled from him in what could only be disgust. Danny was a big joker, but there was nothing remotely resembling jest in his manner now.

"What?" Will demanded.

Abruptly Danny looked at him again, pinning Will to the ground with the intensity of his glare. "Mike? Mike fucking Lebo?"

Will spread his arms wide. "Ye-eahh?"

With a quick glance over at the table, where Eric had rejoined his wife and the other women, Danny took a deep breath and let it out. He was calmer when he looked back at Will, but the disgust had been replaced by something akin to disappointment.

"Maybe you're past it, bud. Me? I still have nightmares about his funeral. It's never gonna be funny to me."

Will felt a numbness spread through his body. His mouth began to gape. "Funeral? What are you . . . wait, no, fuck that. You're saying Mike's dead? Jesus, when did—"

Danny held up a hand to stop him. "Stop." He narrowed his eyes angrily. "When you decide to stop being such a prick, you know where the table is."

In stunned silence, Will watched his best friend turn and walk away.

I still have nightmares about his funeral. That's what Danny had said. But Mike could not be dead. Will had received an e-mail from him just a week ago.

And yet now, as he thought about it, tasted the concept with his mind, he found just a whisper of a memory in his head, something about a hit-and-run.

A funeral.

CHAPTER 3

Up on the platform, Stacy growled into the microphone, smiling mischievously as she sang Sheryl Crow's "Steve McQueen." Maybe a dozen people had abandoned their seats or their quiet corners and gathered to bump and grind in front of the platform. There were several Will did not recognize, but the others were all older versions of familiar faces. Others stood up behind him and started in dancing as well, so that he was caged on either side by laughing, gyrating people.

A frenetic, benevolent energy exuded from them just as surely as sweat and alcohol from their pores, and yet it touched him not at all. The evening's celebration churned all around him but he was no longer a part of it. The colorful dresses on the women seemed tacky all of a sudden, and the laughter perverse. A hollow place had opened up inside of him.

Will felt completely detached, as though he had phased into some gray limbo, passed out of existence completely, and the rest of the world went on around him as though he wasn't there at all. He had had dreams like this, and they had always terrified him. The room had taken on the texture of a dream now, and the air he was breathing was not quite right. The voices were too loud, the music somehow muffled.

He closed his eyes and felt himself swaying, knew he was about to pass out but could do nothing to stop it.

"Will?" a soft voice said, a gentle hand steadying him.

His eyes fluttered open. The delicate, almost otherworldly face of Martina Dienst swam into focus. Her eyes were narrowed with concern, but other than the tiny lines at the edges of her mouth, she looked as though she had not aged a day in the last ten years.

"Are you all right?" she asked.

He stared at her, his throat dry. The woman had changed not at all, and yet it seemed that his eyes had altered, or perhaps what had evolved was his way of seeing. Martina had always been beautiful, but now she was stunning. There was an elegance and grace about her that had always been there but seemed far more vital now.

"Hey," he said, forcing a smile that felt stiff and false. "I'm . . . I'm OK. I've just had a really long week." Will took a deep breath and raised his chin, stood a bit straighter, not wanting her to think he was drunk or high. "You look amazing, by the way."

Her smile was sweet and yet somehow regal. There had always been a touch of majesty about her. "Thank you. You look pretty good, too, if we ignore the pale, nearly fainting part."

Will laughed softly and felt as though some of the color flooded back into the world. The surreal quality of the room rolled back like a wave on the shore, but he was cautious, afraid it would wash over him anew. When it didn't, he smiled again and this time it felt more real.

"Very long week," he reiterated.

"You're not alone," Martina said. "I arrived from Vienna yesterday. I am still not in this time zone."

For a brief instant it seemed to him that he was going to be able to do it, to take a breath and dive back into the flow of the evening. But then Danny's words came back to him, coupled with the ghost of a memory he did not recall ever experiencing before. It wasn't déjà vu. If there was an opposite to déjà vu, that's what this was.

Caitlyn sobbing, face streaked with tears. The strength going out of Ashleigh's legs as she sat down hard on the tile in the corridor, slumping up against a row of lockers.

I still have nightmares about his funeral.

Jesus, Will thought, trying not to let Martina see how shaken he was. *Mike Lebo is dead?*

It was fucking impossible. Completely, utterly impossible. He had no recollection of a funeral—*a sliver of a memory, a rose dropped upon a casket, already in the ground, loose dirt sifting down to spatter the wood*—but Danny wasn't fucking around. Will had seen that in his eyes. He might joke about a lot of things, almost everything, but not about this.

"Damn," Will muttered, shaking his head. Then he focused on her. "Martina, you remember Mike Lebo, right?"

A veil of melancholy was drawn across her eyes. "Of course I do, Will. Who could forget? What a sweet guy. The day they announced it in school, when he was killed, that moment is burned into my mind. He's still the only friend I've ever had die. Maybe that makes me lucky."

Will could not seem to catch his breath. His eyes burned as though he were about to cry, but no tears fell.

"Yeah. Maybe it does," he rasped. That look of concern was back in Martina's eyes, but he could not bear speaking with her even a moment longer. Not right now.

"You know what? I'd love to catch up with you. I've been to Europe once, back in college, and I've always wanted to go again. I'd love to pick your brain, but I'm really not feeling well. Are you going to be at the other events this weekend?"

Martina nodded, frowning. "I'll be around all weekend. You just look after yourself and feel better, all right? Are you all right to drive? Maybe someone should take you home."

"I live in Somerville."

"A hotel, then?" she suggested.

He took another long breath and shook his head, trying not to be too dismissive of her kindness. "I'll be all right."

They said their good-byes and he turned to walk back to the

table. As he did he caught sight of Stacy. With a toss of her hair she strummed out the final chords of a song by the Eagles that had been released before any of them had been born.

"Thank you," she said as the applause erupted. That knowing smile was there again. "It's great to see all of you. I'm going to take a break and then do one more set for tonight. It's really a pleasure to play for you guys. Thanks for having me."

In the lights that illuminated the platform and the microphone stand, the spray of freckles across the bridge of her nose seemed somehow darker. When she put her guitar on its stand and came down off the platform, she had an expression of real contentment on her face.

Will had paused on his way back to the table. Now he waited as she approached him. When she had crossed half the distance that separated them, the smile on Stacy's face faltered and a kind of trepidation crept into her eyes.

"Hey. You all right?"

"No," he admitted, hoping she read the regret in his tone. "I'm really not feeling well. I'm going to head out, I think. Will you be at the game tomorrow?"

Stacy looked pensive, gnawing her lower lip a moment. "Yeah," she said at length. "I'll be there. Feel better, all right?"

"Probably just working too hard," he lied.

She nodded, leaned forward and gave him a light kiss on the cheek, and then turned away. "See you tomorrow. You take care of yourself," she said over her shoulder. Then she was off across the room, threading through the crowd, politely fending off the compliments she received as she went to mingle.

Will pushed her out of his head, along with everything else that had happened tonight. The only way he could put one foot in front of the other, the only way he could function at all, was to purposely avoid thinking about certain things. But he knew he would not be able to put those thoughts off forever.

He went to the table where his friends sat, moving amongst chairs that had been pushed too far out from their places, trying not to knock off jackets that had been hung off the backs. Several people greeted him and Will managed to smile and even shake a few hands, to promise he would catch up with them at the football game the next day.

Ashleigh noticed him first. She was in the midst of a conversation with Lolly and Pix, but her smile evaporated the second she spotted Will. Despite the mire of unsettling thoughts in his head, he could not help but laugh.

"I must really look like shit, judging from the expression on your face."

At his words, everyone at the table turned to look at him. Will did not miss the cold glint of pain in Danny's eyes. It hurt him to see it, to know that at the moment his old friend thought he was a total asshole.

"You do, bro," Eric said earnestly. "Absolute shit. What's the matter?"

"Something I ate, maybe," Will said. His gaze ticked from one face to the next, lingering a moment on Ashleigh until at last he focused on Danny. "I'm headed home. Figure I should get some rest now so I don't miss the entire weekend."

"Good idea," Pix piped up. "You'll need all your energy to watch those cheerleaders at the game tomorrow."

Will didn't have the energy to deadpan a grin, but Eric did it for him.

"We admire them for their athleticism. And all that synchronization. That's a science."

Ashleigh rapped him on the shoulder and scolded him with a look. Then she turned to glance up at Will again.

"Drive carefully," she said, playing big sister. "We'll save you a seat tomorrow."

"You got it," he promised.

Without further hesitation, he headed for the door that would take him downstairs and out of Liam's Irish Tavern, where he could get into his car and drive away from the impossible.

ON THE MASSACHUSETTS TURNPIKE, Will turned the radio up loud and rolled the front windows down halfway, letting the chill air rush in, hoping it would clear his head. The sick feeling in his stomach that had combined with astonishment had been superseded now by a dark anger that surged up like bile in his throat.

Sick fuckers, he thought.

It had to be a joke. The most disturbing practical joke he had ever even heard of—and far more clever than he would ever have given Danny Plumer credit for. There were images in his head, snippets of memory he didn't understand, fragments of emotions that slipped his mind even as he tried to grasp and make sense of them. But all of that might just be the power of suggestion thrown into the mix with what was genuine exhaustion. He was more tired than he had imagined. That part, at least, had not been a lie.

The flag at Eastborough High flies at half-mast. Will's parents have bought him a black suit, and his father is shining his son's shoes. If he lets his eyes close, Will knows he will see the brush moving across shoe leather.

But he wouldn't close his eyes. That was how idiots totaled their cars. Falling asleep behind the wheel.

A cross beside the road, a hasty memorial erected not with wood and steel but with flowers and cards and photographs and candles, flickering candles. In the street Will finds something the police have missed—a broken tooth, knocked from Mike's mouth when the motherfucking hit-and-run murdering son of a—

"No!" Will shouted, snapping his head up, jerking the wheel to the left to correct his course. He had started to fall asleep, started to drift into the next lane.

He shook his head and turned the radio up even louder. With his teeth grinding together, he accelerated, the needle leaping up past sixty-five to seventy and then to seventy-five. He had to get home. There were things he needed to look into, things he had to put his hands on, touch. He knew once he did that, he could flush all of this insanity right out of his head.

Insanity. He didn't like the sound of that word.

The road hummed under his wheels. Taillights glowed ahead, and too-bright headlights glared in his rearview mirror. Will reached up and turned it down to get the brightness out of his eyes.

They still burned, promising tears, but he didn't have anything to cry about. That was the hell of it. After high school graduation he had lost contact with all but the closest of his old friends. He saw Danny the most because he was in the area, but he and Mike had kept in touch. Christmas cards, a flurry of e-mails four or five times a year. Hell, Mike had been at Ashleigh's party the night after they had graduated.

Will knew it. He *remembered* it. They had all been there. Mike had mixed rum and Cokes for everyone and Eric had ended up puking in the shrubs. After Will and Caitlyn had gone upstairs to Ashleigh's bedroom to have a little private time, Mike and Danny had serenaded them from the flower garden outside the window.

"This is fucked," he said, cold wind whipping his face, wide awake, eyes staring at the road ahead. The engine thrummed and he saw that the needle had crept up to eighty. Will slowed down a little, knuckles white, fists tight on the steering wheel.

After graduation, he and Mike had hung out every time a holiday or summer break brought them both home to Eastborough. After college had come and gone, Mike had moved to Phoenix. His address was in Will's book back at the apartment.

The wake. The flowers. Mike's uncle Bill singing "Danny Boy" so softly under his breath that no one else can hear it.

No. Simply no way.

Will pounded the steering wheel and the horn let out a startled beep.

We just traded e-mails last week, he thought. *That night at Ashleigh's after graduation, he signed my fucking yearbook. "To Will, a better friend than most of us deserve."* Will could see the handwriting in his mind, right above Mike's picture.

Mike's picture. How could Mike even have his picture in the yearbook if he had died before those pictures could be taken? The answer was, he couldn't. Mike Lebo could not possibly be dead.

Grimly, Will kept his hands tight on the wheel and forced himself to stop thinking about it, intent on reaching his apartment and finding the proof that he knew lay waiting. Proof that would put the lie to Danny Plumer's ire and disappointment and Martina Dienst's sad recollections.

I still have nightmares about his funeral.

Danny's voice kept playing in his head, but Will wasn't listening.

WHEN AT LAST HE REACHED his apartment, he ran up the stairs. The back of his skull ached dully, but he was not tired anymore. If anything he felt more awake, electrified with determination, or perhaps it was merely desperation. Will unlocked his door and flung it open, then left it that way, the keys jangling in the lock behind him as he hurried down the corridor. Emotions warred within him. Brows knitted grimly, he went into the second bedroom.

His address book sat beside the computer screen.

Will had no idea where Mike would be staying if he had indeed come back to Massachusetts for the reunion. The first guess would logically be at his parents' home, but Will hadn't the first clue as to whether the Lebos still lived in the area, or where.

It didn't matter. Mike had responsibilities back in Arizona—a job, a fiancée, friends. He would be checking his messages from time to time. All Will had to do was call and leave him a message, and then this bullshit would be resolved. And if it was a gag—*it has to be*—and Mike was in on it, well then Will would have a few choice words for him.

As he picked up his address book, Will shivered unconsciously. A chill went up the back of his neck and the book felt strangely heavy. He stared at its turquoise cover and was filled with the impulse not to open it, to simply slide it back onto the desk.

Images he did not want to see flashed in his mind and he squeezed his eyes shut a moment, massaging the bridge of his nose, trying to force them away. The chill was gone. His entire body felt as though it were alive with prickly heat.

Then he scowled, shaking his head, and he flipped through

the book to the *L* section. Mike Lebo's was the second name he had put into that section of the book, the second address listing under *L*.

Only it wasn't.

"No," Will whispered, shaking his head. His face began to feel oddly numb and his eyes began to fill up as though he might weep.

The second listing under *L* was for Angie Lester, a woman who worked in sales for the *Trib* with whom he had gone on a total of three dates several years ago. He glared at the page as though he might be capable of intimidating it into resolving the confusion in his mind, but the conflicting thoughts and memories were still there.

Will flipped to the next page. And the one after. Then there were no more entries for the letter *L*, and he had not found a listing for Mike Lebo.

"Bullshit," he muttered to himself. "Bullshit."

He picked up the phone and dialed directory assistance. When the cold digital voice asked him for the listing and city, he spoke them aloud. "Michael Lebo. Phoenix, Arizona." But he had to bite down hard to keep from shouting into the phone, from screaming that he had just traded e-mails with the guy, that he had talked to Mike on the phone right around the Fourth of July.

But as he waited for the response he bit his lower lip and closed his eyes and a knot of ice formed in his chest, because he knew what the answer was going to be.

There was no listing for a Michael Lebo in Phoenix, Arizona.

His mind began to grasp for understanding. The previous week, he and Mike had made plans to get together on Sunday because Will was reluctant to attend the reunion. He had not imagined it. A nervous laugh escaped his lips and Will slapped the heel of his hand against his forehead. "Idiot," he said, clicking on the computer. He had deleted the e-mail but all that did was move it from the in-box folder to the one for Deleted Items. Some computer systems dumped that folder at regular intervals, but he purposely let his accumulate, having elminated messages he needed one too many times. He nodded his head in rhythm, silently urging the computer to boot up faster, then logged on to the Net to get to his e-mail. As the new messages began to download he clicked over to Deleted Items and scanned down, trying to remember Mike's e-mail address. He checked his e-mail address book, but as he scanned through it he realized he did not expect to find the information he sought.

He sat back in the chair and stared at the screen. His head still hurt but now the ache seemed to spread throughout his body, a dull pain that went deep as the marrow of his bones.

There was a soft ding that let him know his new e-mail had finished downloading. Conditioned by routine, he clicked to open the in-box. There were over a dozen new messages but his eyesight blurred as he glanced at the names, knowing by now that none of them would be from Mike.

How could they be?

Girls in black dresses, a line of people across the ragged lawn at Pine Hill Cemetery, the collar of his new white shirt is too tight and he feels as though he is being strangled, as though he will pass out before the priest falls silent and dismisses them. . . .

Two words leaped out at him from the screen, the return address of one of the new e-mails in his in-box. *Message Undeliverable.*

Shuddering, he bent over the desk, fingers twined in his hair, palms against his forehead. The headache had taken on a new ferocity, the dull throbbing replaced by slivers of ice that shot through his skull, spiking him with pain. Will felt suddenly as though his head could not contain the conflicting images, the contrary memories that were clashing in his mind. There just wasn't room.

"Jesus," he whispered, and though he often spoke that name as a curse, for once it was a prayer.

Will shoved back his chair and stood up so quickly that he nearly toppled it. One entire wall of the room was covered with bookshelves, and as he walked stiffly toward them he felt as though he were wandering. It was only as he dropped to his knees and began pulling at the oversized books on the bottom shelf—the atlases and coffee-table books—that an understanding of his own intentions began to filter into his conscious thoughts.

He clawed at the books and they toppled out, slapping one upon the other and spilling across the floor. Weakly he sifted through them until he found the smooth, thin, blue volume he had been searching for—the one with *Eastborough High School* in gold leaf on the cover.

Holding his breath Will paged through the yearbook. In his mind he could still see Mike's handwriting, and the message that he had written that night at Ashleigh's graduation party. But the image in his mind was blurry now, out of focus, and he could not quite recall the precise phrasing of the words Mike had scrawled above his picture.

Vanessa Lalley, Mark Leung.

There was no picture of Mike Lebo. No message.

As if moving of their own volition his fingers began to turn pages. A prisoner of his morbid curiosity and impaled upon a blade of dread that twisted in his gut, Will flipped to the back of the yearbook. Some part of him—some newly minted portion of his mind—knew what he would find there, just a few pages before the end.

A picture. Not the one that had been in the yearbook but another, more candid shot that had been donated by his parents.

In Memoriam. Michael Paul Lebo. We will never forget you.

"Holy shit." Will let the yearbook slip from his fingers. His right hand shook as he raised it up to cover his mouth. "Holy shit," he said again, repeating it several times like a mantra. His eyes burned and it was only when he tasted the salt upon his lips that he realized he was crying.

Weeping over the loss of someone dear to him.

Grieving for a friend who had died more than a decade before and who would never become a man. Never move to Phoenix. Never have a fiancée.

"What the hell's the matter with me?" he rasped, speaking the question to the shadows in his darkened office, half believing that they would respond, that some voice from the ether would whisper an answer.

Minutes passed before he realized that he was rocking gently back and forth, staring at the books he had spread across the floor. There was the biography on Houdini, whose image adorned the wall here in his home office just as it did at work. And amongst the other research volumes strewn about, there was *A History of Magic*, something he'd picked up for research years before.

Will stopped rocking. He scowled as he lifted the Houdini bio and dropped it on top of the other book. The suggestion of something had flitted across his mind like a flare fired into the night sky only to drop into the ocean and be snuffed. Houdini had debunked all of that crap. How convenient it would have been to be able to blame this on magic. How much easier. He would have happily embraced any other explanation for this than the one that seemed so patently obvious to him.

I'm slipping. My mind is slipping.

The terror that gripped him at this dawning realization was unlike anything he had ever felt before. He shivered as he rose from the floor and then staggered to the bathroom to piss, after which he stepped out of his jeans and somehow managed to navigate his way into the bedroom.

For hours he simply lay there in the dark, staring at the ceiling. Much as he wanted sleep to claim him, to carry him away from the confused jumble of his thoughts and memories, it would not. The ache in his head became a kind of haze that seemed to disorient him.

A night out playing pool during Christmas break, sophomore year of college. Mike was never any good at pool but he has been practicing and he beats Will easily, swigging from the bottle of Rumple Minze Peppermint Schnapps they've been drinking and wiping the back of his hand across his mouth.

As his eyes closed and he at last began to drift off, Will's mind was assaulted by a series of Zoetrope-flashing images. *Mike hands him a tourism flyer about Arizona, telling him to come visit. The two of them on Cape Cod for a weekend the summer after freshman year in college. Singing along at a matchbox twenty concert at the Fleet Center in Boston.*

But those images had already begun to fade, the edges charring and crumbling like burning photographs in his mind. They were simply wrong. Impossible. They could not have happened.

Not when he could remember now, so very clearly, the morning Principal Chadbourne had announced the hit-and-run that had killed Mike Lebo. Not when every moment of anguish in the days that followed was engraved upon his memory. The oh-so-silent wake, where no one had recovered from the shock of it enough to speak about it. The funeral, with the sobbing girls and the fallen roses, and the white collar that was so tight around his neck.

Mike Lebo was dead.

And all these years later, Will's grief was still an open wound.

CHAPTER 4

Aluminum. Rust.

There's a metallic taste in his mouth as though he's been chewing on aluminum foil. Ashleigh is crying, stricken and pale, sliding down the locker to sit hard on her ass. His gaze sweeps the hall. It's between classes and the throng is in motion, or should be. Instead, they're frozen, these kids, just standing there staring up at the ceiling, eyes searching for the speakers from which the hard-edged words have just issued.

In a moment the whispers will begin. Hearts will start to beat again. The kids who didn't know Mike Lebo, or who knew him only from passing him in the hallways, they'll be a little creeped out, freaked at the idea that a kid their age—any kid their age—could die. This isn't the evening news and it isn't some story spun by Students Against Drunk Driving. This is a kid they had passed in the hall at school, who maybe had ridden the bus with them.

That shit just doesn't happen. Not here. Not to someone they know.

He can see it all in their eyes, can read their thoughts in that frozen moment, in that collective intake of breath. There will be counselors at school and cautionary speeches from teachers and administrators and a flag flown at half-mast.

The metallic taste in his mouth is strong enough to make him wince and run his tongue over his teeth in an attempt to erase it. It remains. His skin tingles and he feels oddly thirsty. Ashleigh's crying is stifled as she puts a hand up to cover her mouth, but it is there to hide her horror, not because she is ashamed of her weeping. Her chestnut hair falls across her face. Caitlyn whispers to the son of God over and over, shielding her eyes as though the sun is too bright, though they are in the shadowed corridors of Eastborough High.

His cheeks are numb. His feet are dead flesh, too heavy to lift. His tongue is swollen and tangy with the flavor of aluminum. The fillings in his teeth hurt. At the far end of the corridor, at the foot of the stairs, Brian Schnell has his eyes closed, his lips pursed as though for a kiss. He sways as though at any moment he might fall.

Will watches Brian's eyes open.

People begin to move again, yet now there is a funereal pace to their travels and a whispering shroud has fallen over their voices. Danny crouches to help Ashleigh up, whispering softly to her. Caitlyn is watching him, corpse pale and yet still startlingly beautiful. Her eyes roll back and she stares at the ceiling.

"I can't believe they . . . can't believe they did that. Just . . . just announced it like that, like it's nothing. Like he's fucking student of the month or something. Jesus, like they're announcing a rally for a football game."

Aluminum. His mouth . . .

"Jesus," Caitlyn says again, but now it's a whisper. She stares at him. "Will, you're bleeding. Your mouth is bleeding."

His fingers flutter toward his mouth, wildly, as though they may not find anchor there. When at last they alight upon his chin he feels wetness, sticky and strangely cold. He touches his lower lip and it stings. His tongue runs out over his mouth and the metallic taste is stronger than before.

He gazes down at his fingers, slick with his own blood.

In that moment when the words were announced over the loudspeaker system, he had bitten through his lip. As he traces his mouth now, his finger finds the wound, plays at the edges of it, and idly he wonders if he tried to force it, would his finger push all the way through until his nail tapped the enamel of his bloodstained teeth?

He feels his face collapse, the muscles turning in upon themselves, and the tears come. "Why him?" he rasps. "Why did it have to be him?"

The throng has begun to churn again, to stream and flow toward classrooms and lockers. His friends are all looking at him now and he feels their eyes but cannot meet them. Ashleigh and Danny and Caitlyn—his Caitlyn—he leaves them behind as he forces his feet to move, stumbling along the corridor and around the corner to the men's room.

The door slams open, clacking against the tiles, perhaps cracking the tiles, and it hisses softly closed behind him. He does not enter the first stall but the third, the one he always chooses. Inside that intimate cube he slides the lock across. There is a coat hook on the back of the door—miraculously unbroken—and now he grasps it, nearly hanging on it, holding himself up as his forehead presses against the cold metal of the bathroom stall door.

Aluminum. In his mouth, that metallic tang is joined by the taste of salt. Blood and tears.

His mind flashes back to his bedroom at home, where there are multicolored candles and bits of reptile skin, whittled yew and ash branches, red ribbons, herbs, and dried apples. There are books there as well, two of them stolen from the special collection at the library, shoved down his pants while Brian created a distraction. These things are in a box in his closet, a box he has not opened since the previous year. He has not opened the box because all it contains is bullshit.

It's all bullshit, and yet he thinks of it now and wishes he had not.

Blood and tears.

A spark, a floating orange, a glass of blood, a memory trick, a cut healed as though it never was. Nothing. Games. Foolishness. Certainly not magic.

Bullshit.

There's no such thing as magic.

Only blood and tears.

. . . and then he wakes.

WILL'S EYES SNAPPED OPEN and he inhaled sharply, greedily, convinced in that moment that he had stopped breathing while he was asleep. *Apnea,* he thought, apropos of nothing having to do with his dream or the day ahead. The word popped into his mind and just then seemed far more important than anything else. *Sleep apnea. Stop breathing while you're asleep, never wake up.*

The thought filled him with cold dread, an enemy he could not fight. He took several more breaths and then shook his head to clear it. Maybe he had stopped breathing a moment, but he had woken up instantly. It was ridiculous to be afraid of such a thing.

Will laughed softly, but there was an edge to it that he did not fail to notice. Idly, almost as though his subconscious mind did not want him to realize he was doing it, he licked his lips as if his tongue thought it might find something there. A milk mustache. A ring of chocolate, the way he had so often had around his lips as a small child, thanks to indulgent parents.

"Jesus," he whispered, and then he shivered, the curse/prayer an echo of his dream, though he could no longer remember precisely why. He grasped at the remnants of the dream and it fled him, so that he could now remember only small snatches of it.

The day they had learned Mike Lebo had died. Will sat up in bed now and sighed. He had been a hell of a guy—self-effacing, his presence always calming—and the loss had shaken all of them. In some ways, though, it had also brought them closer together.

Most of them.

A flash of the previous night's events came back to him now, the weird moment of disorientation that had come over him when he and Danny had talked about Mike. Will slipped out of bed and padded to the bathroom, his bladder heavy.

What was that about? he thought. *What's wrong with your head?* How could he have forgotten, even for a moment, that horrible day in the early autumn of their senior year, the scene in the corridor, Ashleigh's sobbing, and the taste of blood in his own mouth? Though he tried to push it away, Will was worried about such a lapse in his own memory. What did it say about his mental state that he could construct in his imagination a fanciful alternative, where Mike had never died?

"What the fuck is wrong with me?" he muttered to himself as he pushed open the bathroom door and flicked on the light.

The fan whirred overhead.

In the mirror his face was pale and there were dark circles under his eyes. *Not enough sleep,* he thought. *Or just troubled sleep.* He knew that after this weekend was over he was going to have to make some calls, try to find someone to talk to. The idea that he had been so haunted by Mike's death that the imminent arrival of the reunion had caused him to go into some bizarre denial was upsetting, but not nearly so upsetting as the alternative, which was some kind of mental deterioration.

Too young for that shit, by far, he thought as he pissed into the toilet, the hissing sound of it hitting the water disturbingly loud in the silence of the apartment.

Will flushed, then shook his head again. He ran water from the faucet and splashed some on his face. This weekend was his chance to reconnect with old friends, some he was intimate with, and some he had lost in the fog of passing time. He had begun that with Stacy Shipman last night, and then he'd had to bail.

Enjoy the weekend, he thought. *There'll be enough time on Monday to find out if you're cracking up.*

Staring into the mirror, he studied the small scar just under his lower lip, that thin white reminder of Mike Lebo's death that had been with him for eleven years, ever since he had bitten into his lip that day and tasted his own blood.

Will ran his fingers over that scar, so familiar and yet somehow also alien to him, as though he had always had it but never managed to really see it before now.

He stared at it, troubled.

THE CLASSIC ROCK STATION Will often listened to was playing the Goo Goo Dolls as he turned off of Union Avenue and into the rear entrance to Cougar Stadium. Ten and a half years ago, when his high school graduation had been held here, there had been only a gravel road and yellowed grass out behind the stadium. Sometime since, the de facto parking lot had been paved over to confirm its use for that purpose. Cougar Stadium was not nearly grand enough to have earned the appellation, but its bleacher seats were modern and numerous enough that *field* had apparently been rejected as too limiting a description.

The paving over of what had once provided parking only to those savvy enough to sneak in the back way did not really alarm him. It was progress, of course, and he could not begrudge anyone that. On the other hand, the idea that the classic rock station was playing the Goo Goo Dolls—a band that had had its greatest success in 1998—got under his skin. Not that there was anything wrong with the band, but the whole classic rock format implied certain things, among them the suggestion that if you'd grown up contemporary with the music, you weren't precisely young anymore.

Will glanced at his watch and saw that it was a quarter after one. He went through the rear gate of the chain-link fence that surrounded Cougar Stadium, but instead of going up into the stands he went around the rear wall toward the front. It was the coldest day of autumn thus far, and he wore a heavy black leather jacket over his favorite Red Sox jersey and a clean pair of blue jeans. Will sipped from the hot chocolate he had picked up at Dunkin' Donuts on his way.

There were groups of parents with giant coffee thermoses threading along the yellow grass toward one entrance or another, and students in small gatherings—boys laughing, girls leaning up against the wall, smoking and eyeing the boys suggestively. In one arched entryway the cheerleaders for Natick High—the opposing team in today's game—were in a huddle, waiting for the festivities to begin.

Around the front of the stadium the cars were parked at every angle, tucked into spots that had clearly never been intended to hold them. Though inside there were concession stands that sold hot dogs and pizza, fried dough and pretzels, there were people barbecuing in the main lot, tailgating, drinking beer. In that way, things had not changed at all since he had been a student here. The lot looked like a miniature version of the tailgating bash that always took place down in Foxboro before a Patriots game.

Will sipped at his hot chocolate, warming his hands on the cup, and steam came from his breath and from the small tear in the lid. He looked at the main gate and saw the people lined up at the entrance and out on the sidewalks. A motorcycle cop pulled up in front of the entrance to Cougar Stadium and dismounted, blue light spinning on his bike.

The parade had arrived.

A broad grin spread across Will's features and he picked up his pace, hurrying along through parked cars until he merged with the mass of people who flanked the entrance to the stadium. He glanced around in search of familiar faces, hoping to run into some of his classmates, but at first he saw only students. The current batch of kids at Eastborough High seemed horrifyingly young. It had only been ten years, but as he studied the faces of the jostling boys and posing girls, he could not remember ever being that age.

That's what we looked like, too, he thought. *Kids. But we never felt that young.* He knew it was true, remembered all too well how worldweary and wise they had all believed themselves to be. Not children anymore, but *teenagers,* with all the presumptuousness that implied. Now he looked at the latest generation and marveled at their youth and naïveté.

And how he envied them.

The first car through the gate was an antique Dodge Charger with the logo of the Eastborough High Cougars painted on the hood. Will laughed out loud. The car had been leading the parade for something like thirty years and had been kept in working order all that time by the kids in the shop class. The driver of the car was Mr. Murphy, who had been Will's English teacher and had been partially responsible for inspiring him to seek a career in journalism. There were other teachers in the car but he recognized only Annelise Berendt, who had come in as principal of Eastborough the year after Will's class had graduated.

They waved GO COUGARS banners and blew whistles, and then another car came through the gate carrying several other teachers and a heavyset, balding guy he assumed was Mayor Aaron Pirkle, if the sign on the side of the car was any indication. There were cheers and some catcalls from the crowd, but then the voices were temporarily drowned out by the sound of thumping drums and blaring horns, and the Eastborough High School Marching Band strode through the gates in perfect synchrony.

The band had always been a source of pride for the school. No matter how many people teased those who took part in it, the members of Eastborough High's marching band never listened. They competed on a national level, even though the school's football team had never won its division.

The band was followed by the first parade float, a masterpiece painstakingly fashioned from paper flowers. It was a bit of rugged terrain, rocks, and trees, and in their midst, a huge cougar, the mascot of Eastborough High. Will stared at it in astonishment, wondering if the thing had really been created by high school students.

There were a couple of other floats far less impressive than the first—obviously the committee had chosen the Cougar float to focus on—and then a rolling exhibition that was not quite a float at all. It was a flatbed truck with the school colors draped over the edges of the bed, laden with what must have been the entire Eastborough football team and the cheerleading squad as well. The cheerleaders—in skimpy uniforms that would not even have been allowed at Eastborough High ten years before— were already engaged in the call-and-answer patter of their discipline, screaming themselves hoarse before the game had even begun.

They were having a hell of a time.

Will grinned as he gazed up at them, at their smiles and the expressions on the faces of the football players. This had to be quite a moment for them. In his mind's eye he could see his own senior year Homecoming parade, could remember the way the air seemed to have a special tang to it, a flavor and a scent that was unlike anything else in the world.

People were shouting and throwing flowers at the players and cheerleaders as the truck passed. Students and parents, mostly, but across the street Will caught sight of a few familiar faces. Martina Dienst, Brian Schnell, Scott Kelso, and Mia Skopis were all hooting and waving to the players with such fervor that for a moment it almost seemed as though they had forgotten a decade had passed since the last time they had stood here and done the very same thing.

In the midst of the crowd, off to their left, he saw Caitlyn.

A shiver went through him that had nothing to do with the

chill in the air. A thousand images like the shards of a broken mirror spun through his mind, just as clear, just as jagged. Caitlyn had hurt him, badly. And yet they had shared so much that he would not trade the years they had spent together for anything. In the crowd, everyone so intent upon the parade, Caitlyn had already noticed him.

Her blue eyes shone even from this distance and she raised a hand, fingers curled in the most delicate and hesitant of waves. Testing the waters. Wondering what would happen.

The oddest thing was the way his own hand lifted as if of its own accord. Will waved back, one side of his mouth lifting in a wistful smile. It hurt, seeing her; it stirred up a melancholy deep within him that would never go away. And yet somehow under these circumstances, seeing Caitlyn as part of the tableau of their past, amidst old friends they both shared, was surprisingly OK.

Then Martina saw him and waved, smiling with such unaffected sweetness that he wanted to hug her. When he glanced back to look for Caitlyn again, she was lost in the crowd. Part of him wanted to speak to her, but even just with the small exchange they'd just shared he felt a sense of relief. Pushing Caitlyn from his mind, he waved back to Martina and edged through the crowd, waiting for a break in the parade so he could dash across to join them. After the flatbed, the cars began to roll through, festooned with ribbons and crepe paper. Another wave of cheers went through the crowd as the current Homecoming King and Queen rolled past in the back of a classic Mustang convertible. There were enough people trailing the car and walking alongside it that Will was able to slip across the street.

"Hey, Marti," he said happily.

Martina arched an eyebrow. "You know, you're the only person in the world who ever gave me a nickname."

"Do you hate me for it?"

"No. It's actually kind of nice."

She kissed him on the cheek and then the two of them turned to face the others. In high school, Brian Schnell had been sort of gawky and unkempt. His shirt was forever half untucked and his hair always needed combing. Childhood baby fat had lingered on him, giving his face a doughy look though he wasn't overweight at all. Adult Brian was still recognizably the same guy, but one look at him and all Will could think of was the bizarre alternate-universe episodes shown from time to time on *Star Trek*. Alternate-universe Brian dressed well and wore his clothes as if they'd just been pressed. He had a goatee and his black hair was well groomed. He was only twenty-eight, but he already had some gray in there.

When he saw Will, his face lit up with genuine pleasure, as if someone had just told him a wonderful joke.

"No shit. Will James," Brian said, and he opened his arms.

Will hesitated, but only for a moment. Once upon a time they had been the best of friends. It hadn't ended in any kind of obvious falling out, really. It had just sort of happened, the way those things did, the two of them drifting apart, finding they had less in common with one another and more in common with others.

Still, that was what this weekend was about. Reconnecting with the people who had drifted away. So when Brian went to embrace him, Will hugged back.

"Good to see you, Bri. How've you been, man?"

Brian broke the embrace and held him at arm's length. "I've been good, Will. Really good."

"You look it," Will told him.

For just a moment, Brian's smile faltered. Will felt an unspoken communication pass between them, as though without words they had just begun a conversation about the death of their old friendship. It was awkward and surprising, since Brian seemed to have been so amiable at first.

Then the moment passed. Brian's smile returned and he shrugged. "Time heals all wounds, they say. You look like you're doing pretty well yourself."

"Will!" a voice shouted, and he looked up to see Tim Friel riding in the back of a ragtop Cadillac with Tess O'Brien, who'd been Queen to his Homecoming King eleven years past. Other reunion class royalty rode by in various cars, all following the reigning pair.

When Will turned back to Brian, Martina had him in conversation, so he said hello to Scott and Mia, catching up with them briefly. Then Martina abruptly broke off talking to Brian and stepped closer to put a hand on his arm.

"We're going to head in. We're meeting a bunch of people inside. Do you want to join us?"

"I'll walk with you," he said, "but I promised Ashleigh I'd come find those guys when I got here."

The last of the parade had already turned into the Cougar Stadium parking lot and the road was filled with people moving toward the entrance. They all fell into the herd, waiting patiently and catching up while they did so. Mia was a buyer for a women's clothing store chain, working out of San Francisco. Scott was an engineer for some tech firm or another; Will had lost the name almost the moment he had heard it. Brian surprised them all by revealing that he worked for a major music label. Even Martina was impressed.

Will had spent many afternoons in Brian's basement listening to CDs and hanging out, singing along and playing air guitar. He was proud of the guy for having turned his passion into his job. Like Will himself, and former-football-star-turned-coach Tim Friel, he hadn't accomplished all of his dreams, but at least he was pursuing them, doing something that made him happy.

"Good for you, Bri. Seriously, that's great."

By then they were inside the gates of the stadium and it was time to part ways. Will stepped to one side and let the crowd flow by and around him. He watched the others for a moment as they were swept away by the human maelstrom. Then he began to glance around.

Teenagers. Families with kids of all ages. A teacher or two that he recognized. At the concession stand just beside the entrance to the bleachers he saw Kelly Meserve and a couple of other former classmates but did not bother trying to get their

attention. He wanted to get settled first. It took him a moment
to visually confirm which bench would be for the home team.
Danny, Eric, and Nick would be seated on the Cougars' side of
the field.

Will started toward the stands.

Beyond the shifting crowd that ebbed and flowed ahead of
him, he saw a single lone figure leaning motionless against the
bleachers. Stacy Shipman shot him that mischievous grin, eyes
sparkling, and he wondered how long she had been watching
him before he had become aware of her presence.

Will arched an eyebrow, pleasantly surprised, and sidled
through the long line in front of the concession stand. The
whole reunion weekend thing had a strange, bittersweet quality
to it—even without the oddness of the previous night's
events—but somehow all of that had dissipated the moment he
had spotted Stacy there.

"Hey," he said as he approached.

"Hey," Stacy replied. "Fancy meeting you here."

That sly grin remained and her chin dropped slightly, a
charming gesture that he was certain was unconscious. She did
not move away from the bleachers or shift her position in any
other way. A spark of hope ignited in his chest that she had been
waiting for him.

Will scratched at the back of his head, unsure how to continue. "Listen," he began slowly. "About last night. If I seemed
weird at all—"

"I always thought you were weird, Mr. James. It's one of the
things I admire most about you."

He blinked and felt his smile grow wider. "I'm going to take
that as a compliment. And by the way, I hope everyone told you
how incredible you were last night. I'd like to hear you play again
sometime."

Stacy arched an eyebrow, the freckles across the bridge of her
nose darker in the sunshine. The chilly breeze blew a thick lock
of dark hair across her face, and with one finger she tucked it behind her ear.

"Time will tell," she said. Then she pushed off from the wall and grabbed Will by the hand. "Come on. Let me buy you a hot dog. They're awful, but it's all part of the Homecoming experience, y'know?"

Will felt her fingers clasped in his own and let her pull him to the back of the concession line. "If you say so."

"I do." And there was that grin again, the look that said she was a woman of great mystery and many secrets, and if he discovered them, he might be just as amused by them as she was.

They waited in the line, which soon grew even longer as the duo running the concession stand seemed incapable of filling even the simplest of orders without at least one mistake. Yet even though Will was vaguely aware of the antics behind the counter—of hot dogs with the wrong condiments and diet Coke instead of regular, of miscounted change and wrongly tallied totals—the delay did not bother him in the least.

Stacy told him about her life after Eastborough High, her disastrous and truncated college experience, and the short stint she had done in rehab, thanks to a certain white powder. She was remarkably candid about the whole thing, but when Will thought about it that wasn't so remarkable at all. It was just Stacy. Her real life of late was far less sexy than her raspy-voiced stage persona would lead one to think. She had always been interested in old homes and architecture. Cocaine had prevented her from getting a degree, but she and a partner had started their own business restoring historic homes, and it gave her a pleasure that was evident in every nuanced word when she spoke about it. Between that and her music, she had found a contented place in her life.

Will grew more and more enamored of her. The woman Stacy had become was even more fascinating than the girl she had been. He wanted to tell her that but was afraid she would think he was only flirting. When they finally reached the counter, it seemed as though no time at all had elapsed, and he felt foolish when he realized he had no idea what he wanted. He ordered a hot dog and a drink and found himself nodding when Stacy asked if he wanted nachos as well. He watched her as she pulled money from the pocket of her jeans and paid the gray-haired man in the booth. The guy must have been sixty-five, but she charmed him in an instant. Will was not certain, but as Stacy pocketed her change he did a mental calculation and thought that the old fellow had forgotten to charge them for the nachos.

Stacy picked up the tray with the hot dogs and drinks before he even had a chance to offer, then pointed her elbow at the nachos. "That's your job. Don't forget napkins. That's a man thing. Forgetting the napkins."

"And straws," Will added.

"Them, too."

They left the concession behind—the line even longer than before—and as they finally made their way up into the bleachers, they discovered that the game had begun. More than five minutes had already elapsed in the first quarter, but neither team had gotten on the scoreboard yet. The Cougars had the ball on Natick's twenty-five-yard line, but it was third down, with seven yards to go. Eastborough's quarterback threw a deep pass downfield and the receiver caught the ball, but he was out of bounds.

"Damn," Stacy whispered.

She paused just ahead of him, unmindful of whose view she might be blocking, and turned to watch the next play. Fourth down, twenty-five-yard line. The Cougars brought their special teams unit in to go for a field goal.

"Come on, you guys," Stacy said. Then she did a little yowl. "Let's go, Cougars!"

Will laughed and she shot him a dark look.

"Sorry," he said, still smiling. "It's just . . . this isn't the sort of thing you ever cared about back in the day."

Her eyes rolled and she gave him a sheepish look. "I know. I still don't, really. But it's our reunion, and Homecoming and all. If we lose it'd be a bad omen. So, go Cougars! Right?"

A cheer went up from the crowd and they both spun just in time to see the ref in the end zone throw up both hands to signal that the field goal attempt had been successful. They had missed actually seeing the play, but the important thing was the scoreboard, which now read: *Home 3, Visitors 0.* Stacy let out that funny little yowl again and resumed walking.

"Where are your friends supposed to be sitting?" she asked, half turning to him.

Before he could reply he spotted them, halfway up the bleachers. There were other familiar faces, but in a cluster along three benches adjacent to the aisle, he saw Ashleigh and Eric, Danny and Keisha, Lolly, Pix, and Nick Acosta.

"Stacy," Will said.

She paused and glanced back at him. He nodded toward the upper rows of the bleachers, where Danny and Ashleigh had now noticed them and were beckoning with frantic waves and gestures, as though they were trying to coax in an airliner.

"Up there. The freaks who look like they're having seizures. Should we run?"

Stacy laughed, skin crinkling at the corners of her soft brown eyes. "I don't run. Although if they don't stop that, we might have to slip casually away."

"They'll just think we went to grope each other under the bleachers."

That eyebrow arched up again. "And maybe they'll be right."

Will opened his mouth to respond but she had already started up the steps toward the others. And he wouldn't have known what to say anyway. It amazed him how easily she could take him off guard like that. But he liked it.

Just as he started up after her, plastic tray full of nachos clutched carefully in his hands, a finger tapped his arm.

"Hey. Is your name Will James?"

Will turned around, brow knitted in curiosity, and found a tall, wiry, redheaded teenager standing there looking decidedly uncomfortable. The kid had a sullen look that he recognized almost immediately.

"Wait a second," Will said, pointing at him. "You're ... I met you yesterday. You——"

The kid nodded. "Yeah. I live in your old house. And it's Kyle. Kyle Brody."

What the hell is this kid doing here? And—

"How do you know my name?"

The kid sighed and glanced around as though he were afraid of being seen speaking to Will. "It's . . . shit, this is stupid. I can't even believe I'm here. Look, this is crazy, but I have a message for you."

"What?" Will asked, staring at the kid. "What are you talking about?"

But even as he asked, Kyle Brody was passing him a yellowed scrap of paper. On it, scrawled in an eerily familiar hand, were two words:

Don't forget.

CHAPTER 5

Cries of outrage rolled like thunder through the stands. In the midst of that cacophony someone shouted the word "Fuck" loud and long, stretching it out so that it became almost a moan. "Fuuuuuuuuuuuuuuuuuuck!"

Will blinked. His throat was dry. His gaze ticked from the yellowed scrap of paper in his hand up to the impatient expression on the pale features of Kyle Brody. He wondered, apropos of nothing, if Kyle's parents had assigned him the same bedroom that Will had lived in when growing up. Once again he gazed at the scrawl on the page. *Don't forget.* What was that supposed to mean?

"Don't forget what?" he asked, barely aware of having spoken the words out loud.

"How'm I supposed to know?" Kyle demanded. Then he shrugged and backed off a step. "Look, I delivered it. Don't even know why I did it, but here I am. And here I go."

The kid turned and started off toward the stairs that led out of the bleachers. For a second Will could only shake his head and stare mutely after him. He spun around and glanced up into the stands. Stacy had made it halfway up to the place where Ashleigh and the others all sat and now stood on the steps watching him

curiously. Everyone else was watching the game. For just a moment he surveyed the faces of his friends, familiar and comforting, and he felt himself drawn to them. There was room on the
bench just in front of Ashleigh and Eric for him and Stacy to sit
down and he felt pulled toward that place. Yet all of that seemed
hazy to him, as though in a dream, the world cloaked in a mist of
confusion and the faintest hint of menace in the air.

His fingers rubbed the yellowed paper. The note had been
folded in two. It was solid, rough to the touch, and it crinkled as
he refolded it. There was nothing around him just then that was
more real than that note.

Will raised his eyes and searched above the heads of the people moving through the stands, trying to find their row. Seconds
had passed. He saw the bright orange of Kyle's hair ahead, perhaps halfway to the steps that led down from the bleachers.
Then, without really even being aware that he was going to go after the kid, he was moving, slipping past people in pursuit.

He caught up to him on the far end of the bleachers.

"Kyle!"

The redhead snapped around as if he'd been yanked, glanced
once at Will, and rolled his eyes. By then Will was in close, blocking out Kyle's view of the stands, trying to keep their exchange at
least semiprivate, there in the midst of the Cougars' fans.

Will held the note in front of him like a priest brandishing a
communion wafer. "Tell me."

The kid scowled, shifting his weight from one foot to the
other. "Tell you *what*?"

A rush of anger and frustration went through Will. Much as
he had tried to block it out, his mind had been slipping gears
since last night. When he had awoken this morning he had been
profoundly unnerved by the tricks his memory was playing on
him. But the note in his hand, rough under his touch, was not the
product of his imagination. It was tangible.

Will shook his head, and for the first time since the kid had
handed him the note he looked into Kyle's eyes, really *looked* at him.

"Listen, kid...Kyle. A lot of weird shit has been happening

to me the last couple of days." He shook the note. "This is just the latest. Not a lot of it makes sense to me. You're here. You came all the way down here to hand me this—"

A frown creased Kyle's forehead. "I go to Eastborough, man. It's Homecoming."

"Yeah." Will nodded. "Of course it is. But, look, you brought this with you. Aren't you at all curious what the hell it means?"

Sullenly, the kid tipped his head to one side, gaze downcast. He shrugged lightly. "I guess."

"You guess?"

Kyle glanced around as if afraid he was being watched. Then he nodded. "All right, yeah. I'm curious. Killed the cat, didn't it? So tell me, then. What is it?"

Aware now of the way his heart was racing, Will nodded toward the bleachers. A few rows up there was room on the end of the bench. With obvious reluctance Kyle went up the stairs and sat down, sliding in so that Will could take the seat beside him.

"Where did it come from?" Will asked.

Kyle watched the game, eyes focused and yet also somehow distant. After a few seconds he gave a soft laugh. "Weird," he said, and shook his head, attention still on the action on the football field. "It really used to be your house? You lived there?"

"Until I went to college, yeah." Will wanted to urge him on but he could tell now that he had to let this kid tell it in his own way or he wasn't going to tell it at all. Around them people shouted and cheered. Popcorn flew, and along the very same row in which they sat, Will saw a kid about Kyle's age tipping a bottle of Jack Daniel's into a half-empty two-liter bottle of Coke as his buddies looked eagerly on.

"Which room was yours?" the kid asked.

"The one at the far end of the hall with the windows in the front. The one with the ash tree just...never mind." The ash tree wasn't there anymore.

Kyle nodded as though that made all the sense in the world to him. "That's my room, too."

"So you found it in your room?"

The kid shook his head. At last he turned to regard Will carefully, meeting his eyes, and there was an unease there that Kyle was doing everything to hide.

"The storage area? Under the house?" the kid began.

"Yeah. We kept all kinds of stuff in there. Wheelbarrow. Storm windows and things. Half the time I think my parents forgot it was there. I hung out in there with my friends sometimes."

Will didn't have to elaborate, didn't have to explain that he and his friends would go there to drink beer and maybe smoke a joint now and again. There was an instant communication between them. Kyle understood those things implicitly because it was his house now and he was of that age and had done the same things.

The edges of Kyle's mouth twitched in a blink of a smile. "My dad put a lock on it last summer. But I copied the key." Then all trace of amusement disappeared and once more the kid could not look at Will. "That's where the problem comes in. I've been down in that hole a thousand times. There's some loose insulation in the ceiling, by a beam—"

Images flashed through Will's mind. He could picture the storage area under the split-level's enclosed porch as if he had just been there yesterday. The door wasn't much, just a few planks of heavy wood and a latch. Inside, the floor was the same concrete as the patio. To get through the door you had to crouch low and duck your head, and even inside you still had to stay down low. Will could not count the number of times he had bumped his head. There was a single bare lightbulb with a chain to turn it off and on, and a couple of thick support beams for the porch ran up through the little room.

And in the insulation that kept the winter cold from seeping into the porch above, there were lots of rips and tears that were perfect for hiding things. Like a dime bag of marijuana, which Will had never really liked but would smoke with his friends if they had some. Or like the Polaroid nudes he had taken of Caitlyn sophomore year and later burned at her insistence.

Will nodded. "You hide things in there," he said, though his voice sounded far away even to him and the roar of the crowd seemed to diminish. He felt as though he were slipping into the same mist that seemed to envelop everything at the moment. But then his fingers rasped on the yellowed paper of that note in his hand and he blinked and turned to look at Kyle again.

The kid was studying him with renewed interest, as though he had never seen Will before at all. Or as though he had just discovered that Will was a brand-new type of creature, something entirely unexpected.

"Yeah," Kyle said. "Sometimes I do." A moment of guilt made him drop his gaze, but then he brought his eyes up again and looked at Will more firmly. "I was in there yesterday, right after I saw you. I was going to get something I had hidden in there, but then I found the note."

His words hastened; his tone became more anxious. "Other than my father, I have the only key. I figured he'd found my . . . the thing I'd hidden. I pulled the envelope down. I was losing it, thinking I was totally busted. But then I saw what it said—"

"What envelope?"

Kyle broke off and gave him a quizzical look. Then understanding dawned and he gave another little shrug. "You don't think it came like that, do you? How do you think I knew your name and where to find you and shit?"

"Do you still have it? The envelope?" Will asked.

An odd sort of slow motion seemed to capture them both. The handful of seconds it took for Kyle to nod and then reach into his back pocket to withdraw the envelope dragged on interminably. As Kyle brought it up and Will snatched it from his grasp, he saw the scrawl on the face of the yellowed envelope. It matched that on the note and was even more familiar, yet he couldn't place it.

Kyle, said the scribble on the face of the envelope. *A guy named Will James used to live in this house. You've met him. He'll be at the Homecoming game. Find him and give this to him. Everything depends on it.*

Will read the words a second time and then a third. A tingle had begun at the base of his neck, and he frowned as he folded the envelope over. With a sidelong glance he regarded Kyle carefully.

A strange prickling sensation raced across his skin, as though his entire body had been asleep and only now was the blood rushing into him again. What were the chances, really, that this kid's story would hold water? This wasn't at all like his confusion of the night before and the way his whole head had felt stuffed with cotton this morning. This was a tangible thing. Someone had done this, had put the note there in the storage space beneath his childhood home.

Someone's fucking with me, he thought.

Immediately he frowned.

Kyle caught the look and flinched. "What?"

"You sure you're telling me the whole story?" Will prodded, eyes narrowed in suspicion. "Seriously, Kyle. I'm not the guy to fuck with today. It's been a long weekend and it's not half over yet. Did somebody put you up to this?"

But before he had gotten the whole question out, Will already knew the answer. He saw the flicker in Kyle's eyes, the surprise and anger, the way the kid got his back up at having his story questioned. If someone was screwing with Will, Kyle's role in that was innocent. The kid was a pawn. But the question was already out.

"I don't need this shit," the kid said. "I don't even need to be here. I was just...I was curious, that's all. But this is too bizarre."

As he spoke, Kyle began to slide off the bench, rising to his feet. Will grabbed his shoulder, spoke his name, and Kyle gave him a hard look.

"You want to not do that," the kid said, and it wasn't a suggestion.

Will let his hand drop to his lap, but at least he had Kyle's attention again. "Sorry," he said. "It's just that, well, hell, obviously someone's messing with me. I wanted to make sure you weren't a part of it."

Kyle started down the steps but hesitated. After a moment he glanced around to be certain they weren't drawing too much attention, and he sat back down in the bleachers next to Will.

"All right. What's it all about, then?" the kid asked.

There was a moment in which Will was tempted to tell it all, to spill the bizarre events of the previous twenty-four hours. But he thought better of it. What was a high school senior going to say, except that Will was losing his head? Instead of an explanation, he opted for the truest answer he could summon.

"I don't have the first clue."

"But you said—"

"I'd tell you," Will interrupted. He shook his head, an ache growing at the base of his skull now, the kind of pain that told him it was only the beginning. He could feel Kyle staring at him, but for a long moment Will only watched the action on the football field. The ball sailed high above the grass, arcing as it soared toward the wide receiver's outstretched hands.

The receiver caught the ball. The clack of helmets colliding resounded through the stadium as a defenseman made the tackle and then others crashed into them, half a dozen teenagers going down in a crush of flesh and plastic, and it occurred to Will that he wasn't even quite sure which team was which. He had to blink and clear his head to realize that Natick High had the ball, that it had been their quarterback to throw that beauty of a pass, and their receiver to catch it.

Abruptly, Will turned to Kyle. "When I figure it out, I'll come find you. I said I'd tell you what it means, and I will. If you still want to know."

Kyle nodded slowly. "I do."

"Fine." Though it had been the kid who seemed so eager to depart, it was Will who stood up now and started down the steps. "I know where you live." He shot Kyle a conspiratorial smile that felt obscenely false, and then he turned away, not wanting to look at the kid anymore, not wanting to think about any of this stuff.

KYLE SAT AND WATCHED Will James go down to the front of the bleachers. He wanted to laugh. The whole thing was just so idiotic. His buds were probably down on the field, watching the game from the barren patch of ground beside the stands. That's where they always hung out, mainly because it made it easy to slip away if they wanted to take off with a girl, or sneak a beer. And here he was with this Matt Damon-looking guy, with...

He took a long breath and let it out, shaking his head. "What're you doing?" he muttered under his breath.

As if in answer he got up and started down the steps that led toward the field, reaching into his jacket pocket for a pack of smokes, then rustling around in his other pockets until he found his lighter, a crappy orange plastic Bic. He paused at the bottom of the stairs, just beside the second set of steps, the ones that led down to the field. As he lit the cigarette that jutted from his lips, Kyle turned to face the crowd in the stands, eyes searching for some sign of Will James, but the man had disappeared into the sea of Cougars fans.

He put the lighter and the smokes away and took a long drag on the cigarette he'd lit. Kyle held the smoke in his lungs and glanced out at the field, where the Cougars were losing by two points. That was all right, though. The game was just getting going.

I'm such an asshole, he thought. He turned and spat over the railing and then left the bleachers, tromping down the steps to the pavement around the field.

Kyle had felt as though he had discovered a genuine mystery. There had been something truly odd about the note he'd found in the storage space under his house. The oddness hadn't disappeared, but now he regretted having followed through on it. The truth was, he hadn't planned on attending the Homecoming game, even though a lot of his friends were here. But that note had changed his mind.

The note. Jesus.

It made his head hurt even worse just thinking about it, and he was glad to have it out of his possession. As he strode across the stadium grounds he took a long drag on his cigarette. His eyelids flickered, and when they did, for just a moment he was back again in the claustrophobic, dusty little space under the house. He had reached his fingers up into that hole in the insulation and pulled out a copy of *Hustler* that Neal Padgett had stolen from his father. When he had drawn the mag out of that hole, the envelope had fallen to the floor in a cascade of dust.

The thing had been coated with dust, like it had been up there forever. Which was impossible, of course. He would have discovered it a long time ago. On the other hand, he really doubted anyone had bothered to pick the lock, sneak in, and plant the thing, to weather it so it looked old and cover it in dust.

So what, then? Kyle asked himself. *Where'd the fucking thing come from?* The whole weirdness of it all was what had made him come down here and give the note to Will James, but the guy seemed clueless, like he was in a daze. Kyle had wanted answers to the odd little mystery from under his house, and he was profoundly dissatisfied that he had come away with nothing but a headache and a queasy feeling in his stomach.

He paused, dropped the cigarette to the ground, and crushed it under his boot.

Forget it. It's out of your hands. Waste of time.

It's over.

WILL'S MIND WAS TANGLED UP with thoughts and doubts and suspicions. How could any of this be? Someone was fucking with him, the note and envelope in his pocket seemed proof enough of that. But that could not explain the gymnastics his memory had been doing the past twenty-four hours. Yet the note—*Don't forget*—seemed a direct reference to the shifting images in his mind.

"Jesus," he whispered as he started up in the bleachers toward where his friends were seated. *I should've worked this weekend.*

He laughed softly, took a deep breath, and tried to let the tension out of his body as he exhaled. No way did he feel like talking about this with anyone. And he had already blown one opportunity to enjoy this rare gathering of old comrades. He shook his head in the very same way he did when he began to feel drowsy behind the wheel of the car, and he vowed not to think about it until the game was over.

When a bit of hot dog roll pelted him in the forehead, Will looked up to see Pix and Lolly howling with laughter, Ashleigh rolling her eyes, and Danny, Eric, and Nick all studiously analyzing the action on the football field, the picture of innocence. A wan smile eased its way onto Will's face and he was surprised to find it was only half forced.

Then Will blinked and he felt his smile dissolve. Stacy was gone. As he walked up the last few steps to where the group was sitting he glanced up farther into the bleachers, then back down the way he had come. By then he had come up beside Ashleigh and she reached up to take hold of his hand. Will glanced down at her and upon her face was an expression of both amusement and sympathy.

"She spotted Trey Morel going by, did a little giddy freakout thing, and then took off with him."

Will sighed and shook his head. *This fucking weekend,* he thought. Nothing seemed to be right, and yet the sky was blue and the sun shone warm upon him, pads and helmets clacked together on the football field, and fans cheered wildly and spilled popcorn and drinks on one another. Someone had churned up dark thoughts and shot his life full of chaos, and the world just went right on spinning as if nothing were amiss.

He took one last glance around, but there was no sign of her. Stacy was gone.

Danny jumped up from his seat, shouting like a madman. The Cougar quarterback had just thrown for a first down. When his gaze swept to the right and found Will, however, his excitement diminished.

"Have a seat and enjoy the game, shithead. Enough with that mopey crap. Dude, I am getting you *so* drunk tonight."

Will gave him a lopsided grin. "You promise?"

"Oh, yeah."

Then Keisha was asking him a question and in the moment when Danny was distracted, Ashleigh tugged on Will's hand again.

"Sit with us. Come on. Just chill. You'll see her tonight."

He nodded and slid onto the seat next to her, wishing that Stacy's abrupt departure were the only thing on his mind.

"Unless you're trying to scare her off?" Ashleigh suggested.

"Why would I do that?"

She shrugged. "You know how you are. The second you think you like a girl a little too much, you send her packing."

Will rolled his eyes. "Why does everyone think I'm afraid of getting close to a woman?"

Ashleigh stared at him, just a hint of amusement on her face.

Will laughed. "All right, besides that. And it isn't true, anyway. I send them packing when I think I don't like them *enough*." He paused, glanced around again as though he might catch sight of Stacy. "Did she say anything?"

Ashleigh linked an arm through her husband's on one side and through Will's on the other. He sensed her relaxing then, settling into the safety of this contact. She had always liked to sit or walk like this, arm in arm with the two of them. Her lover and her best friend. Eric had been forced to get used to it but had not done so without frequently teasing Ashleigh about her penchant for ménages à trois. Inevitably, she would end up rapping her knuckles on Eric's head, and Will wondered if that accounted for his unusual silence this time.

"Ash?" he prodded.

A sly smile touched her lips.

"Did she say anything?"

Ashleigh shot him a sidelong glance. "She said she'd see you tonight and to save her a dance." Her smirk was devastating. "Then she kind of laughed and said on second thought, she hoped you'd save her all your dances."

Will's mouth hung open a moment and then he laughed hesitantly. "Fuck you. She did not say that."

Ash held up her hand as though she were in court. "Swear to God."

All Will could summon up was "hunh." He grunted softly and nodded ever so slightly to himself. Ashleigh nudged him in that universal good-going-champ sort of way, and this time when he smiled there came with it an immense sense of relief.

It was possible that the *entire* world wasn't turning to shit.

"Sort of interesting, the way things change, isn't it?" Ashleigh asked.

"You can say that again."

"Are you feeling all right, Will? Seriously. Between last night and today—"

"I wasn't feeling all that well. But I'm OK now." Will glanced at her. "Just a little stressed, I guess."

Her husband was within earshot and now he leaned forward so he could speak directly to Will, with Ashleigh in between them. "Come on, my friend, relax. You've got nothing to be stressed about until Monday morning rolls around again. You're among friends. Let your hair down. From the looks of things, this weekend's already going better than you could've hoped."

With the last sentence, Eric wiggled his eyebrows suggestively and Will laughed.

"Agreed. I'll take it under advisement."

But Eric's attention had already been diverted away from him. The entire crew—in fact, the entire coterie of assembled Cougars fans—were on their feet booing dramatically.

"Pass interference!" Danny shouted.

"You suck, Ref!" Lolly and Pix cried in harmony.

It was anarchy, but it was familiar and comforting. Just the idea of these two beautiful women, each the exotic opposite of the other, screaming at the ref in unison, was enough to bring him back to another time in his life, a time when he had never been as confused about anything as he had felt in the past twenty-four hours. Teenage boys were all arrogance and swagger—almost laughably so—but there were times when he longed for the kind of clarity of purpose and conscience that he had had in those days.

Anarchy, he mused as he glanced around at people throwing popcorn tubs and drink cups down at the field. *Maybe there's something to be said for chaos after all.*

Nick Acosta slid over behind him, his grin tugging at the scar over his eye, his curly hair even wilder than usual. "Willy!" he said. "What you need is a beer."

Will gaped at him. "Don't even tell me you snuck a cooler in here."

All through high school they had done that for night games, passing the cooler over the fence behind the bleachers. Now Nick just shrugged.

"Okay. I won't tell you. Want a beer?"

On the field the whistle blew for halftime. Will shrugged. "Why not?"

Nick made his way back to his spot in the stands and fished a can of Budweiser out of the cooler. He leaned over to pass it to Keisha, and the beer was smuggled along to Danny, Eric, Ashleigh, and finally Will. There were chips of ice still sliding down the aluminum. He didn't really like beer very much, and Budweiser in particular, but when it was this cold...He glanced around and spotted the tray he and Stacy had gotten from the concession. He had completely forgotten it, and Ashleigh obviously had neglected to remind him, so now the remains of the food were cold. But one of the cups was half empty, so he dumped the rest of the soda on the stairs and poured the Bud into the cup.

Will tipped the cup back and took a gulp.

"I thought you didn't like beer these days," Ashleigh said, a bemused expression on her face.

His upper lip curled as though he'd just tasted something sour. "I don't." Will glanced at Ashleigh, and they both laughed.

As he watched her, a warmth seemed to spread through him. How he had missed that laugh. Ashleigh was a professional woman, an attorney, a mother, and a wife, but in his heart she would always be that girl with whom he had shared everything. He loved her, certainly, but it saddened him to realize that the passage of time could make him forget how much. When she laughed her chestnut hair fell across her face and she squinted her eyes just a bit. Will reached out and touched her hand and she squeezed his fingers.

"It's so good to see you," she said.

Much of the tension in him seemed to drain away. Whatever was happening, whoever was fucking with him, it had already stolen some of the time he should have been spending with her. Will didn't want to lose any more of that time. He wanted to forget all about the bizarre stuff, at least until Monday.

"You, too, Ash," he said. "You, too."

This time when she smiled he had an image in his mind, of this woman all the way back in junior high school, when she had been skinny Ashleigh Wheeler with the braces.

"I don't know if you'd be up for it," she said, "but I was thinking maybe you could come down and spend Halloween with us this year. Take the twins out trick-or-treating."

Will nodded. "I'd love that. We had a good time on Halloween, didn't we?"

"Always. Remember that time you went as Spider-Man and split your pants?"

He rolled his eyes. "You won't let me forget, no matter how much I try."

Ashleigh turned sideways in her seat to face him. "It's when I think about you the most. At Halloween. We really should try to see each other more. Eric tells me all the time that we just have to make the effort. It's weird the turns life takes. I mean, I saw you almost every day for eighteen years. I never thought I'd live anywhere else."

"Yeah, this growing-up thing sucks!" Will said in mock

protest. Then he softened. "Actually, it's not so bad. I wish I could see you all more. What's that saying? 'Life's what happens when you're busy making other plans.' That's true, isn't it?"

Ashleigh frowned. "Not if I can help it."

Will took another sip of beer and grimaced. He had thought he wanted it, that the alcohol content alone would be worth the rusty taste, but now he set it down between his legs and forgot it. "I'd love to come down for Halloween."

"It's settled, then," Ashleigh replied.

Will heard the ghost of her mother in the phrase and could picture Mrs. Wheeler at the kitchen table speaking those same words. She had been a gruff but kindhearted woman, always ready with brownies or candy, but also more than willing to correct a child, whether the kid was her own offspring or not. Mrs. Wheeler had died when they were sophomores in college.

"So, who else have you run into so far?" he asked.

"Oh, my God!" Ashleigh said, the spark of her high school self flashing in her eyes. "Did you see Nyla Leonitis?"

Will grinned at her excitement. "No."

"You heard she was gay, though, right?"

He pictured high school Nyla in his mind. Stereotypes were bullshit, there was no question about that. But with her mannish features, absolute ignorance of anything feminine, and the cut of her hair, people willing to jump to conclusions would certainly have presumed she was a lesbian.

"She's not?" Will asked.

"No, she is," Ashleigh said, waving her hand at him as though he had said the stupidest thing in the world. "First of all, she looks great. But oh, my God, Will, I met her girlfriend and she is such a hottie. I swear to you, *I* would sleep with her."

"Would you film it?"

Ashleigh punched him in the arm, and then continued her weekend-to-date review of the former classmates she had caught up with. She teased him about Stacy—reminding him of her comment about saving all the dances for her tonight—and Will told her about the people he had seen at the parade.

"Martina's still amazing. Things with Brian actually seemed...pretty cool. Not as awkward as I expected. I talked to Tim Friel last night, he's doing well. Cheered when he and Tess went by in the parade—"

"Wait," Ashleigh said, brow furrowing in confusion. "Tim and Tess? Why was Tess in the parade?"

A ripple of nausea went through Will's stomach and he blinked as a sharp spike of pain lanced into his head. His hand went to his temple, and in the moments that followed his mind was filled with conflicting images. Tim and Tess, maybe forty-five minutes ago, riding in the parade as Homecoming King and Queen for his class. Tim and Caitlyn—*his* Caitlyn—riding in that same parade ten years ago, Tim in his football uniform and Caitlyn so beautiful in the dress Will had helped her pick out, a tiara on her head.

"Will?" Ashleigh asked. He felt her hand on his shoulder. "Are you all right?"

He nodded. "Just...just a headache."

"So what was that about Tess? Why was she in the parade again?"

A chill crept through him. He felt the memories sifting, new ones sliding in to cover the old, as though he was shuffling some mental deck of cards. Caitlyn. Before he'd come into the stadium he had seen her in the crowd watching the parade. But even now he could remember looking up and seeing her riding with Tim, waving to him as she went by. Homecoming Queen.

His own laugh sounded hollow to him as he glanced at Ashleigh. "Sorry. I meant Caitlyn. Tim and Caitlyn. Freudian slip, I guess. Maybe secretly I always thought Tess should've won Homecoming Queen."

Ashleigh dropped her gaze. Will's heart fluttered. Had he said it wrong? His thoughts were so confused but he couldn't explain to Ashleigh, not now. Not until he understood what was happening to his mind. He didn't think he could stand her thinking he was losing it.

"She would've been," Ashleigh said softly. Then, without

raising her head, she glanced up at him. "It was the worst, Will. Sometimes I even forget it happened to her."

Ice formed in his gut. "What?"

Ashleigh looked around to be sure no one was paying attention to their conversation. "Tess got the most votes, Will. She would've been Homecoming Queen. But she dropped out that morning and Caitlyn was the first runner-up, so Chadbourne had her take the crown. Tess didn't go to the game, or the dance. She didn't want anyone to know. She was so ashamed."

Will did not want to ask, but he could not stop himself. "Ashamed of what?"

"That Friday night—the night before Homecoming—she was raped."

"Jesus," Will whispered, so low he doubted Ashleigh could hear him. "Jesus Christ."

He glanced around at the faces in the crowd, at his friends. Eric and Danny had gone off to use the bathroom, or maybe to the concession stand. Nick caught Will's eye, concern etched in his features, but Will ignored him. The other women were all caught up in conversation with one another. The air itself seemed to shudder, the sunlight to sparkle with the terrible suggestion that at any moment it might all be torn apart, as though the fabric of the world itself were infinitely malleable.

The taste of beer lingered and Will felt bile rise up in his throat. It was all he could do to keep from throwing up.

The deck of cards continued to be shuffled in his mind. Caitlyn. Tess. Mike Lebo.

Will hung his head and rubbed at the back of his neck. "Jesus," he said again. "That's . . . that's awful. I don't even have the words. And Tess never told anyone? The police, I mean? What was to stop the guy from raping someone else?"

Ashleigh stiffened beside him and said nothing. Will raised his head to look at her, wondering what it was he had said that had upset her. She was staring at him, eyes narrowed in suspicion, lips pressed together so tightly that they were almost white.

"How did you know that? None of the guys knew. Tess swore all the girls to secrecy."

But Will was barely listening to her words. He held his breath as he stared at Ashleigh and he could feel his eyes well up with unshed tears of frustration and helplessness. For even as he gazed at her, she was changing. It was subtle, but it was real. There were lines in her face that he knew had not been there moments before. Her hair was slightly unkempt now and there were a few gray hairs he had not noticed. Ashleigh was wearing more makeup than she had been only a moment before. Brighter lipstick. Eyeshadow. And her eyes. There was something in them he hadn't seen there before.

Pain.

It took a moment for her words to sink in. The fear he had been nurturing in his heart since the previous night blossomed into terror. The impossible was happening all around him, everything he knew to be true and solid seemed to be slipping from his grasp. Will tilted his head and regarded her carefully.

"Ash. Ashleigh, you told me. Just a minute ago. *You* told me."

She shook her head, lowered her gaze. "Don't do that to me, Will." She uttered a sound that might have been a laugh if not for the sadness in it. "Mess with my head enough, I might even believe you."

"Ashleigh—"

Abruptly she looked up at him again, met his gaze with a determined air. "So if you know about Tess, then you know it happened to me, also. How long have you known, Will?"

He could only stare at her. His mouth was dry, his throat closing as if to choke him. Tears began to form at the corners of his eyes but he blinked them away. Will could not reply, could not speak to her.

Her voice dropped to nothing but a papery rasp. "I had to have an abortion. Did they tell you that, too, whoever decided they could share secrets? But I had scar tissue, after. Everyone's always wondering when Eric and I are going to have kids—well, there's your answer. We can't."

She shook her head. "I know I should have told you this. You, if anyone. But I made a promise. And this was a shitty time, and a shitty way, for you to bring it up."

Olivia. Rose. Those were the names of Ashleigh and Eric's three-year-old twin daughters. Olivia and Rose. Will knew this. He had held the baby girls in his arms. Had photographs of them at home. But he knew, now, that those photographs were no longer there, just as Mike Lebo's address was no longer in his book. Because Mike Lebo was dead.

And Ashleigh's daughters had never been born.

The cards were shuffling in his head again, but now some of them had been played. A pattern was forming. Through the haze of his heartbreak and his fear, he could see it happening. Something snapped in Will's mind. The sound, inside his ears the way he could sometimes hear his heartbeat, was like the flick of a playing card when it is plucked from the top of the deck with a flourish.

None of it had ever happened.

But now it had.

Will understood now. This was not in his head. He was not some delusional schizophrenic lunatic. *Don't forget*, the note had said, and though he had not wanted to think about it, he had presumed it to be some coy reference to how ephemeral his memories had suddenly become. Now, though, a wall had been shattered in his mind . . . a wall that he himself had erected out of fear and guilt, using the very skills he had so profoundly desired to forget. For the first time in many years, memories he had hidden away from himself returned, and with them a truth about himself and about the fabric of the world that he had wished never to remember.

It was not his mind falling apart, here. It was magic. Dark, cruel magic.

Will had used it to make himself forget. Now someone else was using magic, twisting his reality, and the shock of it had torn away the veil of forgetfulness he had placed upon his mind.

Ashleigh wasn't the only one with a secret.

CHAPTER 6

October, Sophomore Year...

Like a beehive, the Eastborough High cafeteria was alive with a constant hum of activity. The clatter of trays and plates and the hiss of steam from the kitchen only fed into the white noise of a hundred simultaneous conversations. Lunch monitors patrolled the caf, strolling amidst aisles of rectangular tables and keeping a special eye on the round tables at the outer edges of the enormous hall—the more desirable seats where the upperclassmen always sat.

Will James was in the third row of rectangles, right in the middle of a dining setup that always reminded him of prison movies. PixieGirl and Caitlyn were whispering some gossip or other to his right. Nick Acosta and Brian Schnell were just sitting down across from him, sliding their trays onto the table. Baked manicotti was the choice of the day, and as bland as the pasta and the cheese were, it was at least edible.

Nick leaned across the table, frowning at Will. "We've gotta sit with these pricks?"

Will didn't need to ask for an elaboration. The pricks in question were Greg Bellini, Chuck Wisialowski, and a handful of their asshole buddies from the hockey team. They weren't all bad, but when they hung around Bellini, they might as well be.

"Didn't even notice," Will told him. "It's not easy getting a bunch of seats together."

Nick rolled his eyes. "Pricks." He forked a bite of manicotti into his mouth, then turned toward Pix and Caitlyn and opened his mouth, giving them all a view of chewed cheese and pasta sauce. The girls sighed and went on with their conversation, but Nick and Brian laughed. Will just shook his head. Nick was always happy to go for the easy laugh.

That was when Bellini made his mistake. He had caught sight of Nick's mouthful.

"Yeah," Bellini called along the table, "I heard about you, Acosta. Heard you'll put anything in your mouth."

Will stiffened. His gaze ticked toward Brian. The girls had fallen silent. They all looked at Nick, who only grinned and showed Bellini that same mouthful of food. The short, pug-nosed hockey player sat diagonally across the table from Nick, and had a perfect view.

"Fuckin' loser," Bellini sneered, grinning as he looked at his friends, who chuckled derisively. "Football fags."

Will started to stand up but he caught a look from Nick. In the midst of his grinning, Nick let him know just with that glance that this was his show and he didn't want Will to interfere. Sometimes it seemed that Nick was always prepared to share wisdom with others but never seemed to have enough left for himself.

Still smiling as Bellini went back to his conversation with his friends, Nick broke off a small chunk of the slice of Italian bread on his plate. He cocked back one finger, and flicked it across the table at Bellini. It struck the little bulldog on the cheek, and Bellini slapped at the side of his head as though a mosquito had bitten him.

With wild eyes he glared at Nick. "You're just lucky that didn't have any sauce on it."

Their gazes were locked. Nick's grin remained steady, even manic. He broke off another piece of bread, dipped it into the sauce on his manicotti, and flicked it across the table. It struck

Bellini's shirt, leaving a red smear. There was a collective intake of breath around the table, and it seemed to Will that at that moment a hush fell over the cafeteria. That was ridiculous, of course, as only a handful of people were actually paying attention. It was just in his own ears. In his own head.

Bellini stood and backed away from the table, gaping stupidly at the smear on his shirt. When he lifted his gaze to glare at Nick, his nostrils flared and he was almost shaking.

"Come on, then, shithead. I'm gonna kick your ass."

A prickling sensation went up the back of Will's neck. He stood at the very same moment that Nick did. Bellini and Nick were on opposite sides of the table and they started moving toward the end of the row. Will got in the bulldog's way.

"Why don't you sit down," Will told him.

Bellini sneered up at him, half a foot shorter than any of the other guys at the table, and Nick was taller than any of them. "Wait your turn, Willy."

The air crackled with the tension and the impending violence, the malign intent that rolled in waves off both Nick and Bellini. Will could feel it, as heavy and electric as the moisture and static in the air just before a storm, and wanted to slam Bellini's head into the table.

But then he felt Nick's hand on his shoulder and he turned to find that his friend was still calm, bright-eyed, and smiling.

"Relax, Will. This is my dance."

Will took a quick breath and nodded, then stepped aside, leaving Nick and Bellini to face off against one another. Already they had begun to draw attention. Hockey players had scrambled from their seats and were backing Bellini up, watching to see what was going to happen. Football players were rooting for Nick, who was one of their own. Others students were taking notice, gathering around. Bellini had set the stage now, and there was no way he was going to let the audience down.

"Come on, pussy, let's go," the bulldog snarled.

Nick chuckled, hands at his sides. "After school."

Bellini frowned. "Fuck that. Right here. Let's go."

Pix and Caitlyn were up now as well, but where Caitlyn had a fearful expression on her face, PixieGirl just looked annoyed. "Cut the shit, you guys," she snapped. "Come on, Nick. This is stupid."

Brian Schnell had been watching in rapt fascination but now he seemed to wake suddenly, as though from a trance. He glanced around nervously. "She's right, Nick. You don't need this shit."

Nick sighed, his smile thinning into a bemused smirk. "Look, I'll be happy to kick your ass, but I want to do it somewhere I'll get to finish the job. After school."

"You're a pussy." Bellini took a step closer.

"After school," Nick repeated firmly, his smile disappearing. He shook his head and glanced over at Brian, Caitlyn, and Pix.

Will saw it coming. Nick didn't. In that moment where Nick had turned away, Bellini swung. His fist struck Nick in the side of the face, and by instinct Nick backed up. With the exhortations of the other hockey pricks driving him on, Bellini went after him. Will tensed to jump in, but Nick didn't need him to. The second Bellini got close enough he reached out and grabbed the guy by the head. Nick took a punch to the chest but it barely grazed him. Then he had one arm around Bellini's neck, holding him tightly as with the other he began to pummel his opponent's chest and stomach. Bellini flailed, throwing wild punches that careened harmlessly off the back of Nick's skull. It looked, not surprisingly, much like the sort of fight Will had seen many times at hockey games.

Students had gathered around, but now Will's English teacher, Mr. Murphy, shoved his way through the spectators. Even as he did so, the sound of a chair scraping the floor echoed through the room from a round table of seniors and Joe Hayes stood up. The pale, redhaired Hayes was gigantic; when he shoved his way into the midst of things, students made way for him. Nick was over six feet tall and weighed at least one hundred and eighty pounds, but Hayes grabbed him under the arms and hauled him away from Bellini as though he were an infant. The English teacher grabbed Bellini, and the visual juxtaposition of the four of them was almost comical.

Bellini's lip was bleeding, which seemed odd since Will hadn't even seen Nick hit him in the face. Not once. He wondered if the moron had bit his own lip in all the excitement.

Then it was over. Mr. Murphy thanked Joe Hayes and began shepherding Bellini and Nick out of the cafeteria, obviously headed for trouble. To Will's great surprise the other hockey players didn't bother with any trash talk as they sat back down at the table. In a few brief minutes, all was as it had been, save the absence of the brawlers.

"Well," Brian said, "that was bracing."

"A bunch of Neanderthals if you ask me," Pix said, the consternation in her tone belying the gentle elegance of her features. She was beautiful when she smiled, but without that smile she often looked cold and cruel. Will thought it was a good thing she smiled most of the time.

"Come on, Carrie," Caitlyn said, the one person who still insisted on using Pix's actual name, "you know that's what you love about Nick. His caveman tendencies."

Pix shot her a withering look and Will grinned. Everyone seemed to know she was interested in Nick except Nick himself. Pix wasn't normally shy, but she didn't seem to be in a hurry to mention it to Nick, so nobody else was going to say anything, either. Caitlyn was full of it, anyway. Nick had never been the kind of guy to get into fights, but he also was not going to back down from anyone.

"Can't believe what a loser Bellini is," Will said. He stared down at his tray, picking at the manicotti. It was cold now and the cheese had congealed. A grunt came from his own lips, and he looked over at Brian. "You know why he didn't want to wait till after school."

Brian offered a cynical scowl. "He knew it'd be broken up. If he waited till later, Nick would've wrecked him. Did you see that sucker punch? Bellini knew that was his only shot."

Will raised an eyebrow and studied Brian. Of all the kids who were part of their group, Brian and Nick were the opposite ends of the spectrum. Nick was boisterous and carefree, while Brian was pensive and generally quiet. Usually the two did not have a lot to say to one another, particularly of late. Brian's sister Dori was a freshman, and ever since the first day of school Nick had been lusting after her. The more Dori ignored him, the more Nick wanted her. He'd reached the point where he was lovesick over the girl, though he tried to hide it as best he could.

It got under Brian's skin, though. Deeply.

"Tell the truth, Bri," Will said through a mouthful of manicotti. "That sucker punch made your day."

Brian was embarrassed and even blushed slightly as he glanced at the girls, who were lost in their own conversation. He shrugged as he looked back at Will. "Maybe a little. Can you blame me? My little sister, Will. That's just wrong."

Will laughed softly, shaking his head. "Forbidden zone."

"Exactly!" Brian grinned. "Hey, look, Bellini's revealed to be a big pussy and Nick takes one on the chin. It's a win-win situation from where I'm sitting."

The lunch period was waning. Will and Brian fell silent, then allowed themselves to be swept into the maelstrom of cafeteria noise once again. Brian sucked back the last of his soda, and Will poked at the brown thing on his tray that might have been some kind of cake or brownie, debating whether he wanted to risk it. Beside him, Caitlyn and Pix were talking about the JV cheerleading squad, of which they were both a part, but to Will it was a drone that fed into the white noise in the caf. At least, until Caitlyn leaned over to catch his eye.

Her lavender top had a V-neck and he had the perfect view. The tops of her breasts were pale and lightly freckled and he forced himself to look away, to meet her eyes. In her expression he saw that she had noticed, she had caught him looking, and didn't mind at all. His heart skipped a beat. He had been wanting to ask her out for weeks but hadn't gotten up the guts yet.

"Earth to Will," Caitlyn said, and there was something about the way her eyelids fluttered then that captivated him, something in her smirk that left a mark on his heart.

PixieGirl rapped on the table. "Wake up. You two are like mirror images of each other. Daydreaming. Or catatonic, I can't decide."

Will glanced at Brian. Daydreaming was a trait they had in common, but he had never realized it until Pix brought it up.

"Halloween," Caitlyn went on. "We were thinking we should try to get a group together and go to Salem. They're supposed to do a whole big Halloween theme there. Very spooky."

"Could be fun," Will said, "but what about transportation? None of us can drive yet."

"There are enough parents to go around. We could work it out," Caitlyn said. There was a softness in her eyes that made her seem almost coy. She had never seemed coy to him before.

"It'd be cool," Pix said, her tone making the word sound delicious. "Creepy. All the history there and everything, with witchcraft and burnings and stuff."

Will looked at her. She was right in that it would be cool, and he had also heard that Salem made a big deal out of Halloween. They traded on the hideous and tragic history that the city was renowned for, even had a witch on a broomstick as part of the logo of the city newspaper. It would be fun. But Pix had the facts wrong, and Will couldn't let it go. He opened his mouth to correct her.

Brian beat him to it. "Danvers," he said. "Back in those days, the town and city lines weren't the same as they are now. Most of the witch trials and executions actually took place in Danvers."

"What?" Caitlyn said, brows knitting. "But they always talk about the Salem witch trials. I don't think—"

"No, he's right." Will glanced around at the three of them. "And chances are the men and women who were killed weren't witches at all. Sure, maybe some of them did herbal medicine or that kind of thing, but it was just bullshit, mostly. Like the Inquisition. People who thought differently from the people who made the rules."

"I thought they were Wiccans. Earth worshippers and stuff," Pix said.

Brian shook his head vehemently. "Not even close. Wicca didn't even exist until the twentieth century. Sure, there were pagans. Earth worshippers. Druids. But that was a whole different thing. And none of it's witchcraft."

A ripple of heat ran up Will's back and he felt himself flush. Trepidation made his pulse race. He glanced at Caitlyn and Pix, who were surprisingly attentive, and then back at Brian.

"How do we know?" Will asked, amazed that the words were coming out of his mouth. These were things he had thought and wondered for a long time, but it was the sort of fanciful thinking that his friends had crucified him for in the past, and probably would again. Still, he wasn't going to stop now. "I mean, maybe some of them *were* witches. Into magic and shit."

Brian hesitated, watching Will with a strange caution.

"You mean for real?" Caitlyn asked. "You believe in magic?"

Will knew he should shut up now, but he had already committed himself. "I don't know. Maybe I do. It just . . . some things don't make sense to me without it. I'm not sure if it still exists, but I kinda think that maybe . . ."

The din of the cafeteria, the voices and the clatter of trays and dishes, seemed to disappear in that moment.

"Maybe it did, once upon a time," Brian said, nodding slowly.

The bell rang. Lunch period was over.

But something else had begun.

March, Sophomore Year . . .

There was just a hint of spring that day. The sun was warm and Will had seen a bunch of sparrows earlier. Every time the wind blew, it was a little reminder that winter had not surrendered just yet. As dusk stole the last of the sun from the sky and the darkness descended upon Eastborough, the air had turned cold in a brisk snap, as if the winter had been hiding, waiting for its time.

Spring would come, of course. As always. But until it truly arrived, winter would be tenacious in its hold.

The jukebox in Athens Pizza played En Vogue's "Free Your Mind." Behind the counter, the brothers who ran the place bickered in an odd fraternal shorthand that might have had to do with business, or not. Perry and Arthur were Greek, and their native language crept into their dialogue with such subtlety that half the time they did not even seem to notice.

Will held on to Caitlyn's hand under the table; from time to time, she would spider-walk her fingers up his leg. They sat in a booth with Ashleigh and Eric, who had just started dating. It was odd for Will, knowing Ashleigh was kissing the guy, that he was probably getting into her pants, or would be soon. Not that he was jealous, but Ash was like his sister and he felt extremely protective. Eric was all right, though, and it was clear he genuinely liked Ashleigh. As to where things would go with them, the jury was still out.

There were still a few pieces of pizza left on the metal tray between them, and Will picked up a slice that was heavy with pepperoni. As he lifted it to his mouth he felt that tickling on his leg again and tensed, then shuddered as Caitlyn's fingers crawled up his inner thigh. He could not help fidgeting when she did this, and turned to her with an admonishing grin.

"What?" she demanded, masking her amusement poorly. She tossed her hair back and cocked an eyebrow. "Eat your pizza."

It was this playfulness about her that had greatly contributed to his falling in love with her. Now he reached his right hand out to caress her face and slid closer to kiss her. No matter where they were, or what they were doing, she was unable to resist this kind of intimacy. Will knew it, but he did not use that knowledge to manipulate her. His heart drove him to it, and if asked he would have confessed that he believed she saw it in his eyes and that was why, even now, her mischief ended and she closed her eyes as their lips softly met. Of course, if he had confessed this, he would have been tormented mercilessly.

"Hey, lovebirds, snap out of it for a second!"

Danny Plumer started messing with his hair. Grinning, Will batted his hand away. Danny had his coat on already, always put together, always better dressed than anyone else. Behind him, Mike Lebo was pulling a fleece sweatshirt over his head and Nick was just standing up, jacket in hand. Brian was there as well, but he seemed oblivious to the great exodus of his companions, scarfing down the last of a piece of pepper-and-onion pizza. Typically, there were a couple of stains on his shirt.

Will always enjoyed having everyone together; that was his role in the group. Danny was the natural leader, the pretty boy. Mike was the fan boy, the one who picked the movies and whose enthusiasm was infectious. Nick was the smart one, though he tried to hide it. The three of them played football together. Then there was Brian, the misfit, just as smart as Nick but with few social skills, and Ashleigh, whom they all adored. Eric was on the football team as well, but was there because of Ashleigh, and of course Caitlyn was friendly with Ash, but was Will's girlfriend.

With the exception of Nick and Brian, they all got along. And Will was the one who brought them together, the axis upon which the whole group seemed to spin. He relished that.

"You guys taking off?" Eric asked his football teammates.

"Yeah, what's the rush?" Will prodded.

Danny laughed. "Please. Bud, you forgot we were even here." He glanced at Ashleigh and Caitlyn. "Not that the rest of us boys don't love you, girls, but when you're around, your boyfriends are useless blobs of flesh."

Caitlyn chuckled evilly. "Not so useless."

"Wow," Mike said in amazement. "Get a room, Cait."

Everyone was laughing, but Will was focused on Danny, troubled because what his friend had said was true. "Sorry, bud," he said, all earnestness, using the nickname the two of them nearly always called one another, but rarely used for anyone else.

Danny shrugged. "It's cool. Who can blame you. We're all just jealous because our table only had penises."

Still seated, Brian nearly choked on his pizza, laughing, and had to spit some out into a napkin to catch his breath. The other guys started to laugh at him and any tension that had existed was quickly dispelled. Ancient AC/DC played on the jukebox now, and that was one of the things Will loved about Athens Pizza, the bizarre variety on the jukebox.

"Mike's dragging us to the comics shop," Nick put in, rolling his eyes. "We tolerate his geekdom."

Lebo shot him the middle finger. "A lot of comics are shit, but some of them are really amazing. Plus they're like jazz, man. One of the few truly American art forms. Trashing on comics is un-American." He grinned, pleased with himself. "One of these days you're going to realize what you've been missing."

"Possibly," Nick replied, and then his expression became crestfallen. "And then, tragically, I'll also be the target of cruel mockery." When he lifted his chin, his grin was devilish. "But I'll deserve it, just like you. Fan boy."

Mike shook his head and sighed, used to the ribbing by now. He put a hand on Danny's shoulder and they looked down at Will.

"You're staying at Brian's tonight?" Mike asked.

"Yeah."

"Another meeting of the young magicians' club?" Danny asked. "What is it tonight? You guys still trying to pronounce abracadabra?"

Brian slid to the edge of the booth the guys had just abandoned and kicked Danny in the butt, then quickly assumed an innocent pose, soda cup in hand, straw in his mouth. Danny laughed good-naturedly.

"Nah," Nick mused, shooting a lewd glance at Caitlyn. "They're trying to figure out how to use their wands."

Across the table from Will, Eric laughed and Ashleigh actually blushed so deeply scarlet that her ears were pink. Caitlyn only sat further forward in the booth, leaning in as though to share some secret.

"Actually," she said in a confidential tone, "Will never has any trouble with his wand."

Lebo actually blushed right along with Ashleigh at that one, but Danny and Nick wore expressions of surprise and delight as they hooted and high-fived each other. Will thought it all was pretty ironic. For all her talk, Caitlyn was shy when they were alone together. She teased, but she was nervous about sex. They had spent hours touching one another, but Will suspected it was going to be a long time before they got around to the real deal.

On the other hand, if she wanted to tease the other guys— who sure as hell weren't getting any—and make it seem like the two of them were fucking like rabbits, Will wasn't going to argue. In her way, Caitlyn was defending his and Brian's interest in magic, and he appreciated that. It was a hobby. People had hobbies. Lebo had his comics. Danny hit on girls. Nick lifted weights. Will was glad that he had found someone else who shared his interest in the subject, and Caitlyn didn't seem to mind at all.

"So, tell Superman I said hello," Will said.

"I don't read *Superman*," Lebo said, rolling his eyes at the way Will had so effortlessly turned the mockery back in his direction.

"No," Brian said, still behind them. Will could barely see him past the others. "You only wear the underwear."

Lebo nodded to indicate that he did indeed have Superman underwear. Will presumed he was kidding. Hoped he was. Nick, however, took the opportunity to turn his attention back to Brian as well.

"Speaking of underwear, how's Dori?" he asked.

Brian was used to this. "My little sister hears you talking about her underwear, she'll castrate you, Acosta."

The matrix of lines that connected their group was fairly solid, but there were exceptions. Lolly and Pix, for instance, came and went within the group and weren't permanent fixtures. Nick and Brian, on the other hand, sometimes got along and other times seemed to actively dislike each other. Nick ignored him now, turning to Will. The glint in his eye was not altogether pleasant. There was more than friendly teasing going on here.

"Will, tell Dori I send my best, okay? And if you get a chance, steal me a pair of her panties."

Ashleigh and Caitlyn uttered a chorus of revulsion and, as she was closest, Ashleigh smacked Nick in the chest.

"For a smart guy, you're such a pig," Ashleigh said, her nose wrinkling as though she'd smelled something particularly disgusting.

"True," Nick said, nodding without a hint of penitence. "But so's Danny."

Caitlyn curled her lip. "Danny just doesn't oink quite so loud."

"I'm going to take that as a compliment," Danny decided, zipping up his coat. He glanced at Lebo and Nick. "Let's go."

Will clapped hands with him and said good-bye to the other guys, and in moments they had all gone, save for Brian, who sat at the opposite booth amidst the remnants of a pizza feast, the veritable fifth wheel now that only the two couples remained. Brian didn't seem to notice, and Will knew Caitlyn didn't mind. The three of them had often spent time together of late. But after a few minutes, Eric nudged Ashleigh toward the edge of the booth.

"We should probably get going, too. Gonna be a Blockbuster night."

"What'd you rent?" Caitlyn asked.

Ashleigh stood up from the booth and took her jacket from Eric. "*Witness*," she said. "I've never seen it, but Eric says it's great."

"Very cool movie," Will agreed. "Harrison Ford. Danny Glover."

"And the added benefit of Kelly McGillis's naked breasts," Brian added in between sips of his soda. "Can't go wrong with naked breasts."

Eric smiled. "Wouldn't that depend on who was naked? Like, I really don't think I'd want to see Mrs. Grundy's breasts."

Will clapped a hand to his forehead. "Oh, fuck, that image is like broken glass in my head."

Ashleigh promised to call Caitlyn the next day and reminded Will that her mom was going to take the two of them to the mall in Framingham. There was a moment when Will thought either Eric or Caitlyn would suggest that the four of them go, but no one did, and Will was sort of glad. No matter how deeply he felt for Caitlyn, he didn't want to stop making time for him and Ashleigh to just hang.

After Eric and Ashleigh had left, Will and Brian walked Caitlyn home. Her house wasn't exactly on the way to Brian's, but it was only about a half a mile off their path. Not a big deal at all. Brian was cool with it and didn't even mind waiting on the sidewalk for a couple of minutes while Will and Caitlyn kissed good-bye.

Then it was just the two of them, what Danny had called the "young magicians' club." The name was stupid, just Danny razzing them, but it wasn't entirely inaccurate either. In the time since they had discovered this shared interest, Will and Brian had sifted through every bit of arcane weirdness they could dredge up, even getting their parents to bring them into Boston to sift through the dusty stacks in specialty bookstores and the Boston Public Library. Too often they learned of the existence of certain books but couldn't seem to get their hands on them.

They studied stage magic, even trying to learn to perform many of the tricks they discovered. Will was better at the sleight of hand, the close-up work, while Brian had a better natural understanding of the more complex illusions. Not that they were going to try to build any of them. Their passion did not drive them very far in that direction. Stage tricks, at the end of the day, were just tricks.

Though there was an ongoing conversation between them in which they acknowledged that it was all bullshit, that magic wasn't real, there was also something underlying that conversation that neither one of them wanted to address. The truth was, Will wanted to believe, and he thought Brian did as well. From time to time their hobby would unearth the smallest bits and pieces that supported the idea, and it was at these moments

when Will and Brian would become most vocal about the idea
that magic did not exist. They had read about ancient pagan rituals and modern Wiccan belief, had studied the fictions of H. P.
Lovecraft and the rantings of Aleister Crowley and Gilles de
Rais, and had been briefly fascinated by tales of the alchemists
Fulcanelli and Saint Germain. If one were going to attempt
magic, it seemed to both of them that turning iron into gold was
an admirable pursuit.

Not that they believed any of it. Not really.

Most of the modern books on magic were filled with self-
help bullshit in which they were instructed to commune with nature and to meditate and to perform certain rituals naked under
the moon. A large number of the older texts concerned worship-
ping the devil. Neither of them had any interest in the devil and
they were reluctant to run around the woods in the nude, though
they had a tacit agreement that if nothing else worked they
might try it later when the weather improved a bit.

Aside from Satan and nudity, they had experimented with
every formula and chant they could find without result, but that
did not dim their enthusiasm. It was all very fascinating.

Yet that night as they walked back to Brian's house on Waverly
Street, they spoke of other things. Both boys had other interests.
Brian loved science and music, played the guitar, and struggled
to overcome a shyness that would not allow him to play in front
of an audience outside his closest friends. Will loved movies,
books, baseball, and Caitlyn, not necessarily in that order.

As they cut through the little cemetery on Cherry Street,
climbing the chain-link fence in the trees at the back and moving
along well-worn paths that would lead them in time to the top
of Waverly, they talked about school and television and how
Boston sports teams had come to suck so completely. They
talked about various girls at Eastborough High and which ones
they wouldn't mind seeing naked.

"You and Nick both going to work at Herbie's again this
summer?" Brian asked as they started down the gentle slope from
the dead-end circle at the top of Waverly Street.

Will nodded. Some of the most fun he'd had the previous summer had been behind the counter at Herbie's Ice Cream, and he had gotten to know Nick a lot better since they both worked there. "I need the money," he explained. "Plus, if you've gotta have a job, it's a good place to be. Cool in July. Lots of girls."

They were in darkness, only the chilly breeze rustling in the leaves breaking the silence. From far off Will could hear car engines, but they were distant, down on the main road somewhere.

"So, I've been doing all this reading on Houdini," Will said.

"Houdini was an idiot," Brian scowled. "Sure, he was a genius on the stage, but he was fucking obsessed with mediums and stuff. Went around debunking people who claimed to do real magic."

"Yeah," Will agreed, excitement sparking in him. "But why do you think he did that?"

Brian paused, his sneakers scuffing the pavement as he turned to stare at Will. "What are you saying?"

"If you read about his mother, and his coming from the old country and stuff...I think he was so obsessed with debunking the fakes because he was looking for something real. He was like us, Bri. He was looking for proof. Who knows? Maybe he found it."

"You're high." Brian rolled his eyes and started walking again. Will fell in beside him. "Maybe. Or maybe not."

"Maybe not," Brian allowed.

When Will glanced sidelong at him, the moonlight revealed the tiniest of smirks on Brian's face.

"What?" Will demanded.

The smirk blossomed into a smile. "You'll see."

"What?" Will asked again.

Brian ignored him. They had arrived at the Schnells' house. There was no car in the driveway and the light above the front door was lit, which always meant that Brian's parents had gone out. Will was glad. They were nice people, but with no parents around they could raid the kitchen with impunity and watch R-rated movies on HBO.

As Brian unlocked the front door Will stole glances at him, curious as to what his friend was hiding, what that smirk had meant.

Brian pushed the door open and walked in, Will right behind him. It was only dimly lit inside the house. A rustle and thump off to the left drew their attention, and Will and Brian turned together to see Dori scramble up off the sofa wearing nothing but a pair of high-cut panties. It was only a moment before she snatched her shirt up from the sofa and draped it to cover her, but in that moment her perfectly rounded breasts with their small, prominent nipples were illuminated in the blue light of the enormous television in the living room.

Will was breathless. Dori was tall and reasonably pretty, with short black hair that framed her face nicely, but she had always been Brian's bitchy sister to him. In recent months he had come to truly dislike her, for it seemed the closer he and Brian became, the nastier Dori was to him. She was vicious in a way he felt only siblings ever really were. Now, though, Will saw what Nick saw in her... in fact, he had seen enough of her to make Nick jealous for eternity.

"Dori, Jesus Christ." Brian sighed.

The expression on her face then erased any pleasure Will had taken from seeing her naked. Dori sneered, all her embarrassment coming out as venom.

"What are you looking at?"

There was a jostling behind the sofa and Ian Foster sat up, rubbing the side of his head but wearing a grin. Ian was smooth and always laid-back, the bass player for a band called Deus ex Machina that was supposed to play the spring dance. His sister was in Dori's class, but Ian was a junior.

"Son of a bitch," Brian whispered.

"Hit my head on the coffee table," Ian said. "Way you got up like that... shit, I thought it was your parents."

"So did I," Dori said, still covering herself and glaring.

"Schnell," Ian said, by way of greeting Brian. "And you're Will something, right?"

"James. Will James."

A lazy grin spread across his face. Ian, obviously shirtless, gestured toward his lower half, which was obscured by the sofa. "You'll understand if I don't get up to shake hands."

"Brian, come on!" Dori snapped. "Get the fuck out of here!"

Her brother took a long look at Ian, then turned back to Dori. "We're gonna talk about this later."

Dori's brows knitted in consternation. "Whatever."

With a grunt, Brian turned and started for the stairs. Will felt awkwardly left behind and hurried to catch up, although it was really the last thing he wanted. Brian was going to be in a foul mood now. Not that Will blamed him.

There were framed family photographs on both walls going up the stairs, not just of Brian, Dori, and their parents, but aunts and uncles and grandparents, some old enough they were probably great-grandparents. Will glanced at a picture he'd seen a hundred times before, of Mr. and Mrs. Schnell, Brian, and Dori sitting in front of the fireplace in the living room. Dori was about seven in the picture and there was a strange disconnect in Will's mind, the events of moments earlier having short-circuited whatever his natural response to this photograph would have been. *How could that little girl have grown up to be such an absolute twat?*

He sighed. *Shit. I should just go home.*

"Will."

Brian was at the top of the steps, a dark look on his face, eyebrows knitted together.

"You coming?"

Will nodded, then took the rest of the stairs two at a time. The farther he could get from Dori and Ian, the happier he would be. Although as he thought about it, in retrospect, Dori had a sweet little body. The image of her bare breasts was seared in his mind and he found himself thinking again of the dark, protruding nubs of her nipples.

Snap out of it! he told himself, literally shaking his head to try to erase the image from his mind. It didn't matter how good she looked naked. Dori was poison and Will didn't want to think about her like that, never mind how jealous Nick would be if Will told him he'd seen Dori naked.

With a deep breath, he forced the thoughts out of his mind. Brian had gone into his bedroom and now Will followed him down the hall and rapped unnecessarily on the door as he entered. Brian had taken a seat on the edge of his desk and had the window open, inhaling the cold spring air deeply as if he was trying not to throw up.

Will sat down on the end of Brian's bed and kept silent.

At length, Brian turned to look at him, anger and embarrassment and frustration and sadness all warring on his features. But when he met Will's eyes, all of that seemed to evaporate in a short burst of laughter. Brian shook his head in disbelief, a broad, mystified grin on his face.

"Motherfucker," he whispered. "This is not my life. I cannot believe that just happened." In a startling snap, the amusement disappeared from his face and he glared at Will. "You won't say anything."

It wasn't a question, but Will still felt as though he had to respond. "No way, man. Sincerely."

Though it was clear that neither one of them quite believed that Will would be able to keep the events of the evening in total confidence, Brian seemed satisfied with this response. Once more he shook his head and stared out the window, inhaling the cool air.

"Bri, look—" Will began.

As if stung, Brian jumped up from his perch on the edge of the desk and went to his closet. His blue eyes were stormy with grim purpose, his hair windblown from their walk home. He swung the closet door open and started rifling through the shirts piled on the upper shelf.

"So we've been through it all, right? Fulcanelli. Fucking Rasputin. Every accused witch in every book we could find," Brian said. He shot Will a glance, pushed a hand through his hair, just noticing that it was wild. A thin smile stretched his mouth into a grimace.

"Gotta confess, buddy, I started to think it really was all bullshit. The hobby was getting boring."

Brian shoved his hand in amongst his sweaters and fished around. Will saw the moment that he found what he was looking for. A small grunt of satisfaction escaped Brian's lips. When he pulled his prize from the closet, sweaters tumbled out and spilled into a pile on the floor. Brian ignored them.

So did Will. His focus was on the thing Brian had retrieved from its hiding place. It was a thick book covered in faded burgundy leather, the edges of its pages yellowed and uneven, suggesting age. Brian dropped the heavy tome into his lap and Will caught it. Later he would deny it to himself but there was a kind of spark that went through his fingers then, traveling all the way up his arms. His scalp tingled and his eyes grew momentarily moist.

He felt as though his heart had fallen silent, just for a moment.

There was no title on the weathered face of the book, so he opened it and began to turn pages, the paper rough beneath his fingers. The third page at last revealed the title and author. *Dark Gifts: On the Nature of Magick and Its Uses,* by Jean-Marc Gaudet.

For several seemingly eternal seconds, Will stared at the book's subtitle. *On the Nature of Magick and Its Uses.* Though it was little more than leather and paper and ink, the text had a surreal weight in his hands, as though he held a block of concrete instead of a book.

Static filled his mind, his thoughts all a jumble. He had seen dozens of similar books in the past six months. But there was something... Will looked up at Brian.

"Well?"

"Gaudet was an acolyte of Crowley's. Or maybe it was the other way around. Nobody knows much about him except that a year before anyone had ever heard of Crowley, Gaudet published this. There were three hundred copies bound. Word is there's less than thirty left. Most of them were burned."

Will was breathless. "Where'd you get it?"

That thin smile returned. "It was in a private collection at the Archdiocese of Boston."

For a couple of beats, Will tried to make sense of this response. Then it dawned on him what Brian was saying and his eyebrows went up. "You stole it?"

"Yes, I fucking stole it!" Brian replied, throwing his hands up with an exasperated laugh. "You don't think they loaned it to me."

A picture formed in Will's mind of Brian breaking a window and creeping through the offices of the archdiocese in the middle of the night. But that didn't make any sense. Brian couldn't drive, and no one was going to take him to Boston in the middle of the night. Will almost asked him, then remembered something he had forgotten. Brian's aunt worked at the archdiocese as a secretary or something, and Will remembered that Brian had spent the weekend with his aunt and uncle only a couple of weeks earlier. It was difficult to imagine the machinations necessary for Brian to end up sneaking around the building and pilfering a book of this size without getting caught, yet the proof was right in Will's hands.

"Jesus," he whispered.

Brian smirked. "Yeah."

Will stood up abruptly, dropping the book on Brian's bed. He stood back and stared at it, then glanced at the bedroom door. He ran his hands through his hair and paced back and forth across the room several times. At length he stopped and stared at the book again.

"So . . . spells?"

"Lots of spells," Brian replied.

Will nodded. His mouth felt dry. "So when are we going to try one?"

Off to his right came the sound of Brian clearing his throat, almost as though he were going to cough up a clot of phlegm. "I already did." Brian lifted up a small dish with a candle set upon it, held in place by dried wax. He made that hideous sound in his throat again, and then he spat at the top of the candle.

The saliva and phlegm that shot from between his lips touched the candlewick and ignited, a tiny wisp of red smoke rising before the candle began to burn clean fire that flickered and danced in the breeze from the open window.

Will could barely whisper. "Oh, shit."

CHAPTER 7

Papillon is the French word for butterfly. It was also the name of the gleaming banquet hall where the main reunion event was being held. The place was in Westborough, just off of Route 9, in an enormous building that had been built as a nightclub, only to fail and end up being used mostly for weddings and proms and reunions. The interior was a cascade of white lights that decorated the walls as if a particularly ambitious spider-electrician had strung them about. There were butterflies as well, of course, none of them real.

Will burst through the double doors of Papillon just a few minutes after eight o'clock. One of the doors struck the wall with such ferocity that the inset glass cracked. Will barely noticed and certainly did not acknowledge it. If anyone else had noticed it, they did not bring it to his attention.

His mind was in turmoil. His fingers tingled with tactile doubt as though his every nerve ending knew that whatever he might reach out and touch at this moment could be gone the very next, or if not gone then changed. Altered.

Just as his life was being altered. His world. His friends and his past.

He felt weak and his legs trembled beneath him as he stormed through the foyer of the hall. His eyes burned from weeping and from staring for far too long at the remnants of his history, at the Eastborough High yearbook and his own address book, at photographs he had in albums and others in frames and still more that he unearthed from boxes along with other artifacts from his high school days.

A waitress heading for the main banquet hall stopped and stared at him nervously as he froze and brought up his fist, punching himself in the skull three times in rapid succession. His eyes were closed. He had stopped walking without even real-izing it, teeth gritted together in frustration.

Will shook himself, his whole body shuddering.

Sifting. Cards shuffling. Suicide King. Jack of Hearts. Ace of fucking Spades.

Mike Lebo's funeral. Caitlyn as Homecoming Queen. Ash-leigh changing, just changing right in front of him, all the spark extinguished in her eyes and her children erased from the god-damned universe and how the fuck does that happen? Only he *knew* how it happened. The only way it could have happened.

There were anchors in his mind, things he simply would not allow his consciousness to let go of. He had received an e-mail from Mike Lebo a week ago. He had held Ashleigh and Eric's twin girls in his arms. The thoughts sifted in his brain the way a drunk might lose track of a story, the way a perfectly ordinary word might seem gibberish if he stared at it for too long. The past tried to swallow these anchors, the terrible, churning ocean of his memories tried to suck them down to be lost forever, but he would not allow it.

Shuffling cards. But Will spiked an anchor right through the deck. He had spent the afternoon and early evening doing just that, tracing back through his mind all of the memories that had a double track. The old memories, the original ones, were fad-ing, but they were still there. If he focused he could still visualize them . . . at least partially. Snippets here and there.

He knew he had to do something about those memories be-fore they faded completely.

Other things he remembered perfectly well. In his mind's eye he could still see Dori Schnell's dark, jutting nipples and the weathered burgundy leather cover of the Gaudet book, *Dark Gifts*. That fucking book, that candle, and all that came after with Brian and with Dori and with magic, all of these were memories he had locked up in his mind, the dark secret laden with even blacker emotions that he had forced himself to forget. One little spell. It had seemed so simple.

But now that spell had been shattered. He remembered it all. Someone was altering the past, twisting his mind and memories, and whoever it was had also broken the spell he had cast on himself.

Magic. He gritted his teeth, anchoring himself to the here and now. One hand flashed out and he leaned for a moment upon the wall, the white lights like fireflies around him.

Will grunted in something remotely resembling amusement, but more like disgust. It was almost funny what he had done to himself. Forcing his conscious mind to forget fragments of his past had made him overly sensitive to the subject of magic. He was like goddamned Houdini. Working for the *Tribune*, debunking anything remotely resembling magic, from psychic mediums to stage tricks, decorating his cubicle and his apartment with images of good old Harry, the master debunker. There was no such thing as magic.

But, of course, there was.

"Will?"

His body wavered, his mind fighting for those anchors. His eyes opened and the world swam back into focus. He was inside Papillon. The music from the disc jockey in the main hall flooded out to him, some J. Lo song or other. They all sounded the same to him. Butterflies and white lights surrounded him. A waitress stood with a man in a suit coat who was probably a manager or something. Her eyes were a little scared, but also concerned. His were very clearly disapproving, and he was on the verge of calling the police, Will guessed.

"Will," someone said again.

His hands trembled as he turned. The door to the men's room was about ten feet away. Nick Acosta had just come out of it to find him standing there in the foyer, still dressed in the blue jeans and Red Sox jersey he had worn to the game earlier, completely out of place. Nick himself wore a well-tailored brown suit with a crimson tie that swam up in Will's vision so that it looked like a surgeon had cut Nick open and walked away in the midst of the operation. Will could only imagine how red his eyes must be, how dark the bags beneath them.

"Am I underdressed?" Will asked, hearing the hysteria in his voice but unable to do anything about it. "What do you think, Nicky?"

The sadness in Nick's gaze was more than Will could take. He turned away. Nick moved to lay a concerned hand upon his shoulder but Will shook him off and started for the main hall. He could hear the manager angrily shouting at Nick and Nick curtly vowing to look after him, to take Will out of Papillon himself if he disrupted anything.

Then Nick caught up. "Will!" he snapped, and his hand fell on Will's shoulder. Nick was powerful, his fingers digging into Will's flesh as he turned his friend around to stare into his eyes.

"Talk to me, buddy," he said, maneuvering Will between the closed door of the main hall and a tall potted plant. Nick's gaze was intense. "What're you on? Talk to me, man. We all find our-selves on roads we shouldn't have to travel alone. Don't do this to yourself. Don't go in there like this. You'll never live it down."

Will actually laughed. He had no idea it was coming and then it just bubbled up from his throat, a kind of hideous, hopeless sound. Nick pinched his eyes shut tight and then opened them again, taking a deep breath to try to reason with Will again.

"That's my wise man. I like that traveling alone bit, that was good," Will said. "You're still alive, Nick. Nobody's fucked with you yet. But any second now . . ." He couldn't go on. How could he explain? Drugs, Nick thought. If only it were that simple. Will laughed again and reached up to pat Nick's cheek. "Did I ever tell you I saw Dori Schnell naked? Beautiful tits, man. Nipples like brown pencil erasers. I should've told you. Maybe you don't care now, but I think you would've wanted to know back then."

"For Christ's sake, Will," Nick began again.

With a grunt of effort, Will placed both hands on Nick's chest and shoved him backward. He looked ridiculous, eyes too white set against his olive skin, arms pinwheeling like the scarecrow in *The Wizard of Oz* as his feet flew up from beneath him. Nick swore as he tried to save himself from going down. White lights glinted off the shiny scar that ran through his eyebrow. Then he sprawled on the floor, a great growl growing in his throat as though he was some kind of animal. Only the growl said *son of a bitch.*

Will bolted inside the main hall. The music pumped in cardiac rhythm, Boyz II Men playing now, music of the era. There were people on the dance floor, but for the most part his high school class was clustered in small groups with their friends and spouses, waiting in line at one of the bars on either side of the room. Two enormous chandeliers hung from the ceiling above and the lights were dim, but the crystals in the chandeliers cast little slashes of refracted light all over the room. There were more people tonight than there had been the previous night. Perhaps three times as many. They wore suits and dresses; some of the women even wore formal gowns.

It was the prom all over again.

Faces swam toward him in the sea of light, on waves of music. Everyone he recognized set off another tangent of echoing, conflicting memories in his mind. Things he might have done or said or seen, and now there were so many cards in the deck, so many images shuffling around in his mind, that he found it impossible to decipher if each belonged with his original memories or with those that had replaced them. The false truth. The altered present.

People spoke to him. Stared at him in concern. Pretty women he half knew whispered to one another behind their upraised hands, one of them gently rocking her glass so that the ice in her drink made a bright, clinking noise. Will cursed under his breath

and stopped himself. He brought his hand up and ran it over his
face, fingertips dragging across stubble. The contact was an odd
comfort and he took a breath, trying to slow down the adrenaline that was surging through him.

With a curt nod, a kind of affirmation meant only for himself, he ignored the stares and set off to the right of the dance
floor, moving amongst tables and chairs. Several people called his
name but he paid no attention. A giddy, girlish laugh carried to
him in the midst of the torrent of voices in that hall and Will
recognized it. He glanced in that direction and saw Stacy near
the bar. She wore a bottle-green dress with spaghetti straps, her
hair falling loose over her bare shoulders.

The sight of her pained him. Will was supposed to save a dance
for her tonight. To save all his dances for her. Despite what a fuckup
he'd been this weekend, they had made a connection on Friday
night—and on a bus a lifetime ago—and she still wanted to find
out what the nature of that connection was. She was an island of
normalcy to him now, yet when she smiled so brightly, her whole
face lit up with merriment, it made him feel like throwing up.

What if she's next?

The thought whirled him around; he was unable to look at
her even a moment longer. He forged on through the crowd, familiar faces flickering by his focus like streetlights flashing across
the hood of a speeding car. But he paid them no mind, for he
was looking for one face in particular and one face only. The
music thumping from the huge speakers seemed to match tempo
with the throbbing in his head as he reached the last of the tables
on this side of the dance floor. He turned to head across to the
other side of the hall and nearly knocked Lolly over.

Her brows were knitted together in consternation, her eyes
narrowed. In all the time he had known her he did not think he
had ever seen her angry, so it gave him pause. Somewhere in the
back of his mind a part of him that was merely observing took
note of her regal features, her caramel skin, and recognized that
anger had made her more beautiful.

Lolly glanced around, self-conscious about the number of

people watching her. When she spoke to him it was a hiss between her teeth. "What the fuck is the matter with you?"

A sadness welled up from within him, a melancholy that leeched from him the fury and purpose with which he had stormed into Papillon. The urge to let the words spill out, to talk to her, to share the burden on his heart, was nearly overwhelming.

His mouth opened.

Then over Lolly's shoulder he saw couples on the dance floor, swaying together, grinning at one another, as far away from him at that moment as if they existed in another universe. A guy in a charcoal suit danced close with his date. Will saw his profile at first, and then he swung his dance partner around so that he was in full view.

Brian Schnell. And the woman he was dancing with ... it was Caitlyn. Brian was at the reunion with Will's former fiancée, the Homecoming Queen. She hadn't been the Homecoming Queen, of course. That was one of the truths Will was holding on to, an anchor his mind grasped at. Someone had changed all of that.

"Son of a bitch," Will whispered.

Lolly put her hand, fingers splayed, on his chest to stop him as he started for the dance floor. She spun around, saw Brian and Caitlyn dancing, and Will could see in her eyes that she leaped to the wrong conclusion, thought he was going after Brian out of petty jealousy over a woman who had left him at the altar years before.

"That's what this is about?" Lolly asked, pity and dismissal in her eyes. "Leave it alone, Will. Don't do anything stupid."

But he wasn't listening. Images flickered through his head still, that Zoetrope of shuffling cards, and he pushed past Lolly. His foot caught on the leg of a chair as he slid between two tables and he stumbled, nearly fell down. Will collided with a waiter who carried a huge round tray laden with salads. The tray was upended, bowls and cups of dressing clattering down upon a table, salad showering a woman beside them.

Will kept going. The waiter shouted at him. Lolly called his name.

A number of couples on the dance floor heard the commotion and stopped. Others spun around them, heels clapping on the floor, oblivious to the freight train rolling toward them. Will James was not a large man, but his shoulders were broad and he had a steely determination as he strode purposefully onto the dance floor.

Caitlyn saw him first. Her eyes widened with shock and she stopped dancing, pushed back from Brian, and gaped at Will, a quiver of distaste curling her lip.

"Will?" she said.

As Brian turned toward him, Will sped up. The guy had time only to muster a look of confusion and then Will lunged for him. With a grunt of exertion he sprang upon Brian, momentum carrying them both down to the ground.

Brian's head bounced off the floor with a loud crack.

NUMBER 76 PARMENTER ROAD was dark save for a single light that burned in Kyle Brody's bedroom. His parents were out for the night, celebrating the birthday of Vernon Basque, a creepy little weasel who was one of his father's business partners. Kyle was glad they were gone. He paced in his room with the window all the way open and took a long drag on a cigarette he had stolen from the pack on his dad's dresser. He knew smoking could fuck you up, but it wasn't like his parents could give him shit with a straight face, not when both of them still smoked.

Kyle strolled from one end of the room to the other like an animal investigating new surroundings. He paused at the center of the room and stared at the blazing orange tip of the cigarette. A plume of smoke puffed from his lips and he scowled at the butt in his hand. *Gotta be an idiot to smoke,* he thought.

But he took one last drag on the cigarette before dropping it, still lit, into the Pepsi can on his bureau. It hissed as it struck whatever soda was left, and smoke swirled up out of the can.

"Jesus," Kyle whispered. He massaged his temple with the palm of his hand, feeling a headache coming on.

How the hell did I get pulled into this . . . whatever it is? he thought.

What am I supposed to do? Two questions, the first of which was vital, the second of which was just stupid. He had instructions regarding what he was supposed to do now.

There was nothing funny about it, but the thought made him laugh.

A chilly breeze blew into his bedroom and Kyle shivered, but it occurred to him that there might be more to it than the chill. He stood beside the bureau now, regretting having put the cigarette out. Across the room, half a dozen magazines were spread out on his bed. *Hustler. Penthouse.* A couple of *Playboy*s, but he only ever got the ones with famous girls in them. He had inherited the others from his friend Devon, who had too many of the things, all passed on to him from his older brother. Truth was, Kyle thought the *Hustler*s were sort of nasty. The others were pretty good, though.

But there was something else on the bed.

Kyle kept the magazines in a brown legal expandable folder he had taken from his father's study. When he wasn't looking at them, he stashed the folder deep in the closet under the stairs, where there was an opening into a crawl space.

He had been thinking about that crawl space all day, since even before he had left for the football game. A dreadful tickle had been dancing up and down his spine, drawing his mind back to it again and again. He had brought the note to freaky Will James at the Homecoming game, trying to avoid thinking about the damn thing, about how yellow and dusty it was, about how it had gotten into the hole in the storage area in the first place. But he couldn't avoid it forever, couldn't not think about it. And when he did, that train of thought had led him back to the other place he stashed things in his house.

Would he find something there as well, with the *Playboy*s and *Penthouse*s?

After the game he had come right home, telling his friends he didn't feel well and just needed to get some sleep. His mother had made a sausage pasta dish for dinner that Kyle loved, but he barely tasted it as he ate, just waiting for them to leave, silently willing them to go. And simultaneously wishing they would stay home, so he wouldn't have to check the hiding place in the closet under the stairs.

But they went.

And he looked.

Now, in his room, he stared at the thing that he had found under the stairs, wondering what would happen if he ignored it. The dread that filled him then was far worse and something twisted in his stomach.

Just leave me alone, he thought, hating the infantile whining in his own head. *I don't want any part of this, whatever it is.*

But he understood the truth, that he didn't have a choice. He had been singled out.

And it frightened him.

CAITLYN SCREAMED. There were shouts and curses, and a number of hands tried to reach for Will, tried to tear him off Brian.

"You fucking lunatic!" Will roared, spittle flying from his mouth as he squeezed his hands around Brian's throat and slammed his head against the floor a second time, then a third. "Why? Why are you doing this?"

Brian's face reddened and his eyes began to bulge. Will hauled back his right fist and struck him, knuckles shattering Brian's nose. Blood spurted from his nostrils and Will hit him again and again, pain shooting up his arm with every blow. Will knew he was still shouting, but if words were coming from his mouth even he did not understand them.

Tears burned his eyes. Tess had been raped. *And Ashleigh* . . . He squeezed his eyes tightly closed and punched Brian again, blindly, feeling swollen, pulpy flesh beneath his fist. He could not even think about the changes in Ashleigh.

His eyes snapped open. Baring his teeth with a ferocity he could not contain, he grabbed Brian by the hair and bent over to shout in his face. "Lebo. You fucking killed Lebo! What did he do? What did he ever do to you?"

The last word was choked off by an arm that wrapped around

his neck from behind. Will was pulled off of Brian and he struggled, swinging, lashing out with fists and feet and elbows, trying to get back to the evil bastard responsible for the savage mutilation of reality that had gone on over the past few days.

"Will! Will, just stop it!" Nick snarled in his ear.

It was Nick who was holding him, Nick who had him from behind. But he wasn't the only one. Eric was there as well, and the two of them swung Will around so he was abruptly face to face with the rest of them. Lolly and Pix were both there. Caitlyn. Danny and Keisha. And Ashleigh, hollow eyes filled with a despair that broke his heart again, and he knew that part of that despair had been his fault.

"Will, what are you doing?" Ashleigh asked.

The manager he had seen on his way in appeared now at the edge of Will's field of vision. The man looked smug, nostrils flaring as he announced that he had called the police and they were on the way. Caitlyn whimpered at this but she would not look at Will again. She went down on her knees beside Brian. Several other people were there on the dance floor beside him; one of them loudly announced that he was unconscious.

"You don't know," Will whispered, gazing into Ashleigh's eyes, barely able to speak for the pain in his heart. "You don't know what he's done."

"You're gone, Will. You're fucked in the head," Nick growled.

"Will, talk to me," Eric said, his voice level, the calmest of all of them. "Please, man. Did you take something?"

All along Danny had gazed at him sadly, shaking his head. Now he squeezed his wife's hand and stepped forward. He tapped Nick's arm and in response first Nick, then Eric, let go of Will.

"You don't understand," Will whispered, looking into Danny's eyes.

Danny's eyes were a bright, guileless blue. There was only compassion in them now. "I do, Will. I do. I'm sorry I got pissed at you last night."

For a moment hope surged up within Will. Could it be he

wasn't the only one who had felt it, felt this slippage, this shuf-fling of the deck? But then Danny put his forehead against Will's and there was something odd in his expression, a kind of dark void, a hopelessness that Will had never seen in him before.

"You need help, bud. I just didn't get it, last night. Didn't see it. You need to get a handle on things. Something's going on in your head. You've been acting freaky all weekend. We're scared for you, Will."

Hands were placed on his back and arms and Will's heart sank. They were all there for him. He had just ruined the night, eviscerated whatever pleasant thoughts any of these people had ever had about him, and yet his friends were there for him. But they simply did not understand.

Danny pulled back and looked at him. "You're not right in the head at the moment, bud. We gotta get to the bottom of it." He glanced at Keisha. "I'm sorry, baby. You stay. Eric and Ashleigh will take you home."

Keisha was a kind, understanding woman. "It's all right. We'll be OK. You go."

Most of the crowd was back to busily minding their own business. The music was still playing. The refracted lights from the chandelier cast unearthly slivers of light around the hall. With a groan, Brian Schnell woke up. Will started toward him.

Danny flat-handed Will's chest, stopping him cold. His eyes were hard and unrelenting. "Don't even think about it. We're go-ing. Now. Before the cops get here."

Will drew his hand across his mouth, the copper tang of Brian's blood on his lips, the ache in his knuckles deep and sharp. What an idiot he had been, to think that what had to be done could be done here. Brian had to be stopped, prevented from hurting anyone else, but there was no way Will was going to be able to accomplish that with Danny Plumer playing nursemaid.

Will blinked and took a few short breaths before meeting Danny's steady gaze. "I'm going. You stay." When Danny began to argue, Will held up a hand. "No, shut up, listen. I've fucked up this night enough. I'm not taking you away from your wife. I drove myself here, I can get myself home. I'm not high. I'm not on anything. You want to talk to me, call me in the morning or just come by."

He pointed at Brian, saw Caitlyn helping him to sit up, and could look at them no more. Will felt the bile rise in the back of his throat, his stomach clenching, but he forced himself to stay calm as he focused on Danny again.

"That guy, if you knew what he's done . . . and I'm not talking about Caitlyn here . . . if you knew . . ." Will shook his head. "Just call me tomorrow. If fucking Schnell wants to press charges, you all know where I live. Tell the cops they can find me there."

Later he would realize it was pure astonishment that caused them to let him go. Not a few mouths were gaping, not one of them knowing what to say as he turned and strode across the dance floor. A path cleared before him. He saw Martina, a look of sympathy etched on her face, but most of them looked vaguely embarrassed, as though just knowing him was something they felt ashamed of in that moment.

The manager blocked his way. "You can't leave. The police are on the way. You can't just—"

Disbelief erupted out of him as a burst of laughter. Will stared at the man. "You're kidding, right? I broke a few plates. Send me a bill. You're not the guy who got a beating." Unbidden, a sneer came to his lips. "Course, if you want a real reason to have me arrested—"

The manager stepped instantly from his path. "Crazy bastard," he whispered, but he did nothing more to prevent Will from leaving.

It was all so very unlike him, but Will knew that was a false assumption. The foundation of who he was had been altered. His life and his past were changing. It stood to reason that he himself might well be changing too.

Just before he walked out of the banquet hall he glanced toward the bar where he had seen Stacy before. She wasn't at the bar, however. Other than Will himself, she was about the only one in the entire room who was in motion. She was walking across the room toward him, moving swiftly to get to him before he could leave.

Will flinched, paused a moment with his head turned away from her. He swallowed, his throat tight, trying not to imagine what could happen to her, what had already happened to Ashleigh and the others.

"You all right?" she asked.

He turned. Somehow she had crossed the distance between them in just a few seconds. She gazed up at him with an expression that seemed equal parts sadness and bewilderment.

Will's left hand fluttered up as though he were trying to erase something from the space between them. "Don't," he said. Then he met her eyes. "No. I'm not. Never been worse."

Her face changed then, but not in the horrid way that Ashleigh's had. This was natural, organic. Into her features crept dark resignation and hard-won wisdom. There was no doubt in Will's mind that Stacy had lived through difficult times and he saw them now, etched in the crow's feet around her eyes, the tiny lines at the corners of her mouth.

"Anything I can do?"

Will shook his head. "I don't think so."

She took this in, then nodded sagely. "You'll tell me about it sometime."

It wasn't a question, but he nodded in agreement nevertheless. Then he pushed out through the double doors and into the foyer of Papillon, brightly colored butterflies all around him, tangles of white lights illuminating the path of his exodus. He went out the door and into the night, feeling in his pocket for the keys to his Toyota. The chill night air cleared his head, trying to wash away the old memories, all the images that didn't jibe with the world around him, with this new reality.

But Will was not going to let them go.

The lot was lined with the dark, silent hulks of a hundred cars. Nothing moved but the wind. Will strode amongst those cars, keys jangling in his hand. He reached the Toyota and un-locked it, but as he opened the door a wave of nausea and de-spair rose up in him. He steadied himself against the car, one hand on the roof.

I can't do this, he thought. But even as the words went through his mind he knew they were bullshit. *Who else, Will? You're the only one.*

The question was where to begin. He hadn't allowed himself even to think of magic as real and tangible power in more than a decade. Where to begin?

"Hey."

Will grunted in surprise and spun around, heart hammering in his chest, mind flashing back to the empty parking lot. He was alone in the dark in the lot. Just empty, darkened cars. Alone.

Or not.

The kid was there with him, just a few feet away. In the moon-light his orange hair was dark brown, with hints of red. What the hell was his . . . Kyle. His name was Kyle Brody.

"Jesus, kid. Gonna give me a heart attack." Then Will's eyes narrowed. "What are you doing out . . ."

He never finished the sentence. Possibilities, probabilities, bits of logic snapped into place in his head. For the first time he noticed the dark, heavy shape in the kid's hands. Kyle walked over to the Toyota and dropped the book onto the hood with a thump.

In the distance, police sirens began to wail.

Kyle Brody gave Will a hard look, but he was hesitant and even a little scared, and his voice cracked when he spoke.

"I'm tired of being your errand boy."

Will barely heard him. He stared at the book where it lay, loath to pick it up, even to touch it. The cover was weathered and dark and there was no title. But he did not need a title to know that book.

Dark Gifts.

CHAPTER 8

The wind died. For a moment Will felt as though the world had sped up its rotation, that it might slip out from under him and he would begin to fall, not knowing where he would land. As he stared at the aged face of that terrible book he felt as though it tugged at him with hooks through his eyes and his mind, his heart and his balls. The fluttering in his stomach and the tingle that danced up his spine were equal parts dread and elation, terror and arousal; it was almost like falling in love.

"Fuck," he whispered, the word not a curse but an oath of surrender. A veil had been lifted from his mind and a shroud laid down upon his heart. He had just been about to set out in search of this book, or a copy of it. But somehow he knew that this wasn't just any copy. This was the very same one, the one he and Brian had pored over, on whose pages they had spilled their own blood.

Paper and leather and ink. And our blood.

How he could be terrified of such a thing he did not know, but he was. The book had not even given him time to look for it; instead, it had found him.

"I didn't bring it so you could just stare at it," the kid said. "Tell me, Will. I want to know how it got under my stairs."

Seeing the book again had entranced him somehow. Just the grain of the leather was enough to captivate him, to fill him with trepidation. Kyle's voice broke that trance. Will shook his head, catching only the echo of the kid's words in his mind. *Under the stairs*, he thought, a tiny smile playing at the corners of his mouth. *Of course. That's where I would have hidden it.*

The wind kicked up again, carrying with it the peal of police sirens. Will glanced up in alarm, ears and eyes tracking. They were coming from the west, and not far off now. He had heard them before, but his mind had been occupied with other things. There was no way to be certain they were coming for him, but the manager of Papillon had told him the police had been called, so Will couldn't take any chances.

His fingers hesitated one moment longer, almost of their own accord, then he reached out and grabbed the book off the hood of the car. It was strangely light despite its thickness, as though it did not want to be a burden to its owner. *Deceit,* Will thought. But, then, most magic was powered by deceit.

"Are you fucking deaf?" Kyle snapped, almost stamping his feet as if he might throw a genuine tantrum in a moment. His tough-guy posturing—always slightly undermined by his orange hair—was shattered.

Will shot him a hard look, heart trip-hammering in his chest. "Get in the car," he said as he slipped behind the wheel, placing the book on the seat beside him.

The door hung open. Kyle stood half a dozen feet away. The police sirens were growing louder. Will glanced in the direction of that wailing noise.

"They coming for you?" the kid asked, suddenly frowning, his head tilted in doubt.

"Yes. Get in the car."

Kyle threw up his hands and blew out a dismissive breath. "I don't think so. Have fun. I'm out."

"Fine." Will shut the door, jammed the key into the ignition and turned it. The engine roared to life. He had no idea what the police would do, but knew he might be arrested. His whole body was prickling with the rush of blood through his veins, his heart pumping wildly. Time to get the hell out of there.

There was a rap at the window. Will snapped his head around to see Kyle standing there. His expression was torn. He wanted to take off, but not just yet. Will, though, was out of time. He rolled the window down even as he threw the car into gear.

"Tell me one thing," Kyle said.

Will looked up at the highway. Blue lights splashed off the trees next to the main road and the entrance sign to Papillon.

"Is it magic?" the kid asked.

Will stared at him. "Yeah. Yeah, it is."

He hit the gas, pulling out of the parking space much too quickly. Tires spun on gravel. He kept his headlights off as he drove along between two rows of cars, then turned left, headed for the side of the building. Route 9 was the easiest access to Papillon, but Will James had grown up around here. There was a curb cut at the back of the parking lot that led through a small office park and then onto Chestnut Street. It was the wrong direction to get back to Eastborough, but that was the least of his concerns at the moment.

As he drove behind Papillon he glanced once in the rearview mirror. Kyle Brody was lost in the dark, hulking shadows of the cars in the parking lot. A police car, blue lights spinning but siren now silenced, was just beginning to turn into the lot from Route 9.

Will drove quickly, but as calmly as possible, through the small office park and out into the neighborhoods of Westborough. He remembered the panel at the rear of the closet under the stairs, and the times he had used it as a hiding place. Odd, he thought now, that it took becoming an adult to realize how much of his teenage years had been spent hiding things . . . hiding beer and pot and love letters and smut magazines. Hiding how badly he had wanted to grow up, to be an adult and make his own decisions. All that time spent rushing headlong toward adulthood, only to spend the rest of his life wishing he could go back.

Go back. The words echoed in his mind, shattering things. Will couldn't breathe for a moment. His chest hurt and he pulled the car over, having taken so many turns that he barely knew where he was now. Some suburban street like any other, lots of trees and pretty houses and flower gardens wilted by the October wind. He laid his head upon the steering wheel and let the numbness come.

Oh, Jesus, Brian, what have you done?

For long minutes he sat there. At length he sat up and glanced around, then began to drive again, watching the street signs he passed, attempting to figure out precisely where he had gotten himself. A few hasty turns had brought him to unfamiliar streets. When he realized he was lost, Will laughed softly to himself in the car and then proceeded to drive on, trying to find his way, that dark book his only company. Though he kept his eyes on the road, he could feel its presence almost as though, stained as it was with his blood, the book remembered him.

July, the summer before Junior Year ...

The thermometer at the bank across the street revealed the temperature every ten seconds as though it were an accusation. It was ninety-five degrees, not a cloud in the sky, and the sun gleamed upon the windows of Herbie's Ice Cream in a solar assault that kept the two tables closest to the plateglass windows empty. Customers would rather stand than sit in those normally coveted window seats.

Outside, the rare skateboarder might flash by, or a cluster of kids unconcerned with heatstroke would wander past, headed for one cool destination or another.

Inside Herbie's Ice Cream it was a blissful paradise. Will was actually glad to be working. The air-conditioning was pumped up as high as it would go, and though he was in constant motion, he spent his hours at work bent over massive tubs of ice cream. This was the place to be today, no matter which side of the counter you were on. Over the winter the owner had brought in a guy to paint murals on the walls, all of which involved ice cream, the beach, surfing, and penguins, of all things. Penguins were associated with staying cool, Will figured. But he liked them because they were so silly-looking.

The murals were colorful, at least, which matched the decor of the place. The chairs were an array of bright pastel plastics and the tables were decorated with rainbows and stars. Music pumped from the sound system, loud enough that one couldn't ignore it, but not so loud that the customers couldn't have a conversation. The owner, Jack Herbert—aka "Herbie"—ran tapes of nothing but tunes from the sixties and seventies, but most of the kids liked the oldies just as much as their parents did.

Will finished packing a mint chocolate chip cone, dipped it in sprinkles, and then handed it over to the attractive mom-type who'd ordered it. The woman paid him, told him to keep the change, and Will smiled at her as he punched at the cash register and did the math. The woman strode away, headed for a table of three other women, two with small babies. He counted out the customer's change and dropped it into the tip jar, which he and Nick would split at the end of their shift.

Behind him the milk shake machine whirred. He glanced back to see Nick pouring milk into the tall, silver metal cup attached to the machine.

"Hey! Make me one of those, will ya?" he called.

Nick wore dirty Reeboks that had once been white, black shorts, and a crimson Harvard jersey. He smiled up at Will. "Make it yourself, you lazy bum."

Will hid his hand behind his back so he could nonchalantly give Nick the finger without any of the customers noticing. He knew he would probably be surreptitiously pelted with an empty cone at some later point. That was the best part of the two of them being on duty together.

"Maybe you two should just grow up."

Startled, Will glanced up quickly and was relieved to see Brian on the other side of the counter. He laughed softly. "Don't sneak up on people like that, man."

Brian grinned. "Well, if you two jokers were actually working instead of just screwing around, you wouldn't be caught by surprise by the arrival of an actual customer."

"Hey. It's been friggin' busy in here today. This place, the movie theater, and the mall...people escape here on days like this. July in New England, buddy. Nick and I are performing a public service."

"Oh, is that what you call it?" Brian raised an eyebrow.

Will narrowed his eyes. "Can I take your order, smart-ass?"

"An orange float, please."

At a corner table, Mike Lebo and Danny Plumer ate sundaes and laughed uproariously at some private joke, probably something filthy. Will wished he could have been privy to it, but he was on the wrong side of the counter. Danny and Lebo called to Brian, but he only waved to them, waiting at the counter while Will created his orange float. Though Nick finished with the customer he had been making the milk shake for, he did not come over to say hello to Brian. The two got along fine when the group was together, but otherwise simply chose to ignore one another.

The conversation across the counter was weightless, mainly concerning films they wanted to see and what was going on with Will and Caitlyn these days. But he and Brian carefully avoided discussing the subject that most fascinated them, the topic that had occupied so many of their days and nights in recent months.

Will loved to make orange floats. The smell of the vanilla combined with the orange soda was wonderfully sweet. The biggest problem with working at Herbie's wasn't eating too much ice cream; it was deciding what he wanted. The owner had made it clear he did not mind if the employees sampled the wares, as long as they were reasonable about it.

Once there was a nice vanilla froth on the top of the float, ice cream dripping down into the soda, he brought it to the counter. Brian paid him, and they made plans to go out after Will's shift was over. Caitlyn was going to the movies with her girlfriends, so Will figured he could drag Brian over to Liam's for buffalo wings.

A wicked expression clouded Brian's features. He smiled. "Thanks for the float."

He turned to walk away and Will frowned, wondering about the significance of the strange look Brian had given him. He did not have to wonder for very long. As he watched Brian carefully walk his float over to the table where Danny and Lebo were sitting, he understood.

Brian Schnell's feet did not touch the ground. The soles of his shoes were a little more than an inch from the linoleum floor. Floating in that way, he strode to the corner table and sat down across from the other guys, who had not seemed to notice this little bit of magic at all. Will's heart fluttered in his chest and he felt his face flush, incapable of stopping the smile that split his face at that moment.

Thanks for the float. Yeah, right, he thought. *Smart-ass.*

Anxiety raced through him. Certain that everyone in the place must have noticed this feat of subtle magic, Will looked quickly around. The air conditioners kept humming and music pumped from the sound system, a Led Zeppelin tune, in keeping with the other oldies on the tape. "Fool in the Rain," he thought it was, but he'd never paid much attention to the Zeppelin stuff.

No one was staring at Brian. In fact, the only person in Herbie's who was even glancing toward that table was Nick. When he felt Will looking at him he turned and shook his head. "Tell me why we have to work again?"

"Money, my friend," Will said, feeling numb and removed from his own words. "Capital. Spending power."

The bell jangled above the door and he forced himself to glance in that direction. A couple of twentyish guys in paint-spattered clothes and work boots came in, their sunburned faces streaked with sweat. They were semiregulars, and any other day Will would have shot the breeze with them, offered his sympathy that they had to work outside in this weather. Today he tried to wish them away. The painters did not disappear, but to his surprise and relief, they sidled up to the counter where Nick waited to serve them.

That left Will to focus on Brian. At the table, where he was in animated conversation with Danny and Lebo, Brian paused to glance once at Will. His smile was insufferable. Will couldn't help but laugh softly to himself. *You son of a bitch*, he thought. *You really did it. Fucking levitation.*

But Brian wasn't the only one who had been studying.

There was a small spatter of ice-cream drips on the counter. A baby began to cry. A teenage girl sitting with her friends threw herself back in her chair and let loose a torrent of giddy laughter that caused her to cover her face in embarrassment a moment later. The sun continued to beat down upon the sidewalk outside. Herbie's was like a million other ice cream shops. Perfectly ordinary.

Will turned so that his back was to Nick and the painters. He kept his hands down below the counter so that none of the customers would see the contortions of his fingers. He closed his eyes and whispered a handful of words in French. Most of them were gibberish to him, but he had the gist of what they meant, what the incantation was intended to accomplish. He held it in his mind, and his eyes fluttered open as he repeated the troublesome French words again and again, carefully forming them with his tongue.

There were other accoutrements that went along with the incantation. A white candle, a charred bit of birch bark, black thread and, somewhat disturbingly, human saliva. But the writings of Jean-Marc Gaudet had revealed to Will and Brian one of the fundamental truths of magic, something that none of the poseurs had ever touched upon. An incantation, once successfully performed with the appropriate rituals, became far simpler thereafter, requiring only words and focus. It was as though the power to perform that bit of magic had been indelibly inked upon the magician. That was thrilling, and not a little frightening. Every time either of them performed an incantation, they would be changed forever.

Touched by magic.

Now, as another oldie pumped out of the sound system and

Nick handed the first of the painters his ice cream—a huge pistachio thing in a waffle cone—Will glanced over at the table where Brian sat with Danny and Mike Lebo. Lebo was rolling his eyes and laughing as Danny ranted about something. Brian shoved the blob of vanilla ice cream into his orange soda and took a sip from his straw.

Will carefully contorted his fingers, replicating the position that had been illustrated in fine, spidery pencil sketches in Gaudet's book. His lips quietly mouthed the difficult French words. He could not help smiling.

As he watched, the orange soda in Brian's glass began to darken to a deep red. Leaning forward, chuckling good-naturedly at Danny's ire, Brian took a long sip from his orange float, then recoiled, his face etched with disgust. He threw himself back in his chair, its legs scraping the floor, and spat on the table. Then his eyes locked on the glass and he saw.

"Jesus!" Brian cried, and he batted at the glass as though it might attack him. It tumbled off the table and fell end over end to shatter on the floor, spraying bright, fresh blood across the linoleum.

A tiny island of vanilla ice cream quickly melted in the puddle of warm blood.

Everyone in the shop froze. First they stared at Brian. Then they glanced down at what he was staring at, at the streaks and spatters of crimson. Lebo swore in disgust, Danny in amazement.

Will didn't give them time to adjust. The moment Brian had reacted, even before he had swiped the glass from the table, his fingers had been at work again and his lips silently formed the words to a spell of reversal. In seconds, the blood faded, red becoming orange, and then it was nothing more than sticky soda on the floor.

Brian's mouth was open in a small O of astonishment as he turned to look across the shop at Will, who shrugged as if to say, *Don't look at me.* Which they both knew was bullshit. Brian was clearly impressed. Will was glad. *So much for levitation,* he thought. *Try transmutation next time.* It was not a contest between them, this investigation into magic. But the boys did derive a certain amount of pleasure from astounding one another. Other kids might have used card tricks and coin vanishes. Will and Brian were only interested in real magic, and now that they had discovered it, they were just getting started.

There were staccato bursts of conversation around the shop, the loudest coming from the table where his three friends sat, but Will was relieved that within a minute or so, no one seemed certain they had seen what they had seen. A trick of the light, someone suggested. The mother with the crying baby thought it might have something to do with the heat, or with the linoleum itself. The painter with the pistachio ice cream told his partner that he knew one thing for certain, he wouldn't be drinking the orange soda they served in Herbie's.

The painters paid Nick and he rang up the sale. When he closed the register drawer he glanced over at Will. There was something odd in his expression, as though there was a question on the tip of his tongue that he was hesitant to put voice to. But Nick never said a word to Will about what had happened that afternoon with Brian's orange float.

Not ever.

THE HOUSE WAS QUIET AND DARK. Other than those in Kyle's room, the only light on was the one above the kitchen sink. The entire drive home from that bizarre scene in the parking lot with Will James, Kyle had been buzzing, adrenaline racing through him.

As soon as he had arrived home Kyle had dropped his jacket over a kitchen chair and gone up to his room. He had been on the phone ever since, first to his girlfriend Amie, and now to his best friend, Ben Klosky.

"Did you tell Amie all this shit?" Ben asked.

Kyle had the phone trapped between cheek and shoulder, picking up his room. Now he paused, dirty socks in one hand. "Dude, are you nuts? She'd think I was out of my mind. I mean,

I told her I found the book and all, but I didn't mention that first note. I just told her it belonged to the guy, that he used to live here."

Ben chuckled. "What'd you say, that you tracked him down on the Web or something?"

"Exactly." Kyle tossed the dirty socks into a pile, then grabbed a basket of clean, folded laundry his mother had left in his room and set it on the bed. "So what do you think?"

As he pulled open a drawer and began to put away the folded clothes, he could almost hear Ben mulling it over, could imagine him squinting his eyes, making them disappear into the baby fat that still rounded out his face.

"What do I think? I think you're on crack."

"Fuck you," Kyle grunted.

"No," Ben replied politely. "Fuck *you*."

"I'm serious, Benjy. I'm not making this crap up." With a pair of neatly folded blue jeans in his hands, Kyle paused. A shiver went through him as he thought about the crawl space under the stairs, about that book and the dust on it, and how sometimes it felt heavier than it should, and sometimes it felt lighter. And how sometimes . . . sometimes it felt *warm*. "It's creeping me out."

Ben was silent for several seconds. Kyle waited for his voice on the phone as though he could not move until Ben spoke again. He stood with the blue jeans in his hands and listened to the windows rattle in their frames. The wind had kicked up. One of his windows was open just a couple of inches and the chill breeze seemed to whistle through the gap.

"Hello?" Kyle said, snapping off the word in annoyance that barely covered the tremor in his voice.

"I'm thinking." A gravity had crept into Ben's tone and he paused again for several seconds. "You're my amigo, Kyle. I know better than to ask if you were drunk or on something. Obviously something's going on there. But does it have to be something freaky?"

Kyle let out a tense breath, dropped the blue jeans into the

drawer and slid it shut. He sat down on the end of the bed, ignoring the rest of the clean laundry. The wall began to tick, a familiar sound that always came with the heat going on.

"I'm up for suggestions."

"Anything," Ben said. "You said you first saw the guy on the
street outside your house, checking out his old place or whatever.
Couldn't it be that he broke in there? Locks can be picked. Pro-
fessionals know how to do that shit."

A dry, humorless laugh escaped Kyle's lips. He tried to imagine Will James picking the lock on the storage area under the
back porch. The problem was that Ben had not seen the yellowed
envelope or the thick layer of dust upon it, or Will James's reac-
tion to reading it when Kyle had given it to him at the football
game earlier. And Ben had not seen the book. That damned
book.

"You've seen too many movies," Kyle said.

"Man, come on ... the shit you're talking about—"

"Happened, Benjy. What are you doing to me? I thought ... I
mean, I figured you were the one person I could tell who
wouldn't think I was ... ah, shit, forget it. I gotta go."

"Whoa," Ben said. "Hold on. I'm not saying I don't believe
you. I just think you shouldn't jump to conclusions without
looking at all the possibilities. I mean—"

"These things happened. Impossible things are happening."

Ben sighed. "Kyle. Have you looked up the word in the dic-
tionary? Impossible, I mean."

From time to time Kyle fondly recalled the way his mother's
kiss had brightened his spirit as a child, and how he had believed
with all his heart when she told him her kiss would make it all
better. And so it did. Now, though, there were spiders of fear in
his gut and unwelcome thoughts burrowing in his mind. He
closed his eyes and dragged a hand across his face as though he
might erase the dread. But Kyle Brody was not a child anymore.
He had long since given up believing there was a way to make
anything *all better*.

Ben seemed to sense he had overstepped. "Sorry," he said. "But it's just...it's kinda hard to get my head around it. Maybe if I saw the book..."

Through the gap of the open window, the whistling wind carried another sound. A car engine, purring low, slowing, and the squeak of brakes. Tires rolling on pavement.

The engine died.

A door opened and then clicked shut.

"Kyle?"

"Hang on."

Kyle rose from the bed and went quickly to his window, but with the lights on the glass was almost opaque. Phone still in hand, he went to the bedside table and clicked off that lamp, casting half the room in shadow. Kyle put his face to the window, nose cold on the glass.

A car was parked on the road in front of his house. The streetlights threw haloes of light upon the pavement up and down Parmenter Road, but the Brodys' house was in the middle of a long unlit stretch, so the streetlights in either direction were only enough to shine the promise of illumination their way.

In front of the car was the dark silhouette of a man. Though little more than a shadow, it was clear he was looking up at the house. The only lights visible from outside would be the ones from Kyle's room. The shadow-man would be staring at this window. At him.

"Oh, shit," Kyle whispered.

"What's wrong?" Ben demanded, concern in his voice.

The figure began to stride across the lawn. As it passed the oak tree the man slowed, one shadow-arm reaching out through the darkness so that his fingers brushed the lower branches of the oak, almost a caress. Then he continued on, toward the door.

The light from the moon and the stars was just enough so that as the man neared the front steps, Kyle saw the object he carried in his right hand. It was a book.

He jumped when he heard the knock. His mouth was dry,

heart surging in his chest like a stone skipping across the surface of a pond. Though in his mind he was certain he knew who it was down there, knocking on his door, still he could not eliminate the image of that shadow-man from his mind.

"Kyle, come on, you're killing me."

His knuckles hurt from holding the phone so tightly. Kyle glanced at it. He had momentarily forgotten about Ben, forgotten even that he had been on the phone in the first place.

The knocking began again.

"Benjy. I gotta go."

"Hey. You all right?"

Kyle had no answer for that. "I'll call you tomorrow."

His thumb clicked the phone off and he dropped it on the bed. As if he were entranced he made his way down the hall and paused at the top of the stairs. The light from the kitchen behind him barely reached the landing in front of the door.

Making his decision, Kyle hurried down the stairs. He clicked on the outside lights, unlocked the door, and pulled it open.

Will James stood on the stoop. He looked pale and sick in that wan light, as though he might throw up at any moment. Behind him, the night still seemed alive with menace in a way that it never had before. In his hand was that leather book, and though Kyle felt his gaze drawn to it, he refused to look at it for more than a second or two.

"What is it with you?" he said, staring at Will, trying to ignore the desperation in his own voice, and the book, and the memory of the yellowed, dusty envelope. "So you used to live here. So what? What the fuck do you want from me?"

There was something innocent and boyish about the man's face, about his short blond hair and the way he carried himself. But his eyes were ancient.

"You wanted the truth before, kid. I'm here to give it to you." Will held up the book, the scuffed burgundy leather cover somehow darker than before, even with the outside lights on. "I hope you still want it, because in exchange for the truth, I'm going to need your help."

All Kyle's earlier bravado had disappeared now. "I...I don't think I want to know."

"Maybe you need to." Will took a step nearer, clutching the book against his chest now. His eyes were hollow and lost. "Someone's tearing my world apart, Kyle. Destroying lives. I have to stop it and I can't do it alone."

Kyle had to clear his throat to speak. His stomach hurt. "Did you *really* used to live here?"

For the first time, a weak smile flickered across Will's face. "Yeah. I did."

Kyle closed his eyes. He felt frozen now, and it had nothing to do with the chill in the air. Before he even knew what he was going to do, before he could think about anything else, he pushed his hands through his hair and stepped back from the door so that Will James could enter.

CHAPTER 9

The rest of the world seemed impossibly far away. As he sat at his kitchen table and listened to Will James talk of magic and blood and levitation, Kyle felt as though his house had receded from everything he understood of reality. Out there was the yard he had played football in, the driveway he helped his dad shovel in the winter, the lamppost whose glass he had shattered with a Frisbee. The neighbors walked their dogs on Parmenter Road, kids rode their bikes, and in the summer a battered ice-cream truck went by, driven by a twentyish girl whose smile was far more interesting to the neighborhood boys than ice cream.

Yet across the table from him, face too pale in the unforgiving kitchen lights, Will James gave up his ugly secrets, staring at a spot in the middle of the kitchen as though he could see the past unfolding with every word. And despite how detached Kyle felt, how Will's stories made him itch as though tiny insects were crawling upon his skin, he reminded himself time and again that—once upon a time—Will himself had played football in that yard and helped his father shovel the driveway, had ridden his bike on Parmenter Road and probably looked forward to visits from the ice-cream truck, though for an entirely different reason.

So Kyle sat and he listened to stories about Will James and Brian Schnell, and Brian's little sister Dori's naked breasts, about orange floats and cafeteria fights and about that book. That damnable book. It looked so harmless there on the kitchen table, battered cover dull in the overhead lights, its deep red leather now anemic, drained of much of its color, as pale in its way as Will himself.

But Kyle did not want to touch it again. With every word Will spoke the book's presence there in the kitchen grew more ominous. He wished he had never seen it, never touched it, and though he knew deep down he would later pretend not to have considered it, the thought crossed his mind that he could *feel* a malignance emanating from those pages.

Dark Gifts. It was aptly titled, that much was certain.

" . . . got worse after that," Will went on. A sour expression pinched his face and he glanced up at Kyle, almost as if Will had forgotten he was in the room, as if he had lost track of precisely who his confessor was. "It was a big game. I mean, try to imagine it. Just for a moment, try to imagine that you were the one with the unhealthy little obsession that had finally borne fruit." He chuckled humorlessly. "Rotten, bitter fruit."

Through the open windows Kyle could hear a car engine growl as it went up the street. He hesitated, hoping he would not hear it slow, hoping that his parents had not decided to come home early. But the car went on, the engine noise fading, leaving only the sound of the floral-patterned clock ticking in the kitchen, and their breathing.

"Why you?" he asked doubtfully. "Okay, the book's rare. You and your friend were my age when you found this thing. It's just hard to think something that hadn't worked for other people would—"

"How do you know?" Will interrupted, voice soft.

Brows knitted, Kyle studied him, this guy in his jeans and his Red Sox jersey, and thought he could see in the man's face the teenager he had once been. "How do I know what?"

"That it didn't work for other people? As far as we know,

there may have been hundreds or thousands of genuine magicians just in the past couple of hundred years. What makes you think the world would know? Scientific discovery is a thing of exultation, of celebration. That's what you don't understand, Kyle. Magic isn't like that. Once you've had a taste of it ... it's secret. Something to be savored, to be held close and cherished, but not shared. Magic is dark and selfish."

His eyes were so very far away that Kyle was almost afraid to speak then, to interrupt the connection that Will had in those moments with the dark days of his past.

"After that day in Herbie's—that was the ice-cream shop— Brian and I had a bond that wasn't like anything I'd ever experienced before. Or since, really." Will grunted. "How fucking sad is that? Anyway, even though we had this secret, this thing that was so much ours, all this time we spent learning spells and stuff was just as much about one-upping each other as it was about the magic."

Magic, Kyle thought. *He says it like it's nothing.*

Long seconds ticked by on the clock and Will seemed lost in the past, or in the pain of whatever was happening to him now. Kyle had long since reached the point where he did not know what to believe. Magic was bullshit, but then, the book had come from somewhere. So had the note. And there was nothing ordinary about either of them.

At length, he spoke up. "So ... so what happened? I mean, it's pretty obvious from what you've told me that you and this Brian guy fell apart after a while. You stopped messing with ... all this stuff?"

On the table were two glass bottles of root beer. Kyle's version of hospitality. Will had sucked his down so quickly that he'd had to wipe foam off his lips. Kyle had taken a single sip and now the bottle sat on the table as if daring him to drink. But he was lost now in the story, in the possibilities.

Will gestured to the bottle. "Are you going to drink that?"

"Help yourself."

After he had taken a long swig, Will at last looked at Kyle

again. "Something happened that...scared us. Scared me. Not only that, but it was..." He narrowed his eyes. "You act the tough guy, Kyle, but you're not stupid. I knew that right off. You think of yourself as a good guy?"

This bizarre tangent forced Kyle to take a breath. He blinked, thought about it a moment, and then shrugged. "Yeah. Don't most people?"

"I'd like to think so," Will replied. "I did, too, back then. Thought of myself as a good guy. High on my white horse. I think a time comes in everybody's life when we get knocked off that horse." His gaze lost its focus and then his eyes slid away, but it was not memory that made Will drift this time, that was obvious. He did not want to look at Kyle while he spoke. "I did something shitty, Kyle. We did. Brian and me. I've never forgiven myself for it, and I never forgave him for it, either. But I had to move on with my life. I had to get to a place where I could take it as a lesson learned and try to remind myself why I ever thought I was a good guy in the first place."

Will took a quick sip of the root beer, then held the cold bottle against his cheek. He laughed softly and this time there was a bit of humor in it, a gleam in his eye. "We all have our sins to pay for. For your sake, I hope it's a long time before you have to learn that lesson."

Slowly, very slowly, Will set the bottle of root beer down. There was a despair on his face unlike anything Kyle had ever seen. The man raised his right hand, lips moving silently at first; then his voice rose, but the words sounded like gibberish. Will swore, stumbling over a word, then he started again, eyes closed. He rubbed his thumb across his index and middle fingers repeatedly for several seconds.

He stopped. Fell silent. Opened his fist.

A small flame no larger than what might burn upon a candle's wick danced in the palm of his hand.

Kyle nearly wet his pants. "Oh, shit," he whispered, eyes wide.

Will closed his hand and a tiny tendril of smoke furled up from between his fingers as the flame was snuffed. Then Will leaned toward him so that their faces were only a couple of feet apart, his eyes locked on Kyle's.

"You knew something extraordinary was happening, Kyle. You wouldn't have let me in here if you weren't ready to hear the truth." Will reached for the book, dragged it across the table with a sound like sandpaper on wood, and tapped it. "Someone is using magic—magic from this book—to hurt people I care about. Someone's changing the world right under my nose."

He bit his lip, eyes closed tightly as though to ward off tears. When he opened them again fury had replaced despair. His blue eyes seemed a dismal gray now, as though storm clouds had covered the sky. "I have to set things right. Not just for those people who've been hurt...but also because it's affecting me, Kyle. Changing me. I don't feel the same. And I want to hold on to the person I was long enough to fix it." His voice lowered to a confidential rasp. "You can't imagine what it's like to feel yourself changing, to know it's being done...."

Another car went up the street and this time they both paused to listen. When the engine noise had diminished and the ticking of the clock and the hum of the refrigerator were all that remained, Will pulled *Dark Gifts* into his lap and stared at the cover.

"I need help, Kyle. You have no reason to help me. But someone brought you into this thing already with this book and with that note. You live in my old house. In my old room. I can't believe there's no significance to that. I don't know if I know anyone else I could convince, even with the hocus-pocus shit. And even if I did, I think it's a bad idea to wait. I want to get to this before anything else happens, or before I'm...altered drastically. Or erased."

Kyle stared at him. After a few ticks of the clock he got up, sighed, and began to pace in the kitchen. His head hurt. His chest hurt. The image of that flame in this crazy fucker's hand was going to stay with him, he was sure of that. His parents would be home eventually and he had no idea what the guy wanted him to do. But if that little flame was possible, then couldn't it all be true? All of it.

His gaze ticked over to where the book lay in Will's lap and he shuddered, remembering the way it had felt in his hands. True or not, he didn't like that book. Not at all. The last thing he wanted to do was mess with whatever was inside it.

Striding across the kitchen again, he paused and leaned against the door frame, looking down the stairs at the darkened landing by the front door, glancing into the shadows of his living room, imagining Will James opening his presents there on Christmas morning.

But this was no dream. It wasn't some drug trip. It was impossible, sure. But what the hell did that mean?

"Tell me what's going on. Who's being hurt? Who's in danger?" he said into the shadows of the living room. Then he turned to find Will James watching him hopefully.

"And then tell me what you did that was so terrible."

April, Junior Year

Friday afternoon was a time of bliss, with the whole weekend ahead. There would be plans, of course—the mall, a movie, maybe a party—but of late every weekend began the same way. Will boarded Brian's bus and they sat in the back, windows open, talking about everything except what they were both thinking about, the secret that they shared.

The book.

This particular Friday was no different. The bus rattled, its engine straining as it climbed up Terrace Road, exhaust fumes swirling up and into the back windows. Will and Brian ignored the fumes. That was part of the price to be paid for sitting in back. Once upon a time they would never have gotten these backseats, but they were juniors now, and juniors ruled the buses. Most seniors either had cars or rode with one of their friends, abdicating their regency over the seating arrangements on school transportation.

"What've you and Caitlyn got going this weekend?" Brian asked.

Will smiled. "Wouldn't you like to know?"

Brian rolled his eyes.

"Seriously, not much," Will relented. "I think we're probably going to go to The Sampan tomorrow night. I want to hit the bookstore at some point this weekend, but I don't know if my mother can take me. Can't wait until I get my license."

"No shit," Brian agreed. He nodded slowly, then studied Will. "So you guys are pretty serious, huh?"

Will couldn't stop the grin that spread across his face. "I know. I'm whipped. What can I say? Love's pretty cool."

"I don't even know what that is," Brian told him. "Love."

His tone was layered. There was a level at which he was taunting Will, riding him for his dedication to Caitlyn the way all of the guys did, partially out of ignorance and partially out of envy. But Will heard more than that in Brian's words; on a certain level, he meant what he had said. He really did not understand what love was, and he seemed to regret it.

"Not that I'm a fuckin' expert," Will said, "I'm sixteen, not sixty. But, okay, take a look up there."

Will gestured toward the front of the bus. There were dozens of other students there, laughing and talking, their voices blending into a kind of loud growl that almost matched the roar of the engine. There were many faces he recognized, and a handful of freshmen who were unfamiliar to him. Some of the girls were plain, or simply ordinary, but a few were cute as hell. Dori Schnell was among them, but not only was she a bitch, she was Brian's sister, so he didn't want to use her as an example.

"See Candace what's-her-name? Brillstein?" Will asked.

Brian glanced forward. The girl in question was a sophomore, a friend of Dori's who wore the miniest of tank tops and had long sandy hair, pale skin, and the most amazing eyes Will had ever seen. It didn't hurt the package at all that Candace was a flirt with perfectly round breasts that she seemed extremely proud of.

"How could I miss her?" Brian asked, shooting a lascivious look at Will.

"You could be blind," Will suggested. "If she came up to you at a party and wanted to take you upstairs, go somewhere private, you'd go, right?"

With a sidelong glare, Brian made his answer clear. "Don't be stupid."

"I'm not. I'm making a point."

"Which is?"

"I'd say no."

Brian stared at him in disbelief. "Get out of here."

Will laughed. "I know. Crazy, huh? But true. Not that I wouldn't want to fuck her brains out. But I wouldn't do it. I couldn't hurt Caitlyn like that."

The engine made a grinding noise as the bus driver dropped into a lower gear, taking a turn onto Cherry Street. In this part of Eastborough the roads were lined with lush old trees whose branches hung out above passing vehicles, shading the street. Branches scraped the bus as they turned the corner.

"Whatever works for you," Brian said, arching an eyebrow. "You go, be in love. Just don't forget who your friends are. We'll still be here when she breaks your heart."

Will stared at him, then chuckled. "Asshole."

Brian grinned. "Yep." He paused a moment, his smile disappearing, and then glanced at Will again. "So you up for this, today?"

An odd ripple went through Will. The skin on his hands tingled and he flushed as though he had just been caught doing something terribly embarrassing. His chest tightened as pleasure warred with guilt. That was always the way it was for him with magic. He knew that it was dangerous, that there was something nasty, even dirty, about some of the things they had done. But magic thrilled him, and its allure was impossible to ignore.

Brian was looking at him expectantly, but before Will could respond, the bus began to slow, brakes letting out a high-pitched squeal. Out the window he could see the mini stop sign swing out from the side of the bus.

They got up and ambled toward the front of the bus. Dori

rose from her seat and shot a dark look at them before stepping into the aisle. Brian's sister was pretty, but whenever Will caught sight of her she sneered at him, and that cut into her beauty significantly. He figured it was a kind of guilt by association—she had to hate him because he hung around with her brother—but that sneer always made him feel small somehow.

By the time he stepped off the bus on Waverly Street, Dori was well on her way up the Schnells' long driveway. The bus driver closed the door with a hiss and there was another grinding of gears as it trundled on up the street.

"What's your hurry?" Brian called after his sister. "Do we smell?"

Dori paused at the end of the path that led to the front door and glanced back at them. Her smile was venomously sweet. "Yes, since you asked. But I'm in a hurry because I've got things to do. People to see. Places to go. You two ought to try it sometime."

She started up the walk, a new bounce in her step, exuding triumph.

"Don't you mean people to fuck?" Brian asked lightly.

Dori froze. Will could see her shudder with fury. When she turned to them again, her face was red.

"You know," she said through gritted teeth, "you always ask me why I'm such a bitch to you. That's funny, isn't it? That you'd have to ask." Dori sighed and shook her head. Then her gaze drifted to Will and a bitter smile creased her lips. "In case you're wondering, Will, I'm going to a party tonight. With my boyfriend. And other people. That's called a social life. You should try it sometime. Soon. Seriously. Right now Caitlyn's the only thing keeping the whole school from thinking you and my brother are either in love or building pipe bombs."

She brushed at the air as if dismissing them. "Take a note. Take a lesson. That's as nice as I'm ever going to be to either of you."

Once again she turned away from them, striding to the door

and digging out her key. As she fitted it into the lock, Brian followed her.

"You've really never gotten over Will seeing your tits last year, have you?" Brian asked, a nasty glint in his eye. "But I'm wondering if the reason you're so pissed off is because he never asked to see them again."

Dori ignored him, pushing the door open, then slamming it behind her and locking it again, so that Brian had to dig out his own keys. As he did so he turned and grinned up at Will.

"Guess I hit a nerve."

Will wished he had never come. Then he remembered what they had planned for the afternoon, and another little sizzle of anticipation went through him. Dori was a first-class bitch, there was no doubt about that. She was never quite as evil to him as she was to her brother, but Will still always felt like she looked at him as though he were dog shit on her shoe. He had thought many times how nice it would be if someone could teach the little prima donna a lesson.

Now the time had come.

THE SHADES WERE DRAWN in Brian's bedroom, the sunlight bleeding in around their edges. The door was locked. A circle of white candles burned in small crystal dishes on the floor, wax dripping like tears. Inside that circle, Will and Brian sat opposite one another with a number of objects around them, and between them, the book and a copper pot. According to Jean-Marc Gaudet, the copper was conducive to magic, and as such, vital to this particular spell.

Spell's probably the wrong word, Will thought. And he knew what the right word would be, but he did not want to admit it, even to himself.

Music pounded the wall that separated Brian's room from Dori's. It was loud enough that it had to be giving her a headache, but she would be well aware that it was annoying the hell out of them and that would be reason enough for Dori to turn it up even louder. The wall shook with every beat. Will could imagine Dori in there getting ready for the party tonight, trying on different tops and tossing the rejected ones on her bed. He had witnessed the aftermath of her preparation rituals before, the mess she left behind. Even now she was likely brushing her hair out, touching up her makeup in the mirror.

The party didn't start for hours yet, but Dori would do her best to be gone before her parents got home. Her boyfriend Ian was a senior and drove his father's cast-off Volkswagen Jetta. Will figured they had less than an hour before he picked Dori up.

But if this thing was going to work, an hour was plenty of time.

If it works . . .

Will took a deep breath and let it out, trying to clear his mind but unable to, thanks to the pounding bass beat that shook the house. Dori was a bitch, sure, but she was still Brian's sister. Someone he saw almost every day. And really, how much different was she from a lot of other little sisters, especially in high school?

Even as these thoughts entered his mind, however, they were ushered away by vivid memories of Dori snickering, whispering to her girlfriends behind an upraised hand, of a thousand tiny cruelties, not the least of which was the episode only a week earlier when he had walked into the bathroom, accidentally startling her in the middle of brushing her teeth. Will had not known she was in there, and he had given her a fright, but Dori just didn't handle things the way most people did.

She spat a mouthful of toothpaste at him. "How 'bout some privacy, asshole?"

At first, Will had been too stunned even to be angry. When he eventually called her on it, she had shot him her upraised middle finger and told him he was just lucky she hadn't been taking a shower.

Will stared at one of the white candles, at the dancing flame atop it.

"Hey." Brian waved a hand in front of his face. "You're in space. What's wrong with you? No, no, Will. I know that look. Tell me you're not going to pussy out on me."

The music seemed to pound against his skull now, and his head had begun to ache. Despite everything, he still felt a certain reluctance, and yet Brian wore an expression that was almost desperate, eyes intense, brows knitted angrily.

"Will…"

"You sure about this?" Will ventured. He ran both hands over his hair, making it spike up. "I mean, no secrets, Brian. I can't stand her, but she's your sister. Isn't there someone else we can use as a guinea pig?"

Brian rolled his eyes and grabbed the plastic supermarket bag that had been propped against his thigh. He glanced at the door as if to reassure himself that it was locked and then dumped the contents of the bag onto the floor, spilling out a bruised green apple, a small ball of red yarn, a plastic baggie of mixed herbs, and two other little baggies. One held a clump of hair that Brian had collected from Dori's hairbrush over the course of several weeks. Will didn't want to look at the other bag, but he caught a glimpse of it and his stomach churned. Inside was a blood-soaked tampon.

"Can you think of anyone else we wouldn't mind giving some bad luck to whose hair and blood we could get our hands on?"

Will dropped his gaze, studying the book where it lay open on the floor in front of them. The pages were rough and yellowed, the black print in a Gothic style that often made it difficult to read.

"Hey," Brian prodded.

"No, I'm good," Will replied, raising his eyes. "Besides, it's only for tonight anyway, right? Just to make sure it works. Tomorrow we undo it?"

The grin barely parted Brian's lips, and the amiable effect he was going for did not reach his eyes, which remained grim. "Absolutely," he promised.

Will nodded, making up his mind. Beside him on the floor were a box of wooden matches and a plastic bottle of charcoal lighter fluid he had snatched from his garage at home. Everyone else had gas grills, but his father still liked the old briquettes. He slid the matches and the fluid nearer to the copper pot and then reached for the book. Its leather was not soft against his fingers today. Instead it felt like sandpaper and the book itself had a terrible weight, so that he had to lean in to lift it onto his lap.

It fell open at precisely the place he wanted, the whisper of pages sending a shiver through him. His eyes burned and he had to blink several times to focus on the words, on the spell. The mantra he would have to speak was not in English but in German. Brian had translated it, but Will only remembered some of the translation—bits about flesh and blood and thwarting the fates, about suspending chance and attracting the attention of malign forces.

He had tried to forget. It didn't matter anyway because they had worked out a phonetic version so that they would be able to pronounce everything properly.

Don't want to fuck it up and curse yourself, he thought, more than a little giddy with the surreal feeling that swept through him. Then he pinched the bridge of his nose and picked up the paper with the phonetic pronunciation, placed it beside the book on his lap. Will didn't like that word. Didn't want to have to even think it.

Dori's music still pumped through the house and his temples throbbed, his head aching worse than ever. The slivers of sunlight that peeked around the edges of the shades were not enough to dispel the shadows that seemed to gather even more closely around them, and the candlelight only made them appear to writhe and undulate.

There was a peculiar taste in Will's mouth, as though he had been chewing on aluminum foil. For a moment as he gazed down at the book, his eyes would not focus. One by one Brian picked up the things he had scattered on the floor and began adding them to the copper pot, Will watching to make certain he followed the order of ingredients as prescribed.

With a small paring knife, Brian sliced the apple into quarters and dropped them into the pot. The herbs followed, and then Dori's hair. That hideous tampon went in next. Brian shook it from the bag, not wanting to touch it, and Will tried not to watch it tumble into the pot but could not help himself.

Will's right hand began to tremble and he gritted his teeth and forced it to be still. He felt short of breath and his face was too warm, and with the music slamming the walls from the room next door he was close to just jumping up and taking off. But how the hell would he explain that to Brian tomorrow?

"Come on, man. Hurry the fuck up!" he snapped.

Brian shot him a glance that burned away any pretense Will might have tried to put up. "Relax, Will. I gave you your chance to bail. Too late to turn back now." A smile creased the corners of his mouth. "Besides, we're just getting to the fun stuff."

The fun stuff. The words echoed in Will's head. There was a dark thrill in him, like the time he had caught a glimpse up Mrs. Hidalgo's dress in biology class and realized she was wearing nothing under there. Again he wanted to pull himself back, to tear his eyes away, but could not. Mrs. Hidalgo had caught him looking. She had blushed and adjusted her dress, shifted in her seat, but said nothing.

That dark thrill was delicious, and Will could not pull away.

Brian was staring at him.

"Get on with it," Will told him, breathless.

That smile returned to his face and Brian bent to reach out for the Reebok shoe box that had only days earlier contained a new pair of sneakers. He opened the box and shoved his hand in, withdrawing a small toad, then tossed the box aside. The toad was silent but its eyes darted about anxiously and its throat bulged rhythmically.

Will took a few shallow breaths and then focused on the book and the phonetic translation. He began the chant, forcing his throat and lips around the guttural sounds so unnatural to him.

A moment later Brian joined in the chanting, but he did not have to refer to the book or to the sheet with the phonetics. It unnerved Will a little to find that Brian had committed the chant to memory, but he ignored the feeling, kept going. It really was too late to stop now. Certainly he could have broken it off, but that dark thrill held him in thrall.

Brian held the toad in his left hand, pinching it between two fingers, and then pushed the paring knife into its belly. He sliced it open over the copper pot and when its innards began to spill out, he let the dead creature tumble in with the rest of the ingredients. Blood, yes, but they had Dori's blood. This spell required something else...it required life.

A sudden chill traced icy fingers along the back of Will's neck. The thump of Dori's music seemed oddly muffled. The candles flickered, throwing hideous shadows, and one of them blew out, a trailing wisp of smoke climbing above it. For a long moment Will stared at that candle. His stomach ached and his mind was filled with all manner of recriminations and second thoughts, that dark thrill now just something to be ashamed of.

"Will!" Brian urged.

He nodded, put the book down. Brian kept on with those guttural words as Will took the lighter fluid, upended the can and squeezed a long stream into the copper pot, saturating the contents. His fingers were numb, his mind felt detached from his body, and yet he kept working. He set the lighter fluid down, picked up the matches, removed one and struck it. The fire blazed up instantly, the smell of sulfur in the air. Will tossed the match into the pot and the entire contents erupted into hungry flames.

His breath came slow and ragged. His eyes darted around the room, taking in every shadow, watching the slivers of light around the shades with longing, impatient to be out of here, to be in the sunlight. All of his muscles tensed, prepared. But nothing happened.

Nothing. The spell had failed. Failed to accomplish anything except to make Will feel dirty, inside and out. The kind of dirty no shower could ever wash away.

The spell didn't work, he thought. Some part of him was surprised he was not more disappointed, but in his heart there was only relief. Relief, because it wasn't really a spell at all.

It's a curse.

The music in Dori's room was abruptly silenced. It seemed to echo in Will's ears as quiet seconds ticked by. He and Brian looked sharply at one another, wide-eyed, both of them holding their breath. Had they done it? And if so, what, precisely, had they done?

From outside there came the blare of a car horn. That would be Ian. They heard footsteps, then Dori's bedroom door opened and closed. Her shoes ticktocked along the corridor and then down the stairs, and a moment later the front door slammed. She was gone.

Will sagged as he let out the breath he had been holding. He felt foolish and perverse, but he smiled and shook his head, trying to cleanse those feelings. But when he looked up, he saw that Brian's face was etched with frustration.

"Fuck," Brian whispered. He knocked aside the empty Reebok box. "Fuck," he said again.

"What are you gonna do?" Will said tentatively. "Maybe we just don't have what it takes to curse someone. They don't all work. Some do. This one didn't."

But the hell of it was, it had.

CHAPTER 10

April, Junior Year

Nightfall was still a ways off, but as Dori hurried along the front walk toward Ian's car it seemed to her that the sky had dimmed far sooner than it should have. When she glanced upward she realized that it was not the encroaching evening but the weather that had cast a pall over the day. When she had gotten off the bus with Brian and Will, the sky had been a bright, clear blue. Now it was simply gray, and on the horizon there was a darkening hint of something brewing, thunderheads on the way.

"Perfect," she sighed.

The party didn't start for a couple of hours yet, but she had wanted to be gone before her parents got home. Ian had suggested they go out to dinner someplace nice, but since there was very little that fit that description within the town limits and she didn't want to have to go far, Dori had suggested The Sampan. She loved Chinese food. At the moment, she wasn't very hungry, but the key was avoiding her parents. Not that they were that difficult. They just asked too many annoying questions.

Ian sat behind the wheel, the window rolled down, and he smiled at her as she approached. Dori had on brand-new jeans and a white top with a brown suede jacket one size too small that she left unzipped. With just a touch of eyeliner and the coolest bloodred lipstick, she knew she looked good, but the expression on his face as she strode toward the car was all the assurance she needed.

"Hey, cutie," Dori said, marching around to the passenger door. She popped the door open and climbed in. When she leaned over to kiss Ian, she misjudged and their teeth banged together.

"Oww!" he said, flinching back from her.

"Oh, shit, sorry." Dori put a hand on his leg.

Ian laughed, though a bit hesitantly, and ran his tongue over his teeth. "Let's not do *that* again."

Dori smiled and shook her head, then reached out to close her door. Her fingers slid into the smooth plastic grip on the inside of the door and she yanked it toward her. A sharp pain made her hiss and pull her hand away, and she cursed as she glanced at her hand and saw that her index finger had a slice in it.

"What the hell?" she muttered, sucking on the cut finger as she examined the plastic grip. It was cracked, and one portion jutted higher than the other, jagged and sharp.

"What's wrong?"

She shot him a withering glance. "I cut myself on your stupid car, that's all. Do you have any Band-Aids?"

He raised an eyebrow. "Do I look like I carry a purse? No, I don't have any Band-Aids."

"We'll have to stop at the 7-Eleven."

Ian nodded and put the car into gear, backing out of the driveway. "Not a problem. Sorry about that. I didn't even know it was broken. I'll have to get some duct tape or something, cover it up." He seemed troubled, his forehead creased with concern, but as he drove toward the center of town he lightened up considerably. "You hungry, babe?"

The gray skies and cutting her finger had annoyed her, but Dori wasn't going to let that ruin her whole night. She gave him a warm smile and nodded. "Wicked hungry. And looking forward to the party later. Hoping we can get a room to ourselves."

As he glanced at her, a lascivious grin on his face, the front left tire blew. The shotgun report of the exploding tire made Dori cry out, her heart hammering in her chest, and Ian slammed on the brakes. From behind them there came the screech of tires. An old Ford behind them swerved, but not far enough, and the driver clipped the back of Ian's car, ripping metal and smashing the taillight.

Dori cried out again.

Ian swore and pounded the steering wheel with the heel of his hand.

"You've got to be fucking kidding me," Dori rasped, hands on the dashboard.

Which was just about the moment that she felt a trickle between her legs, and she knew that her period had arrived two full weeks ahead of schedule.

NEARLY TWO HOURS AFTER the flat tire and the fender bender, they sat at a table by the window at The Sampan, staring at one another in numb disbelief. While Ian was exchanging information with the driver of the old Ford and changing the tire, Dori had been forced to sit there and bleed, both from her cut finger and elsewhere. The entire time she had waited in the car, glancing anxiously at her crotch in hopes that she would not bleed enough to soak through her jeans before they could get to a convenience store.

They did manage to make it to 7-Eleven in time, but that was the only thing that had gone right.

Now Ian sat across from her, silhouetted against the window, beyond which the night was coming on and the thunderclouds had moved in. Rain pelted the glass so hard it seemed like sleet, though it was too warm for sleet. Dori was miserable and it was obvious Ian felt the same. Neither of them was very patient in general, but this night would have tested anyone. The appetizers they had ordered had been overcooked and cold, and one piece of steak teriyaki had a fringe of what looked like mold on the edge of it. The Sampan was usually fantastic, but Dori had nearly thrown up at the sight of that and been unable to eat any more of it.

It seemed an eternity before the waiter brought them dinner, and when it finally came, both orders were wrong. Completely wrong. Now they were enduring a second infinite lag and both of them were in a foul mood. They were going to be much later for the party than they had intended. Not that Dori really felt like partying anymore.

Ian glanced around as though the waiter might suddenly materialize out of thin air, then sighed and shook his head. "Can't believe you got your fucking period."

Dori put on a tough-girl veneer, but she made no pretense to herself...it was very thin. Yet it wasn't his words that wounded her. It was the tone, the dismissal inherent in his voice. *You've got your period*, that tone seemed to say. *What good are you?*

"You should say a prayer every time I *do* get it," she said in a low voice, glancing around to be sure no one could overhear them.

"I know. I get it, OK?" he said, softening, shooting her a regretful glance. "But it's like you just had it."

"I did just have it. I'm not due for another two weeks. It's early."

Ian frowned and he looked around again, though not for the waiter this time. For the first time in minutes his eyes focused on her and he leaned in closer. "Is that supposed to happen? I mean, are you all right?"

But she was still stung by his attitude and so she only sniffed and averted her gaze. "Like you care. Asshole. Sometimes it's early, sometimes it's late. But it's never been this early. Sorry I ruined your night."

"Come on, Dori. Don't be like that. You didn't ruin anything. Not your fault, is it?"

Every word seemed to have been torn from him. She could see it in his eyes, in his expression and the way he moved his hands. Ian didn't mean a word of it. He was just saying what he thought he ought to say, and that kind of patronizing baby bullshit made her crazy.

"Do you even want to go to the party?" she asked, her back rigid against the chair, fingernails tapping lightly on the table. She had been ravenous before, but the wait and the hideous appetizer had fixed that. Her stomach had gone from empty to numb, and now the smell of Chinese food made her nauseous.

"What? Of course I want to go. You don't?"

"Do you still want to go with me?" The moment the question was out of her mouth she was furious with herself for how small and weak she sounded. She had meant it to come off as demanding, even bitchy, but now she sounded needy. She abruptly changed gears.

"You know what? Fuck it. I'm not hungry anymore. Let's get out of here."

Ian blinked in surprise as she got up from the table. "What? Where?"

Dori narrowed her eyes. "That's up to you. Take me to the party or take me home."

With that, she turned her back on him and strode out of The Sampan. As she left the restaurant she could hear Ian arguing with the waiter, who still hadn't brought their dinner. Ian was going to pay for the drinks and the appetizer but that was it. Dori hoped he didn't leave a tip, either. She didn't give a shit. No way was she ever going to eat in this place again.

JILLIAN MANSUR'S FAMILY LIVED in a sprawling farmhouse on Grove Street, set back a ways from the road. Her father had been sent on a business trip to San Diego and had taken his wife along, leaving Jillian alone in the house. She had just turned eighteen and they thought of her as a responsible girl in an irresponsible world. That was almost a direct quote, though Dori couldn't remember the rest of it. Obviously, the Mansurs didn't know Jillian at all. *Maybe*, Dori thought, *they've taken one too many business trips.*

The house was a wreck. Beer had been spilled onto the living room carpet and left to soak. Someone had shattered a Zima bottle in the kitchen sink. There was vomit in the garbage can. Under the dining room table, a senior named Jimmy Vons was curled up into a fetal ball, passed out and snoring. He was missing both shoes and one sock.

Dori felt like crying. Frustration burned in her chest and her throat tightened, but she would not allow tears to moisten her eyes. Not here. Not in front of all these people, all these seniors. Some of them had been nice to her since she had started seeing Ian, but many of the girls dismissed her. She was just a lowly sophomore, after all. She didn't belong.

Tonight, she agreed with them.

Off the kitchen was a small pantry that one had to pass through to get to the back door. Dori had fled there, and now she leaned against shelves of tomato paste and soup cans and hugged herself, trying to catch her breath. Her eyes burned. When she raised her hands to push her hair back, her fingers trembled. Her back was wet where someone had spilled a glass of red wine on her neck, staining the collar of her suede jacket and the white shirt beneath and drenching her in that rich, earthy burgundy odor. The jacket was ruined. She could not escape the smell. She had no idea what to tell her parents.

When the drunken bitch had spilled the wine on her, Dori had rushed to the bathroom, hoping to wash as much of it from her jacket and shirt as possible. But when she banged into the bathroom she had found a couple of senior girls snorting coke off the toilet seat, half-naked, groping each other. Trying to find some privacy, she had ended up in the pantry, and only now, as this little bit of intimacy enveloped her, did she feel the dampness at her crotch and realize that she needed another tampon. To get one, she'd have to go out to the car, but Ian always locked it. She needed his keys.

She needed Ian.

Never in her life had she wanted to leave anywhere so badly.

Dori reached out and steadied herself, holding on to one of

the shelves. She took several long breaths and found herself staring at a can of baked beans. For some reason it made her smile.
Though fleeting, that smile was enough to let her breathe again.
Nothing was going right tonight. Not a goddamn thing. The
rain, the flat tire, the fender bender, the fucking Sampan, and
now this party from hell. *Whose idea of fun is this?* she thought.

With the added motivation of not wanting to bleed through
her jeans to complete the ensemble of stains for the evening, she
took a final breath and left the pantry. A trio of guys passed a
joint around and the sweet smell of marijuana filled the kitchen.
One of them was cooking scrambled eggs and dancing along to
Nine Inch Nails or Jane's Addiction or whoever the hell it was
on the sound system.

After her red wine shower, Dori had left Ian in the living
room. She figured maybe ten minutes had passed, but he wasn't
there.

"Son of a bitch," she whispered, glancing around until she
spotted Brad Ghilani, a friend of Ian's. Her skin crawled with a
paranoid unease, for she was convinced that somehow everyone
in the room was tracking her in their peripheral vision, that they
could see she was falling apart. A kind of frenzied panic over-
took her as she strode up to Brad.

Normally brazen, Dori glanced around hesitantly and tapped
him on the arm. "Brad? Have you seen Ian? I'm ... I need to ..."
Flustered, she forced herself to stare at him, chin raised. "I need
his car keys."

Brad was useless. She should have seen the glaze over his eyes
before she had even spoken to him, but somehow she had missed
it. He took a long swig of beer and wiped the back of his hand
across his mouth. "Nah, sorry," he said, slurring ever so slightly.
Then he pointed toward the stairs. "Think he had to piss,
though."

As she walked toward the stairs, a gentle wave of relief began
to wash over her. Why hadn't she thought of the upstairs bathroom? That had been foolish. Not only might it be possible for

her to get a moment alone, but surely Jillian would have tampons. *Just chill out*, she told herself. *Take care of this first, then you can find Ian and decide if you still want to leave.*

There were a few people on the stairs, but the second floor was quiet. The door to the hall bathroom was ajar and the light was on inside, the fan whirring. Dori raised a hand to rap on it. From inside, she heard a soft moan. She rolled her eyes in frustration. Snorting coke in the downstairs bathroom and now this upstairs? Couldn't people pick someplace else to fuck around? She lowered her hand, trying to decide whether to interrupt or just to wait.

Then a male voice reached her from inside the bathroom, a raspy, hitching whisper. "Hey . . . oh, shit, the door. What if . . . what if someone comes?"

Dori's lips parted and she swayed forward, just slightly, her knees weakening. Her facial muscles were slack and her fingers felt numb. She reached out, watching her hand move as though it belonged to someone else entirely, and slowly pressed the door open.

"Mmm," said a girl on the other side of that door, and the sound was followed by another, a moist sound, that Dori had heard before. That Dori had *made* before. "Oh, don't worry," the girl said. "Someone's definitely going to come."

Dori's fingers kept pushing. The door swung open just in time for her to see Jillian lower her head and slide her lips onto Ian's cock. He moaned again, eyes closing, and he pushed his fingers through her hair and then held her head, fucking her mouth. Jillian stroked him with her right hand and sucked noisily, greedily.

Ian shuddered. He opened his eyes and gazed dreamily down at her bobbing head, entranced. Then he must have sensed that the door was open, that someone had come in. Or perhaps he had seen Dori in his peripheral vision, for he glanced up, shock warring with the pleasure etched upon his face.

His eyes went wide when he saw who it was.

"Dori," Ian whispered, trying to pull back from Jillian, though the sink was behind him and there was nowhere for him to go. His hands flailed in the air as he began to panic, and he tried weakly to push Jillian's head away.

The girl continued to slide her hand and her mouth over him, but she glanced upward as she did. Jillian saw that his gaze was elsewhere and she looked to her right. Her eyes met Dori's.

She kept sucking.

Dori took a step back, then another. Her fingers touched the door frame and the nerve endings came alive. Just touching the wooden frame seemed to burn her. Her face felt cold, but hot tears striped her cheeks and she tasted salt on her lips.

That was what broke her. The taste of her own tears.

There was a scuffle in the bathroom as Ian pushed Jillian away. He called her name, but Dori could barely hear him. She was already moving, running down the corridor. Chris LeBlanc tried to stop her on the stairs, to ask what was wrong, but she pushed past him and nearly fell as she hurried down the steps. Conversations stopped all around. People turned to stare. Dori didn't care. The pain in her heart had shut down everything else inside her. She ran to the front door and threw it open, rushing out into the night, into the rain, not bothering to close it behind her.

On the Mansurs' front lawn, she hugged herself and let loose the shriek that had been building inside her, turning her face up to the sky. The rain drowned her tears, ruined the suede jacket she was wearing. Dori barely noticed.

From inside the house, she heard Ian calling her name. She glanced quickly back. The door was still open but he had not come outside yet. Abruptly her pain was replaced by a venomous hatred unlike anything she had ever felt in her life. *Fucking bastard*, she thought. *Scum.* Violent images filled her mind, but despite her desire to do him harm, all she really wanted was to go, to be away from here. From him.

Despite the rain, Dori started away from the Mansurs' house, cutting across the lawn, shoes squelching in the sodden earth. Already part of her was hesitant. On a clear night she could have walked home without difficulty. It was a few miles, but not a problem. Tonight, though...

She paused, felt the rain streaming down her face.

Back at the front of the house, blocked from her view by trees, Ian called out into the rain. Any second now he might actually come out into the storm, might come looking, wanting to try to explain. And the hell of it was, she thought she might listen.

Asshole, she thought. But no amount of profanity could truly express what she felt about Ian just then.

"No," she said, denying the urge to go back. "No way."

She shook herself and started toward the road again, first walking, then lightly jogging on the slippery, muddy lawn. It felt good to move, and she ignored the rain that plastered her hair to her face. Dori started to run, her breath coming more quickly, her heart pounding. She reached the pavement but she kept running, wanting only to put distance between herself and the party. Questions had begun to rise in her mind and she wondered how she would deal with all of this at school...Everyone would know. What was she supposed to do when she saw Ian or Jillian in the halls?

The rain was cold as it sluiced down the back of her neck, and Dori pulled her soaking-wet jacket up over her head like a cloak. She kept up her pace, hurrying along the road, wondering if she should risk trying to hitchhike. Grove Street was a lazy, winding road lined with trees. It was going to be a long, wet walk.

"Dori!"

She spun, still holding her jacket over her head. Back along the road at the edge of the Mansurs' property she could make out a dark figure, silhouetted against the night. Ian had come after her. Bitterness rose like bile in the back of her throat. Did he actually think he was going to be able to explain what she had seen?

"Fuck you!" she screamed.

Ian started to follow her. He called her name again. The pain in her heart returned now, worse than before, and fresh tears burned her cheeks. She started to run across Grove Street.

"Dori!"

She spun around, there on the wet road, and bellowed so loudly that the strength of it bent her over. "FUCK! YOU!"

The pickup truck's headlights washed over her, and as she turned she was blinded by them. Instinct took over. She heard tires screaming on the pavement as the driver tried to stop. Dori threw herself to the left.

One of the headlights shattered as the truck hit her.

THE TICKING OF THE CLOCK seemed impossibly loud. Will James sat in a chair in his kitchen...only it hadn't been his kitchen for years. Everything about it was strangely unfamiliar, and yet it still felt like home, as though there was a thin veneer of falsehood covering the truth of this place, and if he only scratched the surface he might find beneath it the kitchen he remembered from his childhood.

There was a bittersweet quality to each minute he spent here. It felt good and right, and it also made him feel far too much like the adult he had become when his attention was elsewhere.

The clock ticked.

The refrigerator hummed.

Kyle stared at him, eyebrows knitted, and actually flinched back an inch or two. "You're not serious," the kid said.

Will did not turn away. He was fighting the emotional and mental turmoil that threatened to overwhelm him, trying to hold on to memories that his mind kept trying to bury, and he didn't have time for pretense or courtesy.

"I'm completely serious."

The kid stared at the thick book on the kitchen table for a moment, then jerked back abruptly and stood up, crossing to the kitchen sink and turning toward Will as though he had been cornered. Kyle looked frightened, sad, and somehow disappointed. When he shook his head now there was horror in his voice.

"You *cursed* her."

He nodded. "Yeah. We did. I can't be sure all of the shit that happened to her that night was our fault, but neither one of us was enough of an asshole to try to pretend otherwise. It wasn't until a few days later that Dori told Brian most of the story, but the second we found out, that night, we knew we were responsible."

Kyle's chin snapped up and he shot Will a hard look. "You mean she lived?"

Will stared at him blankly. "What? Yeah! Jesus, yes, she lived. You mean you thought—" He let out a puff of breath, shoulders sagging, and felt far older than he was. "The curse didn't kill her. But it could have. If Dori hadn't tried to get out of the way, if the driver hadn't noticed her and hit the brakes…she'd have died. Just like—"

His eyes went wide. He'd been about to say Mike Lebo. His memories had been so badly muddled that he had been about to compare what had happened to Dori to what had happened to Mike, but in his heart he held on to the truth, the memory of what the past had been like before someone had started changing it.

"Just like what?" Kyle asked.

Will shook his head. "Doesn't matter. The point is, we cursed Dori. That truck hitting her broke both her legs. Took her months to recover."

The lighting in the kitchen made Kyle even paler than he was naturally. He stared at Will as though he were some kind of apparition that had appeared with a warning, like one of Dickens's Christmas spirits, and transformed familiar surroundings into something that simply shouldn't be. Will was uncomfortable beneath the kid's scrutiny, but he was not about to be deterred. He figured he had one chance at this. Kyle might not be the only person who could help him get it done, but Will wasn't going to risk it.

"So what happened after?" the kid asked.

Will could not prevent the queasy smile that forced its way onto his face.

"We removed the curse. What do you think happened?" He shook his head. "We promised each other that we were done with magic, that we weren't going near it, weren't even going to talk about it. Not ever again." Once more his shoulders sagged and now he dropped his gaze, letting his mind drift back to those days. They seemed so long ago. His eyes itched with the threat of tears. "That wasn't enough for me, though. I did one last bit of magic. Went through that book and found a spell that would make me forget. Forget it was real. Forget what we did. But I guess the universe doesn't allow that kind of cheating. Whoever's doing this now... it made me remember. But... Son of a bitch," he whispered hoarsely. "We promised."

"Jesus," Kyle muttered. He paced the kitchen. "So... all this stuff that's been happening to you. You think it's this Brian guy?"

One image rose up in Will's mind then, from that night when they had found out what had happened to Dori. Will had been terrified and wracked with self-loathing. He had seen his own guilt and disgust reflected in Brian's eyes, and the two of them had pledged to keep their crime, their sin, a secret. Who would believe them anyway? But they had made a number of promises to one another that night. And hadn't there been a kind of excited glint in Brian's eyes?

He thought there had been.

"When I told him that I was going to do the spell to forget, he swore that afterward he would get rid of the book. That he was gonna burn it. Obviously, he didn't do that."

Kyle paused in his pacing and stared at him. "But I found it under the stairs here. This was *your* house."

Will frowned. "What's your point? You think I left it there?"

Impossible things had been happening for days, so it should not have surprised Will at all when something happened that was merely strange. Yet it did surprise him. The shattering of the spell he had put upon himself, and the realization of what was going on, had pushed him into a kind of madness earlier in the day that had been with him ever since. It made his hands tremble and his skin prickle with pinpoints of heat and his head ache with the conflict of memories and desires and fears. It was a passionate lunacy that had driven him to beat Brian bloody at Papillon and to appear in the dark on the steps of his childhood home to plead with a teenage boy for help.

Yet now, as Kyle studied him again, the kid's eyes briefly ticking toward the wine-red leather cover of *Dark Gifts*, there was a connection between the two of them that Will could not deny. It had been there before. Maybe there was something cosmic about it, maybe not. He didn't really care. All he knew was that in that moment he saw in Kyle Brody's eyes that the kid had recognized this bizarre kinship between them—a man who had once been a child here, and a boy whose life was flowing along a similar path, right down to sleeping in the same bedroom.

Kyle *believed* him.

Will closed his eyes and whispered a silent prayer of thanks. Until that moment he had not realized how little hope he had been holding on to.

"So this Brian?" Kyle said, clearing his throat and standing a bit straighter as he tried to pretend this was just an ordinary conversation. "You said a lot of things about him hurting people, about him changing...your life? Your world? Whatever. How's he doing that, exactly?"

There it was. The biggest question of all. The kid watched him expectantly and for a second Will had to search for the right words. He did not have them, but he was not going to let that stop him now.

"We had found a spell. We never tried it; or at least I didn't. Looking back, I couldn't tell you if Brian did or not." In his mind, the deck shuffled again. Mike Lebo's funeral. Ashleigh's bruises and tears the morning after her rape. "This one spell... According to the book, it was supposed to..." Will took a deep breath and locked eyes with Kyle. "It was supposed to take you back in time."

Slowly, Kyle began to lean backward, looking for something to lean on. He nearly fell over before catching himself on the counter. "You're telling me this guy's done it? Gone back? And he's messing with things then and...and changing them?"

Will nodded, not releasing Kyle from his stare. "And there's only one way to undo it. I have to do the spell myself. I have to go back and stop him from hurting people. I could use help with the spell, Kyle, but there's more to it than that. This place, this house, this was everything to me back then. My home. I know you understand that."

Kyle nodded.

"Just being here in this kitchen, I feel like all I'd have to do is reach out and I could just peel away the time that's passed, wipe it away like a layer of dust has settled in over the years. I'm closer to the past now. More connected. I need to do the spell here. And you need to watch over the spot, so I can find my way back. It's..." He gestured toward the table. "It's all in the book."

"But, my parents," Kyle said, shaking his head. Then he laughed. "I...I want to help. This is completely fucked up, but I do believe you. I've felt that book. . . . I'd never be able to explain it to anyone, but I know there's something powerful in it, something not right. And those notes. And there's something else, too. It *feels* true. It's just... what about my parents?"

Will had already considered this. "We won't do it here. We'll do it in the storage room. Under the porch."

For long moments Will held his breath. Every tick of the clock made it harder for him to hold on to the memories that were slipping away, every second putting more and more distance between him and the past he was determined to alter. All the dangers, all the potential consequences, were on his mind. He knew that he could end up only making things worse. Magic was a tool, and only as subtle as the magician who wielded it.

But he had to try.

So he held his breath until Kyle gave a single, curt nod.

"OK."

CHAPTER 11

"Don't we need candles and stuff?"

Will was halfway down the stairs that led from the back porch to the concrete patio with *Dark Gifts* in one hand and a kitchen carving knife in the other. The bushes that had formed a barrier between the patio and the backyard had been torn down and replaced with a low masonry wall that was attractive but completely unnecessary. It was just as sterile and ugly as the front of the house. Kyle's parents apparently had a bizarre hatred for shrubbery.

He paused on the steps, staring at the patio.

"Will?" Kyle prodded.

"Hmm?" He turned around and saw the kid gazing at him expectantly. Had he asked a question? *Oh, right,* he thought. *Candles.*

"I can't say for certain, and it's been a long time," Will explained, "but I think that crap is mostly for show. I'm not sure if it's for the benefit of the magician or for whatever powers out there in the universe we're supposed to be appeasing. It could also be for focus. I mean, red yarn? Apples? Anyway, we don't need any of that stuff here. I think there are really only a few elements to real magic anyway."

He said this last as he continued down the stairs, and he paused at the bottom to glance back up, waiting on Kyle. The kid had not moved from the top of the stairs. He had a large, heavy flashlight and now he trained the beam on Will, studying him closely, paying particular attention to the knife.

"Like?" Kyle asked.

The knife felt suddenly heavy in Will's hand and he glanced at it, then back at Kyle. "Oh, come on!"

Kyle narrowed his eyes. "You guys had to kill that frog."

Will sighed. "Look, I have no response to this. And no time for it, either. Does the spell require blood? Yeah. But remember how, in order to curse Dori, we needed her blood? This spell requires mine. And a lot of it. Blood, faith, some chanting, and a little artistic skill. All I need from you is some chanting, the holding of the book and the flashlight, some bandages, and then, if it all works, I need you to watch over the circle, make sure nobody fucks with it."

The kid liked to come off as tough but Will saw the hurt in his eyes and instantly regretted getting so harsh with him. But the regret did not last long. There was no room here for regrets, nor for apologies. Later, if it all worked, there would be more than enough time for that.

"Look, Kyle, I need your help. Do I have it or not? Seriously. In or out?"

The boy was thin and sort of gawky, his short orange hair like a marquee that read fuck-with-me, and yet somehow he had managed to overcome that and have a fairly harmless high school career. At least from what Will had been able to decipher. Kyle Brody did not rattle easily.

"Let me get those bandages now. Maybe some disinfectant."

Will nodded. "That'd be great."

Flashlight in hand, he disappeared back inside the house, leaving Will alone on the patio. The moon and stars provided enough light for him to see by even without the flashlight, and when he turned toward that door beneath the porch, he felt the pull of his childhood drawing him toward it. The past was magnetic and it had a magic all its own. He walked to that five-foot-high door with his pulse thumping in his ears, his breathing too loud in his head. The rest of the house had been transformed completely, new flesh built up around the skeleton of his boyhood home.

But this...this was like stepping back through time without the use of any magic other than memory.

"Wow," he whispered breathlessly.

Will tucked the book under his arm and reached for the handle. He'd actually tried to open the door before he noticed the lock and remembered Kyle's talking about it. He placed his hand upon the wood of the door, feeling the paint under his fingertips. How many times had he painted this door himself? Three? Four? The shade was different now, lighter, but in the nighttime, he could barely tell.

Kyle appeared suddenly at his side. Will had not heard him come down the stairs, but now he moved so that the kid could fit the key into the lock. He did not say a word as the door swung open. The flashlight splashed yellow illumination inside the storage area underneath the porch, and he saw trash cans and a rusty bicycle, an old dirt bike and a lawn mower, broken patio furniture that Mr. Brody likely hoped to fix someday, and the glass storm door that would replace the screen at the front of the house when the weather turned cold.

With a soft chuckle, Will shut his eyes tightly and opened them again. His vision adjusted and he saw that there was no dirt bike. That had been an image dredged up from his own mind, a view into the past. It was an old exercise bike that had been relegated to dusty obscurity. Behind the storm door was a metal bed frame, its pieces leaning against the wall, taking up too much space.

"Look familiar?" Kyle asked.

"Like I was here yesterday," Will replied, barely conscious of having spoken.

"We'll have to make some room, I think. How big does this circle have to be?"

Will caught his breath and shook himself from his reverie. It was startling to be here and he felt a surge of warmth in his chest. But much of that good feeling would be lost if he did not defend it. It could be warped, twisted... *he* could be twisted, just like the past.

"Five feet in diameter."

Kyle had his hands on his hips, glancing around and nodding. "We can't move anything out or it'll be noticed. We'll just have to make room."

He went to the rusty bicycle and lifted it, began to shove it along one wall. A moment later, Will went to the broken patio furniture and started to drag it out of the way. At the center of that cramped, low-ceilinged storage space, Kyle reached the single, bare bulb that hung from a beam, grabbed the small chain attached to it, and clicked the light on.

"All right," Will said. "Let's get to work."

SURREAL. That was the one word that kept echoing in the back of Kyle's mind. *What the fuck am I doing down here?* The truth was he did not know the answer to that question. If he wanted to tell this story later, how would he convince any of his friends that it wasn't completely fucking stupid to let some guy he didn't know get him into the storage space under the porch with a goddamned butcher knife in his hand? It was crazy. He was lucid enough to know that. Even if he told them about the note and the book and all of that, they would wonder if he'd somehow gotten brain damage overnight.

But none of them had touched that book, felt the weight of *Dark Gifts* in their hands. None of them had looked into Will James's eyes and known, just *known,* that it was all true.

Yet, even with all of that, there was still a part of him that had detached itself from the proceedings, mentally protesting in the same way he was certain his friends would. In some way, this was all like a dream to him. An exceedingly strange and unnerving dream.

Right up until Will placed the blade of the carving knife

against his palm, resting it there and staring at it with obvious trepidation. The bare bulb under the porch gleamed off of the stainless steel. Will took several long breaths and then lowered his head.

"Shit. I don't know if I can do this."

Kyle blinked, shifted on his perch atop an old patio chair, and it felt to him as though he had just woken up. He glanced at the book and the flashlight at his feet and he started to get up.

"Maybe you shouldn't," he suggested. "I mean, what if . . . you know, what if it doesn't work?" All of a sudden he wanted nothing more than to have this guy out of his house, to get Will James out of his life, on his way, and never have to deal with any of this insane bullshit again. He wanted to pretend he wasn't curious, that the book and the note and Will's story wouldn't haunt him forever.

But he knew it would only be pretending.

So when Will shook his head, took a deep breath to steel himself, and drew the blade across his palm, Kyle did not try to stop him. He only watched, and wondered if he was going to have to take the guy to the hospital, or if he would be able to drive himself with one of his hands sliced open like that.

Will hissed loudly, lips pulled back from his teeth, eyes clenched shut. Blood welled up from the slashed skin immediately, beginning to pool in the cup of his hand.

"Get the flashlight over here," he groaned.

Kyle was breathless, his eyes locked on the knife, on the cut, entranced. But when he looked up to see Will staring at him, that got him moving again. He had put a scrap of paper in *Dark Gifts* to mark the page and now he grabbed both book and flashlight and brought them over. He opened the book to the page Will wanted. It was cold there, under the porch, but the book was as warm as living flesh in his hands, and impossibly light. He propped the book on the floor and held it at an angle so that Will could see it clearly, and then he clicked on the flashlight, the bright illumination washing away any shadows thrown by the single bulb.

On that page was a drawing of a circle with arcing lines within it, and the strangest symbols sketched at what appeared to be strategic locations inside that design. It made no sense at all to Kyle, but now that he had a clear view of it, Will bent to his work, crouching over the concrete floor of the storage area and beginning to re-create the circular design, drawing with his own blood.

The copper smell of it filled the cramped space. Kyle felt a little sick, and shivered as he watched. Will sat on his haunches, holding up his left hand and squeezing it over the floor, letting a steady flow of blood trickle onto the concrete, then using his right index finger to smear the blood, sketching out the circle, making certain it conformed to the image in the book.

The slice in his palm was deep. It took nearly ten full minutes to paint that design on the concrete—ten minutes in which Will had to stop from time to time and open his hand, causing fresh blood to flow again—and he did not stop until it was done. Despite the chill under the porch, Will was sweating, and Kyle wondered if he might pass out.

When the design was done Will stood up as best he could, bent slightly to keep from knocking his head on a beam, and closed his eyes, taking deep breaths. Gritting his teeth, he smeared disinfectant onto the white gauze pad Kyle had given him, then taped the gauze over the slice in his palm. His left fist was closed now, and he knocked it lightly against his hip, as though that might make the pain go away.

Will didn't wait for the blood to dry. He stepped into the center of the circle and sat in one smooth, swift motion, obviously trying not to smear the symbols he had drawn. For several seconds he only sat there, gently nodding to himself the way Kyle had seen some of his friends do when they were drunk or high.

Then Will looked over at him. "I have no idea how long I'll appear to be gone. It could be seconds. Hours. Weeks. I don't have a clue."

If you even go anywhere, Kyle thought. But that wasn't what he said. "I can't stay down here all that—"

"I know you can't. But you can try to keep your father out of here. Make sure the place is locked and that no one gets in but you."

They stared at one another, Kyle suddenly keenly aware of how loud his breathing sounded in that cramped space. Then he nodded. Will gestured toward the book.

"Read it with me. I'll correct your…" he hissed lightly, clutching his left fist against his chest and rocking a bit. "Sorry. I need stitches, I think. Or a healing spell." Will laughed and winced at the same time. "What an idiot."

He focused on Kyle again. "I'll correct your pronunciation."

And he did. Kyle had to creep around, head ducked, and position himself so that he was outside the circle but could still make out the words written on the yellowed page of that terrible book. It chilled him to be so close to Will. The scent of blood was even stronger, and a dark fear began to coalesce in his mind around the idea that if it worked, somehow he could be drawn in as well. Pulled into the past. Trapped there.

They began to read together and when Kyle fumbled over one of the guttural, foreign words, Will helped him until they had it correctly. An ugly, unpleasant thought formed in his mind, that this was not any human language at all, but he was no linguistics expert and he knew how foolish that was. There were hundreds of languages he would not even begin to recognize.

Kyle felt hollow and afraid and oddly fragile, as though a single blow would shatter him. It grew warm, and soon he, too, was sweating. Several minutes after they had begun he finally repeated the spell all the way through without making a mistake, and Will immediately went into it again, pulling Kyle along with the momentum of words. Kyle was completely focused, wanting only to get out of there now, wanting to do it correctly just to have it over with, one way or another.

He concentrated on forming the words, on his voice, on clutching one of the posts that supported the porch above, holding himself away from the circle, just in case. The skin on the back of his neck prickled, and though he was still sweating he felt a sudden chill pass through him. The light from the flash and the overhead bulb seemed to dim, the shadows to thicken, but so intent was he upon his task that Kyle only narrowed his gaze to make certain he did not foul up the words.

At first he did not even notice the way Will's voice seemed to dim with the lights, and then to fade. It was not until it had dropped off almost to a whisper that Kyle became aware of the change. By the time he turned away from the page to look, Will James was little more than a ghostly apparition.

Then he vanished.

All the strength went out of Kyle and he crumbled to the ground. His knee touched the edge of the bloody circle, now dried to brown, and he pulled it back as though stung. He stared at the circle with wide eyes, a light yet impossible breeze moving across his skin as though rushing to fill the space Will James had occupied only a moment before.

WILL DREAMS OF FALLING, air rushing past him, limbs flailing as he tumbles end over end, stomach and fists clenched to prepare for an impact that never comes. Now he cannot breathe. He is falling still, but upward now, and though he knows his eyes are closed he sees stars. Red stars, like crimson tears, or bloody pinholes in the night sky. His lungs burn with the need for air, falling up. . . .

October, Senior Year...

His eyes snapped open and he inhaled, pulling air greedily into his lungs. Will shuddered as he drew another gasping breath. His hands shook as he reached out to steady himself, and only then did he become aware of his surroundings. Pain seared his palm as his fingers touched grass and cool earth. He recoiled from both the pain and from this abrupt attack on his expectations. There had been concrete under him.

Where . . .

Grass and cool earth, and a sheen of dew upon the grass.

Will was no longer in the storage area beneath the back porch of his childhood home. His right hand rose, shaking, to cover his face, and he scraped his palm along the roughness of his chin, staring through splayed fingers at the landscape that surrounded him. In every direction he saw old tombstones, marble and granite grave markers upon which were engraved familiar names. Morrell. Ouellette. Rice. Snowden. At the center of the field of stones was a single statue rising above the rest of the markers, an angel with its face tucked beneath one wing as if in shame, or in mourning. Though he could not see it from here, he knew that the name embossed upon the base of that memorial would be Franzini.

He knew this place.

Trees lined the cemetery on three sides; a wrought-iron fence completed the boundary, separating the cemetery from Cherry Street. The fence had never made any sense to him, however, for the arched entrance had no gate. Anyone could enter. Will had been here a hundred times. The cemetery wasn't far from Caitlyn's house.

You've got to be kidding me.

A rush of disorientation went through him and his stomach lurched. His entire body spasmed and he dropped to his knees, vomit burning his throat as he threw up on the grass. Chills went through him and he shuddered, then sat back and dragged his arm across his mouth.

The tape holding the gauze on his left hand came off and the pad fell away. The long, bloody gash there seemed to wink at him. First things first, he thought, trying to collect himself. In the time they spent exploring *Dark Gifts*, he and Brian had found different interests to focus on. One of the things that Will had been drawn to was healing. Wincing at the pain, he clasped his hands together as if in prayer and muttered the only spell in Gaudet's book that had been written in Latin. He wondered if there was significance in that. When he took his right hand away there was no blood, but his left palm was bisected by a long white scar.

"Jesus," he whispered, taking a steadying breath. He blinked as he glanced around again, trying to fight a new surge of disorientation.

It's real, he thought. *I forgot. I forgot what it was like.*

Will had believed that the spell would work—if he had not believed, then nothing at all would have happened—but he had forgotten the power of real magic. Serious magic. Back in the days when he and Brian had been dabbling with fire and levitation and Will's little healing trick, even when they had cursed Dori, they had never done anything of this magnitude.

"Back...back in time," he whispered, and a light, lilting laugh issued from his lips so abruptly that it surprised even him. In those few moments, he felt more than a little crazy. His hands fluttered around as though trying to find something solid to hold on to. His stomach lurched again and he held his breath, starting to rock forward but fighting the nausea. After a moment it passed, and he took a few steadying breaths.

A battered white van rattled by on Cherry Street with ladders clamped to the roof and a sign on the door that he could not make out from this distance, even as it passed beneath a streetlight. But Will didn't need to read it. He had seen the van plenty of times growing up. The sign on the door said *Murphy Bros. Painting Services* and it belonged to a bearded, beer-drinking guy who lived with his wife and baby daughter a few doors down from Caitlyn's.

That same mad laughter bubbled up inside him again. "Holy shit," he repeated. That van was a piece of his past, but what solidified the truth in his mind was the streetlights. These days they were all covered with a thick plastic shielding, but when he had been a kid in Eastborough they were metal domes with bare bulbs inside. Mike Lebo had once slept over Will's house, and the two boys had taken out every streetlight on Parmenter with a slingshot.

I'm here, Will thought.

But then he frowned and glanced around. *But why here?* The part of him that had no doubt about the reality of all of this had expected to open his eyes and be under the porch of his own house, eleven years earlier. That had been what he had visualized, just as the spell had instructed. Time and place. October, senior year, the night before Mike Lebo was to die.

Will stood slowly, a hand gingerly pressed to his stomach, hoping the nausea was really gone. He glanced around, orienting himself. It had been so many years since he had been here, but in moments the geography began to assert itself in his mind. The paths that led through to Brian's street, the distance to Caitlyn's house and the houses he would pass, and how long it would take him to walk to his own home from here.

Home, he thought. The word resonated within him in a way he had never expected. Before all of the horrors that had happened to him over the past couple of days, Will had been happy with his life. But this place, this time—right until the day he died, these streets and the feeling in the air here would be the definition of home. He tried to picture his parents eleven years younger and in the living room on Parmenter Road, right now, watching *Seinfeld.* Or Ashleigh sprawled on the floor in her bedroom, doing homework. That was home.

Even in this cemetery, absurdly enough, he felt at home.

But why here? Why would the spell—

From the darkness amidst the gravestones farther up the gently sloping cemetery hill, there came a girlish giggle and then a shushing noise. Will stared into the darkness, the shapes of the markers resolving from the shadows, and he started up the slope. The streetlights of Cherry Street did not reach this far.

"Will," a voice said. "Cut it out!"

He frowned. She was talking to him. But how could—

"Hello?" he called.

"Will!" the girl cried, and she shot up from behind the large marble stone that marked the resting place of the Gilmore family.

In the dark he could not make out her features, but her blond hair picked up the moonlight and he knew her by her silhouette. It was Caitlyn. Will held his breath and stared at her, and even as he did a second figure rose from behind the stone.

"Hey," the kid said. "We weren't spying or anything. We just...you all right, mister? Heard you getting sick, and..."

Will took a step backward, then another, and he bumped into a gravestone and nearly fell over. The kid's words trailed off and he put a protective arm around Caitlyn. Will stared at him.

At himself.

It was too much for him, standing there face to face with his own self, eleven years past. Numb and speechless, he backed several more paces away from the couple in the cemetery and then at last he turned and ran, heart pounding, whispering prayers and curses under his breath.

The wind carried his own more youthful voice to him from up the hill. "What the fuck's *his* problem?" asked the young Will James.

The voice was both foreign and familiar, and he recalled how odd it seemed to him every time he dictated notes into a tape recorder and then played them back. His legs pumped beneath him and he nearly tripped over a broken granite slab. Then he was sprinting through the arch and out onto Cherry Street, his chest burning from the exertion. He was out of shape. Not like that kid back in the cemetery. Not like back in high school.

Not like the Will James of *now*.

In his mind he could see the moonlight on Caitlyn's hair, could remember this night—or several like it. He recalled with perfect clarity the scent of vanilla on her neck and how he fumbled to unhook the clasp of her bra with the fingers of one hand. His face flushed as he ran, remembering the perfect smoothness of her breasts and the way she had whimpered when he licked her nipples. Will could practically still feel her hand stroking him through his jeans.

The sense of dislocation nearly paralyzed him, but he shook it off and kept running, passing the houses on Cherry Street, many with their lights on or with the blue flicker of the television inside the windows. A couple of boys, maybe eleven or twelve, sat on the front steps of one house smoking cigarettes they did not even try to hide as he ran past. The boys stared at him and Will stared back, far more astonished by them and by his surroundings than they were by the spectacle of this man running down the street.

Me. That was me. Foolish as it was, the words kept running through his mind. He could picture the outline of his own teenage face in the moonlit cemetery, the arrogant stance, the cocky way he slung his arm around Caitlyn. All he could think about was *A Christmas Carol* and the Ghost of Christmas Past. It was a spell. It was magic. And in that sense Will had thought of this little miracle, this desperate plot to prevent Brian Schnell from altering his own present, as something fantastical and benevolent. The darkness of his past experience with magic had not changed that.

He was filled with an aching sadness and an envy of his old self, of Young Will and all that was in store for him. Meeting him, though, had been profoundly unsettling, and he was having trouble gathering his thoughts, determining what to do next. Will had known he would probably come into contact with his younger self, but had not expected it to happen so soon. Even if he had braced himself properly, he doubted he would have dealt with it any better.

What the hell happened? he thought. *Why did I end up here?*

And then he understood. He had concentrated on the room under his porch, and the spell had brought him to the right day, the right year, but his younger self had acted as an anchor, drawing him to the cemetery. That was the only thing that made sense.

Will tried to focus. He was here now. He had a goal. But how to work toward that goal? He had been angry, afraid, and desperate, had felt himself changing inside.

Changing inside. Am I even that kid anymore? The answer came to him immediately. He was what that kid had become, thanks to his experiences. But by changing his experiences, by taking away his friends and hurting them, Brian was altering who Will had become. The man he was had been forged by his relationships with his family and his friends. Now all of that was being twisted.

He had to stop it, to prevent the crimes that were to be per-
petrated in the coming days. If the spell had transported him to
the night he had focused on, he had twenty-four hours before
Mike Lebo would be dead. Twenty-four hours to intervene, to
make certain events unfolded as they should.

*But you're an idiot. For starters, how the hell are you even going to get
around town?*

Will's lungs burned and his chest hurt. He slowed to a jog and
then stopped entirely, bent over to rest, not daring to turn back
to see if he could still see the little cemetery, to see if Caitlyn
and ... and Will were watching him. He took deep breaths and
then stood up straight.

I'll do what I always did. I'll walk.

He set off toward the center of town. Now that the maelstrom
of his thoughts was beginning to settle, he realized that there was
no way he was going to be able to keep Lebo alive and keep Ashleigh and Tess from being raped unless he had help. If he was going to stick around, he would need a place to sleep and wash up,
not to mention other clothes to wear. Styles hadn't changed so
much that anyone would think his jeans and Red Sox shirt were
out of place, but he couldn't wear the same outfit every day. Plus,
some of the cash in his wallet might be old enough, but most of
the bills were the new design. Something would have to be done
about that. His ATM and credit cards would be useless.

Will was going to have to approach someone, to share the
truth. He knew that there was danger inherent in this plan, that
intruding in any way upon the past was likely to alter the present,
but hard choices had to be made. It was either risk small changes
or allow the sick bastard to rape and kill his friends. No choice
at all, really.

The only question was who he ought to approach. But it
wasn't much of a question. There was only one logical choice.

Now that he had at least the beginnings of a plan, Will
picked up his pace. His mouth tasted of vomit and he felt ex-
hausted, both from the running and, he thought, likely from the
magic as well, but he did not want to waste a moment.

The night was cool but not as chilly as it had felt when he had first regained consciousness in the cemetery. At the bottom of Cherry Street he turned up Ashtree Road. The split-levels, Capes, and ranches of the side streets disappeared and were replaced by old Colonials and even a few Victorians here and there. In the next decade nearly all of them would have been sold and renovated, but here and now most of them were still in need of painting, with lawns that were yellowed and dotted with bare patches.

A collie lunged from the open garage door of 227 Ashtree, claws scraping the pavement as it raced down the driveway trailing a chain behind it. The thing looked like Lassie with mange, and its barking seemed a combination of savagery and panic. Will froze, watching the chain unravel, slinking along the driveway. Finally it snapped tight. The dog let out a yelp and was pulled off its feet, choking.

Will stared at the collie as it stood panting and glaring at him, pulling the chain to its furthest extent. He remembered the dog. Remembered these precise events. The collie had done this to him several times when he had walked the two and a half miles from Caitlyn's to home.

Surreality swallowed him again.

Ashtree took him to the center of town, where it intersected with Winter Street. Will turned left and glanced up at the clock set into the peak of the granite Eastborough Savings Bank building. It was almost half past nine. For several minutes he could only stand on the sidewalk and gaze around, only breathing when he remembered that it was necessary. The windows of the library were dark save for the one just inside the foyer. The librarian, Mrs. Thalberg, always insisted they leave that one light on to discourage vandals.

Will swayed slightly and shook his head. Mrs. Thalberg. He could picture her, a stocky, olive-skinned woman maybe four and a half feet tall whose nylons always made a shushing noise as she patrolled the study carrels making sure the kids were behaving themselves.

He walked slowly along the sidewalk, stepping gingerly as though the entire street might shimmer like heat over summer pavement and simply disappear. The door to Athens Pizza opened and a fortyish woman came out carrying two pizza boxes, followed by twins, a boy and girl of about ten. Will was sure that he recognized them but couldn't remember their names or where they lived. The smell of the pizza was far more familiar. He paused in front of the plateglass window and stared inside. Perry and Arthur, the brothers who ran the place, were behind the counter as always. Perry shouted something at a group of teenagers who sat at a booth, but Will could not make out his words through the glass.

One of the kids at the table was Stacy Shipman.

Will nearly choked on an involuntarily harsh intake of breath. "Stacy," he whispered. An avalanche of emotion and image went through him, not merely from high school but from the previous two days...days that would not come about for eleven more years. In his fear and dread and desperation he had put any thoughts of Stacy out of his head. Now, watching that sly smile, the way she laughed, and the way the spray of freckles across her nose disappeared when she crinkled it up in laughter, he found he missed her. He wanted to find out what was going to happen next.

Next. What a foreign word it was to him at the moment. Next had to be put on hold for now. But just for now.

The nostalgia that the scene inside Athens instilled in him was powerful. He wanted to go inside right then and order a slice, or a roast beef sub the way Perry made them, toasted with butter. It was with great reluctance that he tore himself away from the window.

This isn't your life now. This is then. It's not for you.

The Comic Book Palace was closed, but through the window he could see Glenn, the guy who owned the shop, tallying up the day's receipts at the counter. Will raised a hand to wave to him but dropped it and glanced away quickly, realizing that Glenn wouldn't have a clue who he was.

When he passed by Herbie's Ice Cream, Will did not even have the heart to look inside. It was possible Nick Acosta would be working, and it had been hard enough for him to see himself and Caitlyn... he wasn't ready to see any of the others yet.

On the next block was the strip mall with Annie's Book Stop and The Sampan. But here Will paused and frowned, staring at the front of the store between them. It was a florist—The Flower Cart—with a pretty awning and colorful window displays. The odd part was that he didn't remember it ever having been there. He knew that the shops in that strip had turned over frequently enough; that particular spot had housed a video store, a travel agency, and two separate frame stores. Somewhere in there, he supposed, there must have been The Flower Cart. Obviously it hadn't lasted very long.

A melancholy thought drifted through his mind as he wondered how many other little bits and pieces of his past he had already forgotten, and how much more of it he was likely to lose as the years went by.

Aren't you a ray of fucking sunshine, he thought, and he laughed softly before continuing on.

He crossed to the other side of the road and took a right down Market Street, which was short and dead-ended in the parking lot of Kennedy Middle School, a long rectangular box with windows. In addition to the strangeness of it all, as he walked past the school Will felt almost as though he were haunting the place with his memories. Yet moment by moment the surreal quality that had affected all of his senses from the moment he'd come around in the cemetery seemed to be diminishing. The air around him no longer felt electric. The brick structure of the school was just brick. Real and tangible.

It was not this place that was out of the ordinary, it was Will himself.

Despite everything, he could not help but take pleasure in simply being here. As he walked across Robinson Field behind the school, he glanced up at the night sky and marveled at the stars. Then Will picked up his pace and began to jog. On the far side of the field he found the tear in the chain-link fence and slipped through it, then made his way along the winding path through the woods. He was amazed that even in the dark his memory did not fail him and he navigated without error.

Minutes later he emerged from the woods at the top of Parmenter Road, and his smile broadened. A shiver went through him, and he felt almost giddy. He could picture his parents watching TV in the living room…his father making pancakes on Sunday morning…his mother painting in the little studio she had fixed up for herself in the garage. Al and Diana James had been older than most of the parents of their son's friends, but Will had barely noticed. Now the idea of seeing them then—seeing them here, a decade younger—was fascinating to him.

Will ticked off the names of the families who lived in the houses he passed. Hendron. Panza. Kenney. Carlin. He came around a corner where tall spruce trees blocked his view of the lower half of the street and at last was in sight of his house. He laughed again and shook his head, slowing to a walk once more.

"Son of a bitch," he said. This was what his house was supposed to look like. The triangular walk in front surrounded shrubs and birdbaths, and there were much larger bushes across the face of the split-level home. After his parents retired to South Carolina, the Brodys would tear all of those bushes out and remove the shutters, painting the thing an austere white. But on this night the green shutters were still in place and the house was painted Chatham Sand, a kind of beige Will would always remember the name of because they had spent a number of summer vacations in Chatham on Cape Cod.

This was home.

His steps slowed even further and he took a deep breath, the smile slipping from his features. Of course he could not speak to his parents, could not simply walk up and knock on the door. If he could get a glimpse of them, that would have to be enough. There would be no way for him to stop the horrors of the days ahead without interfering somewhat with the past, without confiding in someone, but he wanted to take as little risk as possible. Talking with his parents would be an unnecessary risk. Unless he could manage to "accidentally" bump into them at the supermarket or something. But that was for later.

Twenty-four hours from now, Mike Lebo was going to be run down by a hit-and-run driver and killed, his skull shattered on the pavement and his ribs crushed by the impact. Right now that had to be his focus.

Will took a deep breath and stepped off the road, away from the streetlights, into the comparative darkness of the Ginzlers' front yard. As he drew nearer to the house in which he had grown up, he could not stop his gaze from roving to the ash tree in the front yard and to the oak from which he had once fallen, earning him a concussion.

And beyond his house, there was a pale blue one with dark shutters that belonged to Herb and Kathy Wheeler. It was Ashleigh's house. Before she had met Eric DeSantis and he had met Caitlyn Rouge, Will and Ashleigh had been inseparable. Even afterward, she had been his best friend. The cleverest, most imaginative girl he would ever know.

Will cut across his lawn and went along the side of the house, then slipped through the darkness of the backyard, happy that his parents had never bought him the puppy he had always asked for. He didn't need any barking dogs at the moment. It unnerved him to be a prowler on his own property, to know that should his mother spot him out the window of her bedroom she would be alarmed, even afraid.

Cautiously he made his way to the line of hedges that separated his property from the Wheelers'. He poked his head through to the other side and studied the rear of the house, the patio, and the tall trees just outside Ashleigh's corner bedroom window on the second floor.

Something shifted in the darkness at the base of the trees and Will froze, narrowing his eyes. A shadow. A silhouette.

Someone else was already there. The shadow reached out to

grab the lowest branch and began to haul himself up into the tree, climbing toward Ashleigh's window.

All the breath went out of Will. Blood rushed to his face. Killing Mike, raping Tess and Ashleigh, all of that had apparently not been enough for Brian Schnell. He had to hurt Ashleigh more. He had come back again. This time, however, he wasn't the only one who knew what the future would hold.

Fury and disgust rippled through Will, and he slipped soundlessly from the hedges and began to rush across the lawn toward the dark figure scrambling up that tree.

This time when he had Brian by the throat, there would be no one to pull him away.

CHAPTER 12

Questions flashed through Will's mind in a confused jumble. The figure in the tree was Brian. One glimpse of his face had been enough to convince Will of that. But from what point in time had Brian returned to this time frame? He had the foolish goatee that Will had seen on him recently, but that proved nothing. Had he already returned to the past and committed the crimes that were to come, and had now made a *second* trip into the past? Or was this his first foray through time? Could Will prevent those crimes by stopping Brian now? Yet as he sprinted across the Wheelers' backyard, those questions were stillborn, buried beneath a torrent of fury and adrenaline. Will breathed in the scent of October, of someone burning leaves and of the chill night air, and he hurtled through the moonlight toward the tree that led up to Ashleigh's bedroom window.

Brian saw him.

"Will?" his old friend whispered. "Oh, shit, Will, hang on." Frantically, Brian began to climb down. Which was an incredibly stupid thing for him to do.

"Son of a bitch," Will muttered as he reached the tree.

He reached up and grabbed the back of Brian's shirt, then

yanked him from his perch. Brian's fingers stretched out, hands scrabbling for purchase, but it was too late. He fell from the branches and landed hard on his back on the grass with a grunt as the air was expelled from his lungs. Brian groaned and began to shake his head even as Will attacked him.

"Stop," Brian rasped thinly, trying to catch his breath. He held up both hands. Will slapped them away, dropped to his knees, and hauled on the front of Brian's shirt.

"Stop?" he hissed. "Did that work when you were raping Ashleigh? What about with Tess?"

His vision seemed to tunnel then, the night deepening around him so that he could see only Brian. Will hit him three times in rapid succession, clutching his shirt with his left fist and striking with his right. Blood and spittle sprayed from Brian's mouth and there were strings of it in his thin goatee.

"Jesus, Will, stop," Brian wheezed. "It wasn't me. I swear to—"

Will wrapped his hands around Brian's throat and began to choke him. The pleading in Brian's eyes only maddened him further, and he slammed the man's head against the ground again and again, feeling thick corded muscles beneath his fingers and digging deeper into his throat.

A hideous little laugh burst from Will's lips. "Wasn't you? How stupid do you think I am?"

But even as he spoke these words, Will moved ever so slightly, so that the full light of the moon could shine upon Brian's bloodied features. There were multiple bruises there, some of them several days old. A single tear slipped out the side of Brian's right eye and slid, glistening in the moonlight, along his temple to drop into the grass. Without even realizing it, Will began to relax his grip on Brian's throat.

Changing his past had changed him. Will knew that. The violence and heartache that had been wrought upon his memories had tainted him. *But how much?* he wondered. *Just how much?*

Teeth gritted in confusion and anguish, he bent over Brian and met his gaze with a primal hatred that unnerved him. "Who else could it have been? I was there, Brian. We were in it together, remember? I saw the look in your eyes when we cursed Dori, and when we promised each other we'd never go near magic or that fucking book again. You had a hard-on for it the way you never did for anything or anyone else."

Brian nodded frantically, licking blood from his lips. When he spoke it was in gasps. "I did. I . . . I liked it, Will. And I lied. I didn't stop."

"And now you've gone too far," Will snarled.

"No," Brian shook his head. "I swear I—"

Will cracked a backhand across his face that sent a satisfying spike of pain through his own knuckles. Brian shook it off, his trepidation being replaced by anger now. He glared up at Will and spat a wad of bloody saliva into his face.

"Listen to me, you dense son of a bitch!" he roared.

On instinct, Will held him down and turned to look up at Ashleigh's window. A figure moved past the glass. She had to have heard, but with the light on she wouldn't be able to see out into the darkness of her backyard.

The room went dark.

"Shit," Will snapped. He glared down at Brian, then grabbed him by the arm and hauled him to his feet. "Come on."

The last thing he needed was for Ashleigh to have him arrested.

Will hustled Brian across the Wheelers' backyard toward the line of tall bushes that separated it from his own, back the way he had come. Brian did not fight him. If anything, he moved faster than Will. They slipped through the bushes and Will spun him around.

"Not a sound," he whispered in the dark.

They stood still, Will listening to the ragged breathing of this man, this guy who had once been his friend, who had lied to him, who had killed and raped and violated every natural law.

Yet there in the darkness, with the scents of October and evergreen in his nostrils, all he could think about were the times they had thrown snowballs or crabapples at passing cars and had to run to hide in bushes or behind houses. How many times had they stood, partially hunched just as they were now, breathing heavily but grinning widely, barely able to catch their breath enough to laugh, waiting in silence for the danger of discovery to pass?

"Hello?"

Ashleigh's voice, a stage whisper, was carrying across the back-yards. Will had often used the tree in the back to climb up and see her. They would talk quietly, him hanging in the branches and Ashleigh sitting comfortably in her window seat. He had learned more of her secrets and her hopes and her fears there in that intimate darkness than anywhere else. Later, Eric had visited her up that tree as well, sometimes slipping into her room, and other times Ashleigh had slipped out. But that wasn't the same. Though he had never been able to say exactly why, Eric's visits had spoiled it for Will, and he had for the most part stopped climbing that tree. He could always talk to Ashleigh on the phone or just ring the doorbell.

It just wasn't the same.

Now, as she called out into the darkness, Will was struck by her voice. Sometimes he dreamed they were all kids again, but in his dreams none of the details was ever right. The truth was, though it saddened him, many of the details were lost to him. He had forgotten what Ashleigh's voice had sounded like at seventeen. For a moment, when she spoke, he couldn't breathe. The world went off kilter and his equilibrium shifted; conflicting memories flickered through his mind, colliding with the truth of his presence here.

"Shit." He sighed. *Enough of that. There's no going back now.*

"Is anyone out there?" Ashleigh whispered.

Will did not dare try to catch a glimpse of her. His grip on Brian's shirt had loosened, and his fingers were wet with Brian's blood. As his heartbeat slowed and the adrenaline rush subsided, he glanced at his old friend's bruised and bloodied face. Brian stared at him intently, despair etched upon his features.

"Listen," Brian whispered.

Will's nostrils flared and he tightened his grip, shaking Brian. "Quiet."

Brian's lips peeled back in a distorted grin, his goatee giving him a devilish air. "Asshole," he murmured. His right hand came up quickly, fingers curled, contorted. He spoke another word, one Will did not understand.

Will lifted off the grass, pitched forward, but did not hit the ground. Reflexively he let go of Brian and found himself levitating three feet in the air. A shout of alarm and anger came to his lips but he held it back, mindful of Ashleigh, wondering if her window was still open. Wide-eyed, he stared at Brian as doubt seeped into his mind.

"You could've done this anytime?" he asked.

Brian ran a hand through his dark hair, gingerly touched his split lip and winced, pulled his fingers back, and looked at his own blood glistening in the moonlight.

"Not anytime," he said. "It isn't easy. It makes me tired. And I have to be able to concentrate. You didn't give me much of a chance."

They spoke in the smallest of whispers and Will's doubts grew. Brian had been willing to take off instead of being discovered by Ashleigh. He had cooperated in remaining quiet. Will stared at him.

"I'm listening."

A dark, unpleasant chuckle came from Brian's throat. "You don't have a choice."

With that, he waved his hand through the air and Will collapsed upon the ground with a grunt. Brian poked his head through the bushes and then withdrew, crouching by Will's side.

"She's got her light back on," he said, wincing from the pain in his face, tracing a finger from his jaw to his left ear, perhaps an aching jaw muscle. Then he let out a short breath and focused on Will again. "I felt it, too. I mean, I'm assuming that's what happened to you. Memories changing. The past...changing. It's like someone's overwriting the disk of this week in my...in our lives."

"Like shuffling cards," Will suggested, putting voice to the image that had been with him all along. "Taking the familiar ones and replacing them with a new hand."

But still his eyes were narrowed with suspicion.

Brian nodded. "I wanted to talk to you at the football game, but there were too many people around. Plus I...well, I figured it was you. I mean, who else could it be? So I had to assume it was you, right up until you came into Papillon and fucking attacked me." He touched the old bruises high on his right cheek. "That was quite a spectacle. I was too confused to try any magic, not that I would've done anything in front of everyone anyway. And I understood why you were doing it."

An unpleasant smile flickered across his features. "But that's a conversation for later." Brian sat cross-legged on the grass. The autumn wind carried his whispered words so that it seemed he was speaking directly into Will's ear. "You didn't show up at brunch the day after the debacle at Papillon. Obviously everyone was worried about you. Caitlyn talked to Ashleigh. Danny had been over to your apartment. None of your neighbors had seen you. On Monday, Ashleigh called Caitlyn back and told her you hadn't shown up at work."

Will's stomach did a queasy flip. "So I don't get back?"

Brian shrugged. "You wouldn't necessarily get back at the same time you left. On the other hand, it's possible you came back here and blew it completely." He ran his tongue over his swollen, bloody lips. "I knew what was happening. No way to explain it to anyone else, of course. But one look at your face Saturday night, the things you'd said, and then you go missing? I knew you had to have done it. And since you hadn't come back, I thought you might need some help."

He gestured toward his battered face. "In exchange, I get a tune-up."

Will couldn't help smiling. "A tune-up? You've been watching too many cop shows."

"That's what you always say."

The humor drained out of Will. It was too strange, too awkward to be Brian's friend right now. "I used to. 'Cause it was true." They sat there in the darkness, hidden from the Wheelers' house by the bushes but in full sight of the Jameses' back porch. The house was quiet, though there was the blue flicker from his parents' television in their bedroom window. Will wondered what time it was.

"I'd done the spell before. Just once," Brian said, unable to meet Will's eyes. "I wanted to see my grandfather again."

Will nodded. "That's how you could do the spell without having the book."

"Once you've done it—"

"It marks you," Will finished. He glanced down at himself as though he might see the invisible traces left on him by the magic he and Brian had performed years before. It had left scars beneath the skin.

"The spell left me right on my front steps," Brian said, brow furrowed in contemplation. "I guess it matches you up with the location of your…earlier self. Good thing it didn't plunk me down on the couch next to my old self. Not sure I could've dealt with that."

Will said nothing. He didn't want to think about himself and Caitlyn in the cemetery. There were things he was just going to have to deal with, but he wanted to take them one at a time.

"So you came over here thinking you could get Ashleigh's help. You figured you needed transportation, maybe money, a change of clothes."

Brian nodded.

"Why Ashleigh?" Will asked. "You guys weren't that tight."

"I knew you'd come back already. I didn't know what day, but I figured we'd both try to get here before all the terrible shit started happening," Brian said. "I knew if you needed help, you'd come to Ashleigh. The young me or the young you, we'd have a hell of a time convincing them. We were arrogant little shits. But Ashleigh...she had more imagination than she ever let on. And she loved you more than anything. You could convince her. And if you hadn't shown up yet, I figured I could convince her, and if I couldn't, I could tell her you needed her help and at least she'd listen to me before calling the cops."

They stared at one another. Will lifted his chin and regarded Brian carefully. "You know this doesn't make any sense. This isn't random. We had that damned book. Me and you. Now someone's using the magic in *Dark Gifts* to tear our lives apart...to hurt people from our past..." He glanced around. "From here and now. It's got to be connected to us, or connected to that book, or both. Your memories are shifting, but unless you're the guy responsible, you don't know the whole story. You know somebody killed Mike Lebo. But Tess was raped."

He lowered his voice even further so that it was barely audible, even to his own ears.

"And so was Ashleigh."

When Will looked up and saw the stricken expression on Brian's face, the pain in his eyes, he could almost force himself to believe his old friend had nothing to do with the terrors that were to come in the days ahead. Brian said nothing, just sucked air in through gritted teeth as though he had been cut or stung. Then Brian shook his head and met his gaze again, as if defying Will to accuse him of such heinous acts.

"There's more," Brian said.

Will flinched and felt his throat constrict. "What do you mean, more?"

"First tell me what happened to Ashleigh and Tess."

As quickly as he could, Will sketched out the sequence of events from the football game: his seeing Tess in the parade and Caitlyn in the crowd, only to have his memories and reality twisted a short time later when Ashleigh revealed what had happened to Tess.

Brian frowned. "But Caitlyn was Homecoming Queen. Are you saying..." He put a hand to his head. "Shit." He nodded.

"Right. Two versions of that. It was Tess, originally. So she dropped out because she was ... was raped."

Will stared at him, studying that face and those eyes in which he saw the echo of his own trepidation. "You said there was more. What did you mean?"

"You did the spell Saturday night. I was around until Monday, remember? I stuck around forty-eight hours longer in our present than you did. In that time, something else changed. Another ripple from the past..." He glanced around, unnerved. "From here. Another ripple from here that altered my memories but somehow hasn't reached you yet."

Will's throat was dry and tight. "What? What else happens?"

"Do you remember Bonnie Winter?"

Something tugged at the back of Will's mind, a memory, and then images crashed inside his head. As if it were a virus that passed from Brian to Will, the new memories raced through him.

Bonnie Winter.

A cool, crisp autumn morning—the Monday after Homecoming—and they arrive at school. Walking through the parking lot they see her, in the shade of the building beneath a towering oak tree. Gold and brown and red leaves blow in the breeze, rustling as they dance around the corpse of Bonnie Winter, her naked flesh gray with death, eyes eternally wide. Her limbs are hideously contorted and a single ant crawls across the gentle slope of dead skin just above her pubic mound.

His chest hurt, all the air in his lungs rushing out as he sat down on the cold ground.

"Jesus, no," he whispered.

Graduation day, Bonnie Winter had kissed him and handed him a note. On it, in her unique, barely legible scrawl, she had written: *Will, now that we're graduating I can finally tell you I've had a crush on you for four years. You're a cutie. Great to know you. Good luck!*

But a dead hand could not have scrawled those words. Dead lips could not have kissed him, red tresses gleaming in the sunlight on graduation day.

He stared up at Brian's bruised features and did not know if he could believe the sympathy he saw there. *Bonnie. Jesus.* The memory of her corpse made his stomach convulse but he forced the image from his head.

"You still think it's me?" Brian asked.

Will stared at him. "I know it isn't me. If it isn't you, I don't have the first clue where to start. You understand why I can't trust you?"

Brian nodded. "Isn't it interesting, though, that I trust you? What does that say?"

Eyes narrowed once again, Will at last climbed to his feet, glaring down at Brian. "Both of us dirtied our hands with magic, Brian. It tainted us. We promised to stay away from it. The difference is, I kept that promise."

Brian scowled. "By using magic! By casting a spell so you could hide from the truth. You're telling me that's somehow more noble than just dealing with it, the way I did?"

This time Will could not meet his eyes. "Maybe not. Guess that depends on exactly what you've done with it since then. Maybe you just liked it too much." He looked up. "So if I'm not ready to believe that the only obvious suspect in goddamn magical time-travel rapes and murders is completely fucking benevolent, maybe you should just cut me some slack."

Once more Brian smiled, and Will did not like that smile at all. "Touché."

Will wrinkled his nose. "Since when did you talk like that? Is that music-industry-asshole talk? Nobody says touché except in the movies."

"Not even on cop shows?"

Will rolled his eyes.

"So, now what?" Brian asked, rising to his feet, the moon once again illuminating his battered features.

"Now?" Will replied. He stepped between two bushes and gazed at Ashleigh's bedroom window. "Now? For a start, we keep Lebo alive."

ASHLEIGH KNEW what she had heard.

Voices. Shouting. A scuffle, possibly a fight. If she had been alone in the house, or if she hadn't been used to boys showing up in her backyard, she would have been anxious, even frightened. Instead, she was curious and more than a little suspicious that some mischief was afoot. Her boyfriend, Eric, was far too laconic to be playing some practical joke on her.

Will was another story. Fooling around in her backyard was just his style, particularly if he was hanging out with Danny, or with Mike Lebo and Nicky Acosta. Nick would've done anything to get a glimpse of Ashleigh in the tank top and panties she always wore to bed. Will, on the other hand, had seen her dressed like that a hundred times and never seemed to notice.

Of course, if the boys had had a few beers, it wouldn't be hard for Nick to talk Will into leading them all on a covert mission up the tree outside Ashleigh's window. She wasn't a flashy girl like Caitlyn or flirtatious in the way that Pix and Lolly were, but she wasn't above relishing the idea that the boys might want to have a peek at her.

Not that she would let them.

Before she turned her bedroom light back on, Ashleigh slipped into a pair of sweatpants. Now she lay on the bed reading *Dune*, but her mind was not entirely focused on the sand worms of Arrakis. Even as her eyes followed the words on the page, her ears were attuned to sounds outside her window. The breeze rustled the leaves, and though the house was only a few decades old it popped and creaked from time to time, so it was difficult for her to discern what sounds might be coming from outside. Still, she felt certain that after that first round of scuffling and voices, she had heard other, quieter sounds, from farther away.

A tiny smirk appeared at the corner of her mouth and she reached up to push a stray lock of brown hair away from her face. This was why she wore her hair in a ponytail when she was reading.

Boys and beer, she thought, *are a hilarious combination.*

With a glance at her window, Ashleigh settled further into her bed, the book propped on her chest. Though it was early autumn yet, her parents had already put the heat on in the house and it was nice to have the cool breeze coming in through the window. As she read about intergalactic politics and sand and spice, the words began to blur on the page and her eyelids fluttered. Her chin nodded drowsily, and several times she snapped her eyes open and tried to focus on the page again. When she had read the same paragraph half a dozen times, she surrendered and slipped her marker into the book and set it down on her nightstand.

"Ashleigh?"

The voice was like the whisper of the wind. The first time he spoke she was not even certain she had really heard it. Perhaps, she thought, it had been the rustling of the leaves outside the window.

But then she heard her name called again, ever so softly, and she shivered, a sour twist to her lips. All of the amusement she had felt only a short time earlier left her. It had to be Will, or Eric, or maybe one of the other guys. But that whisper gave her no familiar voice to latch on to, and there was something dark and insinuating about the way he called to her. There was none of the urgency Will or Eric would have had, yet a great sense of caution.

With some trepidation she clicked off the lamp at her bedside. Though she knew she was wearing her sweatpants she still glanced down self-consciously to reassure herself, the same way her mother always checked that the front door was locked before they left, and then checked once or twice more, as if once wasn't enough.

Ashleigh went to the window and peered out into the darkness of her backyard. The moon was not full, yet it was bright enough to cast the trees and bushes in ominous silhouettes. Nothing moved in the dark, and her heart drummed a staccato rhythm as a strange dread enveloped her. There was something wrong here. Though it wasn't the sort of thing she shared with her friends, she had always had a sense about such things.

And yet...

At the edge of the Wheelers' property was a stretch of woods that ran behind all of the homes on this side of the street. As she surveyed the yard, there came the snap of a branch and the rustle of underbrush from those woods. An animal, she was sure, but when she peered into the woods there was a shadow darker than all the others, a silhouette that was not a tree or a bush. It was human.

She felt it watching her.

The silhouette moved, darting abruptly behind a pine tree. Ashleigh uttered a small gasp and flinched as the lurker disappeared.

She heard her name called again, and was startled to realize that it came from directly below the window. Startled and relieved. Her eyes ticked back and forth between the woods on the other side of the yard and the few trees just outside her window. One hand had flown up to cover her mouth when she had glimpsed the silhouette in the woods. Now she lowered it and pressed her forehead against the screen, trying to peer downward to get a glimpse of whoever was down there.

"Who is it?" she whispered.

"It's Will."

Ashleigh shuddered. "It doesn't sound like Will."

There was a pause. "I...something's happened, Ash. Something...pretty unbelievable. I need your help."

His whispers were rasped and his voice low and grim, but now that he had spoken further she thought it might be Will after all. Ashleigh glanced at the door to her bedroom, careful to keep her voice low so that her parents would not hear her.

"Are you sick? You don't...you don't sound like yourself."

Another pause. "I don't look like myself, either."

Barely aware she was doing it, Ashleigh slid her hands up her arms and hugged herself, a chill spreading through her body. Something unpleasant fluttered in her stomach. Her gaze ticked toward the woods, but the silhouette still had not returned and she had to wonder if she had seen anything there at all. It might have just been a tree branch swaying in the breeze. The alternative was far too unsettling to consider. If there was a lurker, he was likely still there, spying on her window.

"What…what's that mean, Will? You're scaring me."

"I don't mean to."

"Why didn't you just climb the tree like you used to?"

No answer, though she could hear him now, moving around at the base of the tree out there. She pressed her face against the screen again, trying to get a glimpse of him. And then she knew.

"It's because of what you just said, wasn't it? You look different?"

"Yes."

Fear raced through her then. Fear for him. "Oh, my God, Will. What happened?"

"I'll be OK. But I do need your help," he replied, his whispers floating up to her. "Ashleigh, listen. If I…if I didn't look like me…I know it sounds freaky, but if I didn't look like me, what's the one question you could ask me so I could prove it was me?"

The question unnerved her but her mind began to work at it immediately. What was it that no one else would know but Will? He had read portions of her diary, but there wasn't much that was secret inside it, really. Will knew so much about her, when she first got her period, when she had first experimented sexually with Eric…hell, he knew what she had gotten for her birthday every year for her entire life. An image floated across her mind, a glass Coke bottle spinning on a wooden picnic table behind Connie Laurent's house.

"Ashleigh?" that strangely familiar voice rasped.

"Have you ever kissed me?" she asked, peering down into the darkness beneath the trees.

Seconds passed. During that time she realized it was a stupid question. There was a fifty-fifty chance he would guess the right answer, whether it was Will or not.

"I don't look like me." What the hell does that mean?

"No. Not in the way that you mean. I've kissed you, but just, y'know, as friends."

"Did we ever come close?"

This time there was no hesitation. "Yes. Playing spin the bottle at Connie Laurent's. We went behind the fence, but we didn't kiss. It just would've been too weird."

A prickling sensation spread across the back of her neck and Ashleigh found that rather than relief, she felt only more anxious and hesitant. His voice was just wrong. It was Will, but not Will; even whispered, she could tell that.

"Will...I mean, *you* could have told someone."

"I didn't, Ashleigh. Not ever. It wasn't anybody else's business."

"I'm...I'm afraid, Will. If you are Will. I think I should close the window now."

"No!" he called, his voice rising from a whisper though not quite a shout. "Sorry. Shit," he whispered. "Ashleigh, please, ask me something else."

Her eyes closed and she rested her forehead against the window frame. She hugged herself again, and she could feel the gooseflesh on her arms. Will was her best friend, even now. What would be so private that—

"I've got it," she said.

"Ask me."

Ashleigh opened her eyes. She peered into the darkness below, and through the trees and the leaves for the first time she thought she saw a figure. In the night she could not tell, but he seemed too tall to be Will.

"I don't look like me."

"My ninth birthday. What did you get me?"

His sigh was audible even on the second floor. "Jesus, Ash, I don't remember. It was a...it was a long time ago. But... your ninth birthday? I remember you cried that day. You cried a lot."

Her throat went dry and though she wanted to, she could not close her eyes. When she swallowed, it hurt her.

"Do you...do you remember why?"

There was a long pause this time. At length, another whisper carried up to her. "I'm not alone, Ashleigh. I don't know if you'd want me to talk about it."

She froze. "Who's there? Who's with you?"

"Brian."

Her brow furrowed in confusion and she tried to get a better look out the window. She traced her fingers along the base of the screen, tempted to remove it, to thrust her head out and try to see them.

"Brian?"

Another voice, then. Not at all familiar. "Hello, Ashleigh."

"Has...has something happened to you, too?"

"Yes. Yeah, I guess that's one way to put it."

She was more than a little freaked out. Forget about closing the window; her mind had now moved on to the possibility of calling the police. But then it occurred to her that the question she had asked...that was one only Will would ever know. He would never have told anyone that story. No way.

"Brian. Can I trust you to cover your ears?" she asked. It was insane. It didn't even sound like Brian. How could she trust him? But the alternative—completely panicking—would be a bad idea if it turned out that something awful really had happened to Will.

"Yeah. I'll cover them. Got 'em covered now."

"Answer the question, Will," Ashleigh said. She bit her lip gently and her chest hurt. She did not want to talk about this, didn't want to remember.

"It was..." Will began hesitantly, "it was the last time your father ever took a drink. He forgot your birthday. He ate part of your cake. And he...he hit your mother. Your mom, she canceled the party, but you begged her to let me come over. I was the only one there with you, and..."

Ashleigh felt the edges of her eyes burn with unshed tears. "And you held me while I cried." She covered her mouth again and then reached to begin removing the screen. "Will, what is it? What's happened to you? Come up. I'll help. Of course I'll help."

He hesitated only a moment, and then he began to climb. Ashleigh saw the dark figure clutching branches, hauling himself up. Too broad in the shoulder to be Will. But different as it was, the voice was his. And only Will would have known...only Will had held her when her heart was broken.

A snapping of branches across the yard drew her gaze and she spotted it, that same dark silhouette, moving amongst the woods. The figure quickly darted deeper into the woods and then was gone.

"What the hell..." she began slowly, speaking mostly to herself.

From beneath her, climbing nearer the window, Will spoke. "Happened to me? You asked that already. The answer's simple, but hard to take."

Ashleigh looked down and she saw him, his face illuminated by the glow from her bedroom. It was Will's face, no doubt about it. But different. Older. More rugged. This was not a boy, but a man.

"What happened is, I grew up."

All the breath went out of Ashleigh's lungs. A spasm passed through her and dizziness made her stumble backward. Ashleigh believed that people only fainted in the movies, and so she did not faint. Instead, she said a silent, barely formed prayer as all the feeling went out of her legs and she collapsed, eyes wide with horror. She scrambled backward, sliding across the wood floor, and she began to hyperventilate.

Ashleigh pulled her legs up beneath her and hugged them to her, turning to face the wall, her back to the window.

But she did not wake up.

The nightmare did not go away.

"Ashleigh," whispered this man...Will James. "Please."

Her heart trip-hammered in her chest, but she could not deny what she had seen. That face. And what she had heard. His voice and his words and the truth that he had known.

He spoke to her.

And Ashleigh listened.

CHAPTER 13

"You've got to be kidding me."

Kyle stared at the place where Will James had been, a weird, manic grin spreading across his features and a mad little laugh bubbling up from his throat. His body went slack and he just sat there, smiling, running one hand through his hair.

"No way. No. Way."

But his denials were only perfunctory. There was no doubt in his mind as to what he had just seen. Magic. As impressive as the flame-in-hand Will had brandished earlier had been, this was the big time. Serious mojo. Kyle was almost numb with amazement. *Holy shit,* he thought. *Unbelievable.*

So much of his connection to Will James—the note and the book and all of that stuff—had been so creepy, even frightening, that this giddiness that swept over him now was a relief. He shook his head and gazed in admiration at the circle and symbols, all painted in Will's blood. The memory of Will slicing open his own hand was fresh in Kyle's mind, and he had to hand it to the guy, that move had taken more than a little faith and slightly less than all his marbles.

"Wow," Kyle whispered.

The giddy sensation began to subside, and his smile disappeared as he thought about what Will had told him, about the purpose of this bit of sorcery. Silently, he wished the man luck. In all his life, nothing like this had ever happened to Kyle. And it wasn't just the magic. He played it cool because that was how a pale, lanky kid with orange hair had to play it to avoid being completely tortured by his classmates. But he had always had this sense that his life was going to be boring.

Ordinary.

There was nothing ordinary about this.

Despite the unsettling truths about the world he had learned in recent hours, for the first time Kyle Brody thought that perhaps his life was not going to be quite so boring after all. Perhaps it was this factor that caused him to approach his obligation to Will James with a gravity and maturity he had never exhibited toward anything else. Whatever it took, he would safeguard this place until Will returned, and not a word to his parents. This guy's life . . . and the lives of some of his friends . . . might be depending on Kyle. It had happened almost too fast for him to understand the weight of that burden, but now that he did, he could only accept it.

As he began to come down from the high of seeing magic performed, seeing a man slip through time, other concerns began to assert themselves. He was staring at the bloody circle, at those symbols, and it really sank into him what his parents would think if they happened to come into this cold, stooped little room and discovered Will's occult scrawl.

Minutes went by. Kyle stared at the spot where Will had disappeared, but it quickly became obvious to him that unlike in time travel stories he'd read, Will James was not going to pop right back up only moments after he'd left. Soon he grew anxious and started to bounce his heel on the concrete, his leg rising and falling incessantly. It was a nervous habit that drove his mother crazy, particularly when it signified his desire to leave the dinner table.

The complications of all of this began to present themselves.

Will hadn't had a clue what to expect after he'd performed the spell. He'd left it all for Kyle to figure out, and the clock was ticking. His parents could come home any time now. They'd been out to Ken's for dinner with friends; if they lingered, or if they decided on another bottle of wine, they might be there for another hour yet. But if they didn't, they might pull into the driveway at any moment.

"Shit," Kyle snapped, and he got up and hustled, hunched over, to the door. Leaving the light on he slipped onto the patio, ears attuned for the sound of his parents' car arriving.

As fast as he was able he slipped up the back porch steps and into the house. His heart had picked up a strange rhythm, a combination of fear and excitement and guilt. In the living room he paused to glance out the picture window at the darkened street. No sign of any cars. Kyle took several breaths, steadying himself, and then as if at the sound of a starter gun he sprinted down the short corridor and into his parents' bedroom. His mother had a long, squat dresser—what they called a lowboy—with a mirror on it. His father's was a tallboy. On top of the bureau were a nice steel-banded watch, a bunch of loose change, and some receipts his father had unceremoniously dumped from his pockets.

No keys.

His dad didn't keep the key to the storage area on the ring with his house and car keys but instead on a separate, flimsy metal ring that also had a key to the garage, which they never locked, and to the snowblower. Kyle could feel his pulse in his throat and the tips of his fingers as he rifled through the top drawer of his father's tallboy, where his dad kept rings and batteries and keepsakes, matches and—in a container that could have passed for a harmonica box—a small vibrator.

Kyle shuddered at the memory of his first discovering the vibrator. It was just too much damn information. But as his fingers brushed the box aside, the keys scraped the bottom of the drawer. He snatched up the small ring and quickly worked the key to the storage area off of it, then hid the ring behind a pack of playing cards and reorganized a few other things to keep the ring from sight. If his father was going through the drawer, he wouldn't notice right off that a key was missing if he didn't notice the ring itself.

A phone began to ring, but it was not the house phone. It was the trill of his mobile, which was still stashed in his backpack because he had not used it since coming home from school the previous day. He darted across the hall to his own bedroom, grabbed the backpack, and fished through it for the phone. He missed the call, but that wasn't really his priority at the moment.

Back in the kitchen, Kyle dialed his own home phone number, even as he grabbed a Coke from the fridge and a bag of pretzels from the cabinet. The house phone started to ring and he nodded impatiently, silently urging it on as though he had just instantly developed some kind of freaky telekinetic power that could cause the answering machine to cut in quicker. On the fourth ring, it picked up. He listened to his mother's voice on the machine.

"Hi guys, it's just me," he said at the beep, trying to disguise the fact that he was a bit breathless. "I hope you don't mind, but I'm gonna spend the night at Ben's. We rented a bunch of horror movies and we're gonna have a gore-fest, with blood and popcorn. Mom, I know how much you love this stuff, so, y'know, come on over." He laughed nervously and wondered if they would hear the falseness of it in the message. "Anyway, I'll call in the morning. See you tomorrow."

He cut off the call, paused, and stared at the phone a moment, then clicked it over from ring to vibrate. He was going to be right underneath them. If they heard the phone ringing, that would blow the whole thing.

With Coke and pretzels in hand, Kyle left the kitchen and went quietly out the back porch door. Just as he was going down the stairs, he heard the sound of car doors closing out in front of the house. His heart beat like hummingbird's wings and he crept as silently as possible down to the patio. As he opened the door to the storage area he could hear his parents laughing about something as they approached the front door.

Too close, he thought.

And he closed himself in for the night, too late remembering that he had no pillow and no blanket, and that it was going to be cold in the small hours of the morning.

For several minutes he sat on the concrete, breathing slowly. Then he took out his cell phone again and quietly dialed Ben's number.

October, Senior Year...

"You *know* you're not supposed to fuck around with the time stream. It's in every movie."

Will stared through the screen at Ashleigh. She looked so young to him it was hard to imagine this was their senior year. There was something precious about her, something she lost as she grew older. Of course, he suspected that was true of all of them.

"It wasn't my idea," he replied, his voice just loud enough for her to hear him over the music she had put on to cover their conversation so her parents wouldn't hear. "I hate magic. I told you the whole story already."

Ashleigh studied his face. "Yeah. You did. And I get it, Will."

He was in awe of her, and it must have shown on his face, for she became self-conscious and lowered her gaze.

"Why are you staring at me like that?" she asked.

Will laughed softly. "Please. Like you weren't staring at me? I'm just amazed that you're taking this as well as you are."

A slightly hysterical giggle bubbled from her lips and she clapped one hand over her mouth. Over the top of her hand her eyes were more than a little crazy and she breathed as though she feared she had forgotten how.

"Ashleigh, what...I didn't mean to—"

She waved him to silence, at first staring at him and then tearing her gaze away. She pulled away from the window and paced the bedroom in her white tank top and blue cotton sweats. Will could not tear his eyes away, but there was nothing prurient in his interest. Or very little, at least.

With her back to him she first lowered her chin, her pony-tail sliding off her shoulder to hang beside her face. At length she threw her head back and took a deep breath. Will was gravely concerned for her. The girl had freaked out when she had first gotten a look at his face but she had not screamed, had not called for her parents or the police. Once she had calmed down enough and the strength had returned to her legs, she had gingerly approached the window and in hushed tones had demanded that he explain, that he make her believe in the impossible, in magic.

He had thought she was taking it all very well indeed.

Now Ashleigh turned toward the window again, still hugging herself. She glanced at her CD player, as though expecting it to perform some strange action. Then she shook her head again. Her eyes narrowed and abruptly she strode across the room. Will watched the decisive expression on her face as she worked the screen free and removed it from the window. She turned and slid it under her bed.

Will was confused. The last thing he wanted was to upset her more. Did she want him to come inside? Before he could ask, Ashleigh came over to kneel in front of the window in her bare feet, her sweatpants gathering dust from the hardwood floor.

"Don't move," she instructed him.

The plea in her eyes at that moment broke his heart. Will loved his friend Ashleigh DeSantis, professional woman, wife, and mother of twins. But only now, in this moment, inches away from this sweet, clever, baby-skinned high school kid, did he realize how much he missed Ashleigh Wheeler, the girl next door.

Her right hand fluttered up as though out of her control, but then she seemed to recover herself, for she reached out through the open window. Her long, slender fingers traced his features as though she were a blind woman. Will flinched at her touch and another rush of emotion filled him. He had told Ashleigh the facts, the sequence of events, but only what she absolutely had to know. That people would be hurt. That people would die if he and Brian did not do something to stop it. He hadn't told her what could happen to her . . . or what her life would be like if he couldn't prevent that.

Ashleigh ran her fingers over the stubble on his chin.

"Let me see your hand," she said.

Will raised his left hand, resting it on the windowsill.

"No. The other one."

He clung to the branches of a tree he had climbed hundreds of times as a kid, yet his hip hurt where he leaned against the exterior of the house, and his right arm was slung over a thick branch at an angle that made his armpit hurt. *I'm twenty-eight*, he thought. *Jesus, what the hell is fifty-eight going to feel like?* Not that he expected to be climbing trees then.

It took some doing to twist around so that he could switch hands. When he reached up with his right hand, she took it and held it in both of hers. Her fingers traced his palm and then turned it over. With her index finger she seemed almost to be trying to tickle him, and Will frowned and glanced up at her face. So intent was she upon her work that she paid him no attention at all.

Her fingertip paused upon the fleshy web of skin that separated his thumb from the first finger of his right hand.

"It really is you," she whispered, so quietly that he could barely hear her over the music playing in her room.

Will frowned and looked down, and then he realized what it was she had found. There upon his skin was a tiny, pale circle of scar tissue. The scar was so small and so old that he almost never thought about it, yet he could still remember the circumstances of his receiving it very clearly. Will had been seven at the time and his parents had taken him to visit his uncle Harry, at the site where the architectural firm his amiable uncle worked for was constructing a new library. Will had been given a hard hat to wear, which he'd thought was just about the coolest thing ever.

Uncle Harry smoked.

As they stood together gazing up at a crane that was lifting a steel beam high into the air, Uncle Harry let his hand dangle by his side, a lit cigarette between two fingers. The burning tip accidentally brushed Will's hand and the ash had come off, clinging to his skin. Searing. Scarring.

In the darkness, in the branches of that tree, Will looked in the window at the sudden light in Ashleigh's eyes, as though a veil of cobwebs had been torn away, and for a moment it was as though he had not used dark sorcery to travel back in time, but rather had woken up to find that his entire life since this moment, this night, had been one long dream.

"Uncle Harry," he said.

Ashleigh let out a long breath that ended with a tiny laugh. "Uncle Harry," she repeated, and nodded. "And so what happens to us, Will? Me and you? We're still friends, right?" Her shoulders bobbed in the smallest of shrugs and her tone was cautious. "All of us. I know people drift apart after high school, but I have to believe this group will be different."

Will felt queasy. "We probably shouldn't talk about this."

She rolled her eyes. "Please. You're totally screwing up the future anyway. You're here. I've seen you. I believe you're you. You don't think I'm just going to forget that, right?" Ashleigh sat back on her haunches and sighed. "I know you had to come back. People are going to die, blah, blah, blah. But you're here now. So tell me..."

In that moment while she paused, he thought of a hundred questions she might ask. Would she marry Eric? Would Will marry Caitlyn? Where did she live? What did she do for a living? Did she have children? But Ashleigh asked the one question he wasn't prepared for.

"Am I happy?"

Will froze, moisture burning the corners of his eyes. His throat tightened, and try as he might he could not force himself to smile. Looking at her now, the idea of what was to come, what would happen to her, devastated him even more than it had when he had discovered it.

Her eyes widened and a look of anguish contorted her beauty. "Oh, God, Will..." she began, her voice cracking. "What? Tell me, what is it?"

"No."

"No?" she demanded, cold and angry.

Shit, he thought. *This wasn't in the plan.* "You *were* happy. That's part of the reason I'm here, Ashleigh. I'm not going to give you any other details, but yeah, you were happy. Then whoever is messing with us...changed things. I want to stop that from happening."

For several seconds she quietly digested this, and then she nodded slowly. "And the group?" she asked, moving on from his unsettling response. "What about that? We're still tight?"

"Yeah," he replied. "It's pretty amazing, actually. Not that everyone hangs together all the time, but we keep in touch. It's all good."

How could he explain to her the bittersweet nature of the truth? They were fortunate, he knew that much. The group of them had remained friends and that was unusual. But the intensity, the passion with which they had all viewed their friendships and the world around them, was a pale shadow of what it had once been. The things that had seemed so immediate and vital when they were teenagers were fondly remembered, and that was all. Other, more adult concerns occupied their minds now. But that was a lesson Ashleigh would learn for herself as she matured. Even if he told her, she couldn't really understand until she lived it.

"Yeah," he repeated. "It's all good."

Her eyes seemed to focus on his face without the doubt and shock and fear that had been there before. "I feel like I just woke up."

Will smiled softly, remembering all the secrets he and Ashleigh had shared. "From a nightmare?"

She frowned. "Not exactly. More like I was dreaming the world was this ordinary place. Now I wake up and it's anything but. But I feel like I always knew it. Isn't that weird?"

"Not really," Will told her warmly. "You were always wishing for something amazing to happen."

"But when it did happen, for real, you didn't say a word," she chided him, gaze darkening.

Will felt a cold chill pass through him, an icy shiver that lingered around his heart. His nostrils flared and he shot a glance down at Brian, who still lurked at the base of the tree. He shook his head.

"I didn't want to think about it. Not ever." Will resettled himself so that he was more comfortable, the tiny scar from Uncle Harry hidden in the autumn leaves. When he looked at Ashleigh again he could not hide the melancholy in him. "You were hoping for something wonderful. Magic is not that."

Ashleigh widened her eyes. "But you're here. Look at this. Look at you. This is . . . this is fantastic."

Will shook his head, icy tendrils wrapping around his heart ever more tightly. "Is it? Think about why we're here. If magic is this . . . this untapped power in the world, a way to break the code of the fabric of things, then obviously it isn't natural for a reason. This is the code of miracles. The secret pattern of the universe. It's encrypted for a reason, Ashleigh." He stared at her, hearing the edge in his voice and wishing he could banish it. "I know it's all real. I know it exists. But maybe the reason I tried to pretend for so very long is not just that I didn't want to know, but that I realized that I shouldn't.

"Nobody should know how to do this shit. It isn't our place. That's why it's magic. Sorcery. Whatever you want to call it. It's intruding upon the mesh that makes up the fabric of the world, but without the tools to do it right." He gestured down toward Brian, though Ashleigh couldn't see him without leaning out her window. "We're idiots. Screwing with magic gets people hurt, sometimes worse. And this . . . Jesus, I can't believe I did this. You were right, Ash. Traveling in time is like running through a minefield. We're bound to step on something that explodes."

He felt a darkness come over him then, and Will lowered his gaze, brows knitting together. In his mind he still had so many memories, ugly pictures of Bonnie Winter's corpse and of Mike

Lebo's funeral, images of Ashleigh's face changing before his eyes as someone in the past violated her, altering everything she had become.

"Listen to yourself," Ashleigh said, a little too loudly. She glanced nervously around and then quickly scurried over to her door and peeked out. After a moment she seemed satisfied no one had heard her and she came back to the window.

"All of this stuff...I hear you, Will, but don't you understand how cool this is?" She shot him a look of dismay. "*My* friend Will, the guy who still lives next door? He would think it was very cool."

"He *did*," Will said, trying to get through to her. "I did. Until I understood what it is. What it does. You start picking at the fabric of something and it starts to unravel. That's all magic is. Unraveling. I swore I'd never go near it again. Magic is hideous. It would have been easier if I could have been clueless like everyone else. But magic tainted me, and Brian, too. Somehow traces of the old reality stayed with us. And as long as I knew how things were supposed to be, my only choice was to try to make it right."

At last the gravity of his words seemed to sink in, to eliminate the sense of wonder and adventure that had begun to sparkle in Ashleigh's eyes. Now it had been replaced by the glint of fear. It hurt him to see that, but Will knew it was necessary. She had to see what magic was.

"All right," she said. "So what's the plan, then? What do you need from me? What's first?"

Will paused and glanced down at Brian, whose face was barely visible in the shadows. He had not completely abandoned the idea that Brian was involved, but his behavior certainly diminished Will's suspicion. Perhaps they shared some bond now, or perhaps it was just instinct, but Brian's claims had simply *felt* true.

Now that Ashleigh had asked the question, he had to confront the reality that he and Brian didn't really have a plan beyond convincing her to help. That had seemed so insurmountable that they hadn't gotten much further.

"I'm not sure," he said. "We can get by, food-wise, until the morning, I'm sure. Chances are we can sleep in the storage space under my porch..." He glanced at the house next door. "You know what I mean. Under his porch."

"Young Will's."

Will smiled. "I'm not exactly old."

"Older than Young Will. Besides, I've gotta have some way to keep you two separate in my head." Ashleigh crossed her legs and watched him expectantly, helpfully.

"I guess. Anyway, tomorrow's when we're really going to need your help. We have to figure out some kind of identities for ourselves, who we say we are if anyone asks. And we'll need the car tomorrow."

Ashleigh grimaced. "I don't know. My parents only let me drive the Toyota, and my father always takes it on Sundays to go golfing with his friends while Mom does her whole church thing."

The ice around Will's heart had thawed, but now a new tendril seemed to slide into his chest, coiling to strike. "But tomorrow's Saturday. The fourteenth of October."

She thought a moment, but then Ashleigh shook her head. "Nope. No school today, Will. Tomorrow's Sunday. This is Saturday right now."

Suddenly he began to shiver, his head shaking. The music in her room seemed far too loud, and he looked down at Brian, who was gazing curiously upward. He wanted to call down but didn't dare draw the attention of Ashleigh's parents.

"Son of a bitch," Will murmured. He pulled himself to Ashleigh's window now and poked his head in. She backed up, startled, as he twisted around, surveying her room.

"What?" she asked in a harsh whisper.

He looked at her, frantic. "Your clock. Where is it? You... you used to have that one, the cat with the ticktock tail."

"It broke," she said, still taken aback. Then she scrambled to her bedside table and grabbed a small alarm clock from atop it. "It's—wow, I thought it was later than that. It's only quarter to ten."

Will drew a shuddering breath and nodded to himself. "OK. OK, we've got about half an hour."

Ashleigh frowned. "Why? What happens in half an hour?"

"If we don't do something about it?" Will replied grimly. "Mike Lebo dies."

ASHLEIGH STAYED CLOSE to the garage door, out of sight of any of the windows. Her heart thundered in her chest and she stared with wide eyes at the sight of Will and Brian, at these two men who were even now stealing her father's car. With her help.

What the fuck am I doing? she thought wildly, numb as she tried to process everything she had heard and seen this night, everything she had come to believe. Whatever whispered conversations she and Will had had with him perched in the tree in the middle of the night, whatever delicious thrills had gone through her, whatever dark fears had begun to surface in her, all of those things were hers and hers alone.

This, though, this wasn't magic. This wasn't whispers in the dark. This was two grown men stealing her father's car, and Ashleigh had given them her spare set of keys.

Her eyes felt strangely dry; it was as though she could not close them as she watched Will get into the driver's seat and give the key a quarter turn. Not enough to start the engine, but enough so that he could slip the car into neutral. Moving quickly—they had no time to spare—Brian pushed the car out of the driveway while Will steered. Ashleigh was proud of Will, seeing him like this. He was a handsome man. But Brian was the real surprise. He had always been a little doughy and more than a little sloppy. Despite the bruises on his face, it was obvious that he had changed a lot. He was handsome and fit.

It was so strange, seeing him. Seeing both of them. No matter that she already believed all of this. Just looking at them made the skin at the base of her neck prickle with the wrongness of it. They didn't belong here. And yet she was glad they had come. The very air around her seemed ominously heavy, as though there were a storm coming in. Yet the air was dry.

It wasn't that kind of storm.

Ashleigh watched for other cars on Parmenter Road, but there were none. She checked the windows of her neighbors' houses, wondering if irony would surface and she might see the face of Young Will James himself in the corner window of the house next door. But no. No sign of Young Will. Out with Caitlyn still.

The street lamp off to the right was broken, and so as Brian started to push the car again, this time down Parmenter, the two men became shadows. Only then, in the moment when Brian jumped into the passenger's seat and Will started the Toyota up, engine roaring to life, did she remember that dark silhouette in the woods at the edge of her backyard. Her breath caught in her throat now. How could she have forgotten?

Easily enough, she realized. With Will appearing in her window and the shock that had given her, with all the startling things that she had experienced in the last forty-five minutes or so, it had been easy to forget. Now, though, the memory of that shadowy figure chilled her.

Will and Brian didn't want to talk about it, but they were magicians now. For better or worse. This time-travel shit was just one kind of magic. But if the two of them were traveling through time, doing sorcery or whatever, then who had it been back there watching her house? And had he been watching Ashleigh, or watching for Will and Brian? Someone was trying to change the past, hurting people, even killing them.

Ashleigh glanced around, suddenly very cold despite the sweatshirt she had pulled on before climbing down the tree by her window. Without another moment's hesitation she ran back around the rear of the house. Even with the moonlight, the yard seemed black as pitch, and her heart beat so hard she thought it would burst her chest. Her gaze swept to the right and she studied those woods across the yard, gasping several times when she was certain a contorted figure was moving, coming out of the trees at her, only to realize it was the wind, bending branches.

The light in her window was a beacon. She scrambled up the tree to her room faster than she ever had before, scraping the palm of her left hand before at last calming down enough to slip back into her room without making too much noise.

The music was still playing. Madonna.

Ashleigh spun around and knelt before the window again. She reached over to click off the light and then peered out into the darkness, studying the eerie topography of the woods behind the house. Her chest still hurt, and as the minutes ticked toward the moment when, according to Will, Mike Lebo was supposed to die, the only thing on Ashleigh's mind was the question of whether it would have helped them to know what she had seen. Or thought she had seen. Whether it had been important.

She stared out at the nighttime landscape for a very long time.

"TURN DOWN BROOK STREET," Brian snapped. "Come on, haul ass!"

The clock on the dashboard read nine minutes past ten. The way Will remembered it, Mike had been run down at about quarter past. At least that was what the police report said, based upon statements made by people who heard the squealing tires and the noise of the impact as the car hit flesh and bone.

Six minutes, Will thought. *If the clock's right. If the witnesses weren't just rounding off to the quarter hour, or guessing, for that matter.*

"Will!" Brian slapped the dashboard. "Turn here! Brook Street. Turn!"

There was a disconnect in Will's mind then. It had been a long time since he had maneuvered his way through the side streets of Eastborough, and Brian's directions didn't make sense. Still, he hit the brakes, tires skidding as he made the corner.

"This doesn't go anywhere," he said. "Brook just goes to—"

"Juniper Hill School," Brian cut in. He had the window open and was staring frantically at the street ahead, watching the sidewalk for anyone on foot. "There's that access road at the back that comes in the back of Lebo's neighborhood."

Will shot him a dubious sidelong glance, adrenaline racing through him, burning his veins with every second that passed. "There's a big fucking chain across the access road. It's a fire lane or something."

"The chain was always down, remember? It was always down."

"Maybe," Will said, speeding up. "Maybe." If this had been junior year, when the group of them had hung around up here quite a bit before he and Brian had parted ways, he might have been more confident. But senior year... He couldn't remember when the fire department had put the chain back up.

The engine roared. Will returned his focus to the road and held tight to the wheel as they rocketed up Brook Street, nearly taking air over the small bridge that spanned the trickle of water that gave the street its name. The road sloped upward and curved slightly, and the tires hugged the pavement as they sped toward the darkened hulk of the school at the top of the hill. As the headlights of the Toyota washed across the face of Juniper Hill School, he felt the memories in his head shuffling again. He drove around the back where there was a baseball diamond and a larger field bordered by a treeline. Will could not breathe.

"My head gets all confused," Brian admitted, his voice hesitant. "I almost expect to see us playing ball. Or partying."

Will knew exactly what he meant. Images flickered so quickly behind his eyes as he crossed the parking lot and started to drive down the narrow fire road beside the baseball diamond that it was almost as though he could see the ghosts of their younger selves out there now, laughing around a case of beer.

"Once upon a time," he whispered.

"Yeah," Brian agreed. "Once upon a time."

The chain was down.

Relief swept through Will. He slowed down slightly to bump over the thick chain and then he accelerated again, tires spitting sand up behind the old Toyota. They said nothing more as they tore down Delilah Lane. Brian scanned the street and the sidewalks. This was the route Mike Lebo would have taken walking home. In the dark. Under the influence.

At the end of Delilah, Will hit the brakes only long enough to check for oncoming traffic, then tore out onto Hawthorne Road.

"Will!" Brian said.

"I see him."

A hundred yards ahead of them on the other side of the street, a familiar figure strode along the sidewalk with his hands jammed in his pockets. He was just leaving the dome of light cast by a street lamp, but that pale illumination was enough for Will to be certain. It was Mike Lebo.

Walking into the darkness, toward a telephone pole that would in the coming days be his memorial, decked with flowers and photos and remembrances, candles and tears.

Words came from Will's lips but did not even register on his mind. He forgot to breathe. To blink. His heart forgot to beat. His hands clutched the steering wheel and his right foot pressed the accelerator and the Toyota tore along Hawthorne Road. Will's window was up and he freed his left hand just long enough to crank it down.

"There's a car!" Brian shouted. "Jesus, Will. Look!"

But Will had already noticed the vehicle barreling down Hawthorne toward them. Toward Mike. The headlights were off. The sedan was running completely dark. Of course it would. This was no drunk driver. Mike Lebo's death had been no accident. But Will James was about to set it right.

He gritted his teeth and swerved across the street into the path of the oncoming sedan.

"He's going to beat you there!" Brian said.

"The hell he is!" Will sneered and he floored the gas pedal. His skin felt too tight on his arms and it was too hot, as though he had been sunburned. His eyes ached.

The Toyota tore up the street on the wrong side of the road. The oncoming sedan remained dark, sliding toward them through the night. Drunk as he was, it took Lebo a couple of seconds to register the roaring of the engines. He started to turn toward the street, to look up.

"Mike!" Will bellowed out the window. "Get back, Lebo! Back up!"

The sedan seemed to surge forward and Will held his breath. This was some fucked-up game of chicken, he was sure of it. Whoever was behind the wheel of that car had to turn aside. The driver wouldn't risk his own life.

"Will!" Brian shouted as the two cars barreled toward one another. "Will, Jesus Christ, turn! I don't think he's going to... What the hell?"

There was a queer change in Brian's tone just at the last, from terror to bewilderment. But Will was barely paying attention and certainly had no time to respond. He opened his mouth and let out a kind of roar and kept his fingers wrapped around the steering wheel.

The sedan jerked aside, crossing to the wrong side of the road, getting out of his way. No headlights. No blare of the horn. Not even a screech of tires.

In the very same instant, Lebo stumbled out into the street, right in front of the Toyota. Will heard Brian shouting, heard his own scream as he stamped down upon the brake and the tires began to shriek.

Too late.

There was a thump as the Toyota's front end struck Mike, and another as the car's momentum slammed him against the hood and then against the windshield. Lebo's head hit the glass and a spidery crack splintered through it. Blood ran into the crack as the Toyota skidded to a stop. Mike Lebo rolled limply off the hood of the car and fell to the pavement.

Will was already moving. He popped the door open and jumped from the car, ignoring the warnings that Brian called after him. He had felt before as though his skin were too tight, sun-burned. Now he felt like ice. Will staggered around the open car door and went to Mike. He stared down at this handsome, friendly face he had only seen in pictures for a very long time. Blood already matted his hair and ran in a streak down one cheek. It was starting to pool under Mike's head.

Brian grabbed Will by the arm and Will shook him off angrily. But Brian wasn't going to take no for an answer. He grabbed Will by the hair and tugged, forcing him to look around so that the two of them were face to face.

"You're not fucking listening," Brian snapped. "People will be out here any second, Will. We can't be here! Get in the car!"

Will flinched as if Brian had slapped him. *Shit. Oh, shit. We're no one. No identity at all. In a stolen car. Son of a—*

He rushed to the car and slipped behind the wheel again. He slammed it into reverse and was moving before Brian had even closed his door. Will killed the headlights in hopes the car would not be identified. As he accelerated and took off down the street, he was well aware of the irony that he was running dark, the same as the car that had been gunning for Mike in the first place.

Mike. Oh, Christ, Mike. His mind was in turmoil, stricken with the idea that he had been responsible. *It was me,* he thought. But almost instantly his nostrils flared in confusion.

"Why the hell did he do it? Was he that drunk? He saw us coming!"

They were already long gone from the accident scene. Will was sick with the idea that they had left Mike behind, dead on the roadside. But he had been dead already. Nothing good would have come of their staying.

"You think he did that on purpose?" Brian asked.

Will held tight to the wheel and shot him a sidelong glance. "What do you mean?"

"At the last second I looked over at him. He wasn't alone. This guy was there, all in black. Even his face was in black. But it almost didn't look like clothes, Will. It was like the black just clung to him, like moving shadows. He threw Mike out into the street. Like he was waiting for us. Like it was all set up for us to be the … to be the ones."

Will was numb. *Oh, Mike, you poor bastard. I'm so sorry. So goddamned sorry.* For the moment he could do nothing but drive.

Moving shadows. What the hell have we gotten into here?

CHAPTER 14

Monday dawned clear and blue, a pristine October morning complete with a chill in the air and frost on the grass. A lot of seniors wouldn't be caught dead riding the bus, but Ashleigh didn't mind. Especially today. Her mind was elsewhere. She sat in the rear of the bus with her head leaning gently against the window, bouncing slightly when the bus rumbled through a pothole. Her breath fogged the glass, but not so much that she could not see the houses they passed, the pumpkins already on the front steps and scarecrows propped in front of lampposts.

Ashleigh loved October. There was something in the air this time of year, something she could smell and even taste on the breeze that came in through the slightly open bus window. But today there was no lift in her spirits, no sigh of contentment.

She shivered and hugged herself and let her eyes go unfocused as the fog of her breath made the glass more opaque, as though it had suddenly become colder on the bus. And perhaps it had.

Sunday had been a hellish day for her. Sometime during the previous night Will and Brian had returned her father's car, a fact she only discovered when her father shouted for her to come outside. Ashleigh had walked out in her sneakers and sweats, essentially the same outfit she had worn to sneak out the window last night. The moment she got a look at the Toyota she froze, mouth open in that silly little O she thought people only made in the movies, and held her breath.

The windshield was cracked. Not just cracked, but run through with splinters like a spiderweb. Her father had stood in front of the car in his bathrobe, with the plastic-bagged Sunday *Boston Globe* dangling from one hand. His bare feet must have been freezing on the driveway, but he hadn't even seemed to notice.

"I just came out to get the paper," he said, almost comically mystified, his thinning hair wild from sleep. But when he glanced at her and she saw the storm in his eyes, there was nothing funny about it at all. "Ashleigh, do you have any idea how this happened?"

Gaping at the car, she'd shaken her head. "Not a clue. God, look at it."

"I *am* looking!" he'd snapped, then sighed in frustration, trying to show her that it wasn't her he was angry at. "Must've been some little punks in the middle of the night. Can't believe it didn't wake me up." Her father had glanced around, probably searching for whatever had been used to crack the windshield. "Did you? Hear anything, I mean?"

Ashleigh had moved closer to the car. "No. Nothing."

Her mind had been elsewhere, however. She had been, in her way, as mystified as her father. Ashleigh knew who was responsible for what had happened to the car, but had no idea how it had happened. She only hoped that Will had left her key under the floormat like he promised.

You dicks, she thought. *Should've woken me up.* But she had realized a moment later that they had done the right thing. There was nothing she could have done, and waking her would have been too much of a risk.

All day long the curiosity had eaten at her. Every time she left the house, she hoped she would see one of them. That night while she was going to bed, every time she heard a noise she got up to peer out the window, wondering if they had returned. More than anything Ashleigh wanted to know what had happened. Had they saved Mike? How had the windshield gotten broken?

Nothing.

They hadn't made contact at all, and in spite of herself, strange doubts had begun to creep into Ashleigh's mind. Was she really certain these men were who they said they were? She believed, and yet she could not help feeling some hesitation as their absence drew longer and the events of Saturday night continued to be a mystery.

Now Monday morning had arrived. It was the perfect October day, and she ought to have been excited. Homecoming weekend was coming up, and Halloween the week after. There was so much to think about, to look forward to. Yet the events of Saturday night and Sunday morning had cast a shadow over her heart that she could not shake.

She rode the bus, cold and silent, and when it pulled into the parking lot at Eastborough High and she gazed out the window, the only thing she was looking for was some sign of Will or Brian. Not her classmates, but these mysterious men who claimed to be their future selves. She squinted, head aching with all of the thoughts and doubts and fears in her. Will—*her* Will—would have ridden to school with Danny Plumer. Ashleigh could have caught a ride with them this morning, but that was the last thing she wanted.

Her friends could not be avoided forever, though. Not even for long.

Only seconds after Ashleigh had made her way through the chaos of the second-floor corridor and reached her locker, she heard Danny's boisterous, arrogant laugh. Most of the time she could take him, even liked him, despite the amount of swagger in the guy. Today Danny's voice made the hair stand up on the back of her neck and her shoulders hunch.

Her boyfriend, Eric, nearly always arrived at school at the last minute. They never had time together before class. Most of the time it didn't bother her, but today, God how she wished that Eric were here. Not that she would have told him anything. Not Eric. He was smart and sexy but had about a thimbleful of imagination. If he couldn't understand why she would spend her time reading something like *Dragon Rigger*, there was no way in hell he would believe any of this. Nothing frightened her more than the thought that he would laugh at her. Or, worse, think there was something wrong with her.

For the first time, Ashleigh had a moment of clarity in which she understood just how deeply she loved Eric DeSantis and how vulnerable it made her. The knowledge frightened her, and she buried it away inside her heart.

No, she could not have told Eric. But he would have sensed she was upset and he would have held her. Just held her. Ashleigh needed that. The only other person who could comfort her right now was Will, but she didn't think she could confide anything in him without spilling it all. The difference was, Will would believe her. Even if he hadn't already been fooling around with magic, he would have believed. It was who he was, and who they were to each other.

A terrible dread had settled over her, and Ashleigh felt an anxiety like nothing she had ever experienced before. Her nerves were frayed, her every muscle taut as a bowstring, and she felt that if anyone touched her, she might scream.

"Ashleigh."

She froze, teeth gritted together, and rested her forehead against the cool metal of her locker. A moment later her heart and lungs started working again and she took a long breath, forced a smile, and turned to look at Will. His eyes were soft with concern.

"Hey. You all right? You don't look so good."

"I don't *feel* so good," she replied. It wasn't quite a lie.

"Do you want to see the nurse?" he asked.

Ashleigh smiled and studied Will's face. It was so odd to have seen what he would look like someday, the opposite of looking at scrapbooks and seeing what her parents had looked like as kids. She had seen a snapshot of the Will of the future...and never mind the metaphor, she had met the real thing. Any doubt she had evaporated as she looked into Will's eyes and realized they were the same. Of course they were.

"No. It'll pass," she said.

He frowned slightly in confusion, obviously still sensing something wasn't right with her but not pushing it. Ashleigh glanced at Caitlyn and then at Danny. He wore a dark green long-sleeved shirt and tan pants. Most of the guys favored blue jeans, but Danny rarely wore them. Caitlyn had on a skirt with a spaghetti-strap tank top, with a red sweater thrown over it. It was the whole purposefully disheveled look that almost never worked for Caitlyn because she was just too damned pretty. Ashleigh and Will both had jeans on. Obviously, neither of them had wanted to spend any time getting ready for school this morning.

"What about you guys?" Ashleigh asked them. "Friday night was cool, but what'd you all do the rest of the weekend?"

They had all hung out Friday night, gotten Chinese food and played pool in Nick Acosta's basement. Normally Ashleigh would have hung out with Eric on Saturday and seen Will and maybe Caitlyn on Sunday. But Eric's parents had taken him to Connecticut for his great-aunt's birthday or something, and she had not dared try to get in touch with Will on Sunday.

"Pretty quiet," Danny said. "My dad's got me helping him paint the house."

Will and Caitlyn exchanged an unsettled look. Then they shared a secret sort of smile and Caitlyn's cheeks rouged just a bit.

"We went to the gristmill over in Sudbury yesterday. Had a picnic," Will said. "It was colder than I thought it would be, but sunny at least. We hung out on Saturday night. It was the weirdest thing. We ran into this freaky guy—"

There was a loud crackle from the speakers set into the ceiling all through the corridor. It was a familiar noise, the sound system coming on just before someone in the principal's office made an announcement. But it was almost never the principal himself. Almost.

"Good morning, all," came the voice of Principal Chad-bourne, without an ounce of pleasantry. There was a hesitation on the system, a moment where it hissed blankly, before the ro-tund, usually genial man spoke again. "If I may have your atten-tion. It is with profound sadness that I must inform you that we have lost one of our own. Some of you may already be aware, but for those who are not, a member of our senior class was killed on Saturday night in a hit-and-run accident. There will be an assembly at one o'clock in the auditorium, and the counseling staff are on hand all day to speak with anyone who feels like talking. I am sorry to have to share this horrible news with you. We will all miss Michael Lebo."

Cold. Ashleigh was cold all over, ice down to her bones. Her facial muscles were slack and that loss of control spread through her. She felt the tears coming, wanted them to come, wanted to feel the heat of them. When they began to stream down her cheeks, burning her skin, she was grateful. Air slid from her lungs in a long wheeze, and she staggered backward into her locker, the back of her skull striking the metal. Like a mari-onette with her strings cut, she slid down the locker, bones jar-ring as she landed in a sitting position on the ground.

The tears burned, but she relished them.

Will and Brian—the adult Will and Brian—had tried to save Mike, and they'd failed. They'd brought the car back, so she had assumed that everything...*Oh, God, oh, no*...She covered her mouth with both hands to keep from screaming. Mike was dead. They'd failed. So where were they? And how would they explain the cracked windshield?

Mike had been one of them. One of the group. Their friend. Now there was a hole in the world where he had been, a wound in the place he had occupied in their lives. *One of us is dead,* she thought. *One of us.*

And yet the business of Eastborough High went on. Not

everyone had been friends with Mike. Not everyone knew him. Even as she let her head strike the locker again, the shock of the announcement had already worn off for many students. They were moving again, headed for their classes as if nothing at all had happened.

Not everyone.

There was blood on Will's chin. He had bitten through his lip.

"Jesus," Caitlyn whispered, her voice a plea, a prayer for it to be a cruel jest. "Jesus, oh, my God. Jesus Christ." Her hand came up to cover her eyes, her features pinched tightly as she tried to hold in her grief. Then the tears came from beneath her hand in a torrent right along with her prayers to or accusations of God.

Danny was dumbstruck. His gaze ticked from one of them to the next, around the group, as if looking for some kind of explanation. He looked lost. None of them had spoken a word other than Caitlyn's cries to the Lord. Now Ashleigh noticed that Will's attention was drawn elsewhere. He glanced along the hall and focused for a moment. Ashleigh turned to see what had caught his eye.

At the far end of the hall Brian Schnell stood just as paralyzed, just as shattered as the rest of them. His eyes were closed and he swayed slightly as though he was about to faint. Then he opened his eyes, saw Will watching him, and turned to go.

Someone was whimpering with grief, and it took Ashleigh a moment to realize the sounds were emanating from her. She pressed her eyes closed tightly and more tears spilled out. A hand touched her shoulder, and just the tiniest bit of warmth went through her, a little bit of comfort. Will, of course. He was always there for her. She was surprised to open her eyes and find that it was Danny who had laid a comforting hand on her shoulder. Suddenly she felt guilty for having had uncharitable thoughts about him several minutes before.

"Ssshhh, it's OK, Ashleigh," he whispered. "You're not alone in this. We'll help each other. Come on. Let's get you up."

He began to help her up and she let him.

Caitlyn was quivering. Her eyes rolled upward and she stared at the ceiling. "I can't believe they...can't believe they did that. Just...just announced it like that, like it's nothing. Like he's fucking student of the month or something. Jesus, like they're announcing a rally for a football game."

Ashleigh was on her feet, her focus on Caitlyn, when the other girl noticed the blood on her boyfriend's chin.

"Jesus," Caitlyn whispered, staring at him. "Will, you're bleeding. Your mouth is bleeding."

His hands shaking, he reached for his mouth. His fingers touched his lower lip and he winced from the pain. Ashleigh watched as he ran his tongue out and licked the blood from the wound. He glanced down at his fingers, now slick with his own blood from where he touched his chin and lips.

Then Will fell apart. He was her best friend, and it broke Ashleigh's heart to see the grief contort his face as he began to cry.

"Why him?" Will said, the words catching in his throat. "Why did it have to be him?"

Ashleigh started to reach for him, to offer him some kind of comfort, but Will could not even meet her eyes. He pushed past Danny and stumbled slightly as he raced for the door to the men's room. The door crashed open and then whispered shut behind him.

For a long time the three of them stared at that door. Eventually, Danny and Caitlyn both realized they had to get to homeroom, but Ashleigh only said good-bye and promised they would talk later. All of them were hurting.

But Ashleigh did not leave the corridor. She wiped the tears from her face and waited patiently for Will to emerge from the bathroom. When he did, she took him by the hand and forced him to look into her eyes.

"Will," she said. "We need to talk."

TIRED, DIRTY, AND VERY BADLY IN NEED of a shave, Will James stood waiting for Brian outside the Eastborough Savings Bank and wondered if passersby would assume he was homeless. Sunday had seemed to drag on forever, yet somehow the grief and remorse he felt over the events of Saturday night had served to numb him sufficiently to survive the day.

Brian insisted that Mike had been pushed out in front of the car. Will wasn't to blame. Yet the memories of the sickening noise it had made when the car had struck Mike and the blood pooling under his corpse on the pavement lingered in his mind. No matter how many times Will tried to shake those things from his head, he could not.

Yet he had come to learn in recent days that perhaps no memory was permanent. Things could be eroded. Or erased.

For two nights they had slept in the hayloft in Jillian Mansur's barn. They had whispered to one another and argued and wept and Will had wavered back and forth as the hours went by and the sun rose, wondering if there was some way Brian might really be involved in this. He doubted it, not with the pain in his old friend's eyes. But Will was no longer willing to trust anything, not his eyes, not his memories...not even his friends.

Over the course of that Sunday, however, he had made a conscious decision to trust Brian. Will felt he had little choice. And he had to confess, at least to himself, that there was some small comfort in not being completely alone in this.

Sunday had been spent planning and debating. Brian thought that they should go back to Ashleigh, but Will insisted they not risk it. His insistence, however, had less to do with risk than with the simple fact that he could not have brought himself to tell her that they'd fucked up, that they—that he had killed Mike Lebo himself. Bile rose up in the back of his throat every time he thought about it. Telling Ashleigh how her father's windshield had been cracked would have torn him up inside.

So they weren't going back to Ashleigh's, but they still needed a car and they could not steal one when they had no idea how long they might have to survive before returning to their own time period. They also needed food and shelter. Fortunately, they discovered that between them they had forty-seven dollars in bills that were old enough to spend without anyone catching the date and thinking they were counterfeiters.

Forty-seven dollars had gone a long way. The moment the pharmacy opened they had bought a couple of toothbrushes and a travel-size tube of toothpaste. Will was glad that Brian had agreed with him on this part of the plan, because he was compulsive about brushing his teeth and also because Brian had horrible morning breath. They had skipped breakfast, had subs for lunch and pizza for dinner, and still had fourteen dollars and change left over by the time they snuck back into the Mansurs' barn that night.

But by this morning, things that had not been that much of an issue the day before had become more troubling. A two-day growth of beard, extremely wrinkled clothes, and the stale smell of unwashed bodies were going to be a problem for the rest of their plan. After waking up this morning and leaving the barn they had walked to the center of town, where Brian had spent their remaining money on a can of Right Guard and a cheap Eastborough sweatshirt sold in the pharmacy for $9.99.

Only one of them could wear the sweatshirt, but they shared the Right Guard, ducking behind a Dumpster to take an aerosol shower. Will loved his Red Sox jersey, but on its third day he would have been more than happy to replace it with something clean, preferably after an actual shower rather than just a blast of deodorant. For the moment, however, Brian had to be the one with the sweatshirt because he was the one with the money.

Or, at least, Young Brian had money. And Not-Quite-So-Young Brian needed to get his hands on some of it.

And now the plan was under way.

Of course, Will did not think they had a chance in hell of actually pulling it off, but the alternative was living like homeless people in Eastborough while they were trying to stop people from being hurt and killed. In downtown Boston, that would have made them invisible. It would have been a simple thing to move around unnoticed posing as a homeless man. But in Eastborough, it was bound to draw attention.

So, the plan.

Will glanced impatiently at his watch, but even as he looked up from it Brian was walking out of the bank with a satisfied smile upon his face. He had been able to wash up somewhat in the bathroom of the place where they had bought subs for lunch the day before, but even with the blood gone he had several purple bruises from the beatings Will had given him on Saturday.

Brian reached him and kept going on down the sidewalk. "Let's take a walk."

"You can't be serious," Will said, hurrying to catch up, glancing around guiltily and shoving his hands in his pockets as though they had just robbed the bank and he was worried the police might arrive at any moment.

They fell into step beside one another, and a tremor of nostalgia went through Will. This was how it had been between them a long time ago, side by side on missions of exploration that took them all over Eastborough and beyond. It seemed to him that he had lost a great deal in growing up. And now someone had taken even more.

"Talk to me," Will said, and all the lightheartedness was gone from his voice.

"One thousand dollars."

Will stopped short on the sidewalk right in front of Sunshine Cleaners. "You're shitting me."

Brian smiled, and then told him. The Schnells were not a wealthy family, but a large and generous one. From birth he had received toys and games and clothes from his parents, but the gifts from his aunts and uncles and grandparents had always been monetary, not only for his birthday and Christmas but for every important event in his life. Brian had had a paper route from the age of ten until he turned fourteen. His father had helped him deliver the papers but had never taken a dime of the money. The Schnells were also frugal.

By the time he was a seventeen-year-old high school senior, Brian Schnell had eighteen thousand dollars in the bank.

"What, it isn't obvious you're not seventeen?" Will demanded. "So you walk in, fill out a withdrawal slip, manage to remember your savings account number—"

"I still have that account."

Will brushed the words off and kept going. "—So what happened when she asked to see your license?"

Brian smiled, reached up, and scratched at the stubble that would soon turn his goatee into a full-fledged beard if he didn't do something about it. Then he pulled out his wallet and opened it up, police-style, to flash his license inside a plastic sheath. He didn't live there anymore, but Brian still had a Massachusetts license. And the way he was holding it, his thumb covered the birth date.

"She was busy. I told her I couldn't get it out of the plastic but I showed it to her and rattled off my license number while she was looking at it. The woman glanced at it for about three seconds. She matched my face to the picture, then gave me my money."

Will shook his head in amazement. "With those bruises I can't believe she didn't pay more attention."

Brian shrugged. "Maybe she just figured it was none of her business."

"You know you just robbed yourself, right?"

"I'll pay me back."

The two of them stared at one another, there on a sidewalk they'd trodden together hundreds of times before. Will broke first, soft laughter coming from deep within his chest. He shook his head and began to laugh harder, and now Brian joined in. Within a few moments they were wiping their eyes and leaning upon one another, sighing as they tried to quash the temptation to lapse into an outright fit of giggles.

Grinning, Will let out a long breath. "We must look like a couple of lunatics."

"Smelly, unshaven lunatics."

Slowly, Will caught his breath. "You realize we're getting a little hysterical."

Brian frowned deeply. "No. I'm just funny."

For several moments they were silent, amusement slowly seeping out of them as the viral dread that had been the constant third party to their reunion reasserted itself. They had been unable to prevent Mike Lebo's death, had instead been manipulated into the hideous irony of causing it.

Will stared at a crack in the sidewalk as cars rolled past them. He shivered a little, but he was not nearly as cold as he had been in the Mansurs' hayloft. He lifted his gaze to the blue sky, felt the warm sunlight on his face.

At least the sun was out.

"We've got to get the book," Will said, his tone grave now, all trace of nostalgia gone. The calm of despair seemed to fog around him and he turned to Brian. "We fucked up, but it might not be too late."

"Will, come on." Brian wore a pained expression. "We talked about this. Even if the book is where you think it is, even if we got it and we tried to use it, there's no way to know if the spell would work. And you…shit, Will, you feel it just like I do. We had our shot. One shot. That's all we get."

The words seared him but Will could not deny they were true. They'd had one chance to save Lebo. One chance. And the kid was dead. Will had washed Mike's blood off of Mr. Wheeler's car himself. Ever since the moment they had pulled away and left his broken body bleeding on the road, the reality in which Mike had not died, and that other, second time line in which he had been run down by someone else, not by Will and Brian, had begun to fade. Will still remembered *knowing* that there was more than one set of memories, that Mike had graduated with them and been a friend to him for years after high school, but Will recalled these bits of information as though he had learned them by reading about them instead of having lived them.

If he and Brian returned to their own time now, it might well be to a future in which they no longer remembered things any other way, and then what of Ashleigh and Tess and Bonnie? They just couldn't risk it. Their only choice was to go forward, to play it out. To see what the future would bring.

"Let's go." Will started down the sidewalk, pulling the rolled-up want ads out of the back pocket of his jeans. "We've got a lot to do."

Someone or something was here in Eastborough, right now, stalking their friends with malevolent intent. Will hadn't been able to keep Mike Lebo alive. The way things had been altered, Tess and Ashleigh would both be raped on Friday night and Bonnie murdered on Saturday night. But now he and Brian had come back in time and set a third, entirely different time line in motion. There was no way to know what effect that would have. If whoever was responsible for all of this knew that Will and Brian were here, trying to interfere—and Will had to believe that—then the events might not follow the same sequence.

He and Brian had talked it out. They had to start by contacting Ashleigh again and by keeping watch over her. Unless he could stop it, sometime soon his best friend, his girl next door, was going to be raped. The picture of her changing before his eyes, fading into a woman with a scar on her soul, remained with him even now. He thought of Ashleigh's twins and of that look on her face after the altered past had changed her, and he picked up his pace.

Not Ashleigh, he thought. *Not her.*

IN MANY WAYS, ASHLEIGH FELT that the strangest thing about Mike Lebo's death was how little real impact it had on her life. She would never have admitted to such thoughts for fear that someone would misinterpret them, accuse her of being heartless. That was so far from the truth. Mike had not been her closest friend, but he was a sweet, funny guy who was a part of nearly every day for her.

Or had been.

The horror of his death was barely twelve hours old, and it had shrouded her in a cloud of despair and hesitation. She felt as though her reactions to everything were too slow. When someone spoke to her, it took an extra second or two for the words to even register. This kind of thing happened on the news, in other towns than Eastborough. Or it happened to adults. It sure as hell didn't happen to people she had known, to boys who had been stealing chocolate pudding off of her tray in the cafeteria since the third grade.

More than anything, there was an emptiness in her mind where Mike should have been, a wound, bleeding tears of sorrow and the dark truth of the world. The truth was, high school kids didn't only die in other towns, in places she heard about on television.

And yet...

School continued. The Homecoming game was this Saturday and the dance would follow, and though Mike would doubtless be remembered and tears would be shed for him, the momentum of all their lives continued uninterrupted. Only his wake and funeral would interfere, and those not for very long. Mike's death would be woven into the fabric of things, and then the rest of them—the ones who still lived—would move on.

It chilled and saddened her and in the back of her mind there was, omnipresent, the unique perspective afforded to her by her own secret. Will and Brian—the Elder Will and Brian—had more than ten years on their younger counterparts. What was it like for them, she wondered, remembering these days? Remembering this loss? With the numb, hollow feeling at her center, she could not imagine what it would feel like to put a decade's distance between herself and her grief. But she wished she could do it in an instant, that she could move forward away from this day with the same effortless magic they had used to return to it.

Will and Brian, she thought. *What the hell happened to you two?*

All of these grim curiosities churned in Ashleigh's mind as she walked home from the high school. She had been working with the Homecoming Committee on the main float for Satur-

day's game, but though their effort was just as diligent, the spirit
had been leeched from them. The students working on the float
still gossiped and flirted and laughed, but all of it seemed muted
to Ashleigh. Though mostly unspoken, the awareness of Mike
Lebo's fate lingered. A wake would be held Tuesday night;
Wednesday, the school would allow students to skip their morning classes and attend Mike's funeral. As though anyone would
be in the mood for calculus after that.

Her mother had tried to get her to stay home, to distract herself with music or bad television, but Ashleigh had insisted on
going to the Homecoming Committee meeting. The people
working on the float were expecting her, they were counting on
her, and she had felt like being surrounded by people. Now she
wished she had listened. Smiles and conversation were not at all
what she wanted. Which was why when Lolly and Pix offered
her a ride home, she declined. It was only a couple of miles to
her house. She could walk it easily.

Alone in the dark with only the October breeze and the
golden moonlight for company, she quickened her pace as she
moved down Market Street toward Kennedy Middle School.
What happened to Mike had her worried. Her father's cracked
windshield worried her even more. If she needed any more proof
of the incredible identity of her nocturnal visitors, she had it.
They had known Mike would die, had known where and how.

And they had not been able to prevent it.

Now, when Ashleigh remembered the conversation she'd had
through her bedroom window with Will as he clung in the trees,
she could only focus on the expression on his face. His eyes had
been troubled as he looked at her. She'd caught that several times.
It had not bothered her overmuch at the time, but now, as she
approached the silent shape of the school with its dark-eye windows, there was something far too ominous about it.

It had, of course, occurred to her that fate had something sin-
ister in store for her as well. The shadowy figure she had seen in
the woods on Saturday night had not been her imagination. But
Elder Will and Elder Brian hadn't been able to save Mike. If

there was anything for her to fear, she was going to have to fend for herself.

Forcibly she turned her mind from such thoughts and focused on more trivial things. When she got home she would call Eric and ask him about his trip. She would do all she could to avoid talking to him about Mike Lebo's death, but he was going to be devastated. She could picture Eric's face in her mind, his strong features, those brown eyes, and she missed him all the more.

Ashleigh sighed. So much for thinking about other things.

The autumn wind kicked up, whistling along Market Street and ruffling her hair, whipping it across her face. Ashleigh pushed it out of her eyes and shivered, zipping her brown, soft leather jacket up to her throat. She picked up her pace even further, hurrying now, just wanting to be home.

As she walked across the school parking lot a strange feeling crept over her, a cold, familiar feeling, but one she had not felt in a very long time. As a child she had stared at her closet door, slightly ajar, and imagined terrible things therein. When the wind blew, the branches of the trees had scraped her bedroom window like the dagger-fingers of some ravenous ghoul.

Ashleigh stared straight ahead, her cheeks flushing and the back of her neck growing warm. She felt childish, her mind overwrought with terrible imaginings because of Mike's death and things Will had said to her. But if her bizarre meeting with Elder Will on Saturday night had taught her anything, it was that sometimes there really were cruel things in the darkness.

So she told herself that perhaps her suddenly erratic heartbeat and trembling hands were not silly at all but instinct.

The school loomed up on her left and she rushed past it at a clip that was barely slow enough to qualify as a walk. As she left the parking lot behind, like Lot's wife she could no longer withstand the temptation to turn, to look back.

A dark car was rolling slowly down Market Street toward her, headlights off.

Ashleigh ran.

"Stupid, stupid, stupid," she whispered to herself, chanting the mantra over and over. Her legs pumped, her shoes crunching the frosted grass. She listened for the engine, her ears attuned to the slightest change in the ambient sound around her. Bats screeched as they flew overhead. The wind rustled the branches and blew fallen autumn leaves across the ground in whirls and eddies that performed an elegant dance. The world around her took no notice of the terror that now rose up inside her.

There came no roar of an approaching engine, no sudden burst of brilliance from the headlights. The car was not pursuing her. Her mind clicked through possibilities, and Ashleigh wondered if she could dare to hope that the driver of that vehicle meant her no harm. But no way was she slowing down. Her breath was coming ragged and fear seemed to choke her. Ashleigh ran past the school and started across Robinson Field.

Branches snapped as something moved through the trees off to her right, on the near side of the field perhaps thirty feet from her. Ashleigh glanced over, throat constricting further, eyes wide as she watched a dark figure burst from the woods that surrounded Robinson Field and start toward her.

That dark silhouette, erupting from the trees, erased all other thoughts or concerns from her mind. Homecoming, Mike's funeral, her grief, magic...it was all erased in that instant. The only image left in her head was of the shadowy figure in her backyard on Saturday night.

"Shit," she whispered.

Then she began to scream. But even as Ashleigh sprinted across the grass, turning away from the dark man, she knew he had chosen his attack carefully. Not even the janitorial staff would be in the middle school this late at night. The lights were all out. The field was broad, and there were woods separating it from the surrounding neighborhoods.

He had her. Her only chance was to outrun him, to sprint the length of the school and come back around the other side, to race back up Market Street toward the main road, where there would be houses and other cars.

Ashleigh bit her lip as she ran. Her eyes burned but she refused to let the tears come. In the past twelve hours she had been forced to think about her own death for the first time in her life. If Mike Lebo could be so violently deleted from the world, then she could be, too. Hopes and dreams slipped through her mind as though they were slipping from her grasp. Graduation gown. Wedding dress. Maternity dress.

She never expected the shadow to have a voice.

"Slow down, Ashleigh," he said, his tone raspy and insinuating.

And too close.

Ashleigh snapped her head around and saw that he was almost upon her. How had he moved so fast? Panic surged through her as though she had been electrocuted. A single tear escaped, even as she began to stumble, halfway twisted around like that.

She caught herself, the momentum of her stumbling throwing her forward, but she let it carry her faster, used it. Her arms and legs pumped and she bent into it, sprinting so hard every muscle ached. But it was a foolish effort, for she knew that he was too fast. Supernaturally fast. Swift as the shadows themselves.

"Ashleigh, why run? I only want to talk to you. I just want to touch you."

Revulsion curdled her stomach, and she knew that she had to do whatever was necessary to keep the dark man's hands off of her. If he even was a man—with that voice and that inhuman speed she could not be sure.

Ashleigh ran across first base on the baseball diamond in Robinson Field. Grim determination filled her as she spotted the twenty-foot-high chain-link backstop. She poured every last ounce of effort into her run and raced to the backstop. He kept talking, but she ignored him now, refusing to listen, believing that there was something in those slithering words that could trap her, could slow her down.

At the backstop she dashed to the right, just behind it, and she grabbed the fence, her fingers linking into the metal lattice-work. Ashleigh scrambled upward as fast as she was able, refusing to look back, refusing to look down, knowing that he was there, that he was coming, and her chest hurt and she missed Eric and Will and her father, her silly, grumpy old man of a father. Hand over hand she climbed and all she could think of was how much she was going to miss, how the world would continue to turn without her on it, and there would be a whole life she would never see.

Halfway up, just as her fingers closed on another snatch of chain link, she felt his hand clamp on her ankle.

Ashleigh Wheeler did not scream. Her lower lip quaked but she reached upward again, trying to pull free. But his grip was too strong. Then, abruptly, he let her go and the fence started to shudder and rattle as he climbed up after her.

There was nowhere else to go. Ashleigh kept climbing.

Over the thunder of her heart beating in her ears she almost did not hear the roar of the car engine. At the last minute she gripped the metal lattice and turned to see the car charging across Robinson Field, tearing up the lawn and trailing a storm of fallen leaves behind it.

The car skidded to a halt as it reached the backstop, its front end striking the chain link hard enough to knock the dark man off of the fence. Ashleigh's feet came loose but she held on with both hands, dangling there, scrabbling for better purchase.

Handsome, older Will James jumped out of the passenger side and leaped over the hood of the old green Buick, sliding across the metal and jumping down on the other side. The moonlight was just bright enough to show her that Brian was behind the wheel. He put the car in reverse and the tires churned dirt and grass.

The dark man was already up on his feet and running for the trees. He had come from the woods on one side of the field, and now he wanted to escape through the trees on the other side. Will came around the backstop, faster than Ashleigh would have thought him capable of. He managed to grab hold of the dark man's arm.

The blow came too fast for Ashleigh to see. Her attacker's black-gloved fists were barely visible in the nighttime shadows. Will's head rocked back from the punch, but he did not release his grip.

"I don't think so, asshole," Will snapped. "This stops now."

With one hand, Will kept a grip on the dark man's sleeve and with the other he clutched the attacker's throat.

"Not tonight, Will," rasped the dark man, his voice muffled through the black fabric that covered his face. "'... Promises to keep...'"

The dark man slammed his skull against Will's in a savage head butt that echoed up to Ashleigh. She winced at the sound and gaped in alarm as she saw Will stagger backward into the backstop.

"'... Miles to go before I sleep.'"

The dark man might have gone after him but the Buick's engine roared and Brian drove around the backstop, headed for him. Ashleigh held her breath, thinking Brian would just run the man down, and not caring at all if he did. But then the dark man ran, sprinting across the short span that separated the backstop from the trees.

Before he even reached the woods, with the Buick bouncing over the rutted terrain after him, the dark man simply disappeared in a swirl of dark smoke that twisted upward and was swept away by the wind.

The Buick rolled to a stop only feet from the trees. Brian sat unmoving behind the wheel. Ashleigh stared in dread and terror and only tore her eyes away from the place where the dark man had been when the chain link beneath her hands shook with the chink of metal. She looked down and saw Will kicking the backstop.

"Fuck!" he screamed. "Fucking hell!"

Her arms aching from holding on so tightly, Ashleigh began to climb down. She had only just reached the ground, with Will reaching up to help her, when she heard other footfalls on the cold ground, and her head whipped up to see two thin figures running full-tilt across the field toward her, the same way she had come and the same way the car had come.

"Get the hell away from her or I swear to God I'll kill you!" shouted a familiar voice.

Beside her, Will stiffened. The Buick's engine died and Brian climbed out of the car. As the new arrivals ran toward them, Brian joined Will and Ashleigh.

"We were trying to avoid this," Brian said.

"Too late for that."

And Will was right.

"Ashleigh, you okay?" asked Will James. The younger Will James. Her best friend. But all the menace and urgency had gone from him.

Young Will and Young Brian both slowed as they approached, staring in disbelief at the men they would one day become. Ashleigh had been afraid the time travelers would never come back, and she had known that whoever or whatever had killed Mike Lebo might still be out there, stalking them all. She'd had no one to confide in save the only two people in Eastborough who might believe her. And they had, of course. Magic had already tainted them, destroyed their friendship, thrown a shadow over their lives.

But this was something they had never imagined.

"Ashleigh?" Elder Will ventured.

"I told them," she confirmed.

"Holy shit," Young Brian muttered, staring at his older self in amazement. Ashleigh didn't blame him. Elder Brian was handsome, fit, and confident, all of the things he wasn't.

"Come on," Elder Brian replied. "I was a little more eloquent than that."

Elder Will chuckled softly and rolled his eyes, smiling at his younger self. "Meanwhile, I'm speechless. Look at me. When did you ever know me to be speechless?"

Which set Young Will in motion. He pushed his hands through his blond hair and shook his head in disbelief, then strode over to them. With a comforting grip on Ashleigh's arm, as if contact was necessary to confirm that she was all right, he glared at his older self.

"You've got a lot of explaining to do."

CHAPTER 15

Ben Klosky had the approximate build and gait of a grizzly bear, but he could still manage stealth when it was necessary. Not that he enjoyed it. At his size, Ben wasn't used to sneaking around. But when it was called for, he had more grace than most people would have imagined.

The shadows enveloped him as he made his way quietly alongside the bushes beside the Brodys' house on Parmenter Road. There was a silliness about this—skulking about a house whose doorbell he had rung hundreds of times—but there was a bit of a thrill in it as well. Trying not to be seen was a job for spies and thieves, and though Ben would never have applied for either job, he had fantasized about both.

The wind picked up, blowing hard enough that it actually whistled past his ears. He zipped up his heavy navy blue sweatshirt and raised the hood. It was sort of late—well, not late-late, but enough of the night had already slipped by that he wouldn't have ventured out if Kyle hadn't called him and told him he had to come. That he had to see whatever weirdness was going on under the porch.

At six foot five and two hundred seventy-five pounds, Ben Klosky hated the room under the Brodys' porch. He would never have considered himself claustrophobic, but just being in the storage room made him want to punch someone. Usually Kyle. It was a good thing the kid was his best friend.

Ben reached the corner of the house without having made a sound. He poked his head around to get a glimpse of the patio and the porch. The windows were dark, though he could see the glow of lights from deeper in the house. His gaze went to the short, stooped door beneath the porch, an entrance for goblins, he had always imagined. Tonight he hated the images this conceit put into his mind.

The wind gusted, blowing brown and red leaves across the back lawn with a scritch-scratch noise that was like tiny, deadly things crawling up his spine. A frown creased his forehead. Ben wasn't the type to spook easily, but he shuddered and glanced around nervously, no longer anxious about being seen by Kyle's parents, but anxious just the same. All of a sudden he didn't want to be out here in the darkness anymore.

His gaze ticked toward the goblin door again, and it troubled him to realize that even that shelter would be welcome.

Still unnerved, he took another glance at the porch to make sure he was not being observed and then hurried quietly across the concrete patio. He had walked over, so his eyes had long since adjusted to the darkness. When Ben reached the door he hesitated, took a breath, then rapped softly.

His ears picked up every sound, alert for any noise from the house. After a moment there was a shifting, a kind of scraping, inside the storage room, but nothing else. Just as he raised his hand to rap again, there was a click and then the door popped open several inches. Ben actually flinched.

"Get in here," Kyle whispered.

The door swung wide, and Kyle grabbed his sleeve. Ben barely had time to crouch down to avoid cracking his skull on the frame of that goblin door. He shuffled into the storage space, which was illuminated not by the overhead bulb but by a flashlight that lay on the floor. As soon as he was in, Kyle hissed at him to close the door behind him. Ben did as he was asked, and then Kyle clicked off the flashlight and pulled the metal string on the overhead bulb.

Ben's back already ached, and he had a muscle cramp in his neck, but when that light went on he forgot his discomfort. Kyle had cleared off an old, rusty wrought-iron chair for him to use but Ben ignored it. Instead, he stared at the circle on the floor.

A ripple of something that might have been fear went through him, and suddenly he felt the closeness of the walls and ceiling more than ever.

"What is this?"

Kyle laughed softly, but if it was meant to put Ben at ease, it failed.

"The guy I was telling you about earlier, Will James? He was here," Kyle whispered. He smiled and shook his head. "Dude, I swear to God you are never going to believe this. But it's true. It's all true."

Ben hesitated, his unease growing. In the dim light of the single bulb Kyle looked even paler than usual, and there was a deeper red tint than Ben had ever noticed in his orange hair. In his friend's hands was a thick leather-bound book, the edges of its pages all ragged the way really old books were.

"That's . . . that's the book you were telling me about? The one you found under the stairs?"

With a grin, Kyle handed it to him. By reflex, Ben took the book and immediately wished he hadn't. Despite the cold that seeped through the walls and concrete floor of that room, the book was warm to the touch. Its cover felt more like skin than leather, and the instant he made that comparison in his mind he felt sick. There seemed to be a strange smell coming from the book as well, the odor of a match after it'd been blown out.

While Ben held the book, Kyle talked to him. About Will James, and the incredible story he had told. About this book and what it could do. But most terribly, about the things that Kyle claimed to have witnessed Will James do right here in this terrible goblin room.

Ben forced a smile. His hair was too long, and the way the

ceiling was torn, with bits of pink insulation innards hanging down like Spanish moss, it made him feel as though things were crawling in his shaggy mane. In the front of his mind, he knew that they were under Kyle's porch, that his parents were in the house probably having a glass of wine and watching a movie or something, with lights on and locks on the doors. This was a place they'd hung out in the past, though Ben only reluctantly. How many beers had they drunk down here?

Too many, but Ben wished he'd saved a few for right now.

In the back of his mind, in a little room inside his head not unlike this dry, stale, rust-smelling storage space, it felt different to him tonight. Alive and shifting with the hint of some presence, of eyes upon him. Big Ben Klosky was no coward, but when he walked through the woods alone, that was how he felt. As though at any moment something might slither from the bushes or drop from the branches above.

This was the same feeling.

He'd seen the way cats hissed and horses shied from certain people or places, but he had never imagined he could feel what they felt. Now he knew people could get their hackles up just as well as dogs.

He wanted out of there. Right fucking now.

"Kyle," he said, voice low, that rusty smell now coating his throat and becoming a taste.

"Shit," his best friend replied, a look of curdled-milk disgust on his face. "I knew you wouldn't believe me."

Ben felt his fingers stroking the leather cover of the book in his hands and he glanced down at it. Opened it. *Dark Gifts.* Jean-Marc Gaudet. He didn't want to know what else was in it, what kind of shit had drooled out of Jean-Marc Gaudet's brain into this book.

He knelt on the concrete and pushed the book at Kyle, who also seemed reluctant to hold it. Ben wiped his hands on his sweatshirt, back and forth several times, and then he pushed his fingers through his hair to brush out the imaginary insulation maggots that his mind insisted were crawling there.

"I didn't say I didn't believe you," Ben said. The truth was, he wasn't sure what to believe. Kyle wasn't the kind of guy who made shit up, pulled practical jokes. But he'd been known to get carried away with his enthusiasms in the past. Could be he had just found the book and—

Ben froze. As he had begun to move away from Kyle, thinking to leave the goblin room, to get some fresh air in spite of Kyle's insistence that he himself had to remain under the porch waiting for this Will James to come back, his gaze had slid across the concrete floor just beyond Kyle. On his knees, he could make out symbols in the dim light.

Rust. That smell in the room. Only it wasn't rust.

Slowly he reached out to grab the flashlight that Kyle had set on the ground. Ben clicked it on, its light shining a spot upon the wall. He swung it around and pointed it at the dark brown circle on the concrete and the symbols that had been scrawled there.

"Kyle," Ben said, a chill racing up his spine. "Tell me that's not blood."

With a sigh, Kyle slid the book onto the floor. He knelt on the ground in that small space and grabbed Ben by the shoulder, forcing Ben to meet his gaze.

"Benjy, have you not been paying any attention at all?" Kyle asked, his eyes gleaming, reflecting that single bare bulb. "I know it's fucked, but this isn't some game. I'm not fooling around here. Pay attention, Mr. Klosky, 'cause Elvis has left the building, and buddy, he took us with him. Nothing's the same now. If you saw even a fraction of what I saw tonight, you could never—"

The flashlight died.

Both of them glanced down at it. Ben's eyes strayed to the bloody circle again.

Then the bare bulb overhead flickered and went out. At the very same moment the hum of electricity that ran through the house and that was always audible for some reason down there in the storage space simply stopped. The house had lost power.

Darkness swallowed them.

"Shit," Kyle whispered.

"Blackout." Ben blinked several times, but his eyes were not adjusting. All he could see were black and gray swaths of shadow. Yet he had frozen in place not because of the dark, but because of the other thing, the feeling he'd had of eyes upon him. Some primal part of his mind felt that the predator was here and that if he remained completely still, he would be all right.

Upstairs in the Brodys' house, glass shattered and Kyle's mother began to scream, not an angry shout but a horrid shriek of pain and hysterical anguish.

In the dark, Ben heard Kyle whisper one word.

"Mom?"

He sounded so very small.

The screaming stopped.

Swathed in blackness, blind in that tiny room, Ben was in the way when Kyle started for the door. Kyle slammed into him, knocking him backward onto his ass. Ben tried to catch himself and his right hand caught on something sharp. He hissed in pain, then grunted as he felt hands and elbows and knees on him as Kyle, now driven only by an insane, beyond-thought need to reach his mother, tried to climb right over him.

Ben was twice his size. In the darkness he felt along Kyle's body, found his throat, and shoved him back, driving him down to the concrete. There was no light. None at all. Ben could not even see a glint where Kyle's eyes should have been. But he heard the whimpering just fine.

Moments before Ben had wanted nothing more than to leave this room. He had changed his mind.

"Don't even twitch," he whispered to Kyle, his voice cracking with fear, eyes burning with nascent tears. Big Ben bit his lip.

"My...my parents," Kyle whispered. His chest hitched and when he spoke again his voice was choked. "Ben, that...that was my mom."

Ben swallowed, and his throat was so dry it was like eating glass. His face was warm and flushed and yet the rest of him was so damn cold. The darkness was too much. If he could just have seen Kyle's face he might have been able to communicate, been able to explain. But in his heart was the ancient echo of some primeval terror, the first men taking shelter in a cave from something cruel and hungry that stalked the night.

"Ben?"

"Ssshhh." He put his hand over Kyle's mouth, bent close, putting his weight on his friend. "Ssshhh. Not a sound. Not a sound until the lights come back on."

They lay there in the dark like illicit lovers fearing discovery.

Until the first scratching began on the small door of the storage space. There had been no further noise from inside the house, no sound of the porch door opening, or footsteps upon those stairs. Just that scratching, like nails dragging languorously across the wood. Kyle whimpered. The storage space filled with the reeking odor of urine and Ben thought Kyle had pissed himself, and then he felt the dampness in his own jeans.

October, Senior Year...

On the drive back to Parmenter Road, Will kept glancing in the rearview mirror, numb with the astonishment that still lingered in him, even after all of the events of the past few days. For every time he glanced in that mirror, he saw himself more than a decade younger, his hair too short, his eyes ablaze with wonder, a true reflection across the years. The kid in the backseat—with Ashleigh in the middle and Young Brian on the other side—was skeptical on the surface, but Will knew him. Will was him. He knew that beneath that superficial doubt was absolute faith in the truth of the impossible.

"Will!" Brian snapped, and he reached over from the driver's side to jerk the wheel.

With a quick shot on the brakes, gaze straight ahead now, Will barely missed clipping a station wagon that was parked on the street. His heart thundered in his chest, not appreciating the irony involved in his killing them all by accident. He kept his eyes on the road, at least for a moment or two. Gradually, first his thoughts and then his gaze drifted back to the kid in the back-seat, to Young Will, who still had so many mistakes to make, so many lessons to learn, so many days to squander.

A smile crept across his face. Will wouldn't rob himself of those mistakes, those lost days, for anything. *The kid's a lot more resilient than the grown-up version,* Will thought. Ashleigh had told him everything that was going on—a revelation that had torn away the spell of forgetting he had done—and Young Will was rolling with the punches a hell of a lot more fluidly than his older counterpart had managed to.

Will glanced in the backseat again, and this time he caught Ashleigh watching him, her eyes haunted by the attack she had just endured. Will wanted to hold her, but found himself strangely reluctant. It wasn't his place. That other Will, the one in the back, it was his duty. A shudder of recognition, of shared sentiment, went through him as he caught a glimpse of their hands. Young Will and Ashleigh were holding hands, not romantically, but for strength.

Will returned his gaze to the road, but in him was a melancholy more powerful than any this bittersweet homecoming had previously created. Of all the things he missed from his high school days, none felt so painfully lost as the relationship he had shared with Ashleigh. They were still best friends, even now. But not like they had been back then.

That was the way life was. The world turned. The river flowed. And the farther you sailed upon it, the less distinct were the things you left behind along your journey.

He took a deep breath and gripped the steering wheel tightly. They were all haunted by the way Ashleigh's attacker had disappeared from Robinson Field, misting into the dark, becoming part of the shadows. Mike Lebo was dead. That part of his past was irrevocably changed, and he felt that loss. But Ashleigh was safe. He and Brian had been right to fear that their arrival might alter their enemy's plans. Had they not been watching over Ashleigh, waiting for the right opportunity to connect with her again—something they had been about to do when the shadow man appeared—he didn't even want to think about the result.

Ashleigh. Will smiled as he turned the corner and drove them all up Parmenter Road in the shitbox Buick Brian had bought out of the classifieds for five hundred in cash. As he thought of her, of all she had meant to him, he found himself missing home for the first time since his trip back. Not Eastborough home, but home. The time he had come from. His year. His apartment. His job. His friends. And, strangest of all, the Ashleigh of that time, the married lawyer with twin daughters and all the confidence in the world. He missed her.

As they drew nearer to his house, Will slowed.

"They're out tonight," his younger self said in the backseat. "With the Djordjeviches."

Will smiled incredulously. So that was this night? "I remember," he said as he pulled into the driveway. He turned around in the seat, gaze ticking from Young Brian to Ashleigh and then pausing upon his own face. "They're going to be late."

Young Will shook his head. "They only went to Framingham."

"Yeah. But they're going to have to drive Jelena—Mrs. Djordjevich—back to Newton. Long story." Though he saw the confusion and curiosity in his own young eyes he tore his gaze away and looked at Ashleigh. She still seemed skittish. "Now's not the time for this. We should get inside."

They got out of the car, its doors creaking as they were slammed shut, and all of them walked up to the front door together. As Young Will got his keys out, Ashleigh stood close by him. Will and Brian had explained to her what they had been doing the past two days—buying the car, getting a motel room, buying clothes, and getting cleaned up—but fortunately she had not pursued the matter of Mike Lebo's death as yet, and Young Brian hadn't asked where his future self had gotten time-sensitive cash.

But all of those things were going to have to be discussed

now; all cards would have to be put on the table. The shadow man was still out there, still hunting, and there were other victims to come.

Inside the house, Young Will led the way to the kitchen and Will the Elder took up the rear, closing the door behind him. As he followed the two Brians up the stairs he noticed Young Brian lean over to his twenty-something counterpart with a giddy grin on his face.

"I like the goatee," the doughy-faced teenager said. "It's a good look."

The elder Brian nodded. "It works for me. For us."

"So what do I . . . I mean, what do you do?" his younger self asked.

Brian paused and glanced back at Will, who gave an abrupt shake of his head. With a sad shake of his head, Brian glanced at the kid.

"I'm you. I know how bad you must want to know, but you're also me. Do you really think you're going to get me to spill the future, just like that? We've fucked this stuff up enough already."

Young Brian shot him a withering glance.

His older self arched an eyebrow. "I'll tell you this much. We do pretty well. Up until now."

The kid nodded. "Cool."

Moments later they had gathered in the living room. Will had begun to think he was adjusting to all of this, but stepping into that room put the lie to that. As he sat down in a high-backed antique chair with floral upholstery, his hands shook. He flexed them into fists, gazing about the room breathlessly. The mustard-colored sofa was just as ugly as he remembered it, the coffee table as scuffed by his own childhood antics. Above the fireplace was an elegant drawing of a man and woman embracing, sketched out in delicate reds on white parchment. Every knickknack was familiar to him, though some of them were long-forgotten treasures.

Will rose and crossed to a shelf, where he snatched up a brass elephant. He let his fingers run over it as they had done many times. The brass was slightly tarnished and the smell of it was like a gift from the past.

For a moment he just held on to it, his back to the others. Then he turned and tossed it to Young Will, who sat on the edge of the coffee table with Ashleigh. The kid caught it easily and he stared back at Will. On the couch, the Brians were side by side, comfortable, and Will wondered how they could have adapted to one another so quickly when he and his younger counterpart had barely exchanged words.

But then, Young Brian was glad to see his elder. Whereas Young Will would have been terrified at the prospect of learning what the next ten years of his life would be like. Even now Will could see it in his eyes and he knew it was the truth. That was what he would have felt. Terror. To know what fate had in store would take away any passion he might have for his life.

The funny thing was that Will would have loved to tell his younger self how things would turn out with Caitlyn. He had wasted so much time, had borne so much heartache, thanks to her. Now here was an opportunity to prevent that from ever happening, to erase it from his memory, and not only did he know he shouldn't take advantage of it, he knew Young Will wouldn't want to hear it.

Irony sucked.

Even if Will said something, there was no way to know how it would affect the future. Back in the day, Stacy Shipman would never have gone out with him. It was only in the future that the two of them would click. Thoughts of her made Will smile. Nope, it was better, all around, for all of them to keep quiet, no matter how much heartache they could have saved their younger selves ... themselves ... in the bargain.

Impatient, Young Will got tired of waiting.

"So what's the plan?"

Will glanced at Brian, who nodded. Not that Will expected anything else. They were far too deep into this thing to hold back now. His gaze shifted to Ashleigh, who smiled softly when he looked at her and nodded.

"I'm shaken up. But I'm all right. Thanks to you guys." She glanced around. "All of you. If you hadn't come when you did—"

"That's what we're here for," Brian the Elder said, his younger counterpart nodding in agreement.

"It also proves that we can change things," Will said. They were all watching him, expecting him to take the lead. "That doesn't mean Ashleigh isn't still in danger—"

"Why don't you let me worry about Ashleigh," seventeen-year-old Will scowled from the coffee table. "You did such a bang-up job with Lebo."

Beside him, his best friend frowned. "Why don't we let Ashleigh worry about Ashleigh? OK, you saved my ass. I said thank you. It doesn't make me the eternal damsel in distress."

A chill passed through Will as he stared at his younger self, trying to figure out if the kid was being sarcastic, or if he suspected his elders had had a larger role in Mike's death. Will and Brian had debated telling them, and decided it was best not to mention it. There was no way to take it back now, and it would only weigh them all down with guilt, regret, and resentment. The pain that gnawed at Will's gut, that nibbled at his heart whenever he thought of Saturday night, of the sound of the car striking Mike's body, was something he would not have wished on anyone. But this was different...this was selfish.

He kept the dark truth of that night from Young Will because he wanted to keep it from himself, to save himself the pain of that knowledge in the intervening years.

"Look, here's our situation," he said, drawing their attention again, ignoring Young Will's gibe. "Tess O'Brien's in danger. So's Bonnie Winter. Like I said, Ashleigh might not be out of the woods yet. Also, just because Brian and I don't remember anything else happening, that doesn't mean it can't. Our coming back here is changing things. Hopefully for the better, but that could work both ways."

On the sofa, Brian spoke up for the first time. He was

stroking his goatee in a way that aged him further than his twenty-eight years, and there was a shadow of sadness that dimmed his eyes.

"Will," he said, speaking to the younger of the two, an old friend returning, "I've got to tell you something that your mutated self over here took a long time to learn." Brian hooked a thumb toward the older Will but continued to look at the younger. "You're not always right. You're not always going to do the right thing. Shit, that's a lesson you've already learned, isn't it?"

Brian glanced at his younger self, then back at Young Will. "We learned it together. But maybe it's going to take a while longer for it to kick in. You guys both want to know what the future holds, don't you? Of course you do. Well, I'll tell you."

"Hang on," Will cautioned him.

With a hard look, Brian silenced him and continued.

"You're going to have some shit times. You're going to have some grand ones, too. But life? Life is made up of all the times in between. Magic is pretty amazing. It's like getting high or fucking, only better. It takes you away from the mundane, transports you to another place where you don't just think you're the center of the world, you become the center of the world.

"But it's all bullshit," Brian whispered, his voice a rasp filled with hesitant emotion. He dropped his gaze a moment and swallowed hard before raising his chin and glaring around the room. "None of it's real. Magic, drugs, sex... no matter how high up you go, you've always got to come back down. And it's what you've got waiting for you when you come down that matters."

The shush of a car passing on the street outside whispered through the room; the only other sound was the ticking of the clock in the kitchen. They all stared at Brian for a time, until at length the dough-faced teenager he had once been twisted around on the couch to face him.

"I get what you're saying. I do. But what's that have to do with this? With what's going on right now?"

Brian the Elder looked over at Young Will with a gravity he had never been able to summon as a boy. "It means you've got to get over yourself. Knock this shit off. There's no room here for attitude. You, both of you"—he glanced at Will—"we, all of us messed with something we shouldn't have. I can't help thinking, long-term, this is the payback. Magic screws with the natural order of things. It makes ripples. We're feeling them now."

"Ripples!" Young Will shot to his feet and shook his head in denial, shuddering as though he were cold. "Mike Lebo is dead, you asshole!"

Young Brian flinched. "Hey!" he said, and glanced apologetically at his older self.

"Fuck you, too," the teenage Will replied. Then he spun to glare at his older self, and the elder Will knew most of this bitterness was aimed at him.

He understood.

But he didn't have any more time for this crap.

Will strode up to the boy he had once been and reached for him. The kid tried to slap his arms away, but Will embraced him nevertheless. His whole body trembled, the smell of his hair was so familiar, and for a moment he felt that odd slippage in his mind as memories reasserted themselves, some sifting lower in the deck and others higher. For a few seconds it was hard to know which body was his and which was his own, because he remembered this moment with utter clarity.

It was the strangest sensation: he remembered what he was going to say before the words had left his lips, words whose effect he understood completely.

"I know you don't want to believe in this. I know you don't want to think about magic ever again. But I'm you, Will," he whispered, gripping the back of the kid's head. "And without me, without you, more of your friends are going to be hurt. Bonnie Winter's going to die. She kissed us once, do you remember? In the eighth grade, in the closet at Doreen Bianchi's house."

At first Young Will struggled against him, but then he seemed to sink into Will's arms. When he looked up there was a kind of surrender in his eyes, but a resoluteness there as well.

His fingers went to his lips as if experiencing a tactile memory of that one kiss from Bonnie Winter.

"You can't let her die," Will told him.

Young Will pushed away from him and went back to the coffee table, where he sat with Ashleigh. She slid her arm around him.

"So," Brian said, watching Will, "you were saying?"

Will nodded. "I was saying we've got to watch them all."

"It shouldn't be too hard," Ashleigh offered. "Tess and Bonnie are both on the cheer squad with me. If Will and Brian hang out at practice this week, no one will think it's weird. Especially not since Caitlyn's on the squad, too."

The elder Brian shot a mischievous glance at his younger self. "And you'll be able to spend every afternoon ogling cheerleaders and have an excuse."

Young Brian pretended to be scandalized. "I admire them for their athleticism and . . . the synchronization. It's a skill."

Ashleigh shot him a dark look, but Will wasn't ready for them to lighten up just yet.

"That works," he said, "and Brian and I can keep an eye on their houses at night. Will . . . and I can't tell you how weird it is to call you that . . . you'll have to keep in constant contact with Ashleigh when she's not at school or cheer practice.

"Look, Mike's funeral is Wednesday morning. If things actually *do* happen the way Brian and I remember them, Tess's attack will be Friday night. We'll get another shot at the invisible man then, for sure. Meanwhile, the two of us will sleep mostly during the day. We're staying at the Red Roof Inn if you need us during that time. For now we'll split up, start keeping watch over Tess and Bonnie. The three of you try to get some rest. You still have school, and us to answer to if you start blowing off homework and tests."

The five of them paused to glance around the room at one another.

"Everyone good with the plan?" Will asked.

Young Will wouldn't look him in the eye.

"What?"

The kid smiled. "I don't want anyone thinking I've got attitude, but isn't there something you guys forgot?"

Will glanced at Brian, but they were all looking at the kid.

"You don't want to tell us about the future, but between what Ashleigh told us and what you were saying in the car, I get the basic idea. Someone left you this note, and this book, and that's how you figured you weren't losing your mind, that someone was really screwing with your head. If Brian's the only one who knows where the Gaudet book is stashed, then don't you think we'd better put the thing under the stairs—and that note in the storage area under the porch—just to be on the safe side? We have to, don't we? Otherwise none of this would ever have happened."

"That doesn't make sense," Ashleigh said, brows knitting. "How can that be? If it took them coming back to cause the note to be written and the book to be left under there, but it took the note and the book to cause them to come back, that doesn't make any sense."

But Will was not so troubled. "Maybe once the slippage started, once Brian and I kept both sets of memories and started to figure out what was happening, maybe that part, at least, was inevitable. That we would come back, that we would be here, that we would be able to get those messages into the future."

Will noticed a dark look exchanged between the two Brians, and he felt a strange uneasiness enter his heart. They seemed relaxed, those two, but looking at them now he wondered if that was not so much relaxation as resignation.

"What was that?" he asked. "That look?"

Ashleigh and Young Will both glanced at them as well.

The expression on the face of Brian the Elder underwent a change that revealed the fear he had been keeping hidden as best he could. In that moment he looked far younger.

"I've thought about this a lot over the years. Sometimes I think..." He paused and glanced out the window at the night. Then he offered a sheepish chuckle that drained from his face instantly. "Sometimes I think magic has a kind of intelligence all its own. Or if not intelligence, at least ambition. It has twists and folds in it...and shadows. This isn't H. G. Wells. It's Jean-Marc Gaudet's fucking *Dark Gifts*."

Young Brian sniffed and shook his head, eyes downcast. "Yeah, right. Magic is never a gift. It always comes with a price."

CHAPTER 16

The sky was ice blue that Wednesday morning when they buried Michael Paul Lebo. Without any warning from the meteorologists the temperature had tumbled precipitously overnight. If it got any colder, Will knew, he would be able to see his breath. Halloween was less than two weeks away, autumn in full swing, and there was frost on the jack-o'-lanterns in the mornings, but this was still unseasonably cold.

Will remembered this day, but he had forgotten how cold it was, and he shivered in the thick sweater he wore. It wasn't below freezing, but when the wind eddied the leaves in an autumnal dance across the cemetery, it felt like midwinter.

At the graveside stood Father Charles, an austere thirty-something priest who was a friend to the Lebo family. Will knew him, but only in the dimmest sense. In that other set of memories, the set that was fading like old photographs in his mind, Father Charles had attended Mike's graduation party. But there wasn't going to be a party now.

The strangest sensation of all was the visceral, nearly debilitating déjà vu that threatened to overwhelm him at any moment. He wasn't sure if it could really be called déjà vu, however, since he actually had had this experience before. Every time he glanced around, his mind tried to match what he was seeing with his memory of these events. It was an immediate echo, but always from a different angle, a different perspective. This hadn't been as much of a problem on Monday night, speaking with Young Will, because his memories of their conversation hadn't existed until they'd had it. He was making new memories.

This, though...the images from this funeral were etched upon his mind. Several times he had to squeeze his eyes shut from the disorientation caused by his dual perspective. Young Will and Young Brian were near the inner circle of mourners, close to the grave and to Mike's family. Others gathered in grief-stricken concentric rows around the center, including Principal Chadbourne and several teachers. Mr. Sandoval from American history and Mrs. Hidalgo from biology stood on either side of Mr. Murphy, who had grown up in Framingham but knew the area well, and whom all the students really connected with. Mr. Murphy was leaning slightly on Mrs. Hidalgo, and when he glanced at her, Will could see his grim, tear-streaked expression.

There were more than a hundred students there, from the look of it. Will crossed his arms, covering his mouth with one hand as he gathered his composure. They were all there. Caitlyn and Ashleigh, Lolly and Pix, Bonnie Winter and Brian's sister Dori; Will smiled to think how much Mike would've loved to know that half the cheerleading squad had shown up to cry over him.

Danny and Nick were behind the girls, along with Eric, who had come home the previous day. So far Ashleigh hadn't mentioned what had happened to her, but Will thought she would eventually, that she should. That was not the sort of thing you kept from someone you loved. Joe Rosenthal, Tim Friel, and Kelly Meserve were there. He spotted Martina Dienst, her arm linked with Delia Young. Todd Vasquez. Nyla. Chuck. Kelso. Mia Skopis.

He was surprised to see Stacy Shipman there, and found himself staring at her. There was something extraordinarily magnetic about the girl, and he wondered if he was the only one upon whom she had that effect. Her head was tilted to one side, resting on Todd Vasquez's shoulder. Even amongst those who had not known Mike well enough to grieve for him, there was a shroud of melancholy that was to be expected. This sort of thing wasn't supposed to happen.

Will took a long breath and let it out slowly. Intellectually, he knew that Mike's death was not his fault, that he had been used as a murder weapon. But he had been having nightmares about the steering wheel in his hand, the sound of cracking glass and the impact of flesh and bone upon metal. They never kept him from going back to sleep, strangely enough. Perhaps because he felt such night terrors were only a fraction of the torment he deserved.

From his sadness he seemed to come awake, standing there in the cemetery, mind still muddled with the combination of this experience and the memory of having been through it before. As his eyes focused on the mourners ahead of him once more, he saw that Stacy Shipman was looking his way. She wore a curious expression that seemed to say that she felt she should recognize him but couldn't quite place his face.

Will offered her a sad smile, and Stacy returned it. Then the priest gave his final blessing and the mourners began to move forward, forming a line around the grave, shuffling past that hole in the ground where what remained of Mike Lebo now lay. Some of them carried flowers that they dropped into the grave. Beside him, Brian started forward to get in line but Will did not join him. Brian shot him a curious glance, but Will only shrugged. He had been through that line before and did not want to experience it again.

As the mourners paid their respects, Will turned his back upon the spectacle. His heart hurt too much to watch it again. He thought of Mike rummaging through the stacks at the Comic Book Palace or doing his terrible Hannibal Lecter impression during school assemblies to get a laugh.

Will closed his eyes again, wiping them. *I'm sorry, Lebo.*

"Let's go," Brian said, voice low. "I don't want to be here anymore."

"I'm with you," Will replied, though he had a difficult time tearing his attention away from the line of black-clad mourners. When he did glance at Brian, he saw that his old friend was staring at him. The bruises on Brian's face had faded to yellow, and though they were both completely out of place in dark pants and sweaters they could barely afford, he managed to look appropriately somber and clean-cut. On the other hand, Will felt like a mess and hoped he didn't look in quite as much disarray as he felt.

"What's that look?" Brian asked.

"You turned out okay," Will said, surprising himself with the sentiment.

"Know what? I know your thinking is pretty muddy right now, but believe it or not, you turned out all right yourself." Brian took a step closer and leaned in so they were practically nose to nose. "We've still got work to do, Will. Don't fall apart on me now."

Will took a long breath and nodded once, then turned and started across the cemetery lawn. A long line of cars was parked on the long narrow drive that snaked through the graveyard. The two yellow school buses that had carried the students from Eastborough High looked hideously out of place, like clown cars in the presidential motorcade.

By the time they reached their five-hundred-dollar Buick near the back of the line, the funeral had officially ended, and while many of the mourners gathered in small clusters to speak softly about the dead, others had begun to drift amongst the gravestones and tombs, returning to their own vehicles. Will paused as he opened the Buick's door and took one last long look at the grave, at Father Charles speaking to the Lebos, at his younger self standing with his friends, not wanting to leave . . . not wanting to leave Mike behind forever.

He grieved still.

On the far side of the cemetery, up the grave-studded slope, something shifted. His gaze ticked upward and there, in the shadow of a marble tomb, he saw the shadow man.

Despite the sun and the blue sky and all of the people around him, Will felt a cloak of darkness enfold him that was far colder than the October air, and he inhaled sharply. In the sunlight the shadow man rippled like the wind across the surface of a pond.

A larger ripple passed through that night-black figure, and then it disappeared.

WILL AND BRIAN WERE SILENT as they drove back from the cemetery. For the second day in a row they had stayed awake all night, standing vigilant outside the homes of Tess O'Brien and Bonnie Winter. On Tuesday they had slept most of the day in their room at the Red Roof Inn in Westborough, not far from Papillon. That night they had met up with Ashleigh, Young Will, and Young Brian for perhaps twenty minutes.

Young Brian had *Dark Gifts* in his backpack and had seemed to be struggling with the weight of it. None of them commented on this oddity. By now even Ashleigh knew that the Gaudet book had properties that were unsettling. The seventeen-year-old Brian had already scrawled a message inside the book, a fact that alarmed Will at first. At least, it alarmed him until he read the inscription and recognized that handwriting. It was the same as it had been the first time he had seen this message. The instructions to Kyle were identical. It seemed his theory had been correct; the moment Will had begun to realize that someone was altering the past, this particular event had become inevitable. Every possible unfolding of circumstances included Young Brian writing those words and the book ending up in Kyle Brody's hands and delivering it to Will eleven years hence in the parking lot of Papillon.

Kyle. Will had barely thought of him at all and he wondered how long—by Kyle's reckoning—he had been gone. He hoped that the kid was all right, that his parents hadn't found that bloodstained circle under the porch . . . and, most of all, that no one had damaged the circle.

Young Brian had also written the words *Don't forget* on a scrap of paper and slipped it into an envelope, upon which he had scrawled more instructions for Kyle. It was Ashleigh who had pointed out to all of them what should have been obvious. If the note and the book were just stashed in their respective hiding places, they would surely be discovered too soon. They had worried at this problem for a while, comforted by the knowledge that it was a problem they were destined to solve.

At length Brian recalled a spell he thought might help. It took him several minutes to locate it in Gaudet's text, and then the book and the envelope were transferred to Young Will's backpack, and the rest was left up to him. He would get them where they needed to be, and perform the spell that would make them invisible and intangible until the very day they were needed. Will knew just shunting them forward in time wouldn't be enough. When Kyle had found them, they had been yellowed and covered in dust. And they would be again. It was the one thing they could be certain of.

Will replayed all of this on that somber drive back from burying Mike Lebo. His eyes were bleary from staying up all night playing watchdog. It was chilly enough for them to need the heat in the car, but for five hundred dollars, they had gotten what they had paid for: the heat didn't work at all. And the radio only played AM stations.

Classical music hissed with static through the speakers in the back and they said not a word to one another. Until they stopped the guy Will had started to think of as the shadow man and set things right, there was very little for them to talk about. A cloud seemed to follow them as the Buick rolled through downtown. Before returning to the Red Roof they both needed something to eat, but there would be no stop at Athens Pizza, no visit to The Sampan. Nothing familiar. Will had longed to drift through the Comic Book Palace and Annie's Book Stop, to do the pop-culture archaeology he had always loved as a kid. Now he felt that such an excursion would be morbid, that if he set foot inside Athens Pizza or that comics shop, he would become violently ill.

"He was there," Will said, voice gravelly from disuse.

Brian turned in the passenger seat and stared at him, waiting for more.

"The shadow man. I saw him at the cemetery, watching the funeral."

"Huh. I guess I didn't think he could come out during the day." Brian shook his head. "How stupid is that? Like he's a vampire or something."

"It's not stupid. That's magic. It always seems more possible at night."

"You've gotta wonder, though," Brian replied.

Will kept his eyes on the road, driving a little faster now, happy to leave Eastborough behind. "Wonder what?"

"Was he watching the funeral? Or was he watching us?"

ASHLEIGH SPENT THE BALANCE of the week so much on edge that the creak of a floorboard would startle her and an unexpected tap on the shoulder would make her jump and cry out. The latter could be terribly embarrassing when it occurred in biology lab. But a small dose of humiliation was not enough to soothe her nerves. Never in her life had she been so aware of each intake of breath, of the rhythm of her heart, of the faces she passed in the halls and on the street.

Yet days went by that were dreadfully uneventful, such that now, with Friday night upon her, she was perversely relieved. Tonight was the night Will's "shadow man" was supposed to attack Tess. No more waiting.

But she was still holding her breath.

It was the night before the Homecoming game, and the committee was preparing the float in the parking lot behind the high school. Ashleigh had been Tess's shadow all afternoon, from cheerleading practice to pizza at Papa Gino's and now back to school to finish up the float. There were two or three dozen kids in the lot all being herded by Mr. Murphy, the committee's faculty advisor. Every year the Cougars made a float that was a cougar. This year's committee insisted upon doing something a

little different, so they designed a float that was a giant football...with the image of a cougar on the side of the ball. Ashleigh thought it was silly, but everyone else loved it, so she kept
quiet.

Besides, tonight she had other priorities.

It was not quite as cold as it had been midweek, but still chilly
enough that Ashleigh wore a light sweater under her jacket. The
air was redolent with the scent of flowers. The football itself
was crepe paper, but the cougar design on either side was indeed
a floral creation, mostly thanks to hard work by Tess herself.
Ashleigh had lent a hand, but Tess was the one who had pushed
for the inclusion of the flowers and she really made it work.
Most everyone else was occupied with painting white lines onto
the brown crepe paper to represent the laces on a football. It had
taken the presence of the captain of the football team to remind
them that the football needed laces. Even now Tim Friel was up
on top of the float helping Tess add daisies to the cougar.

The strangest sight was Will and Brian—*her* Will and
Brian—helping out with nailing down the green plastic grass
carpeting that would cover the rest of the float. The players and
cheerleaders would be riding there, and it was supposed to look
like a football field. Instead, it more closely resembled the fluo-
rescent grass that came in Easter baskets. Though Will and
Brian weren't part of the committee, they had come down and
offered to help. And though surprised, Mr. Murphy was more
than willing to accept their help. Their job was to keep an eye on
Bonnie Winter, who wasn't really helping, but was instead using
her time to flirt.

The *other* Will and Brian—she would never get used to
them—had not arrived yet, but she figured they would be here at
any time. Ashleigh figured they had slept through the day again
and probably gotten something to eat before heading over. She
hoped that they would arrive soon, because she desperately
needed to pee.

"Hey, Ashleigh."

She turned from her spot on the float, where she was painting

EASTBOROUGH COUGARS in the school colors. The wind blew her hair across her eyes and she pushed it away with the back of her hand, the smell of paint in her nostrils. Then she smiled.

"Lolly. What's up?" Ashleigh glanced past the other girl. "Where's Pix?"

"What, I can't go anywhere without her?" Lolly asked, the parking lot lights gleaming off her caramel features.

"Like peanut butter without the jelly."

Lolly rolled her eyes and cocked out her hip in that completely unconscious, sultry way that she did. "I'm meeting up with her and Caitlyn in a bit. I told them I'd stop by and see if you wanted to come with. We're just doing a little window-shopping at the mall."

"I can't. Don't want to abandon the rest of the committee. I'll see you guys in the morning, though."

"All right. We'll just have to shop on without you." Lolly glanced upward. "You're praying for no rain, huh?"

"Oh, yeah. That would suck."

The pressure in her bladder had been growing, and now Ashleigh hopped down from the float and laid her paintbrush across the can. She wiped the paint from her hands on the threadbare jeans she had worn for precisely that purpose and shot Lolly a bashful grin.

"Girl's gotta go."

"Then go, girl, go. And I'm gone, too. See you tomorrow."

Ashleigh hurried across the parking lot toward the double doors of the high school, waving to Mr. Murphy to let him know where she was headed. He nodded in return. She paused just inside the door and tried surreptitiously to get Will's or Brian's attention, but to no avail. They were too busy hammering nails and watching Bonnie Winter. With a sigh she glanced at Tess, who was still up on the float affixing daisies. There were dozens of students around her. Anyone who wanted to hurt her would have to get through all of them to do it.

Unless they were magic.

The shadow man had become a wisp of darkness right in

front of her eyes. Who was to say if he might appear from nothing, grab Tess, and disappear the same way?

Ashleigh hesitated another moment, but her bladder won out. She raced inside the high school, hurrying down the stairs. Halfway down she slipped and nearly fell, catching herself on the handrail just in time.

"Get it together, Ash," she muttered to herself, her voice sounding hollow and distant in the stairwell.

Then she pushed in through the door of the ladies' room. It echoed with the drip of a leaky faucet and one of the lights was burnt out. Any other night she would have been uneasy about going in there alone in an empty school, but tonight she didn't have time for that kind of thing.

As quickly as nature would allow, she was hurrying back up the stairs. In the back of her mind she had painted terrible images of what might await her when she returned, but when she stepped back out into the lot, nothing had changed. Some of the kids were working, others were just flirting, laughing, and screwing around. Bonnie Winter was demonstrating one of the cheers their squad would use at tomorrow's game. Will and Brian had given up the pretense of work to watch her.

Tess was gone.

Ashleigh could not breathe. She glanced around, saw Mr. Murphy talking to Tim Friel, looked closely at every girl, just in case. But none of them was Tess.

"Fuck," she whispered, sprinting across the lot. She wanted to scream at the guys, tell them to stop watching Bonnie Winter's tits bounce, but everyone would have thought she was a freak. Instead, she ran to Tim and Mr. Murphy, both of whom glanced at her with nearly identical raised-eyebrow expressions.

"Ashleigh?" Mr. Murphy began.

But her focus was on Tim. "What happened to Tess?"

"She had a date." He shrugged. "She just left."

Will and Brian had finally noticed something was up and they strode across the lot toward her. Ashleigh focused on Tim.

"Did she say who with, or where she was going?" she asked, panicking.

"Jesus, no," Tim said. "Chill out, Ashleigh."

"Don't fucking tell me to chill out!" she snapped, heart pounding, eyes burning. She had barely escaped the shadow man. The idea that Tess might be in his hands even now was too much for her.

Mr. Murphy frowned. "Ashleigh, what is it? What's wrong?"

She shook her head. "Did someone pick her up?"

"Nah, she was walking. She only lives on the other side of the lake."

Ashleigh wasn't cold anymore. Adrenaline blazed through her as she spun and nearly ran into Brian Schnell. Will was right behind him. Mr. Murphy called after her but she grabbed the guys by their arms and tugged them along in her wake as she started to run out of the parking lot.

"She's walking home. Around the lake. That's nice and deserted, don't you think?"

Will swore and picked up the pace. The three of them raced out onto Townsend Lane, which ran beside the school and dead-ended in a tree-lined circle that screened out most of the view of Gorham Lake. It was barely large enough to be called a lake in the first place, but walking even halfway around would take a little time, and bring Tess through backyards and then through some woods that were part of a state park where people came to swim in the summer. The only people likely to be down there were young lovers with nowhere warm to go.

Headlights washed over them from behind. Tires skidded as the three of them spun around to see Will—the older Will—jumping out of the driver's seat.

"She's gone," Ashleigh announced before they could say another word. And she explained about the lake and that Tess's house was almost precisely on the other side.

"Shit!" the future Will snapped, and he slammed his fist against the roof of the Buick. "I remember where her house is." He ducked his head into the car. "Brian, get out."

Future Brian complied instantly.

"Ashleigh, you and..." Future Will looked fondly at *her* Will "...you two go to the right. Brian and Brian will go left. I'm staying in the car. I'm going to check every street that goes past the lake. If he has a car...if he needs a car...maybe I can find him. Otherwise I'll get to Tess's house and start backtracking from there."

WILL HADN'T EVEN ASKED how they had managed to lose track of Tess. The truth was, the facts were searing themselves into his mind as memories as they happened. This was a night he would never forget. He only wished he knew how it would end.

Even as he guided the Buick, its engine snarling as it tore along Punch Street, it was as though he was in two places at once, his mind mapping the memory of Young Will's trek through the lakeside woods with Ashleigh, simultaneous with its happening. He could remember fearing for Tess and for Ashleigh and feeling guilt for not having paid more attention. Ashleigh had paint on her jeans and the denim was shredded at her knees.

"Get the fuck out of my head," Will grunted, gripping the wheel as he reached the circle at the end of Punch Street. There were no cars parked there, nothing left behind. He paused a moment, staring through the trees along a path that led to the lake.

Other memories warred in his head, images of Tess as Homecoming Queen and then of her riding in the parade years later during their reunion weekend. He didn't want to think of what might have been happening to her, the pain and humiliation, but one snippet of imagery played over and over in his head like the newsreel of some catastrophe: Ashleigh's face, changing before his eyes as the past was altered, going from happy, successful, sweet woman to numb and hollow.

He had saved Ashleigh from that, or helped to.

No way was he going to let it happen to Tess.

Jaw tight, breath coming in sharp bursts, he raced the Buick back up Punch Street and headed for the next cut in toward the lake. There were three, maybe four, before he got to Tess's road. Will prayed he would catch up to the son of a bitch before he reached her.

Against the backdrop of his memories, his younger self rushed through bare autumn trees, pushing low-hanging branches out of his way. One of them slipped from his fingers and snapped back, slicing his cheek just below his left eye.

Will braked out of reflex, just for a moment. There was no pain, but he could remember the pain.

He put a hand up to his left cheek, and one finger traced the line of a thin white scar he would see the next time he looked in the mirror.

WILL HISSED IN PAIN and turned his back to the tree. One of the branches jutted into his back as he touched his fingers to his cheek. They came away streaked with blood that looked black in the moonlight that streamed through the branches from above.

"You all right?" Ashleigh whispered urgently.

He nodded. "Let's go."

They started off again, sprinting nimbly along a path that was barely a path at all. Will was in the lead, but Ashleigh kept up with no problem. She had always been more agile than he was. His face was cold from running through the chill night, and the blood was warm where it dripped like tears on his face, but he ignored it, did not even try to wipe it away.

In his mind, all he could see was the image of his own face, eleven years older. He was afraid for Tess; seeing the dark man, Ashleigh's attacker, disappear into nothingness on Monday night had freaked him out completely. But as he hustled through the trees with the soft hush of the lake lapping its shores, he still could not erase that older image.

Me. It's me. All week those words had been echoing in his mind, and he could not be rid of them. He could also not shake a terrible dread that had snowballed inside him, a horrid certainty that he and Brian had started all of this. Magic didn't just pop into people's lives, he knew that for sure. You had to invite it in. And once you did...

Now he was faced with a visitor from a future he both yearned and feared to know. Himself. Will James. Every time he thought of it, his mind froze up a little. *I look good,* he thought. *I seem like I'm not too big an asshole. But then there's this. I have to go through this.*

Again.

He burst out of the trees onto the clearing in the state park land that was used as a beach in the summer. There was a parking lot not far off, but it was empty. Nothing there. Ashleigh came up beside him, moving faster, and together they ran along that barren stretch of land just above the place where the state had dumped sand. There were green trash cans and a couple of rusted hibachi grills; at the midpoint was a tall white lifeguard chair.

Will stopped and stared at the chair, thoughts clicking through his mind like trying to find the combination on his locker. He'd heard at least a couple of different guys talk about taking girls down here, fooling around up on the lifeguard chair.

"Ash," he whispered.

She glanced at him and Will saw pain in her eyes. God, she meant the world to him. He had no idea what the future held, and the other Will wasn't about to tell him, but he prayed that whatever happened he held on to Ashleigh. She was more than a friend. What was that saying? Home was the place that when you went there, they had to take you in. That was family. And blood relation or no, Ashleigh was family.

Her fingers gripped his hand and like that they hurried down to the lifeguard chair, coming up on it from behind. They slowed as they reached it, moving with caution, sidling around in front.

There was nothing there but shadows and moonlight.

HIS HANDS CARESSED HER BACK and Tess let her head loll back while he kissed her neck. She ran her fingers through his hair and her pulse raced. With his right hand he cupped her breast and gently stroked her nipple through her shirt, sending an electric shock of pleasure jolting through her.

A soft laugh gurgled up from her throat and she smiled further, knowing how sexy it sounded. She darted her tongue out to moisten her lips and she kissed the side of his face even as he continued to nuzzle her throat. They had planned for him to pick her up at the house, but he had walked down the path to meet her, too impatient to see her. In another guy that would have driven her away, but he was a good-looking bastard, charmingly cocky, and she couldn't deny her attraction.

His hand slipped up beneath her shirt, expertly lifting her bra and pushing it above her breasts. An excited thrill rippled through her and her eyelids fluttered as he caressed her bare skin, gently rolling her nipples between his fingers. She knew this was crazy. It was their first date. She should make him stop. This wasn't the place or the time.

"We...we have reservations," she said breathlessly. "Maybe we should—"

He covered her mouth with his own and they kissed deeply, his tongue dancing with hers, lips brushing against hers. Her arousal burgeoned and she let herself go, kissing him back with a fire that surprised her. He ground against her; she could feel his hardness against her thigh, even through their clothes, and she uttered a tiny sigh of admiration.

Tess shivered with pleasure and kissed him more deeply, tracing her fingers across his face.

His hands ran down over her body, and then his fingers tickled her belly as he began to unbutton her jeans. She froze for a moment, then reached down to push his hands away. Tess didn't think she had ever been this aroused in her entire life. She wanted the same thing he wanted; she wasn't going to lie to herself about that. But she knew how things worked, and there was no way that was happening tonight. Though she might curse herself for it later, she forced her heart to slow down, took short breaths to calm herself.

"Maybe we should actually have a date?" she suggested with a lopsided grin.

He wasn't smiling.

Her own grin evaporated. "Hey, come on, don't be like—"

The blow took her in the side of the face, cracking her cheekbone. He struck her with such force that she spun halfway around and staggered backward.

"If it makes you feel any better," he said, "this was always going to end the hard way. If you'd played along, you would've just been postponing the inevitable."

Tess had no time to whimper, no time to even begin to right herself, to run away, before he hauled back and kicked her in the stomach. A thin tendril of vomit flew from her lips and she fell backward into an old tree someone had stripped of half its branches to clear the path. Tess hit the tree and one of those jagged, truncated, snapped-off branches punctured her shoulder, tearing flesh and scraping bone.

Eyes wide, terror and pain nearly stilling her heart, she opened her mouth and began to scream. Her agony echoed out across Gorham Lake.

But he was just getting started.

CHAPTER 17

Kyle Brody lay frozen on the cold concrete in the darkness of the storage space beneath his back porch, the stench of Ben Klosky's urine in his nose. Half-buried beneath his much larger friend, he could feel Ben quivering, could hear the breath catch in his throat.

"Kyle," the voice at the door whispered. *"Time for you to learn a lesson about staying out of other people's business."*

There was an awful glee in that voice that clawed at Kyle's heart. Even now, with Ben's whimpering in his ear and the mutterings of the whisperer beyond the door, his ears still echoed with the sound of his mother's screaming, and the terrible, abrupt silence that had followed. While Ben trembled, Kyle was rapt with attention. His muscles were paralyzed, his lips pressed tightly together, and he held his breath. Only his thunderous heart was in motion as he strained to hear any sound from inside the house, any indication that his parents were still . . . moving.

Once again there came the sound of something scratching slowly down the door to the storage area.

There was a filthiness to the air now, a clinging, fetid rot that filmed his exposed skin. He could taste his fear, and yet his panic over the fate of his parents, the echo of his mother's shrieking, hardened him against his own terror. It was the only thing that saved him from the abject fright that had reduced his best friend to near catatonia.

The latch, he thought. *I've gotta get to the latch, try to hold it and...* This line of thought withered and vanished from his mind, obliterated by a bit of logic that he grasped for in desperation. *The magic. The magic is keeping it out.*

"Ben," he whispered, desperately trying to get free, to extricate himself from beneath that bulk. "Ben, I think if we—"

"Are you afraid, Kyle? I hope so. That's good. That . . . helps," came that eerie, drifting voice, much too close in the dark.

The temperature plummeted in that tiny room and the air felt too close around him, as though the place were shrinking. Kyle shivered and screwed his eyes tightly shut, transported instantly back to childhood memories of quivering beneath his bedspread on nights when every creak and moan made him bury his face in his pillow. The fear crawled upon him, coating him like the filth in the air, like that intimate whisper.

Ben shook even more uncontrollably. Then, abruptly, he sat up. Kyle felt his weight lift and heard Ben shifting in the darkness, trying to catch his breath. Hands scrabbled along the concrete, searching perhaps for something with which to defend himself.

Kyle stared in what he believed was the direction of the door. His thoughts of a moment before had been uprooted and now tumbled through his mind, and he tried to snatch at them, to make sense of them again. His pulse beat a staccato rhythm that urged him to act, but they were in a tiny room with no windows and no other door, and he knew without doubt that nothing in this room could protect them from the whisperer.

The scratching ceased.

Ben gave a querulous grunt.

The latch clicked and the door began to swing open, a scythe of moonlight slicing into the room. Ben was slightly in front of Kyle and to his left, and in the wash of moonlight his face was almost feral with terror.

Kyle's thoughts began connecting again. Shaken from his paralysis, he turned and scrambled back through the storage area. From the floor where he had dropped it he grabbed the book and moaned with the effort. *Dark Gifts* had never felt heavier. It was like hefting a cinder block, but with both hands he managed to tuck it under one arm. With his other hand he spider-walked his fingers along the cement, its details hidden in the darkness.

The pressure in the room changed. His ears popped.

Fuck, fuck, fuck, fuck.

His fingertips scraped dried blood. A triumphant rush went through him, and, clutching the book tightly to him, Kyle rose to a crouch and stepped inside the gore-painted circle. Even as he turned his gaze toward the door, the room was filled with a kind of roar that seemed to tear from Ben Klosky's throat in an agonized blend of fear, anguish, and aggression, a lunatic growl of escape.

That square of moonlight grew wider, the door fully open now. A cold certainty clasped Kyle's heart. There was no escape through that door. Ben stooped over and charged through the opening and Kyle shouted his name, tried to warn him, to call him back. Didn't he feel it? This was the terrible truth of the title of that book.

Dark Gifts.

"Get out of my way or I'll fucking kill—"

Ben had his right fist cocked back as he lunged through the door. His hair was the first thing to catch fire. With a blast of superheated air and a crackling of burning flesh, his entire body was engulfed in flame. An instant later Ben Klosky collapsed into a pile of blazing orange embers that swirled across the patio and blew away like the ash tapped from the tip of a cigarette.

Where he had been was a shadow figure, blacker than black, silhouetted by the moonlight. It did not so much move as flow into the tiny room under the porch. One hand snaked out and a long finger pointed at Kyle.

"*That,*" it whispered, pointing at the book he clutched, "*does not belong to you.*"

His mother's death cries—for he was certain now that was what he had heard—still rang in his ears. His eyelids seemed to be icing shut with the chill in the air and he shuddered, his breath coming in ragged gasps as he stared at that perfect, human darkness.

"F-fuck you," he said, his teeth chattering.

The shadow laughed. *"Who are you saving it for?"* Its night-swaddled head inclined toward the blood circle on the concrete. *"He's not coming back."*

Kyle squeezed his eyes closed, trying to see if he could sense the magic of the symbols scrawled below him. "You can't have the book. And I'm not going to let you destroy the circle."

This time there came no reply, not in words nor in laughter. He began to cringe, his fear gnawing at him deep as bone, worsening in that dreadful silence.

He shook with the force of the blow to his chest. It took a fragment of a second for the sound of cracking bone to register upon his ears. The book fell from his hands and there was the wet slap of something splashing the concrete. Kyle Brody opened his eyes and glanced down. In the moonlight he could see that the arcane circle Will had drawn had been obscured by a cascade of fresh blood.

The whisperer was gone. The book was gone.

Kyle fell to the ground, unconscious, the left side of his face resting amid a growing pool of his own blood.

October, Senior Year...

Three quarters of the way around to the other side of the lake, Brian and his teenage counterpart emerged from a dense stretch of woods where there was barely a path onto a flat clearing, where a series of large rocks formed an outcropping that jutted up from the lake. His chest burned from the rush through the trees and his arms and face bore light scratches. He smelled pine sap, and his scalp itched with the paranoia that there might be insects crawling there.

"Damn," Brian whispered as he paused in that clearing, one foot on a large rock as he drew deep breaths.

A short, awkward laugh drew his gaze up, and in the light from the stars and moon he stared into his own face...the face that had looked back at him from the mirror over a decade before. The younger Brian was chuckling at him.

"What's funny?"

The kid was also breathing heavy, but not hard, not gasping for air. "I'm just thinking when I get older, I'm gonna have to spend some more time in the gym. You look like you're in good shape, but—" He threw his hands up and shrugged.

Brian tried to shoot him a withering glare but couldn't hold it and ended up laughing instead. "Say shit like that and you might not *get* any older."

"We run any more and I damn well know I'm not getting any older than you are now," the kid retorted with a taunting grin.

A wail of absolute despair tore out over the lake, echoing off the trees and sending something scuttling through the branches above them. Brian looked at his younger self, bearing full knowledge of all of the wrongs he had committed at that age, the sins that had weighed down his conscience, but when he saw the flash of panic and concern in those eyes he felt that weight lifted from him.

Together, the two of them sprinted through the clearing and crashed through the trees on the other side. Those lost, desperate screams continued to tear across the sky. Brian pushed branches out of the way and vaulted a felled birch, drawn on by the sorrow of that voice.

"Tess!" he shouted as he darted through some trees to the shoreline of the lake, where the footing was treacherous in the dark but there were fewer obstacles.

"What are you doing?" his younger self demanded in a harsh whisper, stumbling as he followed. "If you scare him off we'll never catch him!"

"I don't care! I just want him to *stop!*"

Before he had even gotten the words out, the screaming

ceased. The last of it rolled across the surface of the lake, and then the only echo was in Brian's head. He did not want to even begin to think about what had caused Tess to fall silent. For long seconds they hustled along in a wordless chorus of grunts. Then the kid swore.

"Tess!" he shouted. Then his voice dropped to a rasp. "Shit. Oh, shit."

Brian focused on the dark line of the lake rim, and moments later they came to a place where the woods thinned considerably and a wide path weaved through the trees, worn down over the years. The lights from houses could be seen ahead, and Brian knew one of them must belong to Tess's family.

But Tess had never made it home.

She lay curled on her side on the ground. The moonlight turned her blond hair a pale silver and her long, bare legs were those of some apparition, haunting both in the glimmer of the moon and in their horrid implications.

Brian felt all the air go out of him and he gritted his teeth, glancing around for any sign of her attacker. He saw nothing, but that was meaningless when dealing with a man who could merge with the night itself.

"Oh, Tess, Jesus," the younger Brian said behind him.

The kid hurried past him and Brian did not try to stop him. Tess lay on the dirt and roots and leaves, crying softly. His was an unfamiliar face; at least she would recognize his younger self. Even as the kid went to kneel at the girl's side—and she flinched when she heard his voice—Brian was trying to put it together in his mind. His gaze darted back the way they'd come and then farther along the path ahead. If Tess had been caught here, she must have walked the same way he and the kid had. The path to her neighborhood was still a ways ahead—the way that Ashleigh and Young Will would be coming. If the shadow man was on foot, if he hadn't just disappeared, he might well run right into them.

He looked down at the tragic spectacle of this young man— the too-serious, almost goofy kid he had been—comforting the would-be Homecoming Queen, and his heart ached as it never had before. He remembered Tess as a sweet girl, not nearly as stuck-up as she should have been given her looks and her popularity. Now she was half naked, her face darkly bruised in the moonlight, her pale flesh shimmering as though she were some crumpled, fallen angel, and something inside of her had been broken forever.

Something inside of him shifted in that moment. Brian felt it happen. Now that this had come to pass, he could *remember* it, from the perspective of the kid who knelt beside Tess even now. He had wanted all of this to end because it was unsettling, it was wrong, and he felt a vague sense of guilt about the whole thing, as if his own experimentation with magic had tainted them all, tainted this entire time in all of their lives.

Now, Brian Schnell hurt inside. Part of him had been broken as well. Mike Lebo's death had caused him to grieve, to feel wounded. But seeing Tess's face like this . . . it churned him up inside, birthing a rage he had never felt before.

"Stay with her," Brian told the kid.

Then he took off after the son of a bitch, praying that either he or Young Will would catch him before he got to the street, wondering where Will was with the goddamned car now.

In his mind, new memories were being forged, and they slipped into his head like phantoms of the past. As the kid whispered to Tess, one hand laid gently upon her shoulder, it was almost as though Brian could hear the words being spoken.

He's gone, Tess. He's gone, and I swear to God he's never going to touch you again.

Brian only wished that he could be certain of that, but his memories did not include the outcome of this night. That was yet to be seen.

His thoughts were interrupted by the sound of heavy footfalls up ahead and to his left. The moonlight did not filter too deeply into the woods that separated the lake from the neighborhood, but he had to assume the shadow man had reached the path and started toward the street.

Jaw set, an ember of fury blazing in his gut, Brian pushed into the trees, forsaking the path to cut diagonally through the woods. The footfalls sped up—the bastard heard him coming—and Brian found himself lunging through whipping branches. He peered through the dark woods, and in a moment he realized that he could see that dark figure hurrying along the path that led to Tess's neighborhood. This time, though, there was no mask covering his face. Maybe he had magic at his disposal, but he was a man.

In the dark, the moonlight was not enough for Brian to make out his face, but as the shadow man glanced toward him, the darkness seemed to bleed upward from his clothing. In the glimpses Brian got of him between trees, the two men racing toward the point where they would intersect, he saw the shadow crawl over the man's face and become the mask he had worn the last time they had come into contact.

Then he reached the path.

The shadow man was running past him.

Brian tackled him around the waist with the solid thunk of bone colliding with bone and drove him to the ground, wondering when the fucker was going to disappear, to fade to mist. But he didn't. The shadow man was a man after all, beneath that fluid mask of darkness he wore. They each struggled to get the upper hand. The rapist struck him several times, wild blows to the back of the head, as they rolled on the ground. Brian managed to get leverage, to plant his feet, and he lurched forward as if crawling on top of the shadow man, throwing his left arm across his throat.

The image of Tess O'Brien, half naked and weeping in the haunting moonlight, swam into his mind. Guttural, primal noises filled with hatred spilled from his lips, and he held the shadow man down and struck his face once, twice, a third time, his knuckles stinging, pain shooting up his wrist.

It was only a moment's advantage.

The shadow man clutched his throat, pushed Brian up and off of him, then hit him in the temple with such force that for a second even the moonlight disappeared. Brian tumbled off of him and the shadow man was up in an instant.

He blinked, that night-clad face peering down at him, and in a panic he tried to get to his feet. The shadow man kicked him in the face. Brian felt his lip split, tasted the metallic tang of his own blood, fell backward onto the path. He landed on a thick, upraised root, and it knocked the wind out of him.

The shadow man kicked him in the ribs and Brian heard a crack.

ASHLEIGH COULDN'T KEEP UP, but Young Will had heard Tess screaming and couldn't afford to wait for her. She urged him on, shouted at him to leave her behind, but he was already gone. His legs pumped beneath him, sneakers kicking up dirt and leaves as he sprinted. This entire week was a blur in his head. He had withdrawn deeply into himself to avoid the reality of what was happening. Had someone asked him a week ago if he would like to have met his future self, to have learned about what his life would bring, he knew he would have said yes.

Now he knew better. He had questions, of course. He just didn't want the answers. It made him sick inside to think that this was where his interest in magic had led, to remember that day in Herbie's when he had turned Brian's orange float into blood. Just the thought of holding *Dark Gifts* in his hands, of the burgundy leather cover of Gaudet's book that felt so much like skin...it made him sick.

Will didn't care that the shadow man was cloaked in magic, that he could disappear whenever he felt like it. Mike Lebo was dead. In his bedroom, right now, there were probably comic books spread all over the floor, and Mike would have known the story behind every one. For some reason that knowledge cut Will deeply.

And now Tess...

Every step reverberated up his legs. Will bent into his run, arms pumping, the soles of his sneakers slapping the ground and crunching fallen branches and dried-out autumn leaves. As the lakeside path widened before him, he had a better view of the moonlit curve of the water's edge ahead.

The shadow man appeared.

BEHIND THE WHEEL of the Buick, the elder Will flinched and drove the heel of his palm against his forehead. He could not hear Tess screaming. The engine roared too loudly and he was too far away. But as each new moment unfolded for his younger self, the memories scarred him. When Young Will saw the shadow man, Will *remembered*.

The tires laid black patches on the pavement as he turned a corner, crushing a mailbox with the Buick's grille.

THE SHADOW MAN DARTED up the path that led from the lake through to Tess's street. Behind him, Will heard Ashleigh shouting. She had seen him, too. But why didn't he just disappear? Why not simply evaporate in a puff of black smoke as he'd done before? Will wondered if it took too much out of him, or if something had gone wrong the last time. Not that it mattered. What was important was that the shadow man was not disappearing. He was running.

Inside, fingers of cold dread began to wrap themselves around his heart, for as fast as he was, Will could gauge the distance, and he knew that if the bastard had a car waiting for him out on the street he would be gone before Will could catch him.

Still he ran on, pushing himself to move as swiftly as he could manage without falling. Several times he nearly lost his footing but recovered only by throwing himself forward and planting one foot, hoping he would not twist an ankle or slide on decaying leaves.

Too long, he thought. *Not fast enough.*

But moments later he had reached the path. Will turned right, and this time he did slide. Earth and leaves moved beneath his feet and he went down on his hands, refusing to fall. Like a runner at the pistol shot he exploded up from the ground and sprinted away from the lake, away from the moonlight, into the gathering gloom where the path was lined on both sides by deeper woods. His chest was tight and the backs of his legs burned from exertion, but he barely noticed. Through the trees he could see the lights of houses coming closer as he raced along that path.

The sound of a struggle drew his attention, and as he came around a slight curve in the path he saw them. The shadow man, just a darker figure torn out of the blackness of the night, launched a heavy kick at someone who struggled to rise from the ground. Whether it was Brian or his own future self, he didn't know. And it didn't matter. He had eyes only for the shadow man.

Young Will ran at him with such speed that though the shadow man heard his approach, he barely had time to glance up before Will slammed into him, both palms out. He lowered his shoulders, planted his hands, and knocked the bastard off his feet. In his mind he could already see what was to come. He would start kicking, just like the shadow man had done.

But his opponent was quicker than Will had expected. The shadow man fell backward and let that momentum take him into a somersault. Even as Will moved in to kick him, he was on his feet again. The shadow man reached for him but Will knocked his hand away and hit him three times in quick succession, a right to the jaw, a left to the abdomen, and another right to the face.

The shadow man staggered backward.

Neither of them had noticed Ashleigh racing up the path toward them. She hurled something, and when it struck a glancing blow off the side of his head the shadow man swore, his voice muffled by the darkness over his face.

Rocks, Will thought. *She picked rocks up from the edge of the lake.*

"Oh, to hell with this," the shadow man said in that muffled voice. He tilted his head back as if pleading to the sky. "I'm out of here."

There was an instant in which Young Will was certain the shadow man would disappear, that he had guessed wrong, that there would be nothing but that floating tendril of black mist and he would escape again. But nothing happened. Ashleigh threw another rock, which struck him in the shoulder. He swore again, clutching his shoulder, and a frustrated snarl came from his throat as he leaped forward and backhanded Ashleigh across the face. She went down, the other rocks she carried plunking to the ground.

"All right, then, Will," the shadow man snarled, that voice so intimate and familiar, and yet too muffled to be recognizable. He beckoned. "Come on."

To one side of the path, Future Brian groaned and began to stand, one hand clutching his side where he had been kicked. The shadow man glanced at him only for an instant, but it was enough. Or at least Will thought so. He stepped in close and swung his fist.

The shadow man caught it, stopped the punch dead. Will could feel the darkness that covered the man's skin writhing under his touch. Magic. Bile rose in the back of his throat, and his stomach churned with nausea. Then the shadow man caught him in the side of the head with a punch that staggered him, but Will could not back up, could not step away. Not with the shadow man holding his fist.

With a cry of rage and anguish, and not a little vengeance, Ashleigh leaped on his back. Her right arm looped around his throat and she began to choke him.

"Fucking bitch, get off me!" roared the shadow man, clawing over his head, trying to reach her face or snag her hair.

"You want magic, you fuck?" Will screamed. "Eat this!"

He had done so very few spells, really, but all of them had remained with him, ingrained within him, tainting him. Now he conjured a small flame the size of a baseball in his right hand and he slammed it into the shadow man's face, aiming for his mouth beneath that night-black mask that covered his face.

The shadow man screamed. His fingers managed to grab hold of Ashleigh's shirt and he whipped his head and shoulders down, flipping her off of his back. She hit the ground with a little "oh" of pain and surprise.

Then he looked up.

Fabric or dark conjuring, the shadow that covered his face was burning away with the magical flame Will had struck him with. The flesh beneath was unharmed, but as that sorcerous fire consumed the mask of magic the shadow man had worn, Will froze. Even in the moonlight, the face his spell had revealed was unmistakable.

"Nick?"

The expression on seventeen-year-old Nick Acosta's face was part sneer and part grin, that white crescent scar across his left eyebrow gleaming in the moonlight.

"Hello, Will," Nick said.

In that moment, when Will was too astonished to act, Nick reached for him almost as though he meant to embrace him, and then he drove his fist up into Will's stomach. With a grunt Will doubled over, even as Nick brought a knee up into his face, shattering his nose with a spray of hot blood.

His face exploded with pain, he couldn't breathe, and his heart was filled with despair as he sank to his knees.

"Screw this," Nick said, grinning at him, hands outstretched in a theatrical flourish. The magical darkness that had cloaked him in shadow seemed to melt off of him now, revealing a black shirt and blue jeans beneath.

"I got what I came for."

Nick turned and fled toward Little Tree Lane. Will sucked painful breaths into his lungs and forced himself to rise, wiping the blood from his mouth with the back of his hand, but he knew that he didn't have a chance in hell of catching up to Nick . . . to the shadow man.

THE MEMORIES SEARED themselves into Will's mind. So vivid were they that, one hand on the wheel, he clapped a hand to his nose expecting to catch the flow of blood from it.

Nick. Fucking Nicky Acosta.
None of it made sense.
But it didn't have to.
It simply *was.*

WHEN NICK RAN OUT between two of the houses on Little
Tree Lane, he was feeling more than a little pissed off. He had a
little checklist of things to do, and Will and Brian were getting
in his way, screwing with him. Dealing with those guys was not
on his list, but they weren't giving him a choice. On the other
hand, he could still taste Tess's mouth on his lips, and the
scratches she'd made on his lower back stung wonderfully. He'd
broken at least one of the older Brian's ribs, shattered Will's
nose, and clocked Ashleigh pretty good, too.

So maybe the night wasn't a total loss.

He wasn't sure what to do next, but that was a matter to deal
with later, after he was out of here. He'd shown up for his date
with Tess in his father's Jetta, but instead of leaving it in the
O'Briens' driveway, he'd parked it right out on Little Tree near
the path to the lake.

The Jetta was waiting for him. The street was quiet. Down at
the end of Little Tree, cars rolled by. He had to assume that
someone in one of the houses had heard Tess screaming, but so
far he heard no police sirens. As he ran between the houses and
into the front yard, he heard the creak of a storm door and
ducked his head to hide his face.

So much for that bit of magic.

The car door was unlocked. He fished out his keys and tugged
it open, then slid into the Jetta. Nick slid the key into the ignition and turned it, the engine purring quietly, the radio coming
on, some sappy ballad he didn't know. A slow, satisfied smile
crept over his face, his heart still drumming excitedly in his chest.
He dropped the Jetta into gear and at last glanced up, just in time
to notice the headlights that bathed the inside of the car.

Metal and fiberglass crumpled as the other car struck the Jetta
from behind. The collision thrust Nick forward, the steering

wheel jutting into his abdomen and lower rib cage as his head whipped against the windshield. The glass cracked and a bloody contusion erupted on his forehead. His foot came off the brake and the Jetta rolled, propelled from behind by the other car. His body twisted around the steering wheel, fireworks in his head from the impact. He blinked, tried to grab the wheel, but his vision was blurred and out of focus and he could not think straight. It was, in that moment, as though he were drowning, far underwater and without the ability to know up from down.

The engine behind him revved and he blinked several times, clearing his vision enough to see the thick-trunked oak tree just before the Jetta veered into it, driven by the vehicle behind it. All of the side windows exploded in a shower of tiny glass shards and Nick was thrown forward again, his head striking the windshield a second time. This time his skull hit the glass hard enough to splinter it, making it bow outward in the shape of his head.

On the radio, Celine Dion seemed to mock him. He slipped into merciful darkness, swallowed by blood and ache and concussion. Idly, he wondered if this was death and if Celine Dion would sing him all the way down to hell.

His eyes opened and he snapped violently awake, as if pulled from a dream in which he had been suffocating. The car horn was blaring, and for half an instant he thought it was coming from somewhere far away. But no, it was the Jetta. There was a hand on the horn, and it was not his.

Barely able to move, he let his head loll to the left, eyes rolling up to see a dark figure leaning in the shattered window, one hand on the horn. With the other hand, the figure grabbed a fistful of Nick's hair and yanked his head back. The headlights from the car that had forced him into the tree still illuminated the inside of the car, and from this new angle, Nick could see that face.

His upper lip curled. Something was wrong with his head,

with his lips, even. It was almost as though he had forgotten how to form words. Still, he managed to get one word out.

"W-Will," Nick slurred.

Will James...a grown-up Will James an entire decade Nick's senior...glared at him with a blazing hate.

"How's your head?"

CHAPTER 18

The wail of approaching police sirens gave Will and Brian little time to figure out how to explain it all to the authorities. Above all, they did not want to have to answer questions that might lead the police to try to verify that they were who they claimed to be. Will quickly rattled off instructions, and then the two of them ambled between houses on the far side of Little Tree Lane, leaving Young Will and Ashleigh to handle the fallout.

Brian was a mess, his split lip having bled all over his shirt, and he walked with the caution of the elderly, hissing through his teeth with every other step from the pain in his side. The kicks he had taken had likely cracked at least one rib, and Will knew they would have to get Brian healed up as soon as possible. But for now the only priority was avoiding the police.

In the backyard of one house they found wooden slats nailed to the trunk of an oak, a ladder that led up to a well-constructed tree house, complete with roof and windows. Some father had put a great deal of effort into pleasing his son. Either that, Will mused, or some of the local kids had swiped wood from a construction site and built themselves a hangout that was a thousand times cooler than the storage area under his old house on Parmenter Road.

Brian went up first, one arm held against his side as though in a sling. It was slow progress up the ladder but he made it without mishap. With a glance back at the road, where blue lights now washed in waves over the two crumpled cars and over the faces of the houses, Will followed Brian up. His own chest hurt badly and he wondered if in the crash the tug of the seat belt had torn muscles, or perhaps cracked some ribs.

They crawled into the tree house, breathing in sharp, pained gasps. "Give me a couple of minutes," Will grunted, "and maybe I can muster up a healing spell."

But Brian was not listening. He had propped himself against the inner wall of the tree house and was staring out the window at the spectacle unfolding in the street. Will knew they were both silently hoping none of the neighbors had seen them slip away, or at least hadn't noticed where they'd slipped away to.

One hand pressed against his chest—the pressure helped dull the pain—Will sat beside Brian. As he looked out that window, distant blue lights casting them both in a strange, gauzy gloom, he saw two figures emerge from the path that led to the lake. Fully dressed now, Tess walked side by side with Young Brian Schnell, his arm around her in a gesture of protection rather than intimacy. Even from this distance Will could see that he was speaking to her, soothing her.

"You're not a bad guy, you know that?" Will said.

Brian chuckled weakly. "I'm been trying to convince myself of that for a lot of years."

Will frowned and turned to gaze at him in that flickering cerulean light. "Me, too, man. Me, too."

Together they watched as the police hurried to talk to Tess, an officer pulling Young Brian aside even as Ashleigh and Young Will rushed over to talk to him. This was a key moment. Will had worked out the story, but it was up to his younger self to pull it off, to get Brian to play along while the cops were watching. Witnesses from the school, including Mr. Murphy, would say that when they discovered Tess had walked home around the lake and that she had a date, the three teenagers took off in pursuit of her. Ashleigh would testify that Nick had attacked her earlier in the week and that only her friends' arrival had saved her. She had been debating reporting him to the police and had just decided to do so when she found out that Tess was supposed to meet him that same night.

Ashleigh and Brian had followed along the lakeshore, trying to catch up with Tess to warn her. They'd found her there moments after Nick had raped her. Will had taken the car, planning to confront Nick at the O'Briens' house, hoping to beat Tess there, but only arriving as Nick fled, with Ashleigh running after him. Will had known something terrible had happened but had taken his eyes off the road for just a moment, distracted by Ashleigh. He had plowed into the back of the Jetta and broken his nose on the steering wheel.

In the tree fort, the elder Will ran his fingers over the bump on his nose where it had been broken. The bump had appeared there at the very same moment when Young Will's nose had been shattered.

The Buick belonged to Brian Schnell, bought with money he'd taken from his savings account without his parents' approval or knowledge. The title was in his name, after all, and no, he hadn't registered it yet. How they would explain the stolen license plate was something Will hadn't had time to address, but as he sat in the tree fort, the pain in his chest beginning to diminish, a new memory began to form in his mind as though bursting through a splintering eggshell.

"I found it on the side of the road, Officer," he remembered telling the cops, blinking away the blue lights even as he wiped a streak of blood from beneath his broken nose. "Brian wanted to wait to register it until Monday, after he told his parents, but I found this license plate and I figured what the hell, let's take it out for a ride. I know we shouldn't have, but—"

And in his mind's eye, Will could recall exactly what the cop said next.

"Looks like it was a good thing you did."

Will smiled there in the tree fort, proud of the kid... proud of himself. More lights were flashing now, red and white, as two ambulances arrived. Neighbors had come out of their homes and were standing in their front yards watching as the EMTs removed the unconscious form of Nick Acosta from his father's Jetta. Not so terrifying now, he was just a broken, bloody teenager and a big question mark for Will.

"Do you think Tess will testify?" Brian asked, fingers still gingerly exploring his side.

"I don't know. But with Ashleigh and me and you—you know what I mean, *the guys*—they've got an airtight case."

"So it's pretty much done," Brian said.

Something about his tone unnerved Will, who slid around to put his back against the wall of the tree house, letting the exhaustion in his muscles take over at last. He studied Brian's face in the gloom.

"What's on your mind, Bri?"

The other man drew his palm over his ragged goatee. His sickly pallor, even in that blue light, suddenly seemed not entirely due to his cracked ribs. His eyelids fluttered and then he stared right at Will and the tree house seemed very small.

"The memories... it's happening to you, right? New ones are slipping in. You kept saying it was like a deck of cards shuffling in your head, but now new cards keep getting added."

Will nodded grimly. "We're *adding* them." He touched the bump on the bridge of his nose again. "My nose wasn't broken before. And all of this... with Nick and Tess... I've got two sets of memories of it. One's mine and one's *his*." It was strange to refer to his younger self in the third person, but Will was certain that Brian would know precisely what he meant. "And at the same time, other memories are changing slowly, fading, being replaced."

Brian nodded. "Exactly. For instance, I know Nick recovers. And I know he ends up in jail. I sort of remember the trial, at least some of it."

Will could feel it, too. They both testified. The stare of the judge as he spoke each word had felt like a terrible weight because even though the vital facts were all true, there were things they were all hiding. Tess had broken down in tears on the stand, but she had told her story. Will remembered Mr. and Mrs. Acosta sitting in the courtroom and how he hadn't wanted to look at them.

"So do I." A tentative smile teased the edges of his mouth. "But I don't remember seeing us—the older us—again. So I guess it's time to go home. Back where we belong."

Car doors slammed out in the street and he peered out the tree house window. There was no sign of Ashleigh and their younger counterparts; a tow truck had arrived to drag Nick's Jetta away. When Will glanced back at Brian and saw the sickly look on his friend's face, any trace of well-being he had been feeling evaporated.

"What?" Will demanded.

Brian's eyes were downcast. "I did the spell to get back here days after you had already gone. I've got those few days of memory that you don't have. Something's been shuffled into the deck that wasn't there before, a new memory." He lifted his gaze to stare at Will. "We're not the only ones who are changing things. And they're not only changing here."

"What is it, Brian? What's the new memory?"

"A couple of days after you left. I can remember it now, but it wasn't there before, Will."

"What wasn't, damn it!"

Brian flinched. "The family that lives in your old house on Parmenter. There was a . . . a massacre there. Someone broke into the house, killed the parents. I remember seeing it on the news the day after the night at Papillon. The kid, Kyle—one of his friends was murdered, too, but the kid was the only survivor. Stabbed and beaten. In a coma, they said. The police found all kinds of symbols in blood in the room under the house and there was talk of Satanic rituals, shit like that."

Pressure built up in Will's temples and at the center of his forehead. He put a hand to his head and let out a long, shuddering breath. "Fuck," he whispered. "Oh, fucking hell." He had gotten Kyle's parents and best friend killed, and the kid was in a coma. Depending on his wounds, he might never wake up.

Will looked up at Brian. "We have to assume the circle I made is gone. And if mine's obliterated, it stands to reason they got to yours."

"They?"

"Well, if Nick was the one who pushed Lebo out in front of us Saturday night, somebody else had to be behind the wheel of the other car. The one that would have hit him if we hadn't been there."

Brian shifted uncomfortably, groaning as he pressed one hand against his side. "Shit, I guess I just figured it was magic."

"I did, too, but you saw Nick. Someone knew we were here, in this time, and went forward to our time to take Kyle out, making sure even if I figured out how to get back that I wouldn't have a way to do it. I left the door open. Somebody's got enough skill to jump into the future and close it, and probably come back again without much trouble. Does Nick look like he's capable of that kind of magic?"

"No. No, I guess he doesn't. But this isn't the end of the world, Will. I mean, we know where the Gaudet book is. We have your younger, more arrogant self get it for us, undo the spell he put on it, and we can figure out a way to go forward from here. It should work. If we go back early enough, we can get there before this kid and his family are killed."

Will shook his head in disbelief. "Jesus, when does this end?"

With a long sigh Brian glanced out the window. "I don't know, Will. But we don't have much choice. We have to try. Otherwise we're stuck here, and that isn't going to work. We have to go back."

"All right," Will said with a grim nod. "But we can't leave yet."

Brian frowned, eyebrows knitting. "Why not?"

Will's throat was dry again and he licked his lips to moisten them. Gruesome images flitted through his mind and he drew his knees up under him and covered his face a moment, as though he might screen them out.

"We couldn't save Mike and we couldn't stop what happened to Tess, but at least we got the fucker. Nick's going to jail. We both remember it that way, yeah?"

"Yeah," Brian agreed.

"Then how come I still remember Bonnie Winter's murder?"

CUT THE CARDS. *Shuffle the deck. Slip in a few wild cards.*

On Saturday at eleven o'clock in the morning Will James found himself in the bleachers at Cougar Stadium, watching a football game he had seen before. He clasped both hands around his Styrofoam coffee cup and blew through the tear he had made in the lid, trying to cool it down. Memories crashed in waves across his mind, more in conflict than ever.

Eleven years ago: He had watched this game with his friends, barely paying attention, eating too much junk and looking forward to the dance that night and the riotous sex he expected to have afterward. The sight of Caitlyn in her cheerleader's uniform did nothing to distract him from these thoughts. Mike Lebo had been a second-string defenseman in that game, and he'd made a sack on the Natick High quarterback that got them all on their feet. Ashleigh had screamed her voice hoarse. Now Will could barely hold on to this memory. It was as vague and insubstantial as a dream, half-remembered.

Eleven years ago: A week after Mike Lebo's tragic death, the game had gone on. There had been talk of canceling the entire slate of Homecoming weekend events, but after Principal Chadbourne met with the senior class officers and most of the teachers, he decided to forge ahead. The Cougars had played in Lebo's memory. Nick Acosta, one of their best running backs, had scored the deciding touchdown and dedicated it to Lebo. Even this memory was fading, merging with new ones that had taken its place.

Eleven years ago . . . and now: Lebo was dead. Nick was in the hospital with a police guard, under arrest on charges of rape and aggravated assault. The Homecoming Queen had been his primary victim and would not be riding in any parade. Word had only just begun to circulate, in whispers. Will's mind was filled with two sets of memories, all unspooling moment by moment as he watched the game. His teenage self and Young Brian sat with Ashleigh and Eric, but their cheering was halfhearted. Eric didn't have a fucking clue what was really going on, but he knew about Nick and Tess, and he was as somber as the others. They were preoccupied, too, keeping an eye on the players, on the cheerleaders, and on the crowd as well.

It wasn't over. Not yet.

A week ago ... and eleven years from now: Will had sat, and would sit, at the Homecoming football game during the weekend-long celebration of his ten-year high school reunion. It was in the distant future, and yet it was the beginning of all of this. Poor, doomed Kyle Brody would approach him with a note. Two words. Two fucking words that had haunted him every waking moment since he had read them.

Don't forget.

But there was just too damned much to remember, too many conflicting images and emotions, and so much of it was slipping through his mind like sand through his fingers.

Will took a sip of his coffee, barely registering how bitter and stale it was. He dragged a hand across his face, stubble against his palm, and took a deep breath, trying to shake it off, to focus his mind. He stood on the grass beside the bleachers on the Cougars' side of the field, near the place where during night games kids would sneak under the bleachers to drink and get high or spend a little private groping time. Not so much of that kind of thing during the day, but it still happened. Will ignored them, just as he ignored the blaring, off-key clatter of the Cougar band in the front row of the bleachers, the whistle of the referees, the clack of helmet against helmet, even the numbers on the scoreboard.

From time to time his gaze would drift to a spot diagonally across the field, where Brian stood vigilant on the visitors' side. But for the most part, Will's focus was on the girls. On the cheerleaders.

On Bonnie Winter.

Her smile was broad and genuine as she belted out the call-and-response cheer of the moment, her auburn hair flying in her face. Will tried not to think of her pale corpse lying in the autumn leaves, ants crawling on her flesh, but that was one image he could not seem to banish.

Bonnie wasn't alone out there. Will couldn't remember the last names of a couple of the girls, but most of them he knew very well. Or had known, once upon a time. Bonnie. Lolly. Pix. Kelly. And Caitlyn, of course.

God, she was beautiful, he thought as he watched her miss a cue, then twirl into a circle with the other girls, trying to catch up. She laughed, her cheeks flushed from the cold air and the exertion of the cheer routine. The skirt was short and her legs so slender and toned. Her blue eyes sparkled, and her golden hair seemed to glow in the sunshine.

Will knew he still loved her, but just as certainly he knew he loved what she had been to him then, not what she became. This, what they had had in these last days of another age, had been everything he'd hoped for. But it had faded along with everything else from this time in his life. Being with Caitlyn then was part of what made him the person he had become, but it had taken him a long time to realize that his relationship was a relic, an artifact of the past.

Now, looking at her, a hard truth struck him. Caitlyn had never loved him the way he had loved her. This was not self-pity, but simple fact. And he was surprised at how OK he was with that.

It was a long time ago, he thought. Even seeing her right in front of him, breathing the same air he had breathed on those perfect days, he had the perspective of that distance in a way he had never had before.

The coffee cup was still warm in his hands, but the way the sun was moving across the sky he was no longer in the shadow of the bleachers, so some of the chill of that October day was burning off. His back had even begun to feel pleasantly warm. On the field, Tim Friel faded back for a pass, but the Eastborough High line completely fell apart. The Natick defensemen rushed Tim; the way he glanced around, it was obvious he knew he wasn't going to get the pass off. The quarterback ran right. Joe Rosenthal blocked for him and Tim danced out of the way of another defensive back who slipped through, but then he was out on his own, sprinting full tilt down the field. Natick uniforms were closing in on him, in hot pursuit, but Tim had taken them by surprise, and he was fast. Very fast.

The bleachers exploded with cheers. Will found himself shouting and whistling along with everyone else, his coffee cup the only thing keeping him from applauding. He only allowed himself a moment's distraction before returning to the grim purpose that kept him stationed there at the edge of the field. His gaze drifted over the cheerleaders but this time he did not linger on Bonnie or Caitlyn. Instead he studied the crowd on the opposite side, then turned to gaze up into the bleachers over his right shoulder. He searched the crowd for anything out of the ordinary. People were jumping up and down, waving their arms in triumph, and hugging each other. The Cougars had taken the lead, and the students, parents, teachers, and graduates of Eastborough High were celebrating.

All but one.

At the front of the bleachers, Danny Plumer leaned against the railing, surrounded by people in motion. Danny was quite still. He did not cheer or whistle or applaud. Instead his focus remained on a fixed point on the field, a kind of distant, forlorn look on his face.

It sent a jolt through Will, seeing Danny like that. Could he have been that wrong? First Nick, and now Danny as well? His bud? How could he have spent as much time with these guys as he had, believed them to be his friends, and not seen what they really were?

A deep melancholy enveloped Will as he stared at Danny. The crowd settled back down as the Cougars kicked off to Natick and the game got under way again, but Danny only stood there watching the cheerleaders.

The cheerleaders.

Relief flooded through Will as he glanced over at the girls as they shook their pompoms through another routine. Danny was just watching the cheerleaders. Who could blame him? Will glanced out at the field, where Caitlyn dropped her pompoms and took a running start, then vaulted into a handspring and landed on her feet again, just in time to punctuate a loud shout of "Cougars!" from the whole cheer squad. Out in front, Dori Schnell planted her hands on her hips and led off the next cheer, voice carrying. She swung her arms in tight choreography but never participated in any of the groundwork. No splits, no somersaults, no acrobatics at all. Her left leg had never healed right after her accident.

As he watched her, Will felt sadness and guilt envelop him. A long time ago he had used magic to make himself forget. Magic had frightened him, and with good reason. But he had been even more significantly motivated by his guilt, by not wanting to have to feel the weight upon his heart every time he saw Dori, and the little limp in her step. Only now did he realize what a coward he had been. He had earned his guilt. And now he knew that in a way he needed to feel every bit of the sorrow it brought.

Still, she was a part of the cheer squad. The girls all wore bright smiles and their routine had an infectious exuberance. Will enjoyed the show. Sure, watching beautiful girls in motion had its own rewards, but it was more than that. Much as he and the guys often joked about appreciating the talent involved, there was more than a little truth behind the humor.

Reluctantly, Will tore his gaze from the cheerleaders and once more looked up at Danny, whose expression had not changed.

Will frowned, eyes narrowing. Quickly he glanced back and forth between Danny and the cheer squad. Lolly did a handspring that took her all the way to the far end of the lineup, but Danny's gaze did not follow her. His attention was straight ahead, at the girl on the squad's other flank.

Bonnie.

The coffee cup dropped from Will's hands and he was in motion before it hit the grass. He went up the metal side stairs that led to the walkway at the bottom of the bleachers, plunging into the constant flow of people coming down to use the bathroom or visit the concession stand, or headed back up to their seats. A fortyish guy with a tray of hot dogs and sodas bumped him, sloshing ice and Coke onto the dogs and onto Will, who apologized and pushed past the man, ignoring the cursing that followed him.

He had wondered why Danny had not come up to sit with them. Now he feared that he knew.

There were too many people on the walkway for him to move fast. He darted his head from side to side, trying to get a look at Danny, but in the thick of the throng, all he caught was a glimpse of dark hair, the vague impression of someone leaning against the railing.

On the field, Natick High fumbled.

Once more, the crowd erupted.

Frustrated, heart racing, doubt and regret and disappointment rushing through him, Will lost his patience and began to shoulder people aside, muttering empty apologies. A hand grabbed his arm and he shook it off. All around him were broad smiles, victoriously upraised fists, applauding hands, and he maneuvered amongst them with a dreadful urgency.

Will blinked in confusion and stopped short. He was sure he had passed the place where he had seen Danny leaning against the railing. Under his breath he swore, then he pushed through a couple of students to get to the metal rail, leaning out over the ground below to get a good look in both directions.

Danny was gone.

Will felt as though all his strength had left him. He let the railing take his weight, head hung. Someone muttered nasty words about his rudeness but he ignored them; they were right.

His heart felt as though it had turned to stone. He had done the spell to take him back in time to heal the wounds someone had torn in his life. Now he began to wonder if, even if his journey was a success, he might have simply traded those wounds for others, injuries not only to his heart but to his faith in everything.

Son of a bitch, he thought. *What's your story, Danny?*

Will didn't have an answer yet. But the Homecoming Dance was only hours away and he promised himself that tonight, no matter the cost, he would learn the truth.

WILL TOOK CAITLYN to the Homecoming Dance in his father's 4Runner, but the drive over to the school was solemn. By default, his girlfriend had been made Homecoming Queen that day, riding on the float with Tim Friel. Caitlyn hadn't liked that at all. It would have been one thing if Tess had just dropped out or gotten sick, but knowing what had happened, Caitlyn simply did not feel right about it. She had asked Principal Chadbourne to tell the Homecoming Committee to skip the King and Queen's dance.

Showing more sensitivity than Will would have credited him with, Chadbourne had agreed.

Both Caitlyn and Tim felt the entire event should have been canceled, but the principal had explained that the gymnasium was already decorated, the snacks and drinks had already been ordered, most of the student body had no idea what had happened the previous night, and in any case, there was simply no time. People would have shown up to find the doors locked and a sign on the door, all dressed up with nowhere to go. Certainly, Tess O'Brien would not want the dance to be canceled.

He was right about that, but Will doubted the principal had bothered to find out for himself. It was simply easier for him to have the dance than to explain its cancellation. Word would get around. It was already spreading. Will was sure the guy was going to catch hell from parents the following week, but Principal Chadbourne did not want to be the one to cancel the event. And maybe he was right. With the terrible things that had happened in the last week, it might be just what the junior and senior students needed.

For his part, Will was glad the dance was still going to happen. If the shit was still going to hit the fan, his future self insisted it was going to be tonight. Will didn't bother reminding him that he and Future Brian were changing things, that the time line might not unfold the way they remembered it. It didn't matter, because it wasn't just their memories. It was something in the ether, some ominous weight in the air.

Magic. He fucking hated it. Magic corrupted everything it touched. He was certain of that. And yet any misgivings Will had had about the interference of his future self in his life were gone. Before all of this, his worldview had been entirely too simple. Yes, he and Brian had made a hobby out of something dark and dangerous, but Will had managed to convince himself it was nothing, that most of it had been his imagination.

There would be no more denial.

If Future Will and Future Brian hadn't used magic to return to this time in their lives, Nick would have gotten away with all of it. Will didn't like to think about what would have happened to Ashleigh—what *had* happened to Tess—or to wonder how many other girls would have suffered the same fate.

But it wasn't over yet.

He and Caitlyn had driven to the school in near-total silence, their hands clasped over the console between the front seats. Now he unlaced his fingers from hers and put both hands on the wheel, slowing the 4Runner as he rolled through the parking lot in search of a space. There were dozens of people still outside, talking in groups or walking toward the entrance to the gym. Yet just looking at them Will could sense their reserve, the hesitation that had touched them all. Word was spreading, all right.

"Pretty brightly dressed for a funeral," Caitlyn said softly.

Regret surged through Will as he pulled the 4Runner in between a dented Sentra and the Dumpster. He put it in park and glanced over at her. Caitlyn wore an eggshell blue dress with thin spaghetti straps, and her hair was done in ringlet curls that framed her face beautifully. She looked to him like one of the delicate ceramic Lladro figurines his mother collected.

He reached out to touch her face, locking eyes with her.

"We've already had the funeral," he said softly. "Okay, so it won't be the same. Mike should be here. What happened with Tess... what Nick did...I'm not going to tell you I'm not fucked up about it. But you've got that dress on, and my God, you look beautiful. And our friends are waiting inside. There's music, there's dancing, and I know you don't want all of that to go to waste."

One corner of her mouth lifted in the sexy, lopsided grin that had made him fall in love with her in the first place. Caitlyn leaned in and kissed him, her lips brushing gently against his. She rested her forehead against his and Will slipped one hand behind her neck. For a long moment they remained that way, until at last she withdrew.

"Let's go dance."

Even now there was a kind of guilty hesitation in her eyes. Will nodded encouragingly.

"Absolutely."

He had to go around and help her down from the 4Runner. It was chilly, and he felt gooseflesh rise on her arm, but she left her jacket on the seat, not wanting to have to deal with it inside. They walked quickly hand in hand across the lot. Todd Vasquez was smoking a cigarette on the school steps; when he saw them coming, he took a long drag, then held the door open for them as smoke plumed from his nostrils.

His dark eyes fixed on Will. "Nice work, man," he said, voice low.

Will gave him a curt nod and went in, but that small exchange made him even more tense. Moments later when he and Caitlyn walked into the gym he felt as though a spotlight was on him. Word had spread, the story about Tess's rape, and Nick's arrest, and the role Will had supposedly played in capturing him. Even with the multicolored lights flashing around the darkened room and the music pulsing, merging with the chatter of so many voices, he felt squirrelly, like all he wanted to do was run.

"Come on," Caitlyn whispered in his ear.

Then she tugged him across the room toward a table surrounded by cheerleaders and football players. Some of them were his friends as well, but others were very much *hers*. Pix and Lolly were double-dating with Tim Friel and Joe Rosenthal. Kelly Meserve was with Scott Kelso. Dori was with Chuck Wisialowski and Bonnie had come with Trey Morel, who was cocky but not a bad guy. Kelso was in a tux, but it wasn't prom, so the rest of the guys were in suits except for Chuck, who apparently considered himself too cool for a formal dance and had worn a football jersey and khakis.

The girls all started in, talking to one another in close, just loud enough to hear each other over the music. There was none of the glee in their faces that gossip usually produced, however. Unpleasant topics would dominate tonight.

Tim Friel was the first one to greet Will. "Hey, man. Pull up a chair."

"Not just yet. Thanks, though," Will said. "We're gonna dance first."

Kelso nodded toward the dance floor, which was sparsely occupied. "Still in the snack phase. Not much dancing yet."

Will shrugged. "I don't mind leading the way." He glanced at Tim. "Great game, by the way. That run saved us."

"Thanks." Tim gave an inquisitive lift of his chin. "You OK?"

His broken nose was still swollen and tender, but otherwise he was fine, and he did not feel like getting into it with these guys. "I'm good."

Caitlyn continued to talk with her girlfriends, and the guys went back to whatever they had been discussing when he'd arrived. Will let his gaze wander; just off to his right, beneath one of the basketball backboards, he saw Brian watching him. And he wasn't alone. Future Will and Future Brian were there, talking with the English teacher, Mr. Murphy. The three adults—and how weird was it to think of himself and Brian that way—were laughing about something.

"Sweetie, I'll be right back. Just want to say hello to Brian," he said in Caitlyn's ear. Her eyes sparkled as she glanced at him, but she said nothing, only kissed him on the cheek and sent him on his way.

Brian saw him coming and excused himself, walking away from the others. They met up not far from a table of chips and cookies and drinks, and Will glanced around to make sure no one would overhear them.

"They seem pretty chummy," he said.

With a glance over his shoulder, Brian nodded. "Yep. Mr. Murphy was more than happy to have our 'uncles' as extra chaperones. Thought your resemblance to your uncle William was pretty remarkable."

"Yeah, isn't it, though?"

The amusement left Brian's face. "He seemed to think our parents wanted someone to look out for us after last night. I let him go on thinking that." He shook his head in frustration. "No sign of Danny, though. Do you really think he's . . . that he and Nick were working together?"

Will glanced at the floor. "I don't know, Bri. I wouldn't have believed any of this if I hadn't seen it, you know?" When he looked up again, he frowned, staring past Brian. "And right about now, Danny isn't the first thing on my mind."

"What is?" Brian asked, turning to see what had drawn Will's attention.

Twenty feet away, the handsome, confident man Brian would one day become was still talking amiably with their English teacher. But the third member of that group was gone.

"Where the hell did Future Boy slip off to?"

WILL HAD SEEN his younger self come into the gym with Caitlyn but had tried not to watch them. She was heartbreakingly beautiful tonight, and the sight of her brought a bittersweet ache. It was a merciful distraction talking to Mr. Murphy, a teacher he had always liked and who, seeing him now as a peer, insisted upon being called Kevin. Strange, but sort of nice, as well.

Now all those thoughts were gone, incinerated and blown out

of his head the second he saw Danny Plumer slip out of the gym through the big double doors that led into the school. With barely an excuse-me, Will had left Brian there to talk to Mr. Murphy and rushed along the darkened wall of the gym, trying to remain inconspicuous.

He pushed the metal release and slipped through those doors and into the dimly lit corridor, the music echoing off the linoleum floor and the metal lockers that lined the hall. When the door clicked shut behind him the music was muffled but not blocked out completely. Will was just in time to see Danny go into the men's room, and with a quick glance around he started in that direction.

All of the grief and pain and confusion in his heart became a maelstrom of emotion that drove him on, quickening his pace. The soles of his shoes slapped the floor, echoing along the hall, almost as though someone was following him. But no, he was alone. His fists were balled at his sides when he shouldered the bathroom door open. It banged against the tile wall.

Danny wore a charcoal black suit and a white shirt beneath it with no tie. He wasn't traditionally handsome, but so cool that it gave him a certain air, like a young Bogart. Will had expected to find him pissing at a urinal or maybe washing his hands. Instead, Danny was leaning against the far wall under the cracked, opaque window, hands stuffed in the pockets of his suit jacket.

"Hello, Will," he said, voice heavy with resignation.

All the breath went out of Will then. His eyes narrowed and a vein in his temple twitched. "You know it's me? You son of a—" He started across the tiled floor, arm cocking back.

The kid—and he was just a kid, really—held up his hands. "Wait, no, wait a second. You got it wrong. I ... yeah, I know it's you. I've got a good idea what's going on, but I haven't done any-thing, I swear to God."

Shame colored Danny's face and he averted his eyes. "Didn't do anything to stop it, either. But, holy shit, Will, I never thought it would come to this. I knew, though. When I saw you at Lebo's funeral, I knew it had to be you. You and Brian."

Will lowered his fist but did not relax his hands. There was so much anger in him, the truth was he wanted to pound the hell out of Danny. He had felt so much of his past betraying him in recent days, and Danny was a friendly face, a part of that past, and the perfect place for him to unleash his anguish.

But instead he stopped, and he listened. "How did you know?"

Danny slipped his hands back into his jacket pockets as if by doing so he could become invisible, could avoid Will's accusatory glare. "Nick saw you, bud. You and Brian, that day at Herbie's. He saw Brian's little walking-on-air trick, and he saw you do some mojo with your fingers and turn his frappe or float or whatever he ordered that day—Nick saw you turn it to blood. Hell, we all saw the blood, but only Nick made the connection."

Will felt his face go slack with surprise. Nick Acosta had always been a decent guy—or so he thought—but he'd never been accused of being clever. It was nothing short of stunning to learn that he had known these things and Will had never been the wiser. Yet even as these thoughts went through Will's mind, others came, as well. Nick as the shadow man, wielding enough magic to cloak himself in darkness, to make himself translocate, at least once.

"And he told you," he said.

Danny frowned. "Shit, no. He didn't say word one to me. I didn't find out until she told me. By then Nick was bangin' her. Or more likely it was the other way around. She offered him what he'd always wanted. She tried to rope me into it, but I gave her a pass. Not Nick, though. Once he got a taste of that, she had him wrapped around her finger. Maybe there was some magic in it, or maybe he's just that fucking weak. I don't know. But he did it all for her, Will. She'd do whatever he wanted, and so he'd do whatever she wanted. All that pain and tragedy, with that face and body? How could he resist?"

Confused, Will held up a hand. "Wait. She? Who's . . . ?"

And then he knew. In his mind he could even picture it happening. Nick had seen him and Brian doing magic in the ice-cream shop that day. He knew nobody would believe him, but there was one person he would have wanted to impress more than anyone else, one person he would have told, even with the risk that she might laugh.

The final puzzle pieces clicked into place. He had already realized that Nick couldn't have been working alone. His skill with magic had been minimal; at the lakeside, after he'd raped Tess, he had seemed surprised that he didn't just translocate away. Someone else was pulling his strings. The same someone who had been behind the wheel of that dark sedan the night Nick pushed Mike Lebo in front of Will's car.

But there was a further wrinkle, one he and Brian had barely discussed yet were both aware of. Whoever was involved—whoever was destined to kill Bonnie Winter—couldn't have been from this point in time. It had to have been someone from the future, or it wouldn't have changed the past, it would have *been* the past.

Will stared at Danny. "He told Dori."

Again, he looked away. "She's been here about six months. The...the older Dori, I mean." He uttered a nervous laugh. "Fucking with Nick's head the whole time. She moved right into Eastborough, opened up a florist shop downtown. The, what the hell's it called?"

"The Flower Cart," Will said numbly. "It's called The Flower Cart." The first time he had seen it he had known that he had no memory of it, but with the morass his mind had become, he had assumed he had forgotten it.

"That's it," Danny confirmed. Then he swallowed hard, and this time he met Will's gaze. "She told us what you did, man. What you and Brian did to her. You guys did your little spells here and there, a little levitation, a little turn-soda-to-blood or whatever. But she spent years studying this crap, Will. Now she's hurting people, twisting people up.

"And it's all about what happened before, what you and Brian did to her."

Will covered his eyes with one hand, and with the other he

reached out to grab a sink to steady himself. The deck of cards in his head wasn't being shuffled anymore. Instead, someone was playing fifty-two pickup with his life, with his memories, aces and diamonds and hearts and blood and girls with wounded souls all flying through his mind's eye.

Everything made sense now. Terrible, devastating sense.

He pressed the heel of his hand against his eyes, slid it up across his forehead as though he could erase it all, every fragment of half-remembered joy that had been obliterated, every grievous sin that had replaced them. Then, abruptly, Will dropped his hand and up from his chest there came a cry of anguish that tore from his throat in a primal rage. No words, just that sound. And when he had uttered it, he felt hollow inside.

Danny was staring at him fearfully.

When Will spoke again, his voice was weary. "Where is she?"

"I don't know. I haven't seen her in months, just heard about her from Nick. I swear to you." Danny's gaze ticked around the bathroom and he fidgeted, there against the wall, like a junkie in awful need of a fix.

"Danny! I saw you looking at Bonnie at the game today. You know she's on the list. Maybe you don't know why, but I do. Graduation day, bud. Months from now. She gives me—the me you know—she gives me a note that says she had a crush on me all through high school. That's why she picked Bonnie. For that matter, that's why she picked Nick. I'm thinking maybe Nick picked Tess, but I don't know. But it isn't going to end here, Danny. Not unless you tell me where she is!"

He jumped. "Fuck, Will! I said I don't know. It's just..."

"Just what?"

Danny rolled his eyes. "Think about it. If you were her, where would you be?"

Will was in motion before Danny even finished the sentence. His guts were ice as he yanked the bathroom door open and sprinted down the corridor toward the gym. Through the tiny rectangular windows, those multicolored lights splashed pale pastel ghosts into the hall. The music still thudded dully through the doors. Will could hear running footfalls behind him, but heading off in the other direction. Danny, taking off. Getting the fuck out while the getting was good.

The dance floor was packed now, bodies gyrating to the rhythm of the music. Faces flashed beneath the colored lights. He caught sight of Stacy Shipman laughing as somebody tried to whisper in her ear in the midst of the dance. Will felt things shifting around in his mind again, but he felt as though he couldn't latch on to any of the memories there now. His mind was a constant flux of motion and color, and he understood, suddenly, that this was a moment in which nothing was certain.

He scanned the dance floor, then started to rush through the gym, searching each table, peering into the shadows beneath the basketball backboards. Where the hell was everyone? Ashleigh? Young Will? The Brians?

He caught sight of Lolly, Pix, and Kelly Meserve. They seemed to be in the midst of laughing over one thing or another, when suddenly Lolly's attention wavered and she stared at something on the dance floor. A mass of people moved past Will, and for a moment his vision was obscured. When next he caught sight of Lolly her mouth was open, and though he could not hear her he could make out the words.

What the fuck?

Will started toward her, his gaze shifting to the dance floor, trying to see whatever it was that she saw. Then he realized why he hadn't seen any of the others. There were Young Will and Caitlyn. Ashleigh and Eric. Young Brian was dancing with Martina Dienst. And in their midst, Bonnie Winter danced with Trey Morel.

And a swirl of black mist twisted and danced along with them...and became Dori Schnell. A grown woman, an adult Dori he had seen perhaps twice since he had graduated from high school. Always beautiful. Her eyes still so very cruel.

It was as though she had been waiting for Will to arrive, for the instant she appeared she glanced over at him and smiled, then reached out toward Trey. With one hand she grabbed him, pulled him away from Bonnie, and kissed him deeply.

Trey Morel began to burn, his hair and clothes engulfed in flames that devoured him. He screamed and fell to the ground, twitching and kicking, as black smoke furled up from his smoldering skin. Bonnie took a step back, face etched in horror, unable to scream, but it was the only step she would take. Dori reached out and twined her fingers in Bonnie's lush red tresses and hauled her down to her knees.

A chorus of screams rippled outward from the center of the dance floor, from the place where Trey was still convulsing, burning alive. Dori yanked hard on Bonnie's hair and once more she glanced over at Will, but there was no smile there, only the feral eyes of pure hatred.

Danny Plumer's words echoed in Will's mind.

It's all about what you and Brian did to her.

CHAPTER 19

The stink of charred flesh filled Ashleigh's nostrils. Eric grabbed her by the arm and shoved her behind him, but his protective efforts could not shield her from the sight of the horror in the middle of the gym. Trey had stopped twitching; the flames that licked up from his remains popped and crackled, his blackened skin peeled, and his limbs seemed to shrink in the blaze.

Where were the sprinklers? Why hadn't the sprinklers gone on?

"Oh, shit. Oh, my God," she whispered.

Someone broke and ran, and then waves of students and chaperones rushed toward the exits. Ashleigh did not move. None of those at the center of the gym tried to run. All of them were frozen, staring in horror at the burning corpse in their midst and at the two figures illuminated by the flames, orange firelight flickering off their faces, twisting swirls of black smoke from burning human fat hiding them for a moment and then passing.

A raven-haired woman with hatred carved into her features grasped Bonnie Winter by her thick red hair, forcing her to her knees, tugging, making the girl scream.

"What the hell is this?" Eric demanded.

Magic, Ashleigh thought. *This is magic. Once you start, everything unravels.*

Eric started forward to help Bonnie, but Ashleigh grabbed his arm. "No. Don't move. Don't . . . don't draw her attention."

The music still played, too loud, thumping in her chest. Ashleigh glanced back and saw that the doors were open. People were shoving, panicked, trying to get out. Fortunately, this woman didn't seem interested in them in the least. There were still hundreds of people in the gym, their exodus illuminated by the striations of colored lights that twirled through the vast room. But in that center circle, Ashleigh saw that there were still perhaps two dozen people who remained, either entranced by Bonnie's plight or determined to help her. Brian was there, her Brian, though his dance partner had taken off. Tim Friel was there, eyeing Bonnie, cautiously moving forward, thinking he could save her. Ashleigh wanted to shout at him to stop, not to risk it.

Will saved her the trouble. He stepped from a shadowy place in the room where the lights seemed not to reach and put a hand on Tim's shoulder. "Hold up, man."

Ashleigh had studied the elder Will's face enough these past days that she had come to see her Will as boyish, to think of his face as young. But now there was something in his eyes and in the cast of his features that had grown darker and older, and suddenly the difference between him and his future self was negligible.

Caitlyn was crying, muttering to herself. Her face was pinched up into an ugly mask of tears and her hair was a tangled mess. She had one hand up, not quite covering her mouth. Now, without Will to shield her, she turned and ran for the exit.

The raven-haired woman gave another tug on Bonnie's hair and sneered as her gaze ticked toward the retreating Caitlyn.

"Oh, I don't think so," she said.

Her free hand came up, fingers contorted as if speaking in some cruel sign language, and her lips moved silently.

"No!" Will barked, and he moved to get between the witch and Caitlyn, his own hands sweeping the air in front of him, hooked into claws as though the air were a curtain he could tear down.

Caitlyn merged with the dozens of others pushing out through the doors into the October night, her blond hair disappearing in the throng, multicolored lights playing across the frenzied crowd. Chaperones yelled to them to be careful, to be orderly. And one by one, others who had remained behind to gape in horror at the spectacle at the center of the gym began to move cautiously away. Todd Vasquez. Tim Friel. Kelly Meserve.

The woman let them go. All of her attention was on Will. She arched an eyebrow in surprise. "Well done. I guess you and my brother did more dabbling than I thought. Don't worry, I can catch up to Caitlyn later. Anytime I want."

Recognition hit Ashleigh and she gripped Eric's arm more tightly, holding on with both hands as her mouth gaped. "Dori?"

With a dreadful slowness, the witch turned and looked at her, nostrils flaring in distaste. "And don't think I've forgotten about you, honey. Precious Ashleigh, everybody's sweet little sister. Nick fucked up, but that doesn't mean you get a pass. You stay right there until it's your turn."

WILL TRIED TO HIDE his fear from her. Yes, he and Brian had used magic as a game, had tried to impress each other with the little parlor tricks they learned. They'd cast spells and glamours, but they were nothing spells, bursts of light and flashes of fire. There were a few more complicated hexes and things, but they had given up after they'd cursed Dori. Will wasn't capable of anything like what he had seen Dori do—the cloaking shadow, the transloca-tion, the incineration of a human being. By instinct he had blocked her attack on Caitlyn, fending her off with a shielding spell that he and Brian had used when screwing around, dueling with the weak enchantments they'd learned. It was the strongest and only defense he had. Caitlyn was safe, for now, and he had Dori thinking maybe he was a better magician than she expected.

But that wouldn't last. Not if she really planned to kill them.

The bizarre tableau at the center of the gym seemed paralyzed, only the fingers of flame leaping from Trey's corpse still in
motion. On her knees, Bonnie whimpered. Will had wondered
why she didn't fight, didn't try to reach up and claw at Dori's
grip. Now he caught a glimpse of Bonnie's face, barely upraised,
and saw streaks of dark blood on her forehead. Dori had her
hair pulled so tautly that her scalp was tearing, making her bleed.
The witch was too strong. There had to be magic in that as well.

"What the hell are you doing?" someone asked, an authorita-
tive voice cutting through the music.

Mr. Murphy stormed across the parquet floor. He had been
helping to get people out of the gym safely, and the cavernous
room was quickly emptying. A few dozen remained, a herd of
teenagers who wanted only to forget what they'd just seen, to get
away from the fire and the death. But Mr. Murphy wasn't leaving.
Will would have thought anyone would panic, seeing someone
burn to death, but the wiry English teacher was holding it together pretty well. He pushed right between Will and Brian and
pointed a finger at Dori.

"You let that girl go right now, lady. This situation is bad
enough without whatever your problem is."

Dori's face twisted into a predatory grin and she tossed her
hair back. "My problems are your problems, *Mis-ter Murphy.* Obviously, you don't see that. In fact, I don't think you can see a
damn thing."

Guttural sounds escaped her throat and she passed two fingers across her eyes, staring at Mr. Murphy.

The teacher's face went slack and he stumbled backward. His
hands flew up to his eyes. "My . . . my eyes. What'd you do to my
eyes?" he cried. "You fucking bitch, what'd you do?"

Dori's upper lip curled back in disgust. "Stupid question."

Blind, the teacher stumbled away. Will heard him crash into
something but he did not dare to take his eyes off of Dori, not
even for a moment.

In his peripheral vision he saw Eric move. It was too late to
stop him. Will saw Eric pull away from Ashleigh's grip.

"What do you want? What the hell do you want with us?" Eric asked, moving forward but keeping himself between Dori and Ashleigh.

A tiny wisp of flame flickered at the end of her finger as she pointed at him. "With you? Nothing. I don't even remember your name. You were just that cute guy Ashleigh was *not* fucking. I always thought that was a shame. If you'd been my puppy back then, I would've fucked you silly." She rolled her eyes, then shot a glance at Ashleigh. "Curb your dog, you stupid twat."

"Eric," Ashleigh rasped.

Will watched her as she bit her lip, not daring to make a move. Eric took a careful step back.

"Ah, yes, that was it. Eric," Dori said.

Still on her knees, face painted in blood, choking on the black smoke from the fire that devoured her dance partner, Bonnie began to tremble and a sirenlike wail issued from her lips. Dori hauled Bonnie to her feet and forced the girl to meet her gaze.

"Stop. Now. Or burn."

Bonnie fell silent, but tears now streaked across the rivulets of blood on her cheeks. As Dori held on, she shifted her weight back and forth, revealing the limp she had had ever since the night she had been struck by that truck, the night they had cursed her.

Will felt his fear dissipating. He glanced over at Ashleigh and then at Brian, and he could sense it coming off of them as well. Disgust. Fury. There was an undercurrent of guilt in his heart, for he knew that he and Brian had begun the process that had brought them here. They were responsible for that damaged leg that had never healed right, for the humiliation Dori had carried with her after what had happened with her boyfriend that night, all because of the curse. But something inside Dori Schnell had always been rotten. Whatever part Nick had played, Dori had been responsible for everything that had been happening to them, for Mike's death, for Tess's rape. She had just murdered Trey; the stink of his burning still filled the air. And what she was doing to Bonnie... They had cursed her, but they hadn't made her capable of this. Will refused to believe that. Something this dark had to have been lurking in her all along. Not that it mattered now, really, how she got this way. The only thing that really counted was figuring out how to stop her.

He nudged Brian, who nodded slowly.

Will raised his hands, recalling the spell in his mind, and spheres of fire manifested in his palms. He ran at Dori, the flames roaring in his hands, and he reached for her. Bonnie saw him first, blinking the blood from her eyes, and she gasped and flinched away, but was held tight by the fingers wound in her hair.

Dori whipped her head around and pointed at him, lips silently mouthing a single word. Even as she spoke, the air around her head shimmered and Will's eyes widened in amazement as all the moisture in the room gathered there. Then suddenly Dori was drowning, her head and shoulders enveloped in a ball of water. It was like looking at her inside a fish tank. With her free hand she reached for her throat, choking, unable to breathe.

Will glanced at Brian, whose arms were outstretched, fingers dangling as though he had been crucified. Beads of sweat ran down his face and the rotating colored lights played across his features. Teeth gritted as though in pain, Brian shot him a hard look.

"Do it!"

This was a magic he had never seen Brian perform before, a spell that must have been incredibly difficult. Seeing it made Will hesitate, but only for a moment. Then he went at Dori again, dark flames in his hands. He lunged for her.

But his moment of hesitation had been costly.

Drowning in water that had appeared from nowhere, Dori pulled Bonnie Winter to her as though she meant to kiss the girl's crimson mouth. Bonnie's face went into the water. Will faltered. Behind him, Brian moaned softly and fell to his knees, weak from effort.

The water spell collapsed, and it splashed to the floor around Dori's feet. The witch smiled, licked blood from Bonnie's face, and then turned to Will. She twisted her arm at a terrible angle in front of her, fingers pointed downward as though she held something within them. Then with a flick of her wrist she turned her hand palm upward.

Will felt himself jerked off his feet, and he fell onto his shoulder. Something cracked inside him; pain arced down his arm and across his back. The breath was knocked out of him and his lungs burned as he pulled himself to a sitting position, glaring at the witch.

"This is all loads of fun," Dori said, glancing around, "but what I want to know is, where's my brother? And where's Will?"

Will blinked and glanced at Ashleigh, then at Brian, who was shakily regaining his feet.

"What are you talking about, you crazy fuck?" Brian asked. "We're right here."

The hatred with which she glared at him made them all flinch.

"I'm not talking about you, you little puke. Back here," she gestured with her hand to take in the whole room, and beyond, "in the old days, you two didn't have a clue. You can't appreciate what you had. Not really. I can wound you, but it wouldn't be deep enough. And why am I even talking to you?"

Dori looked around, shuffling on that bum leg. "They know why we're here. Come on, boys. Don't keep a girl waiting!"

The techno-beat of the previous song had faded, and there was a moment before the next tune on the party mix began. In that momentary lull, Will could hear Mr. Murphy still shouting about his eyes. He turned to see the teacher feeling his way along one wall, desperately trying to find the exit. From the sound system came a synthesized, syncopated beat. Just before the other instruments joined in, a voice rose above the music.

"I'm here, Dori. I've been here. Just watching the floor show."

Pain lancing through his shoulder, Will scanned the gym, searching for the origin of that voice. There were only a handful of people still in the gym, fewer than twenty, and they were flowing quickly now out the double doors.

All save one.

As they swarmed past him, the man Will James would one day become stood defiantly staring at Dori. He remained motionless as the last of the people exited the building, and Will realized immediately what his older self had been doing. He'd been helping with the evacuation, shielding their exodus, making sure Dori didn't try to attack them or prevent them from leaving. *Watching the floor show,* Will thought. *I don't think so. Getting everyone out of the way, more like.*

Future Will started across the gym toward the small group of people frozen in place around the burning corpse of a kid none of them had known very well. Will found himself hoping his older self had a plan, because for his part, he figured they were all going to die.

HANDS UP as if in surrender, Will walked toward the center of the gym, where Dori had hold of Bonnie and where the remains of Trey Morel still smoldered. Ashleigh and Eric were perhaps a dozen feet from her. Young Brian stood shakily, still drained from the spell he'd cast. On the floor, Young Will sat up with one hand clamped to his shoulder.

It isn't broken, he remembered. *Just dislocated.* He might have tried to heal it, but he didn't dare waste the energy. Regret and guilt weighed upon him. *Healing spells. If I'd just gone to Dori after it happened . . . even if I wasn't strong enough to heal her, if I'd just tried, it might have prevented all of this.* But to do that, he and Brian would have had to reveal to Dori what they had done, and neither of them had been prepared to do that.

Will swore under his breath. More than ever, he wished the strings of new memories that were formed every time he altered his own past would show more, would reveal the outcome of his present circumstances. But the scene playing itself out there in the gym was not over yet. Its outcome was still lost in the mists of fate.

"Well, well," Dori mused, "this is a surprise. You've got balls, I'll give you that. I figured you ran away like Brian."

As he moved closer Will had a better view of Dori. She was still a young woman, only twenty-seven, but hate had twisted her. Her mouth was pinched with sourness and there was poison in her eyes. Around her, the others remained unmoving, unwilling to break the circuit that had suddenly been established between the two of them.

"You used Nick."

"He liked it," Dori mused.

"And it was you who killed that kid Kyle's family, jumping back to our time."

She gave a small pout. "The little puke who was helping you? He didn't die? Shit. All that popping back and forth for nothing. Well, I can always catch up with him later."

For a long moment Will could only stare at her. There was no way to argue with the venom in her veins. He shook his head.

"I'm sorry," he said, and his remorse was genuine. "What we did, Brian and me . . . it was stupid and cruel. I can't even imagine what it felt like, the things that happened to you that night. I'm sure it won't matter to you that we had no idea how . . . effective the spell would be, but—"

"Curse," Dori snarled, her chest rising and falling as hate boiled up within her. "You know better, Will. 'Spell' is such a coward's word for what you did. You cursed me!"

When he had come up abreast of his younger self, in line with the others who formed an odd half-circle around the trio in the middle—Dori, Bonnie, burning Trey—he stopped.

"We didn't know—" Young Will began.

Young Brian interrupted him. "For Christ's sake, Dori, yes, all right? We put a fucking curse on you! We're teenage boys. We were screwing around and you were the obvious target. You hated me! Even with all the bullshit and venom you spewed I still never really hated you, but when we had to pick someone to try it out on, you were my first choice. I wanted to tell you I was sorry a hundred times, but I couldn't, 'cause that would mean talking about the magic, and I figured you wouldn't believe me anyway. And you know what? I'll tell you something. After the first couple of months, I stopped wanting to apologize. You were still as nasty to me as you'd always been. So you know what? Fuck you!"

A small breath escaped Will's lips. He stepped toward Brian, one hand out. "Hang on, Brian. Look, none of that is the point."

Dori had been glaring at her brother. Now a giddy, wild laugh spilled from her and she glanced over at Will. "It isn't? Sounds pretty much to the point where I'm concerned. But no, Will, you've grown up all full of wisdom. Why don't you tell me what the point is?"

Brows knitted in consternation, heart secretly hammering despite his exterior calm, he gestured around the gym. "This. This is the point. Yes, we fucked you over. You were embarrassed and inconvenienced. Humiliated, fine. You lost your boyfriend, who was a prick anyway, by the way. On that count we did you a favor. The truth is, if you hadn't been hit by that car, we probably would have thought the whole thing was a scream. And even if people whispered about you behind your back, you would've gotten over it. But the pain. The hospital. Your legs? We never meant for any of that to happen, Dori.

"But all of this...what you've done? It isn't the same, don't you see that? Are you so completely insane that you don't see what you've done?" His voice faltered, and when he spoke again there was anguish in it. God, he missed Lebo. And now the stink of burnt human flesh was in his nostrils. "You've taken lives. You've ruined the hearts of girls who never did anything to you. And this was all for what? To get back at me and Brian?"

Dori smiled, and for the first time he thought he saw some of the girl he knew in there. But whatever remained of her was shattered and jagged like broken glass. "You, mostly. I always hated Brian. He was a fucking weasel. I expected it from him. It was so much worse knowing you were in on it, Will. I always thought you were a good guy. Until you and my brother took my life away. Made me a laughingstock and a cripple."

He shook his head in horror. "Do you even hear yourself? Look what you've done!"

"I know." With a beatific smile she laid her head back and opened her arms as if to welcome a lover. The lights flashing around the room dimmed and the shadows flowed toward her, collecting around her, clinging to the contours of her body, even masking her face, though the way it formed on her hair it was as though the darkness had enwrapped each strand.

Released from Dori's grip, Bonnie fell sprawling on the floor, a grateful sob escaping her lips. With one hand she wiped blood from her face, and she got up on her knees, trying to scramble away.

With a flick of her wrist, Dori summoned a cloud of shadow from the air. It knocked Bonnie over, pulled her back, thrust itself at her mouth and nose, and began to gag and suffocate her. Bonnie tried to scream, but the darkness choked her. Her eyes were wide; a veil of shadow moved over her retinas, blacking them out completely. She spasmed and bucked against the parquet floor.

"Dori, no!" Young Brian snapped.

Will's younger self ran to Dori, tried to pull at the darkness, but it slipped through his fingers like mercury. Ashleigh screamed as Eric pulled away from her and ran at Dori.

"Eric, no!"

Cloaked in shadows, music and color passing through her as though she were not there at all, Dori turned to face Eric as he ran at her, shouting obscenities. Will wanted to grab him, pull him back, but he knew it was too late. She raised both hands, middle and ring fingers folded back, and as she muttered something she made a motion as though she were pushing down upon the air.

With a double whip crack that echoed across the gym, both

of Eric's legs broke and he crumbled to the ground, crying out in pain and shock. Dori wasn't done. She thrust her tongue out and gave a serpentine hiss. The darkness misted like black spit and floated across to touch Eric's hands. Instantly he began to shout in alarm. His eyes widened in horror as he raised his hands and turned them on himself. Formed into claws, his fingers began to tear into his own face.

The witch scowled at Will. "Makes your little pussy magic act look like card tricks, doesn't it? Now, let's see, what fun have I reserved for Ashleigh?"

"Will!" Young Brian shouted, and both the younger and the older turned to glance at him. "There's no hope for her. Do something!"

Bonnie was dying. Eric was killing himself. Ashleigh was next. Brian was right. This thing his sister had become was beyond redemption. They had no other choice. Eyes locked on Dori's, Will uttered two words.

"Kill her."

WHEN THEY HAD PLANNED this, Brian had never imagined that the monster those words would be spoken about would be his sister. Back in their time, in the future, he had not seen her for more than three years. Yet as he lurked in the shadows and watched, listening to every word, he felt only the smallest temptation to reveal himself, to abandon the plan. They had known that whoever was behind this was far more adept at magic than any of them, that none of the little spells and hexes they had learned would be strong enough to destroy the magician behind the terror of the past week. That made it all the more important for them not to show all of their cards before they were ready.

The element of surprise would work only once.

From the place where he lurked, so close to the ceiling of that cavernous room, he could have reached out to touch the rafters. Of the seventeen spells he had mastered in the time when he had played with magic, levitation had always been his favorite. Of all of them, it was the one he continued to be drawn to over the years. He had sworn off other magics as too dangerous, and somehow unclean. But levitation still felt as wondrous as he had once naïvely believed that all magic would be.

Above the lights, amidst the echoes of the pulsing music whose dancers had all fled in terror, Brian Schnell walked on air.

It was all he could do as he watched the proceedings below him not to cry out. Bonnie was suffocating. Eric's legs breaking made a report like a shotgun blast. The smoke from Trey's charred remains gathered amongst the rafters, and he had to breathe through his mouth. By the time Will gave the word, Brian was ready.

His eyelids fluttered with the concentration required, but he turned himself upside down, controlling his levitation with the tiniest motions of his hands. Then came the most difficult part: wielding two bits of magic at once. With a whispered summoning, white fire engulfed his fists, mystical flame that would tear through whatever defenses Dori erected. Of the four of them—himself and Will, then and now—the elder Brian had the most knowledge of magic.

It was up to him.

Dori glanced at Will when he spoke those words, then she looked at the others—at their younger selves, at twitching Bonnie who was gagging on shadow, at Ashleigh as she tried to keep Eric from ripping his face off—and she shook her head in amusement. She raised her hands, fingers contorted to cast a spell, and pointed toward Will.

Brian plummeted toward her, air whipping past his face, his hands outthrust beneath him. Memories flashed through him, images of Dori as a girl, his baby sister on her tricycle, eating ice cream on the Fourth of July, wearing makeup the first time. Yet they clashed in his head with other moments, with all the bitterness and cruelty, with Mike Lebo's broken, bloody corpse in the road, with the pale, haunted, fallen angel that Tess had seemed at the lakeside, her body and soul violated at Dori's whim.

In spite of himself, Brian wept.

His hands burned.

He gritted his teeth as he whipped down toward her, praying he could reinstate the levitation spell at the right moment, trying not to think about what he was about to do. The faces of his parents kept intruding upon his mind, and his tears seemed to burn him far more than the white fire that roared around his fists.

Kill her, Will had said. And so he would.

He would never know what gave him away.

Dori tilted her head back and looked up at him. Her mouth opened and he thought she was going to scream her rage. But instead of words, flame gouted from her throat in a bellow of infernal heat that engulfed him completely. Brian smelled his hair burning, felt the fire searing his face and arms, his skin peeling, his tears nothing more than steam.

He grasped at the air, twisting his body around as though he might somehow arrest his fall. Then he struck the floor, his spine shattering on impact.

WILL'S HEART WAS NUMB. There was no room to grieve for Brian. Not when he was absolutely certain they were all about to die.

Dori stared down at her brother's burning, broken body, flames leaping from Brian's clothes and hair even as the last embers on Trey's body flickered and were snuffed out. The witch seemed mesmerized by Brian, as though she had forgotten the rest of them completely.

Young Brian fell to his knees, staring vacantly at the fire that was consuming the body...the man he would one day become. "I'm dead," he said, voice flat and dull. "I'm dead."

The shadow form that had been thrusting itself into Bonnie's throat dissipated and she gasped and sucked greedily at the air, face twisted into a mask of despair. The blood was drying on her cheeks, but fresh tears streaked her face.

Just a few feet from her, Eric at last regained control of his hands. His fingers were covered in his own blood and his face was unrecognizable, furrows torn in the flesh. Will could see bone. His broken legs were still twisted underneath him, and Ashleigh knelt beside him, shushing him, her hands fluttering about as though she wanted to touch him but was afraid to do so. A soft keening noise came from Eric's throat.

With Dori still stunned, all of her focus on Brian's burning body, Young Will glanced over at his older counterpart. Will nodded to him and the kid went to Ashleigh's side. He reached out and touched Eric's forehead with his left hand, and Bonnie's with his right.

"Sleep," the kid said.

Mercifully, they did.

The elder Will took a few steps closer to Dori, forcing himself not to look at Brian's corpse. "Ashleigh," he said, without looking at her. "Get Bonnie out of here. Will, snap Little Bri out of it and get him to help you carry Eric. Go. Leave."

Young Will stared at him and shook his head almost imperceptibly, mouthing the word "no."

His refusal was moot. The sound of Will's voice snapped Dori out of the strange trance her brother's death had put her in. Now she trembled as she raised her eyes.

"He tried to kill me," she said, voice quavering, rising in pitch and volume with every word. Her lips peeled back with hatred, and spittle flew from her mouth as she screamed at Will. "You told my brother to kill me! He was going to kill me! You fuck! You think I've hurt you with all of this, killing your past, twisting it around?"

Dori lowered her voice then, and with every word shadows whispered from her lips. She stepped over her brother's burning body and the flames did not scorch her. The witch walked toward Will.

"I'm just getting started."

The music died.

Will saw Dori blink and hesitate, a tiny glimmer of confusion in her eyes.

With a loud pop, the brilliant overhead lights went on, dispelling the shadows. The wreckage of the Homecoming dance was all around them. There was blood on the wood floor, and the parquet had melted to black where the bodies burned.

Then Will saw her, standing by the double doors that led into the school.

"Dori," he whispered.

The witch saw that his eyes were not on her and she turned to see what he had seen. In the glare of the gymnasium lights, the shadows that cloaked her body rippled and gleamed.

Beautiful, raven-haired Dori Schnell, sixteen years old, a junior at Eastborough High, stood just inside the gym. How long she had been there, Will didn't know. In her hands she held a thick sheaf of paper, its significance unknown to him. But the way she held it, with such distaste, as though it was soiled in some way, sent a suspicion scurrying across his mind.

"Well, this *is* a surprise," the shadow witch said. "Come to watch?"

Dori started across the gym, limping slightly. "No, thanks. I've seen enough." As she walked she lifted the sheaf of paper as though it was some kind of offering. "Remember this?"

"How could I forget?" the elder Dori replied.

The girl looked at Will, though she kept walking, approaching her future self but without even the tiniest glimmer of hesitation or fear. "I never liked you, Will. Let's get clear on that. I mean, not liked you, liked you. I never had a crush or anything. You're not my type. But I did think you were a good guy. I hated my brother. It happens sometimes, you know? With siblings. But you always seemed all right, even though you hung around with him. I treated you like crap because you were his friend. You were a shit by association. It made me hate you more, when I found out. When Nick told me about the magic. I hated you both. I still hate you."

At sixteen, Dori had been far more beautiful than Will remembered. Or perhaps it was the sadness in her now that made her seem so.

"It was easy to find the book. As soon as I could get around I searched Brian's room. It didn't take long. *Dark Gifts.* Gaudet wasn't fucking kidding, was he? That's the thing with magic. It's a gift, sure, but there are some strings attached. Magic always costs, doesn't it, Will?"

The girl kept limping, and now she had nearly reached the center of the gym and begun to circle around her future self. The witch glared at her, eyes narrowed. The shadows that covered her face seemed thinner now, her expression more visible.

"What're you up to?" the elder Dori asked.

"What's wrong?" said the girl. "Can't remember this part?"

Dori stopped a few feet from the burning corpse of her brother—the way he would one day be, years in the future—and through the flames she looked at Young Brian, the brother she knew, who was on his knees, weeping.

And Will saw sorrow in her eyes.

"I didn't want him to know that I knew. But I wanted the magic. It had hurt me. Scarred me. And I wanted to taste it." She looked at him, raised the book a little higher. "I made a copy."

A copy, Will thought. *So simple.*

The witch took a step toward her, little tendrils of shadow reaching out from her hands. "What's your game, *Dori?*"

The girl shrugged lightly. "Like I said. I've seen enough." Then Dori looked at Will again. "I forgive you. Both of you."

She dropped the stack of paper, her copy of Gaudet's manuscript, into the pyre of flame that was devouring her brother. The white pages ignited instantly, some of them floating away and some escaping the edges of the flames. But the others burned as if they had been hungry for the fire all along.

The shriek that tore from the shadow witch's mouth was a cry of pure hatred, of true evil. Will would have liked to think it was the voice of something ancient and terrible, something that was not at all human. But he knew better. The magic had tainted them all, but it did not control them.

"You stupid, silly little bitch!" the witch screamed. "Do you have the first clue what you've done?"

Dori nodded. "I've got a pretty good idea, yeah."

They all watched in silent amazement as the shadows began to melt off of the elder Dori. She held her hands up and stared at her fingers as the darkness receded. Then she shook her head as though there was something inside her skull she wanted out.

"No, no, no, no, no!" she chanted, pounding her forehead with the heels of her palms.

Will understood. Her memories were changing. Dori had seen what her future held, borne witness to the blood and death and horror that she was to cause, and she had rejected it. She had chosen another path. Now the rest of them were seeing the future change right before their eyes. The witch's features began to soften.

She froze. Her head snapped up and she glared at Will, nostrils flaring. "No," she said, and even under the bright gym lights he saw that her eyes had turned a bloody crimson. "I won't let it change."

The witch spun on her younger self. "There's a spell. While I still remember. To travel in time. To live your life all over again. We always want to go back, don't we? If I merge with you, you little bitch, I can stop this. I can make sure it all happens my way. All it takes is one little—"

And she lunged at the girl, hands curved into claws.

Dori screamed as the monster her future self had become reached for her. The witch's fingers caught her hair, pulled her close, and she began to utter terrible, guttural words that did not sound as though they came from any human tongue.

"Will!" Ashleigh screamed. "Stop her!"

He was in motion, rushing toward the two of them without any idea what he could do. The witch Dori was so much more powerful than he was. Her magic was fading, but he remembered so few spells, and what he knew was minor, not meant to hurt people. He stumbled over Young Brian, who seemed catatonic on the floor. Will felt a firm hand grab his arm to stop him from falling. Out of the corner of his eye he saw his own face, his younger face, mirrored back at him.

Together they raced to stop Dori.

The witch held the girl, and even as the two Wills ran toward them, they could see the elder's fingers disappearing, being absorbed by the younger. With an ecstatic shudder, the witch threw her head back, her body beginning to merge with Dori's so that they appeared hideously conjoined.

They would not reach her in time.

Magic made the impossible possible. And so perhaps it was magic that had allowed Brian Schnell to hold on to one last spark of life as his body was immolated. His back was broken and his flesh was charred and blackened, but he managed to raise his upper body, to look blindly in the direction of his sister with embers where his eyes ought to have been, to reach out a withered, smoking hand and cast a single spell that caused the elder Dori to cry out in pain and to go rigid, momentarily paralyzed.

His final spell.

When Brian slumped to the floor, pieces of his body fell away in a cascade of fiery ashes. He would not move again.

Elder Dori shrieked and seemed to struggle against the spell. Young Dori's eyes searched fearfully and found Will's, even as her future self began to move again and the merger continued.

But Brian had bought them precious seconds.

Simultaneously, the two aspects of Will James thrust out their hands, their frantic thoughts identical, and reached into their minds for the only spell they could think of, the first magic they had ever done that lingered, that remained with them. It had tainted them so deeply that it required no words. They felt the magic flow from them like a brutal exhalation of breath, of energy. The air that separated them from the witch and the girl seemed to shimmer.

The witch did not cry out. She simply jerked upward, pulling away from Dori, pulling out of her, and went completely rigid for a moment.

Then she fell to the floor. Dead.

Orange soda trickled from her nostrils, sticky and sweet.

EPILOGUE

An angry horn blared.

Will blinked, his eyes clearing, and he inhaled sharply as though for a moment he had forgotten to breathe. He threw himself back against the driver's seat, arms rigid, knuckles white as he jerked the steering wheel to the right, veering out of the path of the fire-engine-red pickup truck that thundered down the narrow, tree-lined road toward him.

He held his breath, heart pounding, jaw rigid. The pickup barely missed clipping the Toyota's rear end. Only then did he realize that he had overcompensated, that in order to get out of the way of the pickup he had cut the wheel too sharply on that narrow road. Trees loomed up in front of the Toyota and Will tried to right the car again, but he was out of time.

By some miracle the Toyota sailed off the road between two trees—one close enough to tear off the driver's side mirror—and crashed through a split-rail fence. The car shuddered as the tires ran over rutted ground and tall grass and Will hit the brakes, bringing the car at last to a stop in a farmer's field.

For long seconds he sat rigid behind the wheel until at last he let out a breath and slumped over, resting his forehead, waiting for his pulse to slow, struggling with a fog of disorientation that enveloped him. What the hell was he doing? Had he fallen asleep at the wheel? He couldn't even recall where he had been going, where he was, or what day it was.

Head spinning, profoundly unnerved, he put the car in park and climbed out, engine still running, to orient himself. The field was part of a large stretch of farmland complete with a red barn and a small silo. In the distance he saw a large, fenced pasture, but it seemed unoccupied. Beyond the farm was a hill lined with orderly rows of apple trees; the field he had driven into was, he now saw, a pumpkin patch.

October. Almost Halloween. Though the sun shone brightly, the wind was cool, and he shivered as he stared at the few pumpkins that remained, mostly broken or misshapen things unfit for anyone's front stoop. He knew this place, had passed it a thousand times. The narrow, tree-lined street was Old Buffalo Farm Road. He had been on his way to Eastborough. On his way home.

"What the hell?" he muttered, glancing around in confusion.

Then, as if in answer, it all came flooding back to him. The deck of cards began to shuffle in his mind, image upon image, all of them in conflict with one another. Will cried out from the pressure in his head and staggered back to lean against the Toyota. He clamped his hands to the sides of his skull and squeezed his eyes shut. It was all simply too much. Far too much.

Will knew. He remembered everything. Every variation, every twist of fate.

"Oh, God," he whispered to himself, doubling over, eyes watering. "Oh, Christ."

As suddenly as it had begun, it subsided. The rush of memories began to assert themselves, to settle into layers of mental sediment. His breath had come in short, harsh gasps, but now it began to even out. Will inhaled deeply several times, slowing his pulse and his breathing, regaining his composure.

The memories sifted and merged and faded, and gradually, an entirely new set began to take their place. He could still recall all of those other versions, including the terrible events of the week he had spent in another time, another era.

A week that now had never happened.

Yet he remembered.

A sudden chill made him shudder. The Toyota purred against his back. Will glanced at his watch in the very same moment that he remembered where he was heading.

It was Sunday morning. Reunion weekend was almost over, but a number of his friends and classmates would be gathering at the Carriage House for brunch. With one more glance around at the farm, he climbed into the Toyota and turned it around, there in the field. He would have to stop back later and offer to pay for the broken fence, but for now the anticipation was too great. His hands trembled on the wheel as he guided the Toyota over the broken bits of fence and between the trees, back up onto Old Buffalo Farm Road. He barely noticed the shattered mirror on the driver's side. It was entirely unimportant.

Much as he wanted to speed, he drove the rest of the way to the Carriage House with great caution.

It was a wonderfully rustic, early-nineteenth-century inn with a small river running across the property. The parking lot was already full when he arrived, so Will parked on the street, climbed out of the car, and trotted around to the side of the building, where the entrance was.

Stacy's eyes lit up when she saw him. She wore a hunter-green turtleneck and brown pants, and the wind blew her black hair across her face so that she had to reach up and tuck it behind her ears. Will felt his pulse quicken; despite all that weighed upon his heart, he could not have prevented the smile that spread across his features then, even had he wanted to.

He trotted up the walk and she came down to meet him halfway. Her hand reached out for his and he took it, bending down to kiss the spray of freckles that decorated the bridge of her nose. The corners of her eyes crinkled in happiness, and she gave him that tiny smile that was always so full of mischief.

It was the most natural thing in the world.

"You're late," she said.

In the new set of memories that had superseded all of the others, the reunion weekend had gone very well between them. Better than well. At Liam's on Friday night he had been mesmerized by her performance, by her voice and her eyes. The guys had tormented him in the way they had always done to one another. Lebo had arrived late, but late was better than not at all. They had celebrated and promised each other that they would make a greater effort to keep in touch. On Saturday, Stacy had been waiting for him at the gate of Cougar Stadium, and she and Will had sat with Ashleigh and Eric, Mike, Nick, Danny, and Keisha.

And that night, she had saved all of her dances for him. It was the beginning of something, and he felt light and agile and happy, as one always does at the beginning.

"I was unavoidably detained," he said. "But I'm here now."

That mischievous smile again. "That'll do."

Hand in hand they walked into the Carriage House, through the main foyer, and along a corridor that led to the large private room the class had reserved for the occasion. Mere seconds after he had stepped into that room, with gourds and Indian corn and pumpkins decorating the antique tables and the autumn sunshine beaming through the high windows, he paused and inhaled sharply.

Mike Lebo stood at the brunch buffet, putting together a plate of fruit for himself. Beside him stood Danny Plumer, who quietly muttered something that made Lebo laugh out loud, then shoot Danny an eye-rolling look of slightly appalled amusement. At a table in the corner, Nick Acosta popped a slice of bacon in his mouth, listening intently to Ashleigh going on about the latest remarkable escapades of her twins. Her husband, Eric, held her hand and simply watched her talk, content just to be in his wife's presence.

His eyes surveyed the room. Tim Friel stood waiting while the chef made him an omelette. He saw them all. Lolly and Pix.

Tess O'Brien. Joe Rosenthal. And standing in the full sunlight beneath one of those tall windows, her red hair radiant, he saw Bonnie Winter.

Stacy tugged his hand. "Hey, you all right?" she asked, brows knitted with concern.

"Fine," he said with a grin. "Very fine."

He slid his arm around her and they walked across the room toward the table where Ashleigh, Eric, and Nick were eating breakfast. Lebo and Danny called out to Will and he waved. More than anything he wanted to go over and throw his arms around Lebo, but he didn't want to make a scene. There would be time later.

Plenty of time.

All of the dark memories remained, but they lingered now only as shadows in his mind, enough to remind him always how much he had to be thankful for, how much he had almost lost and how much he had gained instead. For though he remembered the Will who had touched the magic and gone back in time, though he remembered the younger Will James who had been visited by his future self, he was no longer either of those men. None of it had ever happened, and yet there were ripples. Things had been set right, and then some.

Will had never cast the spell that would make him forget what he and Brian had done to Dori. Though it weighed upon him, in time he made peace with his guilt. Long before Caitlyn had broken things off with him, he had realized that he loved her more than she would ever love him. The end of their relationship had broken his heart. Love could be that way. But their breakup had not hobbled him, and so Will had also made a kind of peace with Caitlyn, and with the way things had evolved for them.

Now here he was with Stacy. Between the way things were developing with her and the promotion to Lifestyles editor he had received on Thursday, he was having just about his best week ever.

As he and Stacy reached the table where Will's friends were

sitting, a cell phone began to trill. Ashleigh reached for her purse. Both she and Eric wore expressions of concern, as any parent might who had left their children at home, so far away.

"Hello?" she said, and immediately she smiled, her mood lightening. "Oh, hey, Caitlyn. When are you guys—"

Her smile disappeared.

Tremors of dread went through Will and he felt a pain in his gut, as though his trepidation had hooked him there, and begun to pull.

"Oh, God, Cait, I'm sorry," Ashleigh said, her voice barely a whisper.

They were all looking at her now. Eric touched her elbow as though to reassure her that he was there to catch her if she should fall.

"All right. All right, I'll call later. I'm . . . I'm so sorry."

Will was staring at her as she clicked the phone closed and slipped it back into her purse. Her eyes were downcast and she chewed her lower lip. Stacy's grip on his hand tightened. When Ashleigh finally lifted her gaze she did not look at her husband or at Nick, but at Will.

"What happened?" he asked, his voice so small he was not even certain the word had come out.

"It's Brian. He's been . . . staying with Caitlyn while he was home for the reunion. You know the two of them have been off and on ever since . . ." Ashleigh stopped to take a shuddering breath, one hand going up to wipe her eyes as the tears began.

"He died." She glanced around at the others, then back at Will. "Sometime during the night. He just . . . the hospital says his heart just stopped. Twenty-eight years old and he's dead of heart failure."

"Oh, my God," Nick said, shaking his head. He was pale, his features stricken. "I can't . . . How the hell does something like that happen? I mean, that young? I don't understand. And he was . . . he was one of us. How does that happen?"

No one had an answer to that. Or, more accurately, no one was willing to offer it.

Stacy squeezed Will's hand and he turned to her. It hurt his heart to see the sympathy in her eyes, but he did not know that he was crying as well until she reached out to wipe his tears away.

"I'm sorry," she said, her voice low, the words just for him. "I know you guys were close."

Close, he thought. But it was true. They had been. The path their friendship had once taken had been altered by magic, by their knowledge of the many different ways in which their lives might have unfolded. They had healed the rift between them during their senior year and remained close ever since. In a way it had even seemed natural to Will that Brian and Caitlyn should gravitate toward one another.

They had wielded a dark power beyond their control—he and Brian and Dori—they had received dark gifts, one of which was that the magic had tainted them enough that they could never completely forget the way the world had been before it had been tampered with. He knew Brian remembered and he was certain that Dori remembered, otherwise nothing at all would have changed and they would have been locked in an eternal loop, repeating those awful events over and over.

Will wondered if Kyle Brody remembered, though in this newly forged reality he had only met Will that one time, when Will had been sitting in front of his childhood home on Parmenter Road waxing nostalgic, annoyed at the way the kid's family had taken all the character away from the house. He hadn't performed any magic, but he had seen it; he had helped. It had probably touched him.

The rest of them, though…at their own invitation, they had received these dark gifts. They had tapped in to the mysteries and secrets behind the veil of the world. That was magic, after all.

There in the Carriage House, with the autumn sunshine streaming in and friends laughing all around, he stood and held Stacy's hand while Eric comforted Ashleigh and the word began to spread through those gathered there that one among them would not be appearing for the day's celebration, nor for any other ever again. His grief was overridden by a terrible melancholy, but there was the strange certainty that somehow he had always expected this, that he had been waiting eleven years for it.

And that Brian had, too.

Will James pulled Stacy to him, kissed the top of her head, and just held her close. Despite the sun, the shadows beneath the tables and chairs and in the corners seemed somehow deeper, darker, and he felt a trickle of fear go through him.

Magic always costs, he thought.

He only hoped the price had been paid in full.

AT THE HOUSE on Parmenter Road, Kyle Brody waited until his parents had gone off to church, and then he went to the closet under the stairs and climbed in. Even with the light from the hall, the crawlspace at the back of the closet was impossibly dark, oil black, and when he pushed his hands into the shadows there it was almost as though they disappeared.

He rooted around in the dark, his breath quickening. All weekend his mind had been filled with strange images, things that did not belong there, memories that did not belong to him and were quite simply impossible. Yet they haunted him, these half-remembered things, dangerous and unsettling, like nightmares that would not be dismissed upon waking. No matter how he tried to ignore them, to forget them, they lingered in his mind until at last he had no choice but to prove to himself that it was all in his head, all just a little fringe of madness that had infected him. People had always said he had an imagination that was too vivid.

His fingers closed on something rough and heavy and unpleasantly warm and he flinched away from it, trying to peer through the darkness of the crawlspace. It was real. For a long moment he held his breath and then, cautiously, he reached into the shadows again and slowly withdrew the book. Its cover was slightly battered, a deep burgundy leather, but with a texture that was like nothing he had ever felt.

Kyle opened it, face flushed, pulse going rapid fire, and he flipped the first few pages until he found the title.

Dark Gifts.

A slow smile crept across his face as he rose and carried the book, which was so much heavier than it seemed it should have been, upstairs to his room.

ABOUT THE AUTHOR

CHRISTOPHER GOLDEN is the award-winning, *Los Angeles Times* bestselling author of such novels as *Of Saints and Shadows, The Ferryman, Strangewood, The Gathering Dark,* and the Body of Evidence series of teen thrillers. Working with actress/writer/director Amber Benson, he cocreated and cowrote *Ghosts of Albion,* an animated supernatural drama for BBC online.

Golden has also written or cowritten several books and comic books related to the TV series *Buffy the Vampire Slayer* and *Angel,* as well as the scripts for two *Buffy the Vampire Slayer* video games. His recent comic book work includes the creator-owned *Nevermore* and DC Comics' *Doctor Fate: The Curse.*

As a pop-culture journalist, he was the editor of the Bram Stoker Award–winning book of criticism *CUT!: Horror Writers on Horror Film,* and coauthor of *The Stephen King Universe.*

Golden was born and raised in Massachusetts, where he still lives with his family. He graduated from Tufts University. There are more than eight million copies of his books in print. Please visit him at www.christophergolden.com.